Praise for Leo Dark's *Mr. Nasty*!

"Leo Darke has constructed a nasty masterpiece for all horror fans. I never knew what was coming next! Such a wild ride!"

—Kristopher Rufty, author of *The Devoured* and *Pillowface*

"I enjoyed this as a fast read equivalent to the lurid, schlocky video nasties we all enjoyed so much back in the day. The author lays on the gore with a trowel and plainly knows his stuff when it comes to the DPP list. Who says a misspent youth is a bad thing."

—Allan Bryce, author of *Video Nasties: From Absurd to Zombie Flesh Eaters*

Praise for Leo Dark's *Pandemonium*!

"History and present day collide, and in the pandemonium that follows, Darke has crafted a quality narrative that is both comedic and dripping with tension. An entertaining folk horror tale a thousand years in the making."

—Dave Jeffery, author of *Tooth & Claw* and *A Quiet Apocalypse*

"Darke lures you in to a tale about a gentle, but ultimately doomed relationship, then slaps you upside the head with shock after shock, extreme gore, surrealistically nightmarish sequences, all building toward a breathless, horrific finale."

–Stuart R. West, author of *Corporate Wolf* and *Ghosts of Gannaway*

Praise for Leo Dark's *Lucifer Sam*!

"Leo Darke has created a heavy metal nightmare made of hard-driving prose, a dark sense of humor, and a jovial nod to 1980s horror fiction. There's sex, gore, and suspense to spare, and it all unfolds to a heavy metal beat. An enjoyable read."

—Ray Garton, author of *Crucifax* and *Ravenous*

"Just like the punk rock era that it so finely evokes, Darke's tale is edgy, dangerous, thrilling, unpredictable, and scary. Lucifer Sam rocks. Hard."

—Stuart R. West, author of *Twisted Tales from Tornado Alley* and *Ghosts of Gannaway*

Other titles by Leo Darke

Lucifer Sam
Pandemonium
Sawney Bone

Writing as Mickey Lewis

Walking Shadow

MR. NASTY

LEO DARKE

A
GRINNING SKULL PRESS
Publication
PO Box 67, Bridgewater, MA 02324

Mr. Nasty
Copyright © 2015 Mickey Lewis

This title was originally published by Samhain Publishing, Ltd., September 1, 2015. Grinning Skull Press edition, October 2024. Reprinted with permission from the author.

No part of this book may be used or reproduced in any manner whatsoever without written permission except in the case of brief quotations embodied in critical articles or reviews.

This book is a work of fiction. All characters depicted in this book are fictitious, and any resemblance to real persons—living or dead—is purely coincidental.

The Skull logo with stylized lettering was created for Grinning Skull Press by Dan Moran, http://dan-moran-art.com/.

Cover designed by Jeffrey Kosh, http://jeffreykosh.wix.com/jeffreykoshgraphics.

Published by Grinning Skull Press, P.O. Box 67, Bridgewater, MA 02324

All Rights Reserved.

ISBN-13: 978-1-947227-97-2 (paperback)
ISBN: 978-1-947227-98-9 (ebook)

DEDICATION

To Guy N. Smith:

Thanks for all the werewolves by moonlight, Slime Beasts, and Crabs, Guy. You were truly an inspiration. Rest easy.

PROLOGUE

"Lights, Camera..."

The Director paused, his voice muffled through the latex mask. The cameraman shifted the Red One digital on his shoulder, focused on the naked young man positioning himself in the bathtub. Fifty quid, cash in hand. A job to die for? It would seem so. To paraphrase the old movie: In the South West of England, life was cheap.

"And... *axe him!*"

The extra assumed his most terrified look. It wasn't very good. But what could they expect from someone with no formal training? Probably his first job. They hadn't even bothered to check. What was the point? He couldn't be much more than twenty-five, a bit of a Rock Dude with his beard and long hair. But he would do. He would do just fine. If this was his debut, then what a debut it was. And not just a debut, but a final bow, too. All to the accompaniment of an axe concerto.

It wasn't until the blade actually embedded itself in his right shoulder that the extra realized he didn't need to act terrified. By the time the axe slammed through his left wrist, half severing it, he was giving the performance of his life. He writhed, screaming, in the bathtub as the axe blows chewed into him. Three, four, five... *Thunk! Thunk! Chunk!*

He tried pitifully to evade the falling blade, to pull himself up the side of the bath, now slippery with his own red stuff.

"Lizzie Borden took an axe," the Director grizzled through his mask as the huge man wielding the chopper swung it up and powered it down again, again, *again,* into unprotected flesh. "...and gave the bad man forty whacks."

The extra had stopped shrieking now. The tub was filling with his blood. His limbs jerked spasmodically as the Axeman stepped back, wiping sweat and gore off his face.

"Cut!"

Part One
Turning...

CHAPTER ONE

"Lights, camera... Atrocity!"

There ya go. A perfect, gift-wrapped, bona fide reason why Tommy should hate Mark. Why, in Tommy's opinion, *everyone* should hate Mark. Because he came out with shit like that.

He didn't want to respond. Didn't want to have to turn around and acknowledge his colleague's latest dumb attempt at attention-seeking. But as he was the only one within earshot of the jerk, he couldn't wriggle out of it without being a jerk himself. So, without any inflection in his voice, and without looking around, he said, "What's that, Mark?"

Mark was strutting his gear, posing beside the vintage Tyrell 003 that had swept Jackie Stewart to victory at the '71 Spanish Grand Prix, and which was now being loaned ever so generously by its current owner to the production company behind *The Man from U.N.C.L.E.* remake. But Tommy was pretty sure the owner hadn't envisioned its role in the movie as the leaning prop for this posturing extra as he strove to charm the pit girl models decorously semi-dressed—and consequently freezing—in the pit lane a few yards away.

Mark leveled his gaze on Tommy. "I said 'lights, camera...atroci—'"

"Yeah, I got that. But why...? Why would you say that?"

Mark folded his arms and relaxed against the polished blue paint-work of the low-slung racer. Its curves were sleek and streamlined, sheer car porn to connoisseurs. Tommy grudgingly had to admit

Mark looked good in his racing gear. He was playing one of the drivers in the '60s period movie. That made it sound like a big part. It wasn't. He was a lowly paid supporting artist—hell, let's call a spade a spade—an *extra* on the new film. But whereas Mark looked slim and handsome in his shiny blue and yellow jumpsuit, Tommy looked shit and shapeless in his grubby gray mechanic's overalls. Another reason to hate Mark. To top it off, the overzealous make-up girl had slathered orange foundation all over Tommy's face to make him look more Italian—the film was partially set in Italy but was actually being filmed in exotic Surrey—though it just made him look... well... *orange* instead.

"This new role I've just been given. Got the text confirming this morning." If smugness was a perfume, then Mark was well and truly doused in it. Tommy could even put a name to his brand: Unctuous, for the smarmy shit in your life. That was the perfect word to describe the thirty-five-year-old with his slicked-back dark hair and smooth, waxy complexion.

"One of the main parts," he continued, undeterred by Tommy's lack of enthusiasm. "It's gonna be big. No: *huge*."

Tommy sighed, hands in overall pockets, squinting against the April sunshine. "Yeah?" His interest was concentrated on the two pit girls rather than Mark, however. The Third Assistant Director was herding them toward the Tyrell as the First relayed instructions to him from the Pit Manager's office a few hundred yards behind Tommy.

The girls sauntered over, shivering ferociously. Despite the bright sunshine, it was freezing at Goodwood Race Track, and the girls wore midriff-exposing crop tops and mini skirts—very easy on the eye but obviously intended more for Mediterranean climes rather than English ones.

Mark noticed them, too. "Yeah," he said emphatically. "Gonna be the film of the year. The decade, man. Huge."

"So...what's it called?" Tommy still wasn't really listening. The pit girls joined them, and Jasper the Third AD, about to pass on instructions, suddenly received new ones, and dashed off toward the Cobra Coupe further down the track, where some of Tommy's fellow mechanics were mucking about with fuel cans. Tommy could see Max poking John up the backside with a nozzle for what had to be the tenth time that morning. Max was Bolivian, very loud, and great fun, but he was definitely making himself visible to the crew for all the wrong reasons.

Vicky's smile brought his attention back to where it should be. She was a stunning model with candyfloss blonde hair that had been teased and whorled into golden bliss by the stylists that morning. Her pouting lips were adorned with a nipple-pink gloss that drove Tommy mad. She was too thin for some of the other mechanics—as if they would ever get to have a choice in the matter!—but Tommy thought she was gorgeous. Thick as a brained pig, of course, but that didn't matter right then on that sunny, cold April day at Goodwood Race Track. He forgot all about his irritation with Mark for one glorious moment as Vicky's cobalt eyes held his.

"So cold!" She shivered, holding out her hands and rubbing them together. Tommy began to reach out his own to warm them, but somebody beat him to it, somebody who seemed to beat him to everything. The best roles, the best girls, the best costumes. Even his hairstyle was way better than Tommy's disheveled crop.

Mark held Vicky's hands firmly in his. "I was just telling this mechanic about my new film role..."

"Oh, cool," she chirped, with what Tommy hoped was only polite interest. But he'd lost her smile now to the driver, who simply bathed in it.

"Yeah, it's a genre-shattering debut by a maverick director. He's going to be the new Tarantino. Bigger, actually! Just got the news today. I'm going to be one of the leads..."

"Low budget, I take it," Tommy sniped, bristling over the "mechanic" jibe.

"It's more of an Art film. He doesn't need excessive amounts of money."

"So what's it called?" Tommy asked for the second time. "Lights, camera, atrocity...hmm. I'm assuming it's a horror film..." He realized how hypocritical his scornful tone sounded, if only to himself. He loved horror films.

Violet, the other pit girl model, was looking bored already. Tommy couldn't talk to her as easily as to Vicky. While she was equally beautiful in an airbrushed way, she didn't exude the same warmth as her friend. She was taller, brunette, equally as dim. Tommy had overheard her asking where Bristol was, and that had annoyed him. Not just because that was his city, but because it was, what, the fifth major city in the UK? C'mon.

"No title as yet," Mark said, still rubbing Vicky's hands. "But expect something spectacular. The director says it's going to impact in a big way. And the lights, camera bit is just one of my lines..."

"So it *is* a horror film. You gonna tell us which agency got you this future blockbuster, then?" Tommy realized he was sounding jealous and thereby playing along to Mark's tune, and that smarted even more.

Mark pulled Vicky into a warm embrace before answering, then smiled at Tommy over her blonde coiffed hair as he hugged her tight. "No agency, my friend. I applied direct. And it's going to be so much *more* than just a horror film."

Jasper hurried back over, followed by Max and John. Max was beaming from ear to ear as he took in the two lovelies. Jasper looked harried. Mark reluctantly released Vicky.

"We're going again," the Third AD told them. "Same scene, but they want more mechanics working on the Tyrell now."

Max was already raising the can with its menacing nozzle, but Jasper was onto him.

"You won't need that." He puffed out a breath. "John, you and Max roll tires from that pile to the Tyrell. Tommy, pretend to be examining the steering wheel or something. Just lean through the window and fiddle. Vicky and Violet, stand here looking pretty. Mark, pretend to chat with them."

"Turning!" The bellow came from the First AD, who had emerged briefly from the Pit Station building to check that everything was cool and dandy. Jasper followed him back in at a fair old clip.

"And... *Action!*" The shout was clear and crisp. Tommy bent through the open window of the Tyrell, pretending to adjust the steering mount with his spanner. He was aware of Max and John rolling tires up behind him, but was unaware of their exact intent until he turned to find they'd blocked him in. Very amusing. He could see the big smirk on John's face as he scuttled over to retrieve another huge tire. Max winked at him as he rolled one up to near the door of the racing car and hefted it atop its fellows.

"Cut!" Mark continued chatting up the pit girls while Tommy climbed over the barricade of tires. Jasper explained calmly and patiently to Max and John why it was a bad idea to block Tommy in while Max clapped the Third on the back mischievously and said "Sure, sure," a lot. John smirked and adjusted his huge, thick-rimmed glasses.

By the third take, Max had somehow persuaded Tommy to climb inside the priceless Tyrell 003 while the cameras were rolling. The look on Mark's face alone was worth it; he'd been expressing a desire to get in the racer for the last two days but had always bottled out. Tommy settled in the bucket seat and grinned through the open door at the wild-haired Max. "Say shee-it," the Bolivian said, and there he was, actually leveling his Samsung S5 cell phone at Tommy while the film cameras a few yards away were still recording, and the click sounded like a gunshot.

Fuck, Max! But Max just took another pic and then closed the door on Tommy and leaned his back on it, chuckling away to John, who had his precious fuel can back in his hand. Tommy could see Mark glaring at him through the windshield, Vicky looking a little perplexed, and this take seemed to be lasting forever. He shuffled across on his backside to the passenger seat, popped open the door. But the interior was so cramped he couldn't maneuver himself out through the opening. He did, however, manage to get one leg out, realizing the movie camera was facing him, and all this would be recorded for posterity.

He sprawled back across the two seats, his leg still protruding from the passenger door, and rapped gently on the driver's window. Max ignored him. He rapped a little louder, each knock sounding like a resounding *thump* to Tommy. Max finally spun round, grinned, and opened the door.

"I can't get out," Tommy pleaded. Max grinned wider, grabbed Tommy's right arm, and pulled. Then he changed his mind and trotted round to the passenger side. He leaned in, chuckling softly. "You in a right fucking mess, no?" He got his cell phone out again and fired off a few more shots, then relented and seized Tommy by both his feet and dragged him from the racing car cockpit. Tommy landed on his backside, and beyond Vicky's shocked face, he could see Jasper inside the Pit Garage, staring up at the ceiling in utter disbelief.

"Cut!"

That was the end of *The Man from U.N.C.L.E.* for Tommy. He heard later that Max went on to play a helicopter navigator in a scene with Hugh Grant, sitting together in an actual Wessex whirlybird, the last one operating in the world. That was Max all over; while Tommy landed on his ass, Max always landed on his feet. And that was quite funny really because Max was a funny guy. You couldn't help but like him. As for Mark? Mr. Unctuous went on to fuck the living daylights out of Vicky and gleefully described the whole act in vivid detail to Tommy by email a few days later.

Things couldn't get any worse for Tommy after that, it seemed. Until he met Mark for the second time.

CHAPTER TWO

Cheating on his wife had become something of a habit to Tommy. He did it practically without thinking now, and almost without guilt.

Why *should* he feel guilt, he asked himself quite regularly. His wife didn't love him, that was clear. She *disapproved*. That was her principal response to everything he did. Disapproval hung over their marriage like a depressing cloud. She disapproved of his comic book collection ("Why on earth would you want to tack a bagged edition of *Batman* 255 to the bedroom wall, for God's sake?"); she disapproved of his large collection of videos and DVDs ("Why do you have so many—surely once you've seen them the first time, you don't need to bother again"); she disapproved of his books ("Can't you put them in the attic, they take up too much room"); she disapproved of his art ("Why should I put up with a painting of a naked woman sitting on a tomb in my own conservatory?"). All right, he'd give her that last one—even if it was a Rick Melton original of the gorgeous Anna Falchi from Soavi's extraordinary *Cemetery Man*.

The fact they were still together was a mystery to most people, but it was thumpingly obvious to Tommy. Neither of them could afford to leave. The mortgage was all paid up, but neither of them earned much. Tommy was lucky to clear ten thousand a year, and his wife pulled in half that on her small wage as a part-time shop assistant. When she nagged at him to get a proper job, he nagged right back that she could always go full time, even though he knew the shop she worked at wasn't offering full-time hours. It was an automatic defense to The Nag. She was very good at The Nag, was Tommy's wife.

And while Tommy had cheated successfully on his wife on a couple of memorable occasions, right now he was getting nowhere fast.

He had found her on an internet dating site—Morefishinthesea. com. Her profile was BlondeVenus. Tommy's was TommySin. She had replied to a couple of his chatty messages, albeit in a non-committal way. But now she had stopped. He'd sent her five messages in the last week, and she'd ignored all of them, although he could see the infuriatingly provocative Online Now status highlighted in green beneath her seductive photograph.

He scrolled down through her profile for the umpteenth time since spotting her, the screen of his Samsung Ace cell phone grubby from the dirt paint Make-Up had supplied him with that morning. *BlondeVenus, 35, Single. Body type: curvaceous. Likes reading, trampolining, skydiving, and Motorhead. Wtf,* he'd first thought when he'd stumbled upon her. Not that he would argue with any of that. All right, he wasn't exactly in a hurry to chuck himself out of a plane, and bouncing up and down for fun without sex being involved just wouldn't have entered his mindset for one second, but the rest he could embrace. And who didn't love the Lemster? Well, actually, quite a lot of people, especially the girls he came into contact with on TV and film sets. Their loss. *Love Me Like a Reptile* was one of the best rock tracks ever written. And don't let him get started on *Stone Dead Forever...*

He'd told BlondeVenus that, of course, which had earned him a token response, but it also made him think she was bullshitting about her predilection for the Filth Rockers from Stoke, for whatever reason. Maybe she thought it made her sound cool? The rest of her profile didn't give much away. Her personal statement was bland in the extreme except for the comment: *No Married Men, Weirdos, Web Cam pervs, or baldies please.* That had made him chuckle. And at least he didn't fit any of those categories... Okay, just the one, maybe. All right: two. He wasn't going to admit to the third. But at least he had his hair.

"What the fuck you up to? Perving again? For fuck's sake, man, put it away."

The exasperated Geordie[1] tones made him jump guiltily. He thumbed the phone off and turned to the tall, ginger-haired man in his early 30s

---

[1] Regional accent from northeast England

who'd just emerged from the bushes behind Tommy.

"Made me jump, ya bastard."

Andy "Whay Aye" Hill was dressed identically to Tommy. Both wore purple tunics with a wolf's head emblazoned on the chest. Their shoulders were clamped with chain mail. Andy's legs looked particularly skinny in his tights.

"Give it a rest, man. You look at that site any more and your eyes are gonna ping pong out your head. They're bulgy enough as it is, fella. Anyway, we're needed for the next shot."

"I'm trying to keep away from Mark." Tommy tucked the cell into his thigh-high boot. "Can't believe he's on this job as well."

"Aye, he's a bit of a knob, man, I'll give ya that. It's always the ones ya dinna wanna work with that follow youse around, like. Cheer up, fer fuck's sake. Could be worse. *I* might not have been picked."

"Yeah. That would have been a blow," Tommy told him as they pushed through the ferns toward the clearing where the TV crew had set up base.

"He's bangin' on about that shit movie he's in again," mumbled Andy. They joined the collection of extras on one side of the clearing— the opposite side to that occupied by the director, First AD, and stars, some of whom were sitting on fold-away chairs planted on the lush green grass.

"The silly fuck reckons it's gonna be huge." Andy chuckled. "And it still hasn't got a title. If they canna even decide on a fookin' title, it doesnae look good as far as makin' a fookin' masterpiece, does it? It's all a load of shite."

Tommy could only agree. Mark had managed to wind up Andy, too, by the sound of it. Mind, that wasn't difficult; the big Geordie was quick to lash out, and a born scrapper. He saw red quicker than a West End traffic queue at rush hour.

Tommy could see Mark standing in the middle of the clearing, dressed in his poncey knight gear, while the majority of the supporting artists were done up as dodgy villains. Of *course,* he was a knight. That was just another stick to beat Tommy with, wasn't it?

Andy was on a roll now. Tommy knew better than to interrupt. "I asked him what production company was makin' it like, and he was all kinds of evasive, ya know what I mean? In the end, he told me. I looked 'em up. Didnae inspire me with much confidence, man."

The runner who had been standing nearby frantically listening to a stream of orders on his earpiece rounded on Andy. "Quiet, *please!*"

"Alreet, keep yer fookin' wig on tight, man," retorted Andy, albeit in a lower voice.

The runner trotted over to them, his young face anxious and stressed. *Wasn't it always?* thought Tommy. Who the hell would want to do his job? He didn't get paid much more than the extras, and instead of playing around in the woods with a sword and generally having a laugh, he was always waiting at the shit end of the production company for all the bowel movements to land right on his head at very regular intervals. But to be fair, he remained polite to the bunch of sixteen extras larking around waiting for instructions. Tommy wasn't so sure he could have stayed so patient.

"Right, we need three of you..." The runner had already earmarked Whay Aye and Tommy, and he just needed a third victim. He found it in Chris, long-haired, bearded, chubby. And by far the campest-without-actually-being-gay *Star Wars* fan Tommy had ever met. The runner marched them uphill toward the cave that overlooked the clearing.

"What've we got to do like?" asked Whay Aye a tad uncertainly as they were led toward the dark entrance.

Tommy turned to see the director, First AD, and all the principal cast were watching them.

"We just want you to hide in here and then come bursting out on 'Action'," the runner told them. "D'you think you can do that? Very easy. Just come running out and pull your swords. Look menacing and angry."

"So what's the special FX team doing in here then?" Andy continued a little more uncertainly as they ventured into the clammy gloom.

The runner waved away the question and positioned them right at the back of the cave. So Andy asked it again: "Not being funny like, but it looks to me like this guy's setting up a bomb."

The FX guy grinned widely as he crouched over the little contraption he'd rigged in one corner of the cave.

A drip of water fell from the low ceiling and trickled down behind the collar of Tommy's tunic.

"Youse gonna blow us up or what?" The gangly Geordie had gone redder than usual.

"It's nothing to worry about," the runner assured him as he began striding quickly toward the exit again. "Just a bit of smoke for atmosphere." The FX guy winked at them, finished fiddling with the timer, and joined the runner in a break for daylight.

"Turning..." came the familiar cry.

"And...action!"

There was a deafening bang, and the "bit of smoke" billowed in front of their eyes, filling the small cave in seconds. Tommy could no longer see his hand in front of his face, let alone his two friends as they stumbled blindly in the direction they hoped was the exit, coughing like heavy smokers. Tommy couldn't see Whay Aye, but he could most definitely *hear* him. A selection of choice expletives delivered in his aggressive Geordie tones signaled exactly where the gangly northerner was, which helped prevent Tommy from crashing into him in the thick smoke, although it didn't prevent him from colliding with the paunchy Chris, who emitted a pronounced and extremely camp squawk as they tumbled through the mouth of the cave together, Tommy landing on top of the bearded extra. Whay Aye joined them a second later, sprawling over their tangled bodies and rolling down the slope toward the crew and the delighted cast, particularly the arrogant tit who played Arthur, who was openly guffawing.

The First AD waved a hand for silence. "Reset. Once more without the swearing."

As Tommy got to his feet, brushing away the thick flour-like substance the smoke machine had blasted at them to simulate ash and debris, he saw Mark grinning along with all the others. Of course, Mark's grin was bigger than everyone else's. "Very menacing." He chuckled. "And *very* angry..."

After three more takes, the director was happy and the three dust-caked "villains" joined the rest of their colleagues for a cup of well-earned coffee from the provisions table erected under a canopy in one corner of the clearing. They sprawled on the grass and chatted idly, watching the crew busy themselves preparing for the next shot. The grips hunkered down under tripods and back-breaking cameras while the cameraman supervised the placing of a dolly track in the ferns not far from the tea table. The First AD chatted to him briefly, tapping the track with his Converse boot and cracking a joke that was not smiled at. Cameramen were serious bastards. You didn't fuck with them or their dollies.

Tommy's attention was diverted by a cell ringtone. *The Teddy Bear's Picnic,* for God's sake. The last person Tommy would have expected it to belong to was Mark, but Mark was indeed the offending owner. The First AD, rebuffed and slighted by the cameraman, turned his ire on Mark, which at least gave Tommy a momentary spurt of satisfaction. "Phone to be switched *off!*" the AD barked. Mark shrugged off the admonition, silenced the phone, and carried his tea over to where Tommy and Whay Aye sat brushing at themselves. He was still grinning.

"Loving your work." He smirked, squatting down next to them.

"Aye?" retorted Whay Aye aggressively. He brushed some dust in Mark's direction. "Better than standing around like a prick doing nothing."

"Oh, this is just downtime for me," Mark said smugly. "My real filming job takes place mostly in the evenings."

"And that would be this low-budget slasher you keep boasting about?" Tommy said, taking a sip from his coffee. "I hardly think you're gonna get much dosh from that—if you get paid at all."

"It will certainly get me noticed when it comes out, as you will see, my envious friends. And I won't have to get covered in flour to do it."

Whay Aye looked murderously at him, his fingers playing on the hilt of his sword in its scabbard as if genuinely tempted to use it. While the supporting artists' swords were fairly blunt for obvious health and safety reasons, you could still do a lot of damage with them.

Mark patted the Geordie's back patronizingly. "But you did it so well. So *very* butch. Especially Chris." He grinned at the bearded extra lying back in the grass, enjoying the spring sun on his face. Chris belched demonstratively. *Butch as you or anyone here,* the belch said. Mark pulled out his phone as someone tried to ring him again, switched it off.

"If you go down to the woods today..." Whay Aye sniggered, "...the only big surprise you'll get is if anyone ever listens to your bullshit. Was that your Mum checking you took your packed lunch to school and telling you not to mix with the wrong sort, like?"

"It was probably Vicky wanting more sex." He smirked at Tommy's expression. "Actually, I haven't heard from that bimbo for quite a while now. No, the Geordie's probably right. My Mum. And I'm *definitely* talking to the wrong sort." He winked at Tommy, ignoring Whay Aye now, perhaps realizing he risked a punch in the face if he carried on much longer. "I've got something for you, though, Tommy." Mark got up and searched for his rucksack, which was stacked with all the other extras' belongings beneath the trees a few feet away.

He came back with a photocopied flyer.

Tommy took it as Mark settled down next to him again. He scanned it curiously. "What's this?"

"Don't say I never do anything for you, my friend. It's a casting call audition."

"For what?"

"You are one lucky son of a whore. It's only because I like you that I'm giving you this opportunity."

"You don't like me. And you know I don't like you. And what opportunity?" Tommy was reading the brief lines on the A5 paper, but they weren't really registering.

"Hey, I'm hurt. I thought you were my friend."

"Is that why you fucked Vicky when you knew full well I fancied her? By the way, whatever happened to her?"

Mark clasped the flyer as if to take it off Tommy. "If you're not interested..."

Tommy tightened his grip on it. "I didn't say that." He read the blurb out loud for Andy's benefit. "Sinema Extreme Productions announce an open casting for their new movie to be filmed throughout May and June. We are looking for young talent, male and female, ages twenty to forty-five. Previous acting experience not necessary but preferred. Applicants must be fit and agile, as some aspects of the filming require stamina and action. Auditions to be held at the Factory Studios, Bristol, May third." He finished reading and glanced up at Mark, who was watching him closely. "What's in it for you?"

"Again, I'm hurt. I'm helping the director out, that's all. I think you'd fit in admirably."

"What about me, like?" Whay Aye Andy piped up.

Mark gave him an appraising look, then said, "No. I don't think you'd fit in at all."

"Fuck youse then. Wanker." Andy got to his feet and stormed off into the ferns, deciding it was time to vent his bladder.

Tommy scrutinized the supporting artist he had come to regard as his rival for a second or two. "Why me? Is it so you can lord it over me and show off that you've got a better part."

Mark laughed. "You really do have a low opinion of me, don't you, Thomas?" He watched the runner talking to Arthur for a moment.

Arthur was berating the lowly runner for interrupting him while he was texting on his cell. Earlier, he had refused to continue acting until a group of curious onlookers and Arthur fans who had gathered on the slope above the TV crew were moved on by the runners.

"You think I'm like him?" Mark asked, indicating the blond ex-public schoolboy, who, at twenty-five, was already one of the higher earning thesps on British TV. "You really think I'm as much of a shit as that?"

Tommy took his time replying. He, too, was watching Arthur bullying the runner. "I don't think you'd find it much of a stretch," he said finally.

Mark got to his feet. "Fine," he said. "But just for the record, Vicky wasn't all that in bed. So you really didn't miss out on much, if that's what's bothering you."

Tommy chuckled wryly. "You mean you didn't do it for her, more like." He squinted up through the sunlight at his rival. "You were batting way out of your league there, Markey Mark."

As Mark turned to go, Tommy added, "What do you really get out of it, Mark? Apart from the ego side of it, I mean. Because I'm sure you'd be expecting me to report back to everyone what a wonderful role you've got."

"Oh, I wouldn't need you to do that. Everyone will be able to see that for themselves once it's released. No, I just thought you might like to take part in it. It's not just a film, Thomas; it's an event."

He stopped as he was on the point of pushing through the ferns, presumably to take a leak like Andy before him. "And you can judge for yourself exactly how uncompromising the director's vision is. Why don't you look up the Sinema Extreme website? The addy's on the flyer." He left Tommy frowning at the piece of paper in his hands and disappeared through the undergrowth.

Andy Hill made sure he was a fair distance away from the clearing before allowing himself to relax. He swore under his breath as he urinated on the thick ferns. He should have been enjoying himself. It was a beautiful location deep in the Welsh national park of Forest Ffawr. The sun was warm and promised a pleasant spring.

The birds were comforting him with their melodies, bluebells clustered around the pines. And Andy wanted to hit someone.

Mark would do, for a start, the twat. What an arse. What a complete dick. Smug fuck. Thought he was a cut above. Just because he had a big role in a new zero-budgeted slasher flick. Deluded tit. Laughing at Andy like he was dog shit on his polished shoes. Not good enough to be in his crappy horror nonsense! Well, they would just have to see about that, wouldn't they? He drew his sword, enjoying the rasp of metal on leather as it pulled free of the scabbard, and swung it in the air. He could imagine burying it in Mark's guts. He breathed deeply and sheathed the sword again. He needed something to calm himself or his diabetes would kick in. He didn't want a hypo right now, for fuck's sake.

Andy leaned against the warm trunk of a pine and pulled "something to calm himself" from out of his tall boot where he'd wedged it this morning after costume had finished turning him into an evil Henchman. He popped the spliff between his lips and lit it.

He rested his head against the trunk and closed his eyes. Bliss. Thoughts of Mark, of Arthur, of the First AD and the runner—the whole fucking up-their-own-arse bunch of 'em—slipped from his mind. He listened to the birds, felt the warmth on his cheeks, and enjoyed them for the first time that day. He took another puff. He didn't hear the ferns rustle slightly as someone passed through them, approaching him. His eyes remained closed as he savored a third toke.

The birds stopped singing. Andy didn't notice right away. He was enjoying the patterns behind his closed lids, the sunlight playing his own private cinema show right there in the dappled darkness. Even when he heard the clunk of machinery, it didn't register straightaway. His mind wondered idly what the heavy, awkward ratcheting sound might be, and a memory of something associated with it popped into his consciousness—*watching* Straw Dogs *with his buddies back home in Newcastle, knocking back the Old Brown when they shoulda been at school*—a second or two before the mechanism swung forward and clamped around his head.

His eyes popped open then, all right. And he wasn't back in his beloved toon watching videos and ogling Susan George's tits during the rape scene with his randy pals, but screaming like a Geordie hog as the world turned red, so red, and the pain was red, so red and it was more than anyone could bear—bear, *bear trap!*

The wicked steel teeth of the mechanism bit deep into Andy's face, into his skull, crushing it like a ginger-haired egg. His guttural screams became mewlings as he tottered away from the tree, hands clawing at the bear trap. The person who had clamped it on him studied his movements for a while. Blood dyed the bluebells red. It daubed the crushed features visible between the massive teeth and cross bars of the antiquated, rusty trap.

Then the watcher grew bored of the agony and hefted the spear. It was a very rudimentary spear, bound at one end with thick animal furs, like a caveman's atavistic weapon. The killer held it a moment, enjoying the feel of the wooden haft, then lunged forward, going deep into Andy's stomach. The killer leaned on it, slamming Andy against the tree. The spear was withdrawn, festooned with a clutch of entrails, then slammed back in, twisted, the killer's huge, raw gloves, also fashioned from animal strips of fur, soon red from the pulse and squirt of blood. The killer turned to smile at the Red One camera nosing out of the ferns, clutched by a kneeling operative. The lens focused on the wound, on the blood on the spear, and on Andy's Bear Trap face.

The killer released the spear—still embedded in Andy's stomach and impaling him against the tree—a little reluctantly. Then, as if the impulse was just too strong, grasped it again and gave it one last twist. If Andy had still been capable of coherent thought—if, in fact, Andy had still been *alive,* come to that—he might have pondered on the choice of the primitive spear as a killing tool, which he certainly wouldn't have remembered as an item of Dustin Hoffman's arsenal in *Straw Dogs.* He might then have gone on to ponder if these particular weapons were actually not inspired by Peckinpah at all, but rather by something else—something, shall we say, a little less revered. But, of course, Andy didn't have the luxury of any of these musings. The fog on the Tyne was all *his* all right, thick and dark and all-embracing.

The hands in the animal gloves let go and reached for something else instead. The killer placed it amongst the gory bluebells, right next to the still-burning spliff in the grass. Then both killer and cameraman slipped back into the trees and ferns. After a while, the birds returned. A robin chided Andy for the interruption, flitted in the branches above his bleeding head, alighted on the object placed upright on the grass at his feet. When it toppled over, the Robin took flight. The spliff glowed faintly red and finally went out.

Tommy must have fallen asleep in the warm sunlight. At first, he thought it was Whay Aye shaking him awake and was about to swear at the gangly Geordie when he realized it was Alex, the runner.

"You're on."

"Hmmm?"

"Wake up, Tommy. If the First A.D. catches you sleeping, you'll never work on *Arthur* again."

"Yeah. Sorry, mate." He stood up sleepily, straightening his tunic, blinking around him.

"Where's Andy?"

Alex was looking frazzled again. The production was behind schedule—weren't they always?—and they still had three scenes to shoot before wrap. Tommy glanced around. The Geordie was nowhere to be seen.

"Probably having a piss."

"That's all he's good for." This was Mark's contribution. "He must have a bladder the size of a pea."

Alex ignored this. "Can you both go search for him," he told them. "And hurry."

"Why me?" Mark was outraged. "He's not my mate."

"I don't care. Now, please."

Mark held up his hands. "I need to be checked by Costume, I believe." He glanced over at Emma, the pretty wardrobe girl, who was busy adjusting Arthur's costume.

Alex's patience was slipping fast. "That can wait. We need Andy now."

"Why's he so important?" Mark wanted to know, but he grudgingly began to follow Tommy as he traipsed through the ferns in the direction Andy had disappeared.

It didn't take them long to find him.

Tommy spotted him first. He stopped, and Mark was about to

tell him to move on when he saw what his colleague was trans-fixed by.

Tommy said nothing. Mark stepped past him, as if fascinated.

"Is...is that real?" he said after a while.

Tommy continued to say nothing. Mark stepped even closer. They heard the greedy drone of flies.

"I mean...is this a special effects scene?"

Mark must have realized how ridiculous he sounded because he stopped talking. He had one hand out as if to check to see if the blood was Karo syrup when his boot knocked an object lying in the grass. He stared down at it. Tommy ripped his gaze away from Whay Aye's ruined face and looked at it, too.

Mark was reaching to touch it when a voice stopped him.

It was Alex who had decided he needed to hurry the search along.

"Don't!" was all he said. But it worked. Mark's fingers stopped inches away from touching the object and slowly withdrew.

Tommy said nothing. He was looking at the video box, too. For that's what it was: a big, old, clunky VHS box, plastic sleeve all shiny in the sunlight. He could see the cover image, a girl wearing sunglasses and screaming in close-up. Woods fringing the back-ground, a crudely drawn log cabin, some other details. He could read the title, too: *Don't Go in the Woods...Alone.*

"Don't," said Alex again, his thin face callow and scared. Then he added, "Oh fuck," and backed away through the ferns before turn-ing and running.

Mark turned to face Tommy. "This is bad." His expression was blank.

Tommy said nothing.

CHAPTER THREE

Slade was enjoying himself.

What was not to enjoy? He was sitting next to his best buddy in a nightclub in Prague, and he had his face in between the best pair of tits he'd ever set eyes on, let alone got his hands on. And he certainly had his hands on.

"Fuck me, this is more like it," he mumbled, in between motor-boating the perfect breasts. They were large and full and tasted of some intoxicating oil that hinted at coconut and drove Slade wild. He motor-boated one more time, trying to get his tongue on an elusive nipple, but the girl deftly twisted away, swinging her lithe body on the table to face Trevor instead.

"Fuck me," Slade said again. Trevor looked happy, too. He sat back in his chair as the tall blonde leaned forward on the table edge to swing her tits in his face. His hands came up to stroke them. Slade fixed his eyes on her shaven pussy.

On the stage in front of them, another dancer was sucking off a guy wearing biker boots and nothing else. *Only in Prague*, thought Slade. *Hell yeah.* He would come here every weekend if he could. Shame he had to be back to shitty England in a few hours. He could still taste the girl's breasts. He tapped on her naked shoulder, and she gave him a slightly disdainful glance, which tipped into a smile as he pulled a batch of notes out of his pocket and flicked them between forefinger and thumb.

She was gorgeous, like so many Czech women. Sleek cheekbones, crystal eyes, slightly tapering at the corners, legs that could wrap both Slade and Trevor in their embrace, and tits to die for. Oh, he could literally have died for them right now.

He leaned forward and spoke into her lovely ear.

"How much to take you back to my hotel?"

She smiled. Eased the notes from between his fingers, pressed her breasts against his face one last time, then hopped off the table and picked up her clothes. "More than you can afford, I think." She whisked off with a little wave and a last cheeky smile, leaving Slade with the taste of her tits in his mouth, a boner, and a big gap in his wallet.

"How the fuck does she know how much I earn? Do I look like a loser to you?" He punched Trevor in the shoulder. "Come on, you twat. What are we doing wasting time and money in here? I've got to get this thing watered." He patted his erection and stood up, finishing his beer.

"Where we going?" Trevor asked, following his friend out of the club. Hot Peppers flashed in huge neon letters above the doorway as they emerged onto the street. A tout[2] homed in on them immediately like a well-tuned shark. Slade met him head-on.

"You want girls?" the tout asked with a sneaky grin.

"You want me to punch you to death?" countered Slade, smiling viciously. He shoved the tout out of his way and beckoned Trevor to follow him.

He hailed a cab on the corner of Wenceslas Square. He told the driver the address, and they were off.

"You serious?" Trevor asked when he realized his mate's intention. "We've got to be at the airport in two hours."

"Plenty of time," Slade replied, admiring his reflection in the window beside him. Handsome bastard. Firm chin, wild eyes. Okay, the gelled hair was receding just a tad, but what the fuck. At least he wasn't jowly like Trevor. "I'm only payin' for half an hour. Plenty of time to shoot me joose."

"You're a classy guy, Slade."

"You fuckin' knows it."

The taxi pulled up at the corner of another square, this one

---

[2] Any person who solicits business or employment in a persistent and annoying manner

smaller and far more sedate than Wenceslas. Offices and sophisticated restaurants replaced nightclubs and sleazy bars.

"You sure this is the place?" Trevor asked.

They stood on the corner between a solicitors and a high-class
café. Well-groomed couples were dining outside in the warm spring
evening. They paid no attention to the two drunk Englishmen peering at the door numbers of the nearby properties.

"Hang the fuck on," Slade said and whipped out his cell. He
dialed the number he'd used earlier and a female voice greeted
him smoothly. "Let me in then," Slade said and shoved the phone
back in his pocket. "You wait here and get the beers in." He waved
Slade toward the café tables. "Unless you wanna blow some gunk
as well?" He chuckled lewdly.

Slade knew Trevor was thinking of his wife and kids when the
other man shook his head. "Nah. I've had enough fun for one night."

"What's wrong with you, man? All you've done is let a tart stick
her tits in your face. That's just a warm-up, you faggot."

A light came on in a narrow glass door to their left, which Slade
had initially guessed belonged to the solicitors. Peering through, he
saw a flight of stairs and a tall blonde descending them.

"Right. That's your cue to fuck off. Unless you wanna watch."

Trevor shuddered. "I'll pass."

"Pussy."

Slade let the woman open the door for him and stepped inside. She smiled at him and held out her hand. He took it, staring
her up and down. Thick blonde waves of hair, piercing blue eyes,
nose slightly curved. Good, tall body, tits jutting firmly out from
the white dress. Long legs. He felt himself stiffen. He was gonna enjoy her.

"Are you Judita?" he asked as she led him back up the stairs.
She nodded and smiled artificially.

She made him shower first, which he did, impatiently and reluctantly.

He left the bathroom wearing a towel around his waist and stepped
into the bedroom, where she waited for him. She was standing by
the bed. Soft music was playing. Incense burned along with two tea
lights. A lamp glowed gently on the bedside table. She smiled at
him and let the dress fall.

"They're nice," he said as he stared at her naked breasts. He
brought his hands up to them, a little perturbed by how rock-hard

they were. Not soft like the table dancer's at Hot Peppers. A new boob job, he guessed and frowned. He squeezed them. It was like crushing two rugby balls. Oh well. Never mind. Tits were tits. At least they were large, if not exactly jiggly, which was how he liked them best. He dropped his towel as she knelt on the bed, and he joined her, running his hands over her breasts, teasing the nipples, bending down to suck at them. *At fucking last. Finally got a nipple in my mouth, for fuck's sake.*

His next surprise was that she let him kiss her. But he would probably pay extra for that later when she gave him the bill. He didn't give a fuck about that right now. He slid his fingers between her pussy lips and was impressed to feel moistness. Well, hell... She must actually like him. He pushed her gently on her back and thrust his penis between her breasts. She craned her head forward and darted her tongue over his head briefly before reclining again. He thrust harder, enjoying the sensation of firm breasts enclosing his cock.

Then he scooted higher up her body on his knees and eased his cock into her mouth. She opened her lips wide to take it, swallowing him to the hilt, sliding her lips up and down until he groaned and swore.

"How much extra to cum in your mouth, sweetheart?" He withdrew from her to allow her to answer.

She reached for a laminated price list on the bedside table, consulted it for a second. "Ten Euros."

"Thought you would know that by heart, love. Now lie back and open your mouth and let's have a bit of fun." He began furiously pumping his cock with his right hand.

"Don't say I'm not generous," he said as he mopped thick pearly drops from just below her eye with the towel after he'd finished.

He handed her 50 Euros and gave her a quick kiss on the lips. "Cheers, love." He didn't bother showering again. She watched him from the bed as he left the flat, giving her a cheeky wave as he did so.

Trevor was sipping a lager at one of the tables outside the café when Slade emerged. He chucked the used towel in his colleague's face and checked his watch.

"We've got fifty fuckin' minutes to make the airport. Get that beer down your neck and get the fuck off your ass."

Trevor removed the cum-stained towel from his face and sighed. He stubbed out his cigarette and got to his feet. "How you got where you are in the force will never fail to astonish me," he said.

DI Slade guffawed lewdly and turned to search for a taxi. "Yeah, yeah. Heard it all a fuckin' million times before. Now stop whingin' and get your wallet out. I've blown all my corona on whores, and we need to get back to Blighty. Crime won't fuckin'crack itself, y'know..." He lit a John Player and winked at his DS. "And if you tell anyone down the station how I spent the weekend, I'll tell Flora what you been up to as well."

DS Trevor Whitley shook his head and reached for his wallet. "I don't need to say a word, guv. They all know what you're like. It's a miracle you keep your bloody badge."

Slade laughed and waved at a taxi rounding the corner. "They know how bloody good I am at my job, that's why. There's only one Howard Slade."

"Yeah, yeah, I know: And thank fuck for that." Slade said it before Trevor could as they climbed into the taxi.

He wasn't in the best of moods as he stood in the middle of a shitty wood in the dark in... *Wales,* of all places! Couldn't the Super have assigned somebody else? Wales wasn't even his patch. The bastard knew Slade had just got back from Prague. But then Slade had the most experience...and a pretty successful track record, it had to be said. His phone had started blaring at him as soon as he boarded the Easy Jet flight, and it hadn't shut up until he touched down in Bristol. So much for a sodding early night. Murder most foul on a TV set in Wales. If he hadn't been so fucked, he might even have found it interesting...

He let Trevor do most of the work. He knew the DS hadn't put quite as much away as he had in the seedy clubs of Prague. And he had a much better temper. It wouldn't do to go firing off at these Am Dram wankers, even if he did feel like pounding the pompous director who kept whinging about his fucking filming schedule. And as for that arrogant twat who played Arthur... Slade took a breath, tried to curb the rising fury. What was his name, his real fucking name? The actor had already told him once, but he was fucked if he could remember.

Oh yeah: Pyres. Justin Pyres. Piles, more like, judging from the expression on the scornfully good-looking actor's face. He rubbed his brow to clear the haze. That had no effect. Maybe punching a pearly white peg out of that well-groomed mouth might do the trick. His fist clenched. "So, how well did you know the victim?"

Pyres looked at him like he was insane. "*Know* him? He was an extra. I don't socialize with extras."

Fuck fuck fuck. This was gonna be hard. Luckily, Trev came to his rescue.

"Did you realize he was missing?"

"You've already asked Bertrand that. Why would we? It wasn't as if he was an essential element of the show. Just a hired henchman for the day."

"Okay, I get that he was just a piece of scum fouling your dainty nostrils, but maybe *Bertrand* could tell us if he had any particular need to be in the woods away from everyone else at the time he was murdered?"

The director shook his head slowly, wisely keeping his thoughts on the hierarchy of cast and crew to himself. He seemed a better judge of character than Pyres and could sense this particular Detective Inspector was not the best disposed toward theatrical types. He also looked white as a ghost, even three hours after being informed of the incident. This was way out of his league. His voice shook slightly as he spoke. "I think you would perhaps be better off asking his friends that question, Detective Inspector. He certainly wasn't there for any scripted reasons. I'm sorry, but that's all I can tell you. I wasn't even aware of his name until you told me."

"Oh, I will ask them, that's for sure. But you can kiss your precious filming schedule goodbye for the next few months at least."

Bertrand acquired a whole new shade of pale. "Is that really necessary, officer? I'm sure you can see this whole unpleasant incident was certainly nothing to do with the principal cast or crew. We have a tough itinerary to keep. Any delays to our schedule might be disastrous. Our American producers would be most unhappy."

Trevor Whitley momentarily closed his eyes. *Shiiiit. Stop right there, Bertrand. For your own good.*

Slade actually smiled. "Bert. Bert, my friend. I'll tell you who's not happy here." He took an evidence photo out of his inner jacket pocket and showed it to the director. "Besides me, that is. *This* poor fella, for one. You know, the guy whose name you're not even aware of. The *hired henchman* with his guts round his ankles just over there in the trees."

Now Bertrand looked sick but couldn't avert his gaze from the disgusting crime scene photo. Pyres tilted his head back, not giving in to temptation. "Are these intimidating techniques really necessary, officer? We've told you all we know."

"Shall I tell you what *I* know?" The DI stuck his red face right up against the actor's. Pyres wiped a trace of the detective's spittle from his cheek, and Whitley was just in time to catch his superior officer's arm as he sensed what would follow. He swung Slade around and away from the director and his lead actor.

Slade was breathing heavily. "I was gonna twat 'im, Trev. Proper land one on 'im. I need some fuckin' sleep, man. Can't take this shit. I've still got cum in me pants and a nose full of Charlie. I either get some sleep very soon, or I start swinging."

"Do you want me to finish off here, guv?" DS Whitley looked at his boss a little worriedly.

Slade breathed deeply, then fished a JPS[3] from a battered pack in his jacket. He cleared his throat, wiped his eyes, spat in the grass. A female production assistant watched him with open disgust.

"We're not making any friends here, guv," Trevor said in a low voice. "If we want them to open up, we need them on our side."

"Trev... You're fuckin' right as always. Fuck knows what I'd do without you to keep me on the straight. Look, don't worry. At least I got me end[4] away in Prague. Things ain't so bad. Tell you what, you interview the extras, find out what the fuck that twat was doing in the woods on his tod[5] in the first place. I'll finish my nice little chat with these lovelies..."

"You sure, guv? I can help you."

"Sergeant, just go ask your questions. I'll join you in a minute."

Whitley shrugged and made for the collection of tired and scared-looking extras, now wearing regular clothes—their costumes had been confiscated by forensics. They were huddled miserably around a gas heater rigged to a gen. The woods behind the clearing were taped off. POLICE DO NOT CROSS—blue letters on yellow plastic. As he approached, a scene of crime forensic officer emerged from the trees, ducking under the tape. He saw Whitley and made his way over. He

---

[3] Brand of cigarettes
[4] British slang for penis
[5] On his own

was clutching an item in a plastic evidence bag.

"What have you got, Jim?"

Jim Tavell pushed the white forensics hood back from his head. He raised his eyebrows and nodded in Slade's direction. "Is he all right, Trev? Looks a little woolly to me. But then, doesn't he always..."

Trevor decided to ignore the jibe. It wasn't the first time he'd heard it. Wouldn't be the last. "Nothing a good night's sleep won't cure. He's still the best man for the job."

"The only one they've got, you mean. He really should watch his back, Trev. There's a lot of shit being talked about him back at the department." *And not all of it shit, either.* Trevor Whitley was not oblivious to his superior's reputation. How could he be? He had seen things that would have got Slade fired instantly—and earn him a sentence to boot. But the fact remained he got results. He hit targets. Sometimes a bit too violently...

"Yeah, I know. DinoSlade. I've heard it all. He may be a T-Rex in terms of police procedure, but sometimes that's what you need. But he's always got me to hold his hand, keep him just this side of the law." He pulled a pair of forensic gloves from a bag in his jacket pocket and put them on, then took the bagged item off Tavell and examined it. Arc lamps had been erected in the clearing, reflecting off the shiny video box inside the bag.

DS Whitley shook it. The box rattled. *"Don't Go in the Woods,"* Whitley read aloud. He looked up from the garish cover art. "Mean anything to you?"

Tavell shook his head. "Looks old. Eighties, probably."

"Prints?"

Tavell shook his head. "Nothing obvious. We'll check it out properly back at the lab."

"The tape inside might reveal something. Practical joke, maybe. Or an allusion of some kind."

The SOCO[6] shrugged. "If it's a joke, it's a very vicious one. Allusion to what?"

"Who knows." Whitley buttoned his jacket as the late April night grew perceptibly colder. "I suppose I'd better chat to this bunch of sorry bastards." He turned toward the extras, some of whom had actually been provided with chairs. The rest of the cast and crew, make-up girls, wardrobe, hairstylists, were all seated a little distance

---

[6] Scene of the crime officer

from the costumed extras, and Whitley noted wryly how, even in the midst of a horrendous crime such as this one, the signs of hierarchy were still in place.

"When can we move the body?" Tavell wanted to know as Whitley began to move toward the medieval henchmen.

Whitley stopped, looked back. "When Slade's finished with the top boys. We're gonna have one last look at it, and then we'll give you the okay."

The extras—all men ranging in age from about 19 to their late 40s—looked at him with something like resigned horror as he approached. It had been three hours since the murder had been discovered, and they were all desperate to get away from this awful place. Whitley could hardly blame them.

He'd already spoken to the two who had found the body. The statements were uniform. They'd discovered the corpse of Andrew Hill at 4:30 that afternoon. They hadn't realized he was missing until the runner, Alex Dunning, had sent them to look for him. Nothing to suppose either of them were lying, though Slade hadn't been too keen on them. But then, right now, DI Slade wasn't keen on *anyone*.

He spoke to them again, asking if they knew of any reason why Hill should have been targeted. Were they particular friends of his? He mentioned the VHS tape and asked if it might have any significance for them or relate to Hill in any way. Did they have any ideas why he was in that particular part of the woods alone?

Mark Hamm took the questions in his stride, even the ones he had already answered an hour before. Tommy Wallace seemed a little more reserved. Something to hide? Slade would find the pressure points. But in the meantime, there was nothing else that could be said or asked. They were all tired. Probably best to send them home.

Slade appeared at his elbow, red-faced and huffing slightly. He lifted his right shoe and examined a smear of excrement on the sole with no small amount of disgust. "I don't fucking believe it. Who the *fuck* let dogs in these woods?" He glowered at the two extras belligerently as if they might be to blame.

"Any luck with Pyres?" Whitley asked him, leading him gently to one side.

Slade sighed. Whitley could still smell the stale Czech Republic alcohol on his breath despite the mints he's swallowed. "Stuck up twat. Right fuckin' Eton Rifle. I only just stopped myself from lampin' him, Trev... But I don't think he's got anything. I leaned on all the likely pressure points, and he seems squeaky. Clean as. That limp wrist of a director looked scared shitless, too. But I think he's far too worried about his precious shooting schedule to risk interrupting it to slaughter a fuckin' extra. Shit. This is why I never go to the movies anymore. Way too much bollocks."

"Do you want to speak to Hamm and Wallace again, guv? Or any of the others? They all look done in. Maybe we should send them home."

"To their nice, cozy beds? Fuck that. Their mate's impaled to a tree wearin' a fuckin' animal trap as a fashion accessory and they wanna go home and have a hot chocolate. You are *way* too fuckin' soft, Trev. Besides, there's something about these two I don't fuckin' like." He snorted phlegm, hawked it into the grass.

He stepped up to Mark and Tommy

"So, is *someone* going to tell me why your pal was in there on his own?"

Mark leveled his gaze on the detective. "I assume he went in there to urinate, officer."

"To urinate?" Slade considered that. "Do all you extras normally take a piss with a great big spliff in your hands?" He watched their expressions carefully. Not a flicker. Had they seen the doobie lying in the grass along with their mate's intestines?

"You..." He jabbed Tommy in the chest. "Did you know he was a smoker?"

Tommy shrugged. His eyes were wide. He looked scared, which was fine by Slade. They should *all* look scared. But was there something else there, that the scruffy-haired man wasn't telling them?

"Don't know. Maybe. I think he said he liked to have one on his way in every morning."

"Well, isn't that a nice routine? Pull over in a lay-by for a quick read of *The Sun* and a toke on a doobie?"

Tommy shrugged again.

"Was he a particular friend of yours?"

Tommy paused. "I liked him, yeah."

"You *liked* him." Slade rounded on Mark. "What about you?"

Mark continued to meet his gaze. "I *didn't*."

"Didn't what?"

"Like him."

The fucker continued to eyeball Slade. "Really? Why was that?"

"He was a Geordie asshole."

Slade laughed. Turned to Whitley. "Isn't your old dear from New-castle, Trev?"

Whitley nodded. "Yes, she is, guv."

"Now, see what you've done. You've gone and offended the D.S. here."

Mark shrugged. "He *was* an asshole. I'm not going to lie, officer."

"Did he give you any particular reason for disliking him?"

Mark hesitated, considering the answer. "He swore a lot."

Slade smiled at Whitley again. "That's fucking awful. But then, so does D.S. Whitley's mum, eh, Trev?"

"Like a trooper, guv."

"I think you'll find it's a vital part of their dialect, son."

"Is this discussion going anywhere, officer?"

Slade straightened to his full 5'11", spread his hands wide. "Where do you want it to go, son?" A wild look came into Slade's eyes. He pushed his face into Mark's, just like he'd done to Pyres earlier. "I've got news for you, my friend: I don't like *you*. I don't like what you do for a living, either. None of you are fuckin' real. You play. And I grew out of playing a long time ago."

"Inspector, if you continue to swear, I shall have to speak to someone about police harassment."

Slade smirked. Not as if he hadn't heard that one before. "Okay, son. I'll make it easy for you. I ask you a question, you give me a straight answer. Do you think you can manage that?"

Mark shrugged again, face impassive. Giving nothing away. *Pity it wasn't you hanging from that tree with your tights full of shit and your guts in the grass.* Slade cleared his throat, fetched another cigarette. "This is for both of you to answer." He looked up at Tommy suddenly, as if to catch him not paying attention. Wallace—in his late 30s, possibly even early 40s, Slade guessed—looked too worried to do anything *but*, however.

"This is my last question for now, and then me and my good buddy D.S. Whitley here are gonna go back in those woods and stare at your mate again. Examine the dried blood all over his face, maybe step on some of his intestines by accident—it *is* dark—and smell the defecation he dropped in his pants. Think you'll both agree that's not a nice job. Certainly didn't expect to be doing that when I woke up this morning in a bright, clean hotel room in Prague. So I think you can forgive me if I'm a little fucking out of sorts, and don't think too badly on me for expecting you to be a little fuckin' forthcoming with your answers... But please keep 'em nice and simple. No more than two syllables if you can help it."

"I'm sure we can manage that for you, officer," Mark answered wryly. Tommy nodded.

"Good. Excellent. Well, then, here it is..." Slade took a deep drag on his JPS. "*Don't Go in the Woods Alone*. Great title. Catchy, don't you think? No? Maybe I have different tastes to you fine thesps. I can't be arsed with high-concept bollocks and arty shite. Nope, give me a trashy-flashy, brain-dead flick anytime. Something like *Don't Go in The Woods*, in fact. But what about you two? Are you familiar with this particular classic?"

Mark pursed his lips. Tommy looked away into the trees.

Slade cupped his right ear. "Don't hear you..."

"No," said Mark. "As you say, it's not my sort of thing. And your assistant has already asked this question."

"Tough titty: *I'm* asking this time. What about you, Mister...er." He glanced at Whitley.

"Wallace, guv."

"Thanks Trev. You're my rock. Wallace. You ever see *Don't Go in the Woods*, Mister Wallace?"

Tommy cleared his throat. Slade's cigarette smoke seemed to be getting to him. Good.

"Can't say I have, sir," he said.

Mark held his hand up like a primary school kid in class. Slade frowned aggressively at him.

"Now I've answered your questions, officer, can I ask you one?" His face was unbearably smug, not intimidated at all.

"Go ahead. Anything that keeps me from that corpse is a welcome delay, son."

"Are you a big fan of *Life on Mars*, by any chance? The T.V. series, not the Bowie song. You know, the one about the dinosaur detective out of sync with the modern age and raging against it. Always calling his female colleagues 'love' and bashing the crims when he's supposed to be interrogating them. He swore a lot, too."

Slade laughed, and this time, it was a genuine one. He nudged Whitley, who winced, fearing where this would take them.

Slade scratched his cheek, looked down, brushed ash off his beige trouser legs. He put his arm around Mark's shoulder. "Never watched it, son. Sounds like a bit of a fuckin' pussy to me." Then he placed his right shoe on top of Mark's instep and carefully smeared the dog shit he'd trodden in all over the extra's pristine white trainer. Trevor looked away. Tommy's eyes got wider. Mark didn't react. Not a word.

"I've changed my mind, son. I *do* like you, after all." He patted Mark's back and then beamed at Whitley. "Now, then, Trev. Haven't we got a mutilated corpse to look at?"

CHAPTER FOUR

BlondeVenus was still playing hard to get.

He'd sent her three messages on Morefishinthesea.com in the last two days, but not a sausage. So he moved on to WildEmma36, blonde (if there was one thing Tommy had a weakness for, it was intelligent blondes). WildEmma36 was—hey, what a surprise—36. She had an average body type, brown eyes. Her interests: horse riding, tennis, gambling (and he was beginning to think they really should have renamed this website WTF.com). His hands hovered over the laptop.

I'm a caring, thoughtful girl who looks younger than her age. Can't argue with that, Tommy nodded as he read along. She was slim and fit. Nice hint of cleavage revealed by the tight red T-shirt she was wearing in the profile pic. *I am looking for someone honest, funny, and kind. No married men or players. And if you expect me to just drop everything at the last minute for a wild date, you can jog on. I have a two-year-old boy to care for.*

Tommy jogged on.

Another quick check on BlondeVenus. Her online indicator was glowing green. She was *always* online! But nothing in his inbox. He tapped the laptop pensively. The bedroom door opened behind him, and he slammed the laptop closed guiltily. He turned slowly, as if he had nothing to hide. She was standing impassively in the doorway, a disappointed look on her face.

Trish was in her early thirties, a slender brunette with worry lines beginning to gather around her dark eyes. She'd started dying her hair to hide the odd thread of gray, and Tommy had been diplomatic enough not to comment on it. Her lips were thin, as was her nose, but she had a stubborn chin. This was set defensively now as she watched him, disapproval tugging at her lips and eyes.

"Looking at porn again?" Her voice was a croak. He guessed she'd been asleep again. He hoped she hadn't been crying.

He sighed dramatically but didn't bother answering. Why did it always have to be like this? The constant head-butting, the disagreements, the resentment, and worse still, the apathy. And that's what he felt right now: nothing. He had passed the point of despair, of pain, of loss. She was gone already, though neither of them had the guts to admit it yet.

"What do you want, Trish?"

"Not you, that's for sure."

"I know." His voice sounded sad, even if he didn't feel anything.

"I'm going out." She began to turn.

"Where?"

"Do you care?"

He shrugged. "It's nine o'clock, Trish. Just wondering where on Earth you could be going to at this time of night. Is that unreasonable?"

"It is when you don't really give a damn. Why pretend? I'm going to Laura's. I'm going somewhere where there won't be policemen knocking on the door."

He shook his head incredulously. "You think that's my fault? You think I had something to do with killing my own *friend*? I hold my hands up to many things you've accused me of before. Yep, even the porn. But you are way out of line there."

"So why do they keep coming back?" Her eyes were narrow.

"Are you *serious*? Because I was the one who fucking found him, that's why!" He turned his back on her. "Goodbye, Trish."

He heard the front door close a few minutes later. He blew out a long sigh, considered opening the laptop again but managed to resist the impulse.

His phone let out a trickle. A text. He thumbed the button. Mark: *Have the rozzers been to see you?*

He texted back his answer, adding: *They asked exactly the same questions. AGAIN. Trish is pissed off with it, even though she was out when they came. Scared, I guess. Hopefully not of me. You should make a complaint about that bastard Slade. He actually assaulted you.*

He can't get away with behavior like that.

A minute later, the reply: *Hardly class wiping dog shit on me as brutality. I've had worse. His turn will come, I'm sure. We just need to find a bigger dog. You going to the audition?*

Tommy had forgotten all about the casting. No surprise there, really, what with his mate being impaled, gutted, and bear-trapped. *Not sure.*

The response came immediately. *You should. It is going to be huge. This director REALLY knows what he's doing.*

Why do you care, Mark? Tommy thought. *We're not mates.* He thought of Whay Aye, the laughs and jobs they'd worked on together. Working with Andy reminded him of his brief time on a building site after leaving Uni, the same all-lads-together camaraderie. Andy had been the type to stick by a mate.

He turned back to the laptop, opened it, and typed in SinemaExtreme.com.

The screen went dark. One word floated to the surface. ENTRANCE. Cute. He clicked on it. The screen remained dark. Tommy's patience began to run out. He was about to close the laptop when the screen crackled with video snow, like the leader tape in an old VHS. A closeup on a pair of female eyes. Blue. Scared. And maybe a little familiar. Had he maybe worked with her? It was hard to tell. A whimper on the soundtrack. Muffled sobbing. *So this is the next big thing, according to Mark? Just the same old low-budget torture porn. I'll pass, Marky Mark. Hey, thanks awfully, though...*

Then there was a series of long shots of a blonde girl wearing just knickers in a dark bedroom, her back toward the camera, again naggingly familiar. Tommy waited for her to turn or for a close-up of her face but was teasingly denied. A close-up of her breasts, though, small and cute, and her taut stomach. Then back to just her eyes and held on them. Scared. Blue. A female scream morphed into a synthesizer drone on the soundtrack, then sounds of ecstasy and female orgasm, again distorted electronically, becoming amplified shrieks of shivering agony that disturbed and excited in equal measure. Tommy's interest sharpened, intrigued despite his cynicism. The screen began to darken, the eyes slowly fading from blue to black. And then an email address flickered up in a lurid red font.

But did he really want to be involved in a horror flick, with Andy butchered horribly just the day before? Did he want to be reminded of the slow lazy buzz of flies hanging around Andy's ripped head, waiting for Tommy and Mark to leave them to their pleasures? *But this would be a fiction*, he told himself. It might even be cathartic. *Bullshit!* There was no way reliving murder and mayhem on film would get rid of the memory of Andy hanging from that tree, his tongue half out of his mouth... If he wanted to do this film, it was for his own selfish reasons. It could be a break, like Mark said. *But Mark is an egotistical ass and cares about nothing but his own career.* Was that how Tommy wanted to end up? Well, if Trish had anything to say on the matter, he was already halfway there...

On a whim, he left the bedroom, went downstairs to the lounge. Trish had left the light on and the curtains wide open so everyone passing in the street outside could see their possessions. Not that they had many, apart from the giant mother-ship of a plasma Tommy had insisted on plonking in the small room.

He stood in front of the bookcase stacked tightly with DVDs as if pondering what to spend the next couple of hours of his life watching. Then he came to a decision, left the lounge, and entered the spare room next door. This room was the same size as the lounge but looked smaller thanks to the bicycles leaning against one wall and the pile of coats, jumpers, and handbags that Trish had dumped on top of the now invisible wooden rocking chair in the center. He navigated his way around the trailing coats, stepped on a CD fallen from a tilting rack that Trish must have knocked, cursed when he realized he'd cracked the case; it was *Goat's Head Soup* by the Stones. Bollocks. He picked it up ruefully, retrieved a couple more that were waiting to be stepped on next time (the *Best of the Damned* and Johnny Winter), and slotted them carefully in the rack, rearranging it so it wouldn't topple. Then he opened the cupboard in the corner.

Here were all his dusty, old VHS cassette tapes, bought years before. He'd stopped collecting them now, much to Trish's relief. He'd been known to spend up to fifty quid on some of the rarer ones. He slid his fingers along the fat plastic spines. Exotic if brutal titles ranging from *Nightmares in a Damaged Brain* to *Shriek of the Mutilated*. But the one he wanted eluded him for a moment, and he was beginning to think it had gone altogether when he found it right at the back, hidden behind *Snuff*.

He pulled it out, examining the garish cover.

Slade would have had a field day if he'd found this.

Slade! What a joke. What an absolute cartoon character of a copper. Was that the best they could get for a murder case? Tommy would have laughed if it hadn't been for the memory of the blood squeezed from Andy's crushed face, the right eyeball egging out of its socket from the brutal pressure of the trap's jaws.

He took the cassette with him into the lounge, squatting in front of the Sony DVD/VHS combo player on its shelf under the plasma TV. He popped the tape out of its clam case and loaded it into the player.

Then he took a seat, wondering who it was Slade reminded him of as *Don't Go in the Woods Alone* began to play after a brief flurry of video snow.

If Tommy had returned to the spare room and rifled through his CD selection, he might just have realized exactly who it was that Slade reminded him of: the cover of *Concrete*, a 1981 release from the pop punk band 999 would have shown him. He would have seen Detective Inspector Howard Slade's major source of inspiration, at least visually. The singer was stocky with a square face and short-cropped, dark brown hair, wearing a knee-length trench mac—very similar to the one Slade was wearing now as he stood before the whiteboard in the incident room. If Tommy had said to him, "Holy fuck, you look like Nick Cash from 999," Slade might have clapped him on the back and forgiven him, much impressed that this Supporting Fartist had even *heard* about the band—hell, he might even have resisted crunching his instep or punching him in the guts... Tommy might well have blown it, though, by adding, "After he'd been crunched in the face by a breeze block." But Tommy wouldn't have added that last bit. That would have been stupid. Tommy wasn't stupid.

Slade's nose was flatter than Nick Cash's for sure, and his lips looked like they'd been splayed by a few too many fists—which wasn't far from the truth; Slade was a born scrapper—but he bore the same devil-may-care crook or copper ambivalence that marked out the old punk. They both had another thing in common, and this was where Mark had been far off the...mark: Slade had never seen *Life on Mars*, but he and Cash loved *The Sweeney*.

"You got any word on that bear trap yet?"

DS Whitley leaned back in his chair. "Still on it, guv. Checking all the local farms in the area, it's taking a while..."

Slade grunted, staring at the SOC photo of Andy Hill projected on the whiteboard. "Can't be many of those things around these days. I wanna know if any have gone missing, or if any of the farmers look dodgy when you mention a bear trap. Any agricultural museums around? Check them, too. It's too old and rusty to be a new purchase, but check online for antique animal traps. And get on to forensics: I want everything they can tell me about the animal skins found on the spear."

Trev nodded and reached for his desk phone. Slade turned to an attractive black girl in smart pinstripes sitting just behind Whitley. "Black coffee, two sugars, please, love." He looked at the whiteboard again, deep in thought.

"I think you mean Detective Constable Nandu, sir."

"Hmm?" Slade faced her, puzzled.

"That's my name and rank." Her eyes were large and challenging, unwavering.

Slade nodded his head slowly, measuring her up. Good, taut body, pretty face, small tits, though. "How long have you been in this squad, *Detective Constable Nandu*?"

She didn't flinch. "Three days, sir."

He pursed his lips, moved over, and sat on the edge of her desk. She remained where she was, staring him right back in the eye. Whitley, still on the phone to forensics, grimaced. Several of the other DCs, hardened murder vets, grinned at each other. Some of the rawer recruits watched and listened carefully.

"This your first murder case, D.C. Nandu?" He folded his arms.

"Yes, sir. But I don't see how that can possibly affect the manner in which you address me in the workplace."

Slade nodded in mock self-chastisement. He rubbed his chin.

"I'll tell you what... You rack up a few more murders on your C.V. and prove your mettle and I'll address you however the fuck you want. Until then, me and the grown-ups will continue to work hard tracking down the fucker who did this, and you will do whatever the fuck I ask you to. If you don't like it, I hear St. Paul's needs a new policewoman for social liaison." He winked at her. "Coffee, black, two sugars. *Please.*"

Whitley put down his phone and shook his head disapprovingly. Slade got off Nandu's desk and held his hands out in a WTF gesture.

Whitley waited until DC Nandu had slowly, resentfully got to her feet and left the incident room before speaking in a tone so low that the rest of the squad couldn't hear.

"You've got to be careful, guv. This isn't the seventies. The complaints are racking up. You know that."

"And so are the bodies. Or they will be if they didn't have this squad to stick their fuckin' finger in the breach." Whitley winced at the minced metaphors.

"You think there's more to come?"

Slade didn't answer straight away. He glanced at the whiteboard again, at the blow-up of the video box that had been recovered next to the body. "Forensics finished examining this, Trev?"

"No prints. On the box or tape. The tape contains exactly what it says on the box. No hidden extras, no obvious messages. It's clean. Old, battered, and filthy, but clean. Same with the spear. They're still working on the skins."

Slade turned to address the whole room.

"In reference to D.S. Whitley's comment, yes, I *do* think there's more to come. Call it a hunch, an instinct, and maybe I'm going out on a limb here, but this stinks of a cornflake." Looking up to see DC Nandu had returned to the incident room, resentfully carrying a vending machine coffee, he added, "That's serial killer to you, love." There were a few chuckles from the more experienced detectives, but Slade's tone was serious now and his expression had lost its playfulness.

"This was a particularly nasty homicide. Forensics believe the victim was already dead from injuries sustained by the bear trap before the assailant used the spear. That seems to be for—and this is relevant, considering there was a sodding T.V. crew filming a few hundred yards away—dramatic effect only, for whatever twisted reason. I want every member of that cast and crew re-interviewed, from the director right down to the asshole who changes the shit-roll in the portaloos. You got that? I don't care how many of them whinge. Someone must know *some* reason why this Geordie lad bought the farm. It's not a stretch to guess it's got something to do with this shitty video. Has anyone heard of it before?" He leaned forward on the back of a chair and scrutinized his attentive squad.

A hand rose hesitantly in the air. Slade's eyes widened just a tad. He straightened up and hitched his trousers up an inch. "Detective Constable Nandu...?" He sounded gruff and a little awkward.

When she spoke, the female DC's voice was, in contrast, confident and professional. "It's a nineteen eighty-one slasher flick made in America, sir, directed by James Bryan, pretty much his sole credit, but I'll check further on that. Very low budget, no big names attached, no links with the U.K. that are obvious, and none to the *Arthur* T.V. crew. US title: *Don't Go in the Woods*. The *Alone* suffix was added by the British distributors. Found itself on the video nasty list and was subsequently banned. There have been no releases on D.V.D. or any other format in this country, although it is available in other countries, including the U.S., Japan, Germany, Holland..."

Slade tilted his head back, impressed. "Video nasty, eh? Haven't heard them mentioned in a while. Fuck's sake. Any obvious link between this film and the Geordie?" He was addressing her alone now. She answered instantly.

"Nothing obvious, sir. I can interview his family, if you like? His flat has already been checked, but there are no links to horror films there, banned or otherwise."

"Have you seen it, D.C. Nandu? *Don't Go in the Woods Alone,* I mean?"

"No, sir. If forensics have finished with it, I can watch it tonight."

"With popcorn and a date?" a few DCs started to titter again, but Slade held up his hand. "You've done good work there, D.C. Nandu. Watch it and let me know if there's anything that ties it in with this lad from Newcastle. Check his full record while you're at it. I want to know everything about him, where he shops, where he drinks, who he fucks... And yes, get on to the family. With your sensitive nature, you're probably the best woman for the job. Good." He scanned the rest of the squad. "While D.C. Nandu's busy with the victim, I want the rest of you all over the others, like I said. Start with the extras, work upward. I want to hear about every T.V. episode or film Bertrand and his crew have ever worked on. I want to know if Pyres is gay or straight. I want to know who's financing *Arthur.* If anyone on that crew has ever had even a fuckin' parking ticket, I want to hear about it. If an extra got involved in a bar scrap, let me have it. Grudges, animosity, particularly in reference to Andy Hills—I want it in writing. Statements had better be squeaky tight and loophole free or I'll visit each one of your homes with my C.D. collection. And if you ask D.S. Whitley, that's something you really don't wanna invite. We all clear?"

There were assorted nods and grunts. Slade dismissed them and crossed to Whitley. "What do you know about video nasties, Trev?"

Whitley shrugged. "Not a lot. Like most of us, I've probably watched the odd one in my time. When I worked in vice, there were loads being confiscated. I might have watched a few of them."

"Well, you can watch this one after Nandu's finished with it. Just to get a male perspective on it. Or is that too un-P.C. for you?"

"I've given up worrying about your politically correct qualities, guv. But I think what you really mean to say is you want a more experienced detective to give it the once over." He raised his eyebrow.

Slade chuckled. "Just couldn't bring myself to say it, could I? Must be a dinosaur after all. Old fuckin' habits die hard. But watch it anyway." He approached the whiteboard again.

"I've got a nasty feeling about this one, Trev..." He grimaced at the DS. "No fuckin' pun intended."

CHAPTER FIVE

It was the eyes that decided it. Blue and scared and hauntingly familiar. The eyes, and the fact that now *Arthur* was on hold, Tommy had no work. So when the email came through, he had already made up his mind he would go to the audition.

The message was very bare and basic: *thank you for your inquiry. We are pleased to invite you to a casting call at Sinema Extreme Productions on 3rd May at Factory Studios, 11:00 a.m.*

That was it. No names, no other directions, no clue at all as to what part he would be auditioning for. He contemplated contacting Mark but didn't want to get into a conversation with him. He didn't want his rival to think his taunts and condescension had worked and Tommy was actually going to apply.

The tweets didn't help. *This is proving to be a remarkable shoot. So realistic, so powerful, #Serioushamm.* Mark was all over Facebook, too, or at least the group belonging to the casting agency they were both affiliated with: *If ever there were a horror film that deserved the tag, then this is it. Will put the likes of* The Exorcist *and* Texas Chainsaw Massacre *to shame.*

Now, all of this, of course, had elicited quite a few responses from curious tweeters and members of the Facebook group alike. The interesting thing was that despite his bold statements and apparent efforts to incite envy and resentment by implying he was the only supporting artist working on anything remotely good, his answers to those aroused enough to discover more from him were decidedly non-committal. But then again, that was Mark Hamm's style. He boasted, he strutted. *Sharing* had never been a game he liked to play.

Tommy had almost weakened and posted his own message, but then he could have run the risk of sounding as if he, too, was influenced by Mark's bragging, and he didn't want that. Oh no. #Notfuckingbothered. But, of course, he was auditioning anyway—he just didn't want Mark to know about it yet. And there was always the horrible thought of the added pleasure it would give Hamm if Tommy failed the audition. Better just to keep quiet.

On the morning of the audition, Trish caught him looking at Morefishinthesea.com. He didn't hear her come in. She stood for a while looking at the page full of female profiles over his shoulder, and then she said quietly, almost to herself, "I'm leaving you, Tommy."

Tommy's head whipped around, his face slack with shock. Automatically, he went to close the laptop, but she prevented him, her hand firm on his. "No, you can carry on. You might find someone. Let's be honest with each other for the first time in years. We've both known this marriage is dead in the water for a long time."

He lowered his head for a second, saying nothing. Then he looked up, expression sad and lost.

"I'm sorry," he said. It was all he could think of. But it wasn't enough. He'd been saying sorry for the six years of their marriage, and while she could accept it for the first year when she had loved him, now it no longer washed.

"Me, too," she said finally. "I'm going to move in with Laura for a while." She paused on her way out. "Be happy, Tommy."

He watched her leave from the upstairs window. She wasn't taking much. Laura got out of her Mini Cooper and looked up at him. Trish did not. The Cooper took the turn and was gone. Tommy was a hollow oak of a man, empty and cold. He walked from room to room of the mid-terraced house, as if confirming his new freedom, as barren as it felt. On the coffee table next to the TV, the garish *Don't Go in the Woods* box stood up to attention, the video still in the machine waiting to be finished. He'd only been able to endure half the film before the relentless droning and high-pitched shrieking of the cheap synth score had driven him up to bed. But that hadn't been the only reason. Remorse had pricked him: it was almost as if he had been ghoulishly savoring the connection between the *Arthur* crime scene and the video nasty. He thought of Andy, remembered finding the dead Geordie... He reached out to pick up the video box, then stopped himself. He had half an hour before he needed to leave for his audition. His stomach started to churn, although he wasn't sure whether that was caused by Trish walking out or the forthcoming casting call.

He changed into a plain black, long-sleeved shirt and some black jeans, then looked at himself in the mirror. Untidy dark brown hair, a rather pinched face, a thoughtful (lost?) look in his eyes, and a serious slant to his mouth. He needed to laugh more. He needed to *love* more.

He shrugged into a tight-fitting AllSaints leather jacket and left the house. The Factory Studio—an old, concrete ex-tobacco warehouse used by bands for rehearsal and recording that resembled an Eastern European pre-war abomination—was in an industrial estate only a twenty-minute drive away on the outskirts of Bristol, and he made it with fifteen minutes to spare. He parked his VW Polo next to the Studio and headed for the shadowy entrance, hunched against a late April shower. A row of bells, two of them marked Studios One and Two, respectively, the bottom affixed with a temporary sticky label that read simply SINEMA EXTREME PRODUCTIONS in biro[7]. Not an auspicious start. He thumbed the bell and waited. And waited.

He couldn't see anything through the single dark glass door apart from his own reflection, and when another image suddenly appeared behind his, he stiffened with a jolt and an involuntary grunt. The reflection bared white teeth, and Tommy spun to face the girl standing behind him, her smile scorching right through him.

"I made you jump," she said in an accent Tommy couldn't place but was certainly not Bristolian. He gaped at her like a fish, completely clueless as to what to say. She waited for him to think of something, that smile burning him up, her teeth gleaming behind the ultra-shiny pink gloss of her lips. Her hair was long and a dirty tawny blonde, tangled around her dark brown eyes. She couldn't

---

[7] Ballpoint pen

have been much more than 5'1" or 2", and she had boosted her height with some wicked high heels as pink as her lips. Her hands were in the pockets of her leopard-print jacket, which looked more like a coat on her small figure.

Tommy finally thought of something. "Er, yeah." Brilliant. Top marks. "Yes, you did, I mean, just a little." He smiled back, careful not to reveal his silver-crowned tooth, which he had only recently had done and was still a little conscious of.

"I'm Jasmine," she said and held out a dainty, little pink-nailed hand. He took it and stammered his own name.

"You here for the audition?" she said, and now he could detect what was possibly a slight Trans-Atlantic twang.

He nodded and gestured at the door. "Yeah, but there's no answer."

She leaned past him and pressed the bell again, and he was caught up in the intoxicating smell of her. The fake fur of her coat was warm and cuddly as she brushed past him. His body was electric for the brief second she was close. Then she stood back and smiled again. "It's because we're a bit early. I dare say they'll answer soon." As if her honeyed voice was the cue, a grating set beside the door emitted a harsh rattle and the door clicked. Tommy tested it, and it swung inward into a dark hallway lit only by a dim bulb.

It was a short hall, ending in a concrete stairwell. They hesitated for a moment, then Jasmine reached for his hand and led him forward. As surprised at her familiarity as he was, Tommy certainly wasn't going to reject it. He let himself be gently pulled up the first flight to an equally gloomy landing. A door on the right proclaimed it to be STUDIO ONE, but it was closed and dark. The second floor yielded similar results, and Jasmine led him up the final flight to an even gloomier landing. The notice above the door on the third floor was a makeshift banner with SINEMA EXTREME AUDITIONS in bold, black font against a red background.

They could see through the glass into a small, empty space beyond. The door swung inward as Jasmine pushed, and they entered the waiting area. Six or seven folding chairs were lined up against the near wall, while opposite them, another door, this one of dark wood, remained closed. There was no other furniture. Tommy moved to open the far door, but Jasmine, still holding his hand, pulled him to one of the chairs instead.

"They know we're here," she purred. "They'll come get us when they need to."

Tommy sat next to her, basking in her warm, honey presence. Jasmine more than compensated for the bleakness of the surroundings. He didn't care about the fly-specked dim bulb above their heads, or the breeze-block interior design, or the patch of mold to the right of the peeling door. Sitting with Jasmine was like being next to an effervescent Roman candle fizzing with pink sparks.

She linked her arm in his and leaned close, so that his senses reeled with her scent and her physical proximity. She had a little mole nestled in the hollow of her neck just above her breastbone and a beauty spot darker than the faint honey freckles on her cheeks. He wanted to know all about her, but she seemed keener to find out about him. Her eyes held his, warm and brown and twinkly. He had forgotten all about the audition until the door to the landing opened behind him and a young couple entered—he assumed they were here for the casting call from their general bewildered air. Tommy resented them irrationally for interrupting his private Jasmine moment, but apart from smiling at them briefly, she didn't seem bothered about speaking to them. They ignored Tommy completely and sat together a few chairs down.

"So why do you want to audition for a horror film?" Tommy finally managed to get a question in.

"It doesn't matter that it's a horror film," she trilled. "It's an opportunity. One that hopefully will give us a chance to shine. I've acted in several short films and one feature, but this is offering a real chance of proper exposure."

"But how did you hear about it? I haven't seen it advertised on any of the industry websites?"

"Well, that's part of its charm. It seems to be very much word of mouth. They're being extremely selective, so if you've been invited to audition, that's a fantastic complement." He was rapidly becoming acclimatized to Jasmine's seemingly inexhaustible enthusiasm for everything. It was quite infectious, and while her endless positivity could have been potentially cloying, Tommy found it endearing in a naïve way. He lapped it up. Lapped her up.

The door opened.

A man stood in the doorway. A huge man, like a bouncer on steroids. His tight dark suit—two sizes too small, but Tommy wondered if he could even buy in his correct size—restrained him like a straightjacket. His eyes were obsidian, expressionless. He was completely bald, and he didn't smile. He spoke simply and without ceremony: "Jasmine Paal." His eyes scanned the row of applicants, settled on Jasmine as the object of his search—she was smiling at him radiantly, so it wasn't difficult to guess she was the one he wanted—and stepped aside for her to precede him into the room beyond.

Jasmine sprang up from her seat, kissed Tommy on the cheek, gave him a dinky wave, then disappeared into the room. The huge man closed the door after her. For a moment, the kiss still tingling on his cheek, Tommy felt like following her. The whole setup was slightly sinister, and the bald, unfriendly giant wasn't helping the ambiance. He glanced at the two other applicants, a young girl and boy in their early 20s. If this all turned dodgy, these two student types wouldn't be able to help out. He got up and paced the room, ignoring the couple who watched him, maybe feeling the same trepidation as Tommy.

He found himself thinking of Trish, and a wave of sadness broke through him. The phenomenon that was Jasmine had driven all thoughts of his marital problems from his mind, but now they returned twice as hard. But did he really care, or was he just scared of being alone? He stopped pacing and reached inside his pocket for his phone, torn whether to ring Trish and ask for one last try. Then he thought of Jasmine—that cute little mole on her neck, the radiant smile, the *pinkness* of her lips and fingernails... He put the cell back in his pocket and sat down again.

Twenty minutes, half an hour passed, and Tommy's fears began to resurface. What the hell were they doing in there? He assumed there had to be more people involved in the audition than just the big man—he hadn't struck Tommy as much of the casting-director type. The two students were looking equally impatient now. The girl was relatively pretty, quite strident, with dark, bushy hair and a big chin. The young man fidgeted next to her. Tommy guessed he was a wannabe boyfriend but was too fat and slobby to stand a chance of that: buddy material only, no charm but a good laugh on a night out. Tommy had heard Fatboy declare a good ten minutes ago that he would give it another five minutes and then fuck off. A further ten went by before the door opened and Jasmine emerged, all giggles and leopard print.

Tommy glowed inside when he saw her and jumped up to take the hand she offered him. "How did it go?" he asked her, aware of the bald hulk waiting in the doorway behind her.

"I'll tell you later. Good luck, hun." She was making for the door.

"What? Oh. Okay. But..." He didn't even have her number, and the big man was staring right at him like he was an insect that should probably be squidged.

"Tommy Wallace?" He had somehow identified which applicant on his list was Tommy and kept his eyes firmly on the supporting artist as Tommy turned reluctantly away from Jasmine. She stepped through the outer door without a further word. *Oh well, there goes another one*, Tommy thought, stepping past the big man.

He found himself in a small, dark room. A lamp on a metal table in one corner, the rest of the room shadowed. He could see a pair of legs wearing jeans and trainers on the edge of the lamplight, the rest of the body and the chair it sat upon lost in the dark. *Okay... Not at all creepy...*

He waited for the big man to give him some instructions, but the giant merely stood by the door—to prevent Tommy from leaving? But Jasmine had been allowed to leave. He cleared his throat, waiting for the man in the chair to move or say something, his unease raising a notch or two.

The legs finally moved as a shadowy figure got to its feet, still remaining theatrically hidden.

"Hello...?" he said at last, nerves strained by the silence. "I'm Tommy Wall—"

"I know who you are," said a voice Tommy recognized all too well. His breath came out in an involuntary gasp of relief. He took a step toward the circle of light by the table.

"No. Wait there. You have to perform your audition in the dark."

"Really?" Tommy peered around the shadowy room, looking for any sign of a casting director or anyone else in the room besides himself, the big man, and his good buddy Mark. "Who do I perform to?"

"To whom, you mean. Tut. Grammar. Why, to me, of course." Mark stepped forward a little, though his face was still obscured. "The director trusts my judgment."

Well, that's me screwed then, thought Tommy. So, this *was* all just another platform for Mark to display the size of his ego.

"I might as well leave now then..." He forced a laugh.

"Why would that be?"

He decided not to go down that route. "So what do I do?"

"The director wants to judge your reactions to extreme stimuli..."

Tommy resisted the urge to approach Mark again. This melodramatic act was beginning to irritate him now. "Sounds fun..."

"You might think so." As he spoke, a projector screen flicked into view on the far wall. The sudden bright light harshly picked out Mark's smug features. And yes, he looked smugger than ever. "Your reactions will be recorded by a fixed camera to your left. All you have to do is react to the images we're about to show you."

Tommy automatically looked to his left, where the hulking doorman waited in the gloom. He could just make out a security cam at head height in the wall next to him.

A spotlight clicked on directly above his head, making him blink. The spot picked out his face for the camera. *Very clever*, he admitted grudgingly. He turned back to the screen as a wash of color filled the room. He stiffened. Vicky, the model from Elite Agency he'd fancied on the set of *The Man from U.N.C.L.E.*, was sitting on the edge of a bed in a nondescript room. She was wearing clothes not so dissimilar to her costume in the film: a crop top and mini. Her blonde hair was piled on her head; her blue eyes stared straight at the camera, wide and trusting and a little freaked out. And now he knew why those blue, scared eyes had been so familiar in the website promo. Following an off-screen instruction from a gruff voice, she began unbuttoning the top.

Tommy looked over at Mark, whose features remained inscrutable. "What the fuck?" he said, confusion and anger in his tone.

"That's a reaction for a start." Mark's eyes remained fixed on the projector screen. "Keep watching."

Vicky had removed the crop top. Her bra was shiny pink, hugging her pert little breasts. She waited for the next instruction. When it came, she obeyed without much compunction, though her eyes looked even less confident—and there at last was the touch of fear captured in the promo clip. She was doing as she was told, but something was scaring her. Acting? She hadn't been that good in *U.N.C.L.E.* She unhooked the bra, let it drop to the bedspread.

"Fuck's sake, Mark! Is this a joke?" Tommy deliberately stared at the other man, although *very* aware of Vicky's pink nipples out of the corner of his eye.

"Take a look, Tommy. You know you want to."

"No. This is all a wind-up. Fuck it! I'm out of here." He turned toward the doorman.

"But you can't leave yet, Tommy. The audition isn't over."

"Yes, it is. It never was an audition, was it? Just an opportunity for you to gloat. You knew I fancied Vicky."

"Then look. Look at her. Don't lie to yourself, to your own body. You *want* to look..."

And Tommy couldn't help himself. He looked. Vicky was standing up now, the mini riding down her sleek thighs. She paused, naked but for pink, shiny panties.

"And you're wrong, Tommy. This *is* the audition piece. It's not created especially for you. How egotistical of you to even think that. You are experiencing the same visuals that the couple outside will experience. The same that the rather attractive lady who preceded you experienced. So I'm sorry to disappoint you, Thomas: it's not all about you."

And Jasmine had emerged from the audition giggling! Maybe she had been turned on by this... Tommy didn't know exactly how that made him feel. But he would have been lying if he didn't admit to a little trill of excitement. He resisted the urge to go over and smash Mark, and carried on watching.

Vicky took another look at the camera before pulling down her panties. Tommy heard the rustle of material as they slid down her thighs. She posed elegantly, a little shy, yes (a little scared, too), but aware that she had a beautiful, slender body.

Then the screen went dark. Vicky was still there; Tommy could hear her startled breathing. There were no more off-screen instructions, but Tommy could tell by the sound of heavy boots and a clink of metal that someone else was in the room. The metal sound came again, and Tommy thought of tools clanking together. It was a dull sound, unnerving in the context.

Then came the sound of a blow—of a heavy object thudding into soft flesh—and the first scream.

Tommy jerked. He glanced toward Mark's dim figure, implacable beside the table, then at the doorman, then back at the pitch dark of the screen. Vicky was sobbing uncontrollably. A plea rose from the dark. "Don't, please! What are you *doing*?" Tommy heard what sounded like a machine being loaded, *clink, clink, clink*. Then a metallic percussion and a zip of sound. Another *thud*. Another scream. The percussion sound again, the *zip*, the *thud*, the scream.

And Tommy had heard that sound before... An image of a workman riveting a sheet of metal in a factory he had worked in for a week or two one summer during Uni. The percussion of the nail-gun trigger, the *thud* of the rivet slamming through steel, although there had been no whoosh of air parted by the projectile, and certainly no rip of flesh that he was hearing now. No screams either. He would definitely have remembered those...

"Switch that fucking thing off *now*!" He ducked out of the spotlight and made for the shadowy figure of Mark. The doorman moved instantly, a hand as big as Tommy's head clamping around his bicep, immobilizing him.

The screen flicked to plain white again and then switched off completely. Mark was clapping slowly, sardonically.

"You're not right in the head, Hamm," Tommy said, pulling futilely against the giant's grip.

"Horror Story," Mark replied, completely unperturbed by Mark's reactions. "We're making a Horror Story, Thomas, or did you forget? What did you expect from your audition—gags and a comedy soundtrack?"

Tommy was breathing fast and heavy, and very aware that he was back under the spot and the red eye of the security camera was still fixed on him.

"Switch that light off!"

The spot went dark above him.

"Mister Wallace is leaving now," Mark said matter-of-factly. The giant released him instantly. Tommy controlled his breathing and made for Mark again. The giant followed him warily.

"You really don't need to worry, Thomas. The lovely Vicky is alive and well and probably stripping for someone else right now. She was paid well for her scenes, I'm told."

"That was sick. She sounded terrified."

"Maybe she was a better actress than you gave her credit for."

"She wasn't an actress at all. She was a model. And that didn't sound like an act."

"Oh, I'm sure some of it wasn't. They wanted to keep some verisimilitude, you know. But I'm told she was completely unharmed, albeit maybe a little unnerved."

"Fuck this. Let me out of here."

"Of course. The door is unlocked. Thank you for coming. We'll be in touch shortly."

Tommy snorted and stepped around the bulky shadow of the giant and groped for the door. After a bit of fumbling, he found the knob and swung the door open.

Out in the waiting room, the two students looked up expectantly.

Tommy emerged into the relative brightness and felt the relief dawn brings after a particularly upsetting nightmare.

"Good luck!" he said to the students with heavy irony. They gaped at him uncomprehendingly.

Tommy pushed through the outer door and thumped down the concrete steps, still nauseous and unsettled. Had he just been the recipient of a very unpleasant practical joke? Or was it indeed a rather twisted take on the typical audition piece, all done to record the gamut of his reactions, just as Mark had said it was? Either way, he felt sickened and abused. And he didn't believe for a moment that Jasmine had been subjected to the same process. If only he'd had her number, he would have rung her.

He emerged into daylight, futilely hoping she would be waiting for him out in the unremitting drizzle. He looked up resentfully at the gray abomination of '60s architecture. He thought about deleting Mark's phone number from his contact list (it wouldn't be for the first time) but dismissed the idea. He hadn't finished with Hamm yet; he wanted some proper answers. He climbed into his Polo and drove off through the rain.

CHAPTER SIX

But Tommy didn't speak to Mark again for quite some time. Two days after the audition he received an email that stated simply: Sinema Extreme Productions would like to thank you for attending the audition on May 3rd. Unfortunately, you have not been selected on this occasion but we would like to wish you luck on future projects.

Although he tried to pretend to himself that he wasn't bothered, Tommy was, in all honesty, more than a little pissed off. Not just because he was missing out on a feature film, no matter how dubious it sounded, but also because if Jasmine had succeeded in her own audition, he would be missing out on her company as well. But what else had he expected with his arch-rival—and the supporting artist he disliked most of all—in charge of auditions? And what idiot would give him that responsibility? Not the sort of idiot that could be relied on to make a good film, he told himself in an attempt to lift his spirits.

As it turned out, he didn't need to look for ways to make his life more worthwhile: a few days later, on a sunny morning in May, his agency stepped up, and they did a pretty good job of that for once. They had generously booked him on a popular British Sci-Fi TV show as one of the main monsters. And what made it even better: there was no Mark Hamm dogging his steps, chasing all the Walk-Ons and lines, and trying to edge into camera frame every chance he got.

Tommy arrived at the Cardiff studio in a fine mood. The walk up from the residential road where he'd parked had refreshed his mind and heightened his expectations. Cardiff Bay twinkled cheerily in the sun, and gulls perched on the maritime sculptures along the sea wall of the Barrage greeted him with cheeky cries. He was going to enjoy today despite everything.

He checked in at reception and waited in the refectory to be collected by the Third AD. He looked around at the smattering of minor celebs munching on their subsidized breakfasts. Most of them were part of the weekly A&E drama that shared studio space with Doctor Who (the Sci-Fi show Tommy was working on today), and though he vaguely recognized some of them, he wasn't overly keen on *Casualty,* so couldn't have identified any of them for sure. He spotted the main star of Doctor Who collecting a full English breakfast from the serving counter, and Tommy's curiosity was aroused. He had just taken over the role—the part had been interpreted by several actors over the years since the show had begun in the '60s—and was clearly still enthusiastic about it. He joked cheerily with the kitchen staff and then took his tray to a table near Tommy, smiling warmly at him as he passed.

Well, that was a good start. Many of these A-listers didn't bother giving you the time of day. He considered getting some breakfast for himself but decided to pass. He'd managed to grab a bowl of cereal before dashing out of the (empty) house... He pushed thoughts of Trish out of his mind. He had created this scenario; this was the bed he wanted to lie in, so if the house was empty, that was his choice, and the brief stab of regret he felt was a natural and understandable reaction to separating from someone he'd been married to for six years. On impulse, he pulled out his Smartphone and thumbed the Facebook icon on the menu screen.

Jasmine Paal. He found her straight away and wondered why he hadn't thought of searching earlier. She was wearing a leopard print in her profile pic, too, and her slightly sharp teeth were bared in a cup-your-balls-gently smile. He checked out all the details that were revealed to a non-friend, and that wasn't much. She lived in Bath, was single, born in 1986, and that was it. Her friends list was hidden. There were a couple of inspirational posts from her that had been liked by a couple of (male) unknowns. Several posts from another male acquaintance dating from November that had been ignored. He pressed the Request Friend button and put the phone away. The Third AD was approaching him, a chubby blonde with a wide smile. Too early in the day for the stress to show, he thought and stood up to greet her.

"Are you Tommy?" She was clutching a call sheet and trying to listen to a voice in her earpiece at the same time as she waited for Tommy's response. He gave it, and she grabbed his wrist. "I'm Charlie. Let's go. You're the first to arrive, but we can get you settled in right away."

He followed her across the refectory and through a door she activated with her pass key. Then along a metal corridor and through another pass key-operated door and into the studio block, which was *Doctor Who*'s home.

Framed photographs of scenes and monsters from previous episodes of the long-running series decorated the long corridor that led to the sets. Tommy glanced at them as he passed, but Charlie's grip on his wrist was pretty relentless. She took him through a final door and into a large set dominated by towering alien pillars and hunks of machinery that looked a little fake in their coats of new paint and without the lighting that would bring them to life but were nevertheless impressive enough.

There was a cluster of prop guys and monster wranglers around the three Daleks (the main adversaries of Doctor Who in the show), and Tommy approached them curiously. Charlie released him, told him to wait here for a few minutes while they waited for the other two supporting artists to arrive. He watched her trot off toward the monitor in one corner of the room where the director sat, huddled in conversation with the sound guy and cameraman. They looked vaguely familiar. Tommy worked on so many different shows that it was inevitable he would come across the same faces, and the directors, cameramen, grips, and make-up and wardrobe crew were all chasing the same opportunities for work on as many varied productions as Tommy, just for different pay scales.

He approached the large pepper pot-like shell of the metallic monster he would be operating. It was a TV icon, and Tommy had grown up hiding behind the sofa watching these alien meanies along with so many others of his generation. It was therefore thrilling to see one in the flesh, so to speak, and to know he would be inside it. The Dalek was painted bronze and moved on small castors. A gun stick emerged from the center of the fiberglass body, next to a long rod ending in a sucker. As the top section had been removed for the operator to climb inside, Tommy could lean over and peer in.

There was a simple wooden bench for the operator to sit on, the gun stick handle jutted a few inches inwards, and that was it. No pedals, certainly no steering wheel. This baby would be propelled by foot power and brute strength. He wondered how easy it would be.

One of the monster wranglers saw him and came toward him, scooping up the domed top section as he came. There was an eyepiece near the apex of the dome, but Tommy guessed this was for effect only. He would be required to see through the mesh girding the top of the base section, which was head height—or would be once he was sitting down inside.

"You ever been in one of these before?" the man asked. He looked tired and harassed, in his late 50s with gray whiskey hair and fluffy sideboards.

"Er...no," Tommy confided.

"Oh, for fuck's sake," the wrangler turned to his mate. "Another fucking virgin," he moaned.

"The agency didn't tell me I needed experience," Tommy explained.

"Fucking desperate, were they?" He sighed. "And where are the other two?"

Tommy shrugged. "Charlie said they were coming."

"Did she now." He consulted a folded sheet of paper he tugged from his back pocket, then grunted. "Matt and Claudio. Thank fuck for that. At least they know how to operate these bastards."

As if on cue, a runner pushed through the door from the corridor with two other supporting artists in tow. They shook hands with the wrangler and nodded to Tommy. He nodded right back. One was a real Alpha Male, 6'3" at least, with a big quiff of hair and a bullishly handsome face. His friend was podgier[8], though still tall, and sported a scruffy wisp of beard and a ponytail. This one introduced himself to Tommy as Claudio in a decidedly Italian accent that was rendered a little surreal by the tinge of Welsh mixed in with it.

They chatted with the wrangler for a while and ignored Tommy until Charlie joined them, all breathless, flushed, and smiling. She ran through the shooting plan for the day with them. It all sounded simple enough. They were to operate the alien Daleks around the studio floor, pretending to board an enemy spaceship and simulate attack, engaging in combat with some soldiers, who would be arriving

---

[8] Chubby

later.

"You'd better get in and try it out," the wrangler—whose name, it turned out, was Graham—said to Tommy grudgingly. Despite the latent hostility directed at him, Tommy was determined to enjoy himself. He climbed up the little stepladder that was positioned beside the machine he was to inhabit with no little excitement. He lowered himself down into the cockpit and settled on the bench. The collar was above his head, but he had partial vision through the mesh in front of him.

"Head coming on," the wrangler informed him, and Tommy's world darkened as the dome was slid into place on top of the casing and clicked shut with a slight twist. "Switch the light on," the man barked. Tommy fumbled for the switch at his side, grafted next to a bulky battery strapped to the inside of the casing. He flicked it, and the eyepiece glowed above his head. "Okay, try moving forward."

That was easier said than done. The casing was heavy, and the three castors were far from fluidly mobile. The one at the front kept swiveling, basically locking Tommy to a standstill, but with practice and determination, he managed to grunt it forward a few feet.

"Keep it straight, for fuck's sake," he heard the old man grumbling. "And hold the gun-stick up; don't let the fucker droop. The front wheel needs to be straight at all times."

Tommy did as he was told and pushed his shoulders against the inside trim of the casing. This time, the machine rolled forward a bit more easily.

"Spin it around," the wrangler instructed him. "The movement needs to be smooth."

Tommy tried revolving in a circle on the spot but could manage no more than a sequence of jerky movements.

"Try it again," the man sighed.

Tommy lifted his feet up this time and pushed against the right side of the casing with his shoulder with as much force as he could manage. The machine spun.

"Better. Try it again. And again. Needs to be smooth."

This went on for another ten minutes or so. Tommy could see the other two machines occupied by Matt and Claudio going through their paces very efficiently. A man who looked vaguely familiar to Tommy announced loudly that they would be shooting in ten, and Tommy guessed he was the First AD. He heard a babble of voices from behind him and spun the machine to investigate. Through the meshed grill he could see a stream of men and women dressed as futuristic soldiers entering the room. They were bubbling with excitement and cradling their impressive hi-tech-looking but inevitably fiberglass weaponry with obvious pride. Charlie huddled them into a group and relayed their instructions. A few of them crouched and pretended to fire at Tommy, Matt, and Claudio with their blasters until the short-tempered First barked at them to stop fucking around and listen.

Tommy sat in his casing and waited. Finally, the soldiers were arrayed behind crates and huge plastic breezeblocks in defense positions, and Tommy and his two monster comrades were ordered to reverse against the opposite wall while the cameras were set up.

"For rehearsal," barked the First. "Turning..." Then the familiar cry: "Action!"

Tommy pushed off with his feet, leaning against the bulkhead to give him more impetus. The machine rolled forward obediently, and the wheel remained blessedly unlocked. Matt and Claudio were accompanying him to either side.

The soldiers were pretending to fire. Tommy waggled his gun stick at them. A couple of soldiers collapsed backward, flinging their arms out in extravagant death throes.

"Cut!"

"For a take this time," the First barked, striding around in his big boots with dramatic élan. "But curb the death cheese, please..."

Tommy reversed with his two companions and prepared for action.

Curb the death cheese.

For take after take, Tommy grunted and shoved the dustbin monster up and down the set until finally the sadistic First was satisfied and called Lunch.

A couple of the soldiers decided to shed their uniforms, steaming with sweat. Tommy breathed in the relatively fresh studio air gratefully when Graham hoisted the lid off and set him free. He climbed down and followed the troop of supporting artists and crew as they made for the refectory.

Graham stayed behind alone, fussing with the battery connections in his monsters, some of which had stubbornly refused to work.

It was quiet in the studio now, and Graham relaxed for the first time that day. He hated the chirpy recklessness of the extras, who didn't really give a fuck if the props worked properly or whether they happened to drop an expensive gun Graham had spent hours creating. He examined the base of the Dalek Tommy had occupied and tutted when he spotted a fresh paint chip on its front bumper.

"Clumsy fuck," he hissed to himself. He fetched a pot of paint and a brush from the props cupboard and knelt down to touch up the damage, completely unaware of the door to the corridor opening behind him. He didn't notice the figure shrugging into a discarded soldier uniform either, donning a futuristic helmet complete with visor. Instead of a rifle, the new arrival carried a small camcorder in one hand. The other held a drill.

It was a fairly bulky drill with a power pack attached for cordless use—although the manufacturers had certainly never envisaged the purpose it was going to be put to today. The intruder stepped slowly toward Graham. If the wrangler had turned, he would have seen the red light on the Sanyo glowing constantly and would have smiled for the camera. Or, more likely, scowled in irritation, suspecting another supporting artist prank.

When the figure was halfway toward him across the large studio space, Graham finally turned. He peered at the intruder, at the camera, at the drill. As if on cue, the "soldier" pressed the starter, and the drill twirled into buzzing life.

"What the fuck are you playing at?" Graham took a step to meet the intruder, but something made him hesitate. It wasn't just because the figure—and Graham couldn't recognize the features through the tinted visor—was holding a drill (and holding it like a fucking gun) or even the camera in the other gloved hand filming his confusion that caused Graham to stop. It was more down to the decidedly menacing bearing of the intruder, the unhurried gait.

"Did you hear me?" Graham's voice cracked slightly, and that was embarrassing because he wasn't scared (not yet), and now this bastard had his display of weakness on video. "Yeah, very funny. Put that fucking drill down and fuck off to lunch right now before I call your agency." He straightened to his full 5'10". He might be nearly sixty, but he was a solid 250 pounds of no-nonsense Brummie[9]. If this tit wanted a scrap, he would give him one. The figure continued its implacable approach, the drill whining, the camera recording...five steps away now, Graham squinting to peer through the visor...

The driller watched Graham frowning uneasily through the tinted plexiglass and revved the drill with a flick of a black-gloved thumb. The bit whirled faster. The Sanyo camcorder clutched in the driller's left hand was steady, the view screen framing Graham perfectly in black and white.

The stocky man would put up a fight. That was obvious from the aggressive expression and bunched fists. But the intruder was ready for that. The drill could easily compensate for those dry knuckles. The driller closed the gap quickly in one sudden jab of motion, and the drill lunged for Graham's paunch. The wrangler moved at the last minute, and the bit missed its intended target and ground into the fleshy bags under his left bicep. The victim screamed horribly, and behind the mask, the killer's face formed a rictus grin of mixed frustration and pleasure deferred...

When the drill sank into his arm, Graham realized in a tear of agony that this was no SA or crew member pulling a stunt. This was only too deadly real. He gaped at the gushing wound as the twirling drill bit withdrew from its bloody socket and let out a howl of primitive, raw pain.

He fell back against the Dalek he had just been painting, clutching at the wound uselessly. Blood foamed through his fingers. The masked intruder lifted the drill for another assault. Weeping in agony, Graham darted to his left, around the large pepper pot-shaped prop, putting its bulk between himself and the madman.

---

[9] Someone who comes from Birmingham.

The intruder hesitated for a moment. Graham's assailant appeared lither and fitter than the middle-aged wrangler, and it wouldn't take long for Graham to be chased down if they continued this deadly game of tag. Graham threw back his head and shouted as loud as he could. "HELP! HELP MEEE!" There had to be someone still hanging around, surely to God. Please let there be somebody as diligent as himself, some crew member or runner who just had to finish one little job in the studio before following the rest of the herd to lunch. He shouted again, his voice cracking like a youth hitting puberty, and as he strained to hear any hint of a reply or sound of a door opening over the fizz of the drill, the assailant seized the moment and came round the side of the machine with frightening speed.

The wrangler realized his mistake and tried to push himself away from the Dalek to make a dash for the door. The intruder slammed him back against the machine with one shoulder and steadied the camera, red recording light unblinking, the counter now reaching five minutes ten seconds, then lunged again with the drill.

The bit dug deep into Graham's belly, and he squealed, writhing like a fly on a pin against the empty machine, the machine he had so lovingly restored for the latest series. One pudgy hand gripped the protruding gun stick as he jerked against the fiberglass surface, as if the wrangler were willing the gun to exterminate his opponent. But the gun was a prop, and there was no FX guy in the world who could help him make it real right now. The drill chugged as it bored into solid fat, gristle, and finally, intestine, but before the attack could prove fatal, the intruder dragged the drill out of its borehole and stood back as if to survey a spot of handiwork. Then the drill leaped forward again, and this time, the bit went for the money shot while the camera filmed it all in close-up and Gorevision. The intruder leaned into the job, exerting full strength and pushing the drill bit into the center of Graham's wrinkled forehead.

Et voila! The drill had found oil! Blood welled and bubbled around the twisting bit, masking Graham's agonized features behind a mini waterfall of red stuff. Chards of bone were dug out from Graham's forehead, pattering against the intruder's visor. The killer ignored the drizzle of brain fragments that obscured the Plexiglas and forced the drill bit deeper until it clogged and the power stalled. Graham had ceased to move now, flopped back against the hollow Dalek, one out-flung arm draped over the gun stick. Blood had given him a dark red apron, tinged his jeans, dyed his hair, and splattered the machine behind him.

The driller, finding the bit was embedded too deeply in Graham's skull to withdraw, patiently switched off the camcorder, placed it momentarily on the floor, and then detached the bit from the drill handle. The intruder then placed the drill on the floor beside the camcorder, bent to seize the corpse around its blood-soaked knees, and, gasping with exertion, heaved the body up the flank of the prop and let it fall inside. One foot remained stubbornly hanging over the open top. The killer ignored it, carrying both drill and camcorder to a nondescript rucksack discarded by the door earlier and placed them carefully inside. Then the driller shrugged out of the bloody uniform and left it draped over a plastic chair. One last thing needed to be done. From a separate pocket on the outside of the rucksack, the driller removed a VHS box with a particularly gruesome cover and carried it back to the bloody Dalek Tommy had such trouble maneuvering. The killer dropped the box inside. It slid down Graham's ruptured stomach and came to a rest against his chin.

The driller killer turned again and strode casually toward the door. There was no need to hurry; there was still a good half hour of lunchtime, and there was no chance of anybody disturbing the fun. Charlie's pass key opened the door at the end of the corridor, and the killer walked toward the refectory. There might be time for a quick sandwich before the Third even noticed her key was gone. It would be found soon enough discarded in a waste bin, a bit like Graham stuffed upside down in his own receptacle.

Tommy had enjoyed his Chicken Masala and chips, although his pleasure had been spoiled somewhat upon spotting Mark Hamm entering the refectory when he went to collect his chocolate dessert. The smug extra saluted him ironically from across the room. He was dressed in a blue male nurse's uniform, and the familiar smirk was plastered on his face, as if to say, *Hey, you just know I'm gonna get a Walk On and a line today.*

Tommy ignored the salute, paid for his dessert, and left the serving counter. Hamm blocked his way.

"Hello, Tommy! How's things?" He stuck out a hand, which Tommy promptly ignored.

"I thought just once I might get to do a job without you turning up," Tommy said.

Mark pretended to be taken aback. "Harsh! But I'm not on the same job. I assume you're doing Doctor Who? I'm down the corridor playing a nurse in Casualty." He smiled amiably. "But I hope you're not still upset over that audition business. We could tell from your reactions that you were perhaps a little too sensitive for the part. It was nothing personal."

Tommy nodded. "Whatever, Mark." He made to step past, but Hamm grabbed his arm.

"Hey, don't worry. I'll keep you up to date on the film's progress. And you can always ask your new friend Jasmine..."

Tommy looked at him sharply.

"Oh, she told me you both hit it off wonderfully before the audition. Lovely girl. She'll fit in perfectly..."

One last smirk and he minced off, leaving Tommy with a turmoil of emotions to digest along with his dessert.

All too soon, Charlie was ushering them back to the set. Tommy watched her pause before the electronic refectory door, rummaging through her pockets. The First appeared next to her. "What's up? Lost your key?"

Charlie nodded miserably. The First held out his own and slid it down the key groove. "You really should keep it around your neck, Charlie. I'm sure that's not the first time you've been told." He walked ahead of them through the open doorway, and Charlie, even more red-faced than normal, gestured to the assembled extras to precede her.

The First was waiting for them at the studio door, and the group sauntered along the corridor, some of the soldiers joshing Matt and Claudio about how they were gonna blast their fiberglass asses. Claudio responded by describing the soldiers as Dalek Road Kill. Tommy stayed out of the banter. His encounter with Mark had dampened his enthusiasm. Just as it always did.

It was one of the soldiers who noticed there was a problem. He was one of the first into the room, a shy and rather earnest 22-year-old called Ben. He had shed his uniform before leaving the set, and upon going to retrieve it now, found that although it was still draped over the chair where he had left it, it had magically accrued a coating of sticky crimson. By the time he had realized it was blood, not to mention brain matter, Tommy had advanced far enough into the room to see that his Dalek was similarly covered in grue. He stopped abruptly. Charlie came up behind him, irritable due to her public dressing down from the First. "Hurry up. Straight back inside. Lots to shoot this afternoo—" She froze, having realized exactly why Tommy had stopped, staring at his machine.

They had both seen the foot poking up from the open collar. The slip-on shoe was painted with blood, as was the sock emerging from it. Neither Tommy nor Charlie made any effort to step closer and peer inside. They waited for the First to do that. Curb the death cheese.

Charlie was starting to sob. The First swaggered up like a Staff Sergeant, ready to bark at her again. Then he spotted the foot, too.

"What's this? Someone pranking me?" He peered over the collar of the machine, stiffened, and then slowly withdrew. His fulsome expression had drained, like someone had pulled out the plug on his face.

He turned toward Charlie, as if to admonish her for this latest delay, and then vomited his Chicken Masala all over her spotlessly white tee.

CHAPTER SEVEN

"Can't we hear something else, guv?"

Whitley's ears were bleeding. He had a headache and really wasn't in the mood for any more 999.

Slade didn't need to drive the Bentley. The squad had plenty of designated drivers for that. But he loved it. He loved throwing the vehicle around street corners at 60 miles per, throwing Whitley against the passenger door in the process. It made him feel well... Sweeney.

"Fuck's wrong with you? Great stuff this is."

The track was "Homicide"—Whitley knew that from repeated playings, and always when they were summoned to a SOC. Appropriate, if nothing else. And while it was punchy and catchy enough (even if it was played at Fuck You decibels), Whitley couldn't help feel this kind of shit only added to Slade's reputation as a loose cannon back at the department.

"Don't you think he looks a bit like me?" Slade took another corner at double the mandatory speed limit. Then they were leaving Cardiff City Center and heading up Bute Street, one of the rougher areas of the Welsh city.

"What? Who?"

"Nick Cash. There he is on the cover of that C.D." He gestured to a CD case stacked on top of a disorderly pile that was threatening to topple from the open glove compartment. Whitley pulled it free and examined the cover cursorily.

"Which one? You don't look like any of 'em, to be fair."

"The fucker in the trench coat, dickhead."

"The one with the receding hairline?"

Slade flew through a red light. The Bentley hummed as it bullied its way toward the docks where the BBC studios were located.

"Is he the singer?" Whitley sniffed and chucked the CD case back in the glove box. "Doesn't look much like a singer."

"Don't you think he looks like me?"

Whitley shook his head at his superior's childishness. "A bit. But you're fatter. Older. Nastier. Apart from that, spot on."

"Fuck you."

"But to be honest, guv, I think you're a bit too old to be listening to this shit."

"Cheeky cunt. What do you think I should be listening to then, Taylor Swift? Fuckin' Snow Patrol?" He snorted in disgust, throwing the Bentley into top gear as they reached the Opera House and floated through another red.

"Well... Yeah. Or James Blunt."

The Bentley screamed to a halt, narrowly missing a fat woman with a pram trying to use the zebra crossing.

Slade turned to his DS. "Any more of that shit, and you can get out and walk. Now where the fuck is this studio?"

Whitley peered through the windscreen at the signs ahead of them. He ignored the woman who was passing them, muttering obscenities. She raised a middle finger, and Slade cheered loudly.

"Follow this road around the Opera House, then straight on," Whitley announced after a moment's deliberation. The Bentley kicked forward again, tossing Whitley back against his seat.

"Did you watch that video?" Slade asked as they cruised around the large, elaborately designed Opera House.

"*Don't Go in the Woods?* Yeah. Bit of a tough job. Thanks for that."

"Well?"

"Pretty much as D.C. Nandu described it, guv. There was a bear trap used as a murder weapon and a spear wrapped in animal skins. The perp's M.O. copied the killer in the film."

"Exactly?"

"Pretty much. But there were a lot of murders in the movie. Our perp just picked the choicest. The most dramatic. Oh, and he combined two methods; the spear and the bear trap were used on different victims in the video."

"What do you conclude from that?"

"Apart from the fact our killer's a sick fuck?" Whitley shook his head. "Bad movie buff? Flair for the melodramatic, twisted sense of humor? Who knows?"

The Bentley cruised past the docks, the water choppy in the breeze that had picked up. The studio was to their right. They pulled up directly outside the main door, behind two patrol cars and an ambulance. Slade nodded at a uniformed constable guarding the door.

"Anything new to tell me?" he asked the younger officer.

The PC wet his lips. "Nobody's been allowed in or out since the incident was discovered, sir."

"Carry on," Slade entered the reception area, flashed his badge at the pale security man behind the desk. There was a row of monitors above his head, all showing different parts of the studio complex.

"What did these capture?" He spoke to the security officer, indicating the monitors.

The man looked even more uncomfortable. "Absolutely nothing. The C.C.T.V. in the studio where...where it happened...isn't working."

"Why is that? Malfunction? Or did someone tamper with it?" Slade squinted at him suspiciously. "Were you on duty at the time of the incident?"

"Y-yes, sir."

"And you didn't leave for any reason? Quick piss, a dump?"

"No. I have relief cover for that." He indicated a thin black man sitting just inside the security staff quarters to the right of the main desk. "I was here all the time. But if someone knew what they were doing, they could knock out the C.C.T.V. in there. I..." He paused nervously. "...I only found out it wasn't working after the incident."

Slade raised an eyebrow. "Do you have a sign-in book?"

"Yes sir," the security man was on firmer ground now. He handed over a thick journal open to today's page. Slade scanned the entries briefly, then passed it to Whitley. "Okay. Anybody enter that wasn't marked down?"

"Never. Not on my watch."

"What about on his?" Slade jerked his head at the guard in the staff room.

The security officer didn't reply.

"We'll speak to him later. And my D.S. will check all these names. You sure nobody left just after the incident, which was approximately..." He looked enquiringly at Whitley.

"One-thirty, guv."

The security man shook his head. "Nobody that I saw."

Slade looked at the monitors again. He could see himself and Whitley standing in the lobby. "What about the cameras out here? I'll need all the tapes from the whole day, and any from the rest of the complex that actually work." The guard winced at the implied criticism and nodded.

Slade left the security desk and stepped through the automatic doors into the refectory. More police officers were interrogating witnesses and copying down statements. Slade spotted several celebs among them, including the gray-haired actor who played *Doctor Who*, now looking decidedly sorry for himself. Slade would look forward to putting the pressure on him later. *Might even get an autograph out of the bastard*, he thought. Though what the fuck he could do with that was beyond him. Sell it on eBay? As they stood looking around, a plain-clothes officer with a balding head and a salt-and-pepper mustache moved over to greet them.

"D.I. Hughes. Don't mean to be rude, exactly, but I don't see what this case has to do with Avon and Somerset." His Welsh accent was soft and lilting—from the Valleys, Slade guessed. He nodded curtly. "D.I. Slade, D.S. Whitley. And yeah, we know we're out of our jurisdiction strictly speaking, but we're assuming this incident is linked to a similar one we're already assigned to."

"The Forest Ffawr murder? That should have been one of ours, too. You already assuming the two incidents are linked?"

"We were called in to help. If that itches your balls, take it up with the Super." Slade's courtesy had stretched way past its usual limits. He was never one for territorial politics at the best of times. "I'd rather be drinking coffee and farting happily back at my cozy department in Bristol rather than fucking around out here in the valleys chasing sheep, believe me. But unfortunately, I've got previous experience in these sorts of cases, and maybe a little more seniority, so we're both stuck with it. You can help me, and get one of your boyos to fetch me a coffee, or you can pull your mustache and lose more hair. Either way, this is my baby. We cool?"

Whitley looked at his feet. The Welsh D.I. shook his head in disbelief. "Fuck me; they were right about you. Knock yourself out, sunshine. Just don't step on my toes or I'll fuckin' stamp on yours." His Valleys accent deepened noticeably as his dander got up.

Slade grinned wolfishly. "Excellent. I think we're gonna get on like a sheep and a horny Welshman!" Hughes's heavy features darkened. Whitley cut in quickly: "So where's the S.O.C.?"

Hughes took them through the electronic door to the corridor. Slade noticed one of the uniforms activated it with a pass key, as he did to gain access to the *Doctor Who* studio. He took the pass off the PC and examined it as they followed Hughes up the corridor to the main set. "Does everyone in the building have one of these?"

"I already asked the head of security here," Hughes answered gruffly. "All full-time staff, regular crew, and actors are issued with them."

Slade glanced at the framed stills on the walls curiously. "What about the extras?"

"Eh?"

"The extras, D.I. Hughes... Supporting Artists, bit players, whatever they're fucking call themselves these days. Do they have passes, too?"

They were entering the set now, and SOCOs were all over it, not looking out of place at all in their white, hermetically sealed gear amongst all the futuristic props and scenery. A couple more uniforms were watching the forensic work carefully; one of them, a plump sergeant, nodded at Hughes and glared a little balefully at Slade and Whitley. Slade ignored him. He left Hughes to chat with his officer and headed for Jim Tavell, the chief SOCO.

Jim left his detailed examination of the scene to greet him. He peeled off the polystyrene mask and smiled grimly.

Slade peered past him at the blood-spattered Dalek. The victim's foot was still protruding from the top.

"We waited for you, Detective Inspector," Tavell said curtly. "Body's where we found it."

"Where who found it exactly?" Slade approached the dustbin-shaped prop and the corpse tipped upside down inside it.

Hughes answered for him as he sauntered over, not wanting to miss out. "A supporting artist called Tommy Wallace. He was returning from lunch and—"

"Tommy Wallace?" Slade whirled on him. "Open and shut fucking case then, I would say. That's the same bastard who was first on the scene at the Forest Ffawr incident, too."

"Maybe, but he's got a good alibi. He was in the refectory at the time of the murder." Hughes looked happy to contradict his rival detective from across the River Severn.

"Any witnesses to that?"

Hughes looked a little less happy. "Nobody definite. He ate alone."

Slade grunted. "Did he have a pass key?"

Jim Tavell answered for the Welsh detective. "We found the pass key that was used in a bin in the refectory. Charlie Spavins, a Third A.D. on *Doctor Who*, reported it missing. We've dusted it for prints. Only Charlie's were found. We've also got this..." He gestured to a female SOCO who Slade could tell was pretty even with the mouth mask and tightly drawn hood pulled around her head. She handed Tavell an evidence bag with a particularly lurid item clearly visible inside.

Slade looked at it without touching the item and smiled grimly. The big VHS box sported the mother of all grisly covers: rivers of blood trickled down a close-up of a man's screaming face while a drill bored into his forehead. Slade read out the title and tagline: "*Driller Killer. The Blood runs in rivers...and the drill keeps on tearing through flesh and bone...*" He glanced up at Whitley and sniffed. "It's the same sick fucker, all right. Get it dusted, but I'm guessing you won't find anything."

Slade turned back to the Dalek that had housed Tommy Wallace earlier that day as he battled so happily with the soldiers. Some of the forensic guys were still snapping photographs. He walked around it, peering at the corpse stuffed unceremoniously inside. "Ready to get this sleeping beauty out of his pit?" Tavell nodded and signaled to his men. The corpse was pulled gingerly out of its fiberglass tomb and laid out on a stretcher.

"Same M.O. as Forest Ffawer. This bastard likes his video nasties a bit too much. Gore Film Copycat. That's a new one on me." He picked at his teeth to dislodge a bit of the bacon sarnie he'd wolfed down on the M4 from Bristol and addressed D.I. Hughes. "Both these incidents have been on Welsh turf. You got any nutters on your books who like horror films? Particularly of the nasty variety?"

"We can check. Can't think of any offhand. But we do have a lot of nutters on the loose around these parts."

"I don't doubt that for a minute." He squatted next to the corpse. The blood had congealed around the ghastly wound, and the drill bit stuck up from the forehead like a short metal arrow.

"So, who was he?"

Hughes was obviously sulking a bit from the last remark as

he took his time answering. "Graham Croft. B.B.C. staffer. Fifty-six. Looks after the props and articulated monsters on *Doctor Who* and various other shows."

"Any links to Andy Hill?"

Hughes looked confused for a minute. Whitley nudged his memory for him. "The Forest Ffawr victim."

Hughes pulled a dumb face. Slade straightened and gave Whitley an arch look. "We'll check it for you, Taff. No worries." Hughes was about to object, but Slade raised a hand for silence as he saw another SOCO examining the bloody soldier's uniform slung over a plastic chair. He approached the SOCO, Jim Tavell following.

"Worn by the perp?" Slade asked, glancing at the gore crusting the black uniform.

"We think so," Tavell answered. "We also think it was discarded by one of the extras when he went for lunch."

"Find out who and grill him," Slade said to Whitley. "Okay. I'm done here. Jim, bag that poor bastard and get me everything you can double quick. But I'm guessing it's all gonna be as clean as the furs and the spear on the last job."

Jim Tavell nodded and stepped away to speak to his crew.

Slade rounded on Hughes again. "Why was Croft alone in here, and why didn't he go for lunch like everyone else? Did he recognize the perpetrator? And did the killer nick the A.D.'s pass key to get in or just make it look that way?"

"I don't get you."

"No. You probably don't. Maybe the killer already had a pass key. Either way, it's time we spoke to our little group of film stars in the canteen. Who knows, the killer might still be among them. What do you think, Taff?"

"I think if you call me Taff one more time, I'm going to bend your nose for you, *boyo*..."

Slade laughed. "I like you, D.I. Hughes. You're funny. Even if you don't know what the fuck you're doing. Which is why I'm taking over this case permanently." Before the Welshman could argue, Slade clapped Whitley on the shoulder and headed for the door.

Hughes shouted after him, his face red and flushed. "I've heard all about you, Slade. You're a fucking liability. Think you're a maverick, don't you? Think you're all cool playing your kids' music and shagging every whore you nick. There's a word for coppers like you, Slade...but I'm aware this is a crime scene, so I won't embarrass everyone by using it."

Slade waved back at him cheerily without turning.

"Don't push him too far, guv," Whitley warned as they followed the uniform with the pass key down the corridor. "This is his territory."

"Yeah, and he doesn't know which finger to use for scratching his own ass. I've been given seniority on this job, and he's doing his best to do absolutely fuck all to help." He waited as the PC activated the door into the refectory. "So what are the chances of our perp still being here, Trev? And what a coincidence our friend Tommy Wallace is on the scene, too. Let's see what other surprises we have in store when we question them."

The first surprise was finding they had not just one extra on hand at both crimes, but two. Slade spotted Mark Hamm sitting patiently at a table, waiting his turn to be questioned, and wondered how he'd failed to see him earlier. But then he'd been too curious about the actor playing *Doctor Who* to look around at the extras properly. The same went for Tommy Wallace. Slade finally checked him out sitting on his own, head lowered, hiding behind a big, red rucksack. Well, that wouldn't do him much good.

When Wallace saw him coming, he visibly paled. *Guilty as fuck,* thought Slade.

"We meet again, Mister Wallace," he said as he sat opposite the supporting artist at the refectory table. Whitley settled next to him. Wallace declined to answer, clutching his bag tightly. Then, as if realizing his body language was a giveaway, he released it and sat back in his chair, affecting nonchalance.

"Two murders on two different T.V. sets. And I'm seeing the same face at both." He leaned forward, screwing the extra with his eyes. "*Your* face."

Wallace scratched his nose. "Two faces."

"Say what?"

"I wasn't the only one at Forest Ffawr who's here today."

"Oh, you mean your friend Mark Hamm?"

"He's not my friend."

"Fallen out, have you? What was that over?"

Wallace shifted, not liking Slade's line of questioning. "We were never friends to start with. Look, what's this got to do with anything?"

Slade changed tack. "Bit of a coincidence...you being on both sets *and* being first on the scene of crime. I don't like coincidences. They give me indigestion. You ask D.S. Whitley." He winked at the Detective Sergeant. Whitley remained impassive.

"I didn't ask to be on both sets. My agency booked me. So, yes, it *is* a coincidence." He was clutching the straps of his rucksack again.

"Did you know Graham Croft well?"

"No. This was the first time I'd ever met him."

"And how did you find him?"

Wallace cleared his throat, shrugged. "Bit grumpy. Harmless enough."

"You knew Andy Hill, though, didn't you? Was he a bit grumpy, too?"

Wallace shook his head. "What are you accusing me of, Inspector?"

"Well, duh! This *is* a murder inquiry. Work it out."

"Then it's probably time I spoke to a solicitor."

"All in good time, Tommy boy. Relax. We just need a statement first. Don't rush the process."

Wallace obviously picked up on Whitley's strained look, as if it was the sergeant who suffered from indigestion and not his superior. "Are you *supposed* to be treating me like a suspect? I'm getting the impression you make a habit of riding roughshod over correct police procedure."

Whitley's left eyebrow raised. Slade chuckled and leaned over the table to square Wallace with an unflinching gaze. His tone was low when he spoke. "Seems like you've grown an attitude since last we spoke, sonny. Copying your bessie mate Hamm, no doubt. I don't much like you, Wallace. I can sense you're a wrong 'un. There's a smell about you."

"Now you're just getting personal."

"Laugh it up. This ain't a joke, son. Someone's had their head used as a screw socket. And you look the likeliest candidate for the job."

"Not so likely, seeing as I was having my lunch in here when the murder took place."

Slade became aware of a figure standing just behind him and turned. DI Hughes was watching him carefully. Waiting for him to slip up so he could ease back into the cockpit?

"The director on *Doctor Who* wants to speak to you." Hughes's voice was hard and sulky. "Seems he needs to crack on and wants permission."

Slade stood up slowly, turning his back on Wallace. "Am I tripping?" He rubbed his eyes theatrically. "Has somebody slipped me some 'shrooms? *Needs to crack on?* What in the Holy Whore is wrong with these people? I'll show the bastard how to crack on..." He turned to Whitley. "Is *nobody* taking this seriously?" Whitley shrugged on cue. Slade faced Hughes again, "Tell the bastard there will be no *cracking on* until this case is solved. He can post his shooting schedule up his turd alley for all I care." Spittle pattered on the Welshman's jacket collar as Slade raved, his face red as a Man United strip. "And Inspector Hughes... Don't let anybody out of this room until every statement is extracted. That'll be *your* job." He sighed loudly. "Meanwhile, I'm gonna speak to the star, see if he can shed any light on why a prop man gets a third eye on his show. Then, if I'm really bored for things to do, I might keep the director busy for a few more days playing paper airplanes with his statement and getting him to recite it in Latin until I'm really, truly satisfied he's sorry for asking to crack the fuck on. Are we clear here, dear? *Fuck!*"

Hughes glanced at Whitley, then at Wallace, who'd heard the rant in its entirety. "You're an embarrassment, Slade. A disgrace. I'm gonna speak to the Super, get you removed from the case."

Slade laughed as if he'd just heard the mother of all punch lines. "Join the queue, Welshie. But I'm warning you: it tails around the block a few times. Fact is, they won't take me off cos they know I always come through. Swallow that with some leeks, boyo."

Slade leaned over the table for one last glare at Wallace. "And we ain't done either, son. I think we'll be talking again real soon." He pushed away from the table and, accompanied by his best mate, wove through the packed refectory in search of Doctor Who.

CHAPTER EIGHT

"He suspects me, Wayne. I'm his numero uno."

Wednesday had brought another light spring shower and a small northern man to the city of Bristol. The small northern man was called Wayne, and he liked video nasties. He liked them so much that he was hell-bent on collecting every single nasty on the infamous banned list produced by the Department of Public Prosecutions in 1983. This was no easy task, as some of them were rarer than British Eurovision Song Contest winners. But he had persevered, had Wayne, and could now count amongst his collection a solid 30 out of the hot 39 wanted by the Plod back when he was just a wee nipper.

It was chasing elusive video nasties that had first brought Wayne into contact with Tommy several years before at a horror film festival. Tommy had been flogging a few from a shoe box in the foyer, and Wayne had bought half his stock. Now, he wanted the rest. And right now, Tommy was only too happy to give them up.

"But you've got solid alibis for both murders," the small man from Burney insisted. They were sitting in a biker pub in St Nick's Market, drinking Trooper Ale. The picture on the tap label showed a zombie Crimean Soldier waving an English flag ripped from an Iron Maiden CD cover, which was probably why they were drinking it. It was three in the afternoon, and both of them had drunk maybe one more Trooper than was probably good for them. "But don't let that put you off flogging me your vids," Wayne added hastily.

Tommy sighed. "That's all you care about. You just want to get your hands on my nasties."

"I'm doing you a favor, and you know it," Wayne insisted. The pub was fairly quiet at this time of day. There were a couple of long-hairs playing pool and a fat biker at the next table with a tattoo of Ozzy Osbourne on the back of his neck chatting to a lady with a set of equally greasy-looking tatts decorating her ample flesh.

"You know they're worth more than you're paying."

"Look, I'm running a risk, too, taking 'em off your hands." Wayne looked righteous. His collar-length hair was dark and unkempt, his eyes small but bright and canny. "This Slade copper could be follow-ing you. Which means he'll have me on the radar, too."

Tommy sipped at his Trooper. "Just take 'em. All of them. Sooner you get them up to Burnley, the better. The cops could raid my house at any time."

Wayne nodded eagerly. "So you've got them stashed in the ceme-tery at the moment? Hope you remember where you put 'em. And I hope they're not rain-damaged."

"I wrapped them carefully in several polythene bags; don't fret. They're wedged in a gap under a tomb not far from my garden wall. I couldn't exactly keep them in the house, could I?" He took a large gulp of Trooper, the warm fizz in his head calming him slightly, and was almost beginning to relax a little for the first time in days. "I bet you'll sell them all at FearFest, won't you? Creaming a nice profit out of me in the process, eh?"

"That's not for a few weeks yet. And I've got to look after poten-tially incriminating property until then. But I'm not selling them at the festival, don't worry. I'm keeping them for myself. Always wanted *Don't Go in the Woods...* Just a shame you haven't got *Werewolf and the Yeti*, but I suppose it *is* one of the rarest..."

"Just do me one thing," Tommy said, and his tone became serious.

"What's that?"

"When you're at Fearfest, check out the people buying video nas-ties from the stalls, or at least anyone who seems to have more than a healthy interest in them. Just keep your eyes open for anyone strange."

"That'll be every fucker there," Wayne retorted. His brow creased as the implication of Tommy's words sank home. "You think the mur-derer might be at FearFest?"

"Could be. Whoever did it has got to be buying nasties from somewhere. Seems like a good enough place to find the freak."

"There'll be plenty of those there. At least, if you believe *The Daily Mail*."

Tommy nodded. "Thought that rag had given up chasing video nasties."

"They never give up. It's a personal war for them. Always has been, since the original 'nasty' phenomenon in the eighties. Pure headlines, dear boy. They're loving these latest nasty-linked atrocities."

"So why did the police leak the details, I wonder..." Tommy looked into the distance, forgetting Wayne for a moment. He was momentarily back in the past, breakfast time in the Wallace household, and his father's stern face was staring up at him from the newspaper on the table, a bit of milk spilled on the photo from where Tommy had been clumsy with the jug. His Dad hadn't been happy about that either. Though he had been happy about being in the paper, Tommy remembered. And that had been the *Mail*.

"Who knows," replied Wayne, jerking him back into the present. "Maybe to nudge people into reporting anything suspicious related to nasties. In which case, you and me should keep our heads down. Especially you..."

"You think I don't know that?"

Wayne looked thoughtful for a moment, then peered down into his dark beer. "Weird though, ain't it?"

"What is?"

"That two murders have been committed, and each time a video nasty has been found at the scene of the crime. And you have both of them at home."

Tommy leaned closer to Wayne. "Keep your voice down, for fuck's sake. I think maybe I'm being targeted. Framed."

"How d'you work that out?"

Tommy hesitated. He opened his mouth to speak, but just then, his cell blared out a raucous ringtone from the pocket of his jeans. "Hang on..."

He checked the screen for the caller and didn't recognize the number. He paused for all of two seconds and then thumbed the accept button. "Hello?"

Wayne watched his features suddenly light up. He sniffed and sat back. It was a rum business, all right, as his Dad used to say. A reet fookin' rum business, if you asked him. He'd known Tommy for eight years, and he knew he was a good sort. But even a man who is pure at heart and says his prayers by night…etc. In truth, did anyone *really* know their colleague, their friend, their neighbor? People were fucked up. So many conflicting impulses and dark, primitive instincts, with only a thin veneer of civilization to cover them. It was hardly surprising that they broke through sometimes, these rude shark-fin interruptions on the smooth surface of normality. Deep that… Fuck. About time he had a sniff. He was getting pretentious. Besides, Tommy looked busy on the phone and wouldn't miss him right now.

He got off his stool and ambled over to the handicapped toilet in the corner of the bar. He locked the door behind him and looked around in a proprietorial fashion. Then he pulled out his wallet, extracted a twenty, slipped his baggie of coke from his other pocket, and shook a little cluster on top of the porcelain flush housing above the toilet. He tidied the pile into a line with his Visa card, then rolled the twenty tightly. He took a deep toot, nearly clearing the line, then went back to finish the job. Better.

He made sure he hadn't left anything behind, took a piss, and washed his hands. He started singing (badly) along to the *Don't Go in the Woods* theme tune. It was a travesty of "The Teddy Bear's Picnic" that played over the end credits, and Wayne could remember all the lyrics.

"Don't go into the woods tonight, you probably will be thrilled.
Don't go into the woods tonight, you probably will be killed.
There's a friendly beast that lurks about,
And likes to feast, you won't get out,
Without being killed and chopped up in little pieces."

All in all, he was quite chuffed his mate was flogging off his nasties. He'd often thought of starting up a band just so he could do a cover of this version of "The Teddy Bear's Picnic." He was sure it would go down a storm at gigs...

When he emerged from the toilet, the last thing he expected to see was a gorgeous, tawny blonde in a leopard-print jacket sitting opposite his mate. He already felt a zing of energy surfing the rapids of his veins, and this new turn made it zing just that little faster.

They both seemed engrossed in conversation and didn't notice Wayne until he'd been standing watching them for all of thirty seconds, arms folded patiently. The blonde looked up at him with lioness-brown eyes, and her lips parted in a bright smile, revealing slightly sharp teeth that only added to the animal sexiness she exuded. Fuck. Where did Tommy magic *her* from? This was such a dominant thought that he felt impelled to voice it. "Fuck, Tommy. Where did you magic *her* from?"

The girl trilled with giggles, then stood up quickly. "Have I taken your chair?"

"Yeah, but don't worry; there's plenty more. The pub ain't exactly heaving."

She giggled again and settled back down on the stool. "I was in the market shopping, and when Tommy said he was here, I couldn't resist meeting him."

"She got my number from that dick, Hamm. Can you believe that he's actually come through for me for once."

The blonde giggled and slapped his arm playfully. "Don't be mean! Mark's lovely."

"I've heard he's a right twat. But why would you want to meet Tommy in the first place?" Wayne sniffed, realized the sniff was a bit obvious (although neither Tommy nor the girl seemed to notice), and took a hasty sip of his Trooper.

"Cheeky bastard," Tommy answered. "She knows a star when she sees one. This is Jasmine, by the way. Jazz, meet my mate, Wayne. He's from up North, but don't hold that against him. Jasmine's working on a new film with Hamm."

"The movie you couldn't get on, you mean? She's obviously a better actor than you, mate." He winked at Jasmine. Her giggles were definitely infectious, and while Wayne could never be called a giggler by any stretch of the imagination, he was charmed into a guffaw by her.

"So tell me about it," Tommy prompted Jasmine. "Have you actually started shooting yet?"

"Not our scenes yet, no. Though I believe the director's got a lot in the can already." She took a sip of her Rioja and let out a little gasp of satisfaction. "But I'm really looking forward to it. The director sat us down and showed one of his earlier short films as a warming-up exercise. He didn't want to show us the footage he's already shot on this film as he wants us to see the complete item when it's all done. And, of course, we'll be in it by then. What we saw was a kind of promo. A prototype. And..." She paused, grimaced. "It was a bit rough, to be honest." She shuddered melodramatically. "Very bloody and disturbing." The shiver was followed by a girlish giggle that contradicted her disgusted tone. "But he clearly has some kind of progressive talent."

Tommy was so full of questions that he could barely stop them all from bursting out at once. "How many are there in the cast?"

She shrugged. "I've only seen myself, Mark, and two others so far, Simon and Jane—they were in the audition waiting room with us. It's a low-budget feature, so cast and crew are deliberately small, but—"

"What's the director like?" Tommy interrupted, sensing Jasmine was about to embark on a gushing promotion of the film's modest yet thematically important qualities, and he wasn't particularly in the mood for that.

Jasmine paused. She was obviously trying to find the right words and struggling. Eventually, she shrugged. "He's different," she managed. "Very concentrated. Definitely knows what he wants. I've only met him the once, so it's difficult to form an opinion yet."

"He's a bastard then," Wayne interjected.

Jasmine trilled in a mock-outraged way. "Noooo! And I think he might be disfigured. He wears a—a latex mask. Not a Halloween mask or anything. It's a normal, rather bland plastic face, maybe representing Mister Average... I think it's a symbol of some kind. He's an artist; the mask is his beret." She thought about what she'd said and tittered.

But Tommy had more serious topics on his mind. He leaned forward, watching her carefully. "Didn't you find the audition disturbing?"

Jasmine took another sip of wine. She looked straight at Tommy. "Mark told me the actress in the audition clip was a friend of yours." Was there a challenge in those soft brown lioness eyes?

Tommy looked away briefly, then back. "It was horrible, Jazz. I had to walk out. And she wasn't an actress, that's why—"

"You fancied her, didn't you?"

"'Course he did," Wayne butted in, sensing an awkwardness in the air. "He fancies anything in a bra."

Tommy shook his head at Wayne's crassness. Jasmine smiled carefully and said, "You know it wasn't real, don't you, Tommy?"

He took a big gulp of Trooper, finished the pint. He nodded at Wayne, who had just sniffed quite loudly in a sudden period of silence from the jukebox. "Your round, Mister Sensitive."

Wayne wiped his nose self-consciously and got to his feet. "Another wine, Jazz?"

She shook her head prettily and touched the northerner gently on his rough hand in a token of silent gratitude. Tommy noticed the gesture. She was very tactile. He just wished she would keep it solely for him.

"I'm happy for you, though, Jazz. If you think the film's got promise, then I'm glad."

As if reading his thoughts, she reached out and stroked his hand, too. The nerves in his hand felt like they'd been touched by a live wire. His blood sped up, and his cock tightened.

"I just wish you could be in it, too," she breathed huskily.

"Perhaps it's better I'm not," he answered. "I don't like being around Mark at the best of times."

She frowned at him. "What *is* it between you two?"

Tommy thought about that. "I guess he's just everything I'm not. He's super confident, super smooth, egotistical, has all the best putdowns ready to go at all times..."

"He's not so bad," she said with a little laugh. "I think you two just rub each other the wrong way."

"Too bloody similar if you ask me," Wayne added, arriving back at the table with two foamy Troopers. "Beats me why he asked you to audition in the first place."

Tommy lifted the Trooper to his lips. "Oh, I know exactly why he asked me..."

Wayne sniffed again. "Do tell..."

"He just wanted to rub Vicky in my face. Again."

"Sounds fun," Wayne sniggered. Tommy ignored him. Wayne thought for a moment, then said, "But it's not down to Mark, is it? About who gets the part, I mean?"

"He was in charge of auditions for some reason. He seems to have the director's ear. Would you say they're close, Jazz?" He looked at her, his heart still a little warm after that Electro touch.

"No..." She thought about it. "No, the director doesn't get close to anyone. And as I said, we haven't seen much of him yet."

"Does he have a name?" Tommy leaned forward over the beer-slopped table.

She frowned again. "You'll think I'm daft, but I don't know it. He's playing everything very close to his chest. He hasn't even given the movie a title yet."

"The Film with No Name, eh?" Wayne winked at her. "Very mysterious."

"And how about you, Jazz?" Tommy said, ignoring his friend. "How close do you keep things to *your* chest?"

"Maybe not as close as *you'd* like to be to her chest, sunshine." Wayne sniffed demonstratively.

"Wayne, why don't you go in the Disabled for another snort and leave us to chat in private for a bit? I think that would be a plan."

"Don't know what you're referring to, but I can tell when I'm not wanted." He glanced from Tommy to Jazz, waiting for them to contradict him. When neither did, he got to his feet and took a big slurp of beer. "Okay. I'll leave you two to get it on. Popping down to Tescos to get some baccy. But don't get up to anything naughty, cos I'll. Be. Right. Back."

"Wayne," said Tommy with an embarrassed grin. "Fuck off...and take your time."

When his friend had gone, Tommy sat back in his chair and re-laxed a little. "Sorry about him. He's a liability."

"Oh, he's sweet," she giggled.

"Sweet as a dose of the pox. But where was I?"

"I'm not sure. It sounded like you were coming over all Detective on me," she answered with a cheeky smile.

"Shit, I wouldn't wanna do a Slade on you." When she looked puzzled, he told her all about the Detective Inspector dogging him, and, inevitably (reluctantly), about the murders on the sets of *Arthur* and *Doctor Who*, respectively.

When he'd finished, she was quiet for a second or two. Her face was set and serious. Did she think he was making this shit up to make himself sound more interesting or something?

Then she reached out her hand and touched his again. The same shock ran through him. She held his hand for a moment, silence between them, her gorgeous brown eyes never leaving his. Then she got off her stool, leaned over him, and kissed his cheek.

It was as she was pulling away that he grabbed her, pulled her down onto his lap so he could kiss her properly. To his utter delight, she did not pull away. Her arms came up to embrace him, and she kissed him back. Lingeringly at first, lips gently melding, then tongues flicking at each other, seeking, playing, then passionate. Too soon she broke away, got up quietly, and sat down on her stool again. She looked slightly flushed and smiled guiltily at him. He guessed he was equally as flushed, judging from the burn he could feel in his cheeks. He tasted her on his lips, and his smile was huge.

"Well, if that's the response I get, I'll be a murder suspect any day."

She gave him a little teacherly frown. "You mustn't say that!" Then she reached out for his hand again. "I'm so sorry you're going through this."

"Then you believe me? Because that's really important. That you know I had nothing to do with these deaths..."

"Of course, I believe you."

"Why?"

That seemed to throw her off guard. "What d'you mean?"

"Why should you believe me? I mean, Slade may be a prehistoric moron, but he's right, isn't he? I was on the scene of both murders, and pretty much the first to find the body in each case. It doesn't take Sherlock to figure out I'm in the frame."

"But from what you've told me, there were a lot of people present at both scenes..."

"Yeah, Mark-bloody-Hamm, for one."

"Besides Mark. Didn't you say there were similar crew members on both productions?"

"I did say that. I think." He paused, considering. "But yes, that's right. There were cameramen, sound bods, make-up girls that were present on *Arthur* and *Doctor Who* ..."

"Well, then, this Detective must be aware of that."

"Well, if he is, he's keeping it to himself. He *likes* the idea of me being the bad man."

They were interrupted just then by the return of Wayne, who was eyeing them suspiciously to see if he'd missed out on any fun. Tommy was tempted to tell him exactly how much fun it had been but resisted. He didn't want to appear too keen in front of Jasmine. If he'd learned one thing in his relations with women—and a sad note struck through him as Trish's face popped up in his mind like a reproachful Jack in the Box—it was never to play his hand too soon, never be taken for granted. Although he couldn't deny it, *he'd* certainly taken his wife for granted, too.

He took a gulp of Trooper and smiled at Jasmine. The sadness soon faded, and for a precious, ever-so-fleeting moment in time—and he somehow knew he'd better make the damn most of these next few hours—everything felt like it was going to be all right in Tommy's world.

CHAPTER NINE

Trevor Whitley was trying to breathe through his mouth, but that didn't help much. Slade wrinkled his nose and felt the familiar vileness of death clawing at his throat. He'd been in the force twenty-odd years, and it still got him every time. Anyone who told you it didn't was lying through their fucking asshole. That was just a charade to make rookies feel bad. Truth was, *everyone* felt sick in the presence of a rotten one, from seasoned detectives to raw constables on the beat. And this was a *rotten* one.

"How long, Jim?" Slade didn't look away from the corpse in the bathtub. The body was sprawled in a dried scum of his own gore, a blood ring that had circled the tub and left its crusty tide mark. Bits of brain clogged the drain, clung to the sides of the bath, nestled in the victim's beard and long hair. Great rents in the young man's skull showed the sheer savagery with which the axe blows were dealt before the final slam of the weapon had resulted in it being firmly buried in the victim's crown.

Slade took his eyes off the cow-like bulging eyes milking over with green putrescence and glanced at the big VHS box clenched in one rigor mortis-stiffened hand. *Axe. At last... Total Terror,* screamed the tagline. The box art showed a huge axe buried in what could have been a head, could just as easily have been a log. Unfortunately for the young man in the tub, the killer had taken the first interpretation for inspiration.

"Six weeks, maybe more," Tavell answered, opening an evidence bag to take the video box.

Slade snorted. "It's like an A-to fucking-Z of video nasty slayings. Fuck me, I'm gonna *slaughter* this cunt when I catch him." Trevor Whitley's eyebrow lifted at the irony of his boss's words, but he said nothing. "If it is a him," Slade added, eyeing the SOCO.

"It's a him, all right, judging by the strength of the blow. It took considerable muscle to bury the axe-head this deep."

"Who found him?" Slade had regained his composure.

Tavell waved a couple of his team members forward to collect the corpse now that the detectives had seen enough. "Neighbors had been complaining of a smell for some time, apparently, but it was a homeless vagrant who finally came forward. Wanted an abandoned tenement to kip down in, and this fitted the bill admirably."

"Apart from the putrefying corpse in the bathtub," Whitley added wryly.

"The whole place derelict?" Slade asked his partner.

Whitley rubbed his chin. "Looks that way, guv, but I'll check the neighbors about any potential owner."

"Do that. On the way out. And ask if they saw anyone suspicious in here over the last couple of months." Slade turned back to Tavell. "Was this his first one, I wonder?"

Tavell bagged the video while one of his team began to search the body.

"It certainly predates the other two. And it breaks with the M.O. as well. No T.V. or film set here."

"Maybe the fucker was just trying his hand out. A dry run?"

"Could be. Let me have that..." Tavell spoke to his junior assistant as the young woman retrieved a wallet from the corpse's back pocket. The pretty SOCO handed it over and continued the search. Tavell flipped the wallet open while Slade watched carefully. A crumpled fiver, a few receipts, a VISA and an N.H.S.[10] card.

"Student," said Slade thoughtfully. "Wonder if that links with anything. Trev, I'll need you to check what course he was on. If it's media or film, we could be onto something. Find out whether he's ever been an actor or extra while you're at it." While Whitley pulled out his cell to phone through instructions to the murder squad back in the incident room, Slade read the name of the victim aloud without

---

[10] National Health Services

touching the bent card held in Tavell's gloved fingers: "Harry Cribb. Twenty-five. University of the West of England. Wonder if this poor asshole's ever worked with Tommy Wallace or Mark Hamm, by any chance..."

Tavell didn't reply. He gestured for his team to remove the body, then bagged the wallet.

Slade watched the forensic team carry the corpse away on a stretcher. He glanced around at the filthy, mold-infested bathroom. More members of SOCO were dusting the place diligently, but Slade didn't hold out on them finding anything, judging by the killer's track record so far. But then again, if this was the first murder, was it unreasonable to hope the perp had made some little slip? That thought cheered him slightly. "Give me everything, Jim. Fibers on his T-shirt, D.N.A. under fingernails, spittle in his beard—if you can detect it amongst all that dried blood and brains. Even sperm. The bathtub could be indicative of a sexual motive, though I somehow doubt it. This fuckwad seems driven by other needs entirely."

He clapped Whitley on the shoulder, left the SOCO to get on with his job, and led his DS down the uncarpeted landing. They checked both rooms on the first floor. Each was as dilapidated as the bathroom, and some of them showed signs of fairly recent occupation. A grimy sack draped on a rusted bedstead; cigarette butts scattered on the bare boards; a scummy sock stuck to the floor; empty coke cans. The rooms stank of piss, and there was human defecation curled in the corner of one of them.

"Dirty bastards," Slade hissed. "Get that fuckin' tramp checked out as well, Trev. I wanna know about all his mates who ever dossed down here."

The ground floor was just as shabby, and just as rancid-smelling.

Back out on the street, Slade breathed deeply, then glanced back up at the abandoned two-story, terraced house. A couple of windows were broken. The door had been kicked in. And while it stood out a little from the rest of the street due to its sheer dilapidation, the houses to either side were only a few steps up in terms of respectability. "Good luck with the neighbors," Slade quipped and strode back to the Bentley, leaving the DS to get on with the door-to-doors. He hated areas like this. He knew exactly what reaction Whitley would receive and had earned his turn to sit back.

DC Nandu was looking pleased with herself. She had a load of printouts fanned out before her on the desk next to a battered paperback book with a lurid cover. The title of the book was *Video Nasties: When Our Living Rooms Became Lawless*. It was the first thing Slade saw when he entered the incident room. Probably because of the drill boring into a man's head on the cover. Well, if she wanted to get his attention, she'd done a good job of it.

He strode up to her desk. "Looks like you've been busy, D.C. Nandu. Okay, refresh me: what exactly makes a video nasty?"

She tried not to beam. "This list makes them, sir." She held up a photocopied piece of A4 with a long list of titles. "Back in nineteen-eighty-three, a list was drawn up by the Department of Public Prosecutions to potentially prosecute any video shop proprietor stocking any of these particular titles. These were films deemed to be an affront to public decency. They encapsulated every moral outrage and act of violent barbarism capable of being depicted on film. A peculiarly British phenomenon, the video nasty furor was instigated by English tabloids, particularly the *Daily Mail*, and used as a platform for certain conservative M.P.s to gain an attentive audience in terms of protecting children from unsuitable material and to coerce the British Board of Film Classification and the British Government into a clampdown on uncertificated videos, which eventually came to pass in nineteen-eighty-five." She paused, pleased with the attention her little speech was receiving from several other detectives in the room.

"Go on, D.C. Nandu. Just don't take all year."

"Well, sir, that's it in a nutshell. There were thirty-nine titles classed as most likely to deprave and corrupt and successfully prosecuted under the Obscene Publications Act. Any video shop proprietor caught with any of these titles on their shelves was looking at a fine—and in some cases imprisonment." She tapped the list in front of her. "I've been checking out the whole video nasty phenomenon to see if it holds any clues as to the current series of crimes, sir. I've copied out a plot *précis* of every film known to be on the list that was forwarded for public prosecution."

"Have you, now?" Slade sniffed and looked dubiously at the

sheaf of printouts. "So what have you got that I can actually *use...*"

Undaunted, she held up the book. "Well, sir, the perpetrator's M.O. definitely seems to be derived from the films discussed in this book, which constitute the D.P.P. thirty-nine list. I thought that by going through each film, I might pick something up."

"Do you have copies of the actual films at home to watch, D.C. Nandu? Is that how you spend your downtime? *Driller Killer* and a hot cross bun?"

Nandu ignored his facetiousness. "No, sir. But we are holding three tapes as evidence. I've watched the first one, and with your permission, I'd like to view the other two."

"By all means. Knock yourself out. But it strikes me we're watching these films retrospectively for clues to crimes that have already been committed. We need to be looking at future films on the list to stop the fucker from perpetrating any more."

"I can source some of the films on D.V.D. or download, sir," she replied instantly.

"Do it, D.C. Nandu."

"Yes, sir." She allowed a little glint of white teeth to betray her satisfaction. Slade perched on the edge of her desk. "Just don't get too turned on. As you said, these films are accused of being liable to corrupt and deprave..."

"Well, that was the historic indictment of them, yes, sir," she said, ignoring his barbed levity. "But I'm of the opinion that a lot of them won't be anything like as bad as their reputation. Some will be rather dated compared to some of the material that's freely available on the internet and in retail outlets—even on T.V.—these days."

He frowned at her, mulling over her words. "Short-list the most controversial ones, the most violent and depraved. We need to guess which direction this sick fuck is heading in." He picked up the book, began flipping through the pages. "Would you say the ones he's used as his M.O. so far are among the strongest ones on the list?"

She paused. "I need to watch more to come to a firm opinion on that, sir. But the book seems to indicate that while *Driller Killer* is up there with the most notorious—although it's now legally available on the high street, uncut—the other two are definitely second-tier nasties. There are far more repulsive entries..." She began reading from the list she'd compiled herself earlier after skimming through the book. "*I Spit on Your Grave*—protracted rape scenes, totaling around twenty-five minutes. Castrations, hangings, death by outboard motor. *Anthropophagous the Beast*—cannibalistic killer rips out an unborn fetus from a pregnant mother and eats it. *Nightmares in a Damaged Brain*—highly gruesome axe murders and decapitations. *Zombie Flesh Eaters*—woman has her eye pierced by a long shard of wood, another girl has her neck ripped open by a Conquistador zombie. *House by the Cemetery*—an estate agent has her throat stabbed repeatedly by a poker, a babysitter has her head sawn off by a kitchen knife. *Cannibal Ferox*—guy has his eye gouged out by cannibals, then has his penis chopped off and eaten—" There was a brief burst of sardonic laughter and applause from a couple of the more grizzled veterans who were listening from the nearest desks. Slade glared at them, and they quickly turned back to their PCs.

Slade nodded slowly at Nandu. "I get the picture. They ain't gonna show on Children's T.V. any time soon. Save the rest of the list for your report, or we're gonna be here all fucking day. But one thought does strike me. If the perp *is* a copycat killer, I'd say he's gonna have a job getting a load of cannibals to eat someone's dick around here. Even in Knowle West." A few chuckles greeted this observation.

Slade turned to address the whole incident room, raising his voice. "So it occurs to me our killer's fitting the films to his own purposes. Opportunity and situation keyed to violent content. The videos have to be relevant, not just nasty." He surveyed the group of attentive detectives occupying the desks in front of him. "I want to know why those particular films. There's a link to woods with the killing of Andy Hill at Forest Ffawr, but what about the other two? The bathtub have any significance? The science fiction setting? And why are the killings taking place on T.V. and film sets in the first place? Apart from the first axe killing, which we believe may have been a prototype. I need to know."

"I think it could be part of the Snuff ethos, sir." DC Nandu waited for him to cue her.

Slade glanced across at Whitley, who was on the phone with forensics. "Fuck me. You after Trev's job? You certainly fill that suit better than he does his, the podgy bastard." A couple of titters broke out.

Some of the glow left Nandu's cheeks. She frowned. "Do you want to hear this or not, sir?"

Slade belched. Dropped the book on the desk with an air of disdain. "Snuff films... That's an old eighties crock of bullshit. No evidence of any such films was ever found. What makes you think our killer's playing snuff?"

She rubbed her small, pretty nose, glanced at the *Video Nasties* book. "A hunch, sir. The murders are linked to video films and actual sets where filming is taking place. A fascination with the media, with film-making, maybe? Real killings and simulated killings. Just a theory, sir."

Slade digested this. She was far smarter than he'd given her credit for. If she was right, of course. And there was still a chance she was way off target. "Film fanatic, maybe? A frustrated film-maker who never made it in the business? Worth pursuing, D.C. Nandu. Check out all students who've attended a film course around here in the last five or so years. Particularly ones who failed. Then cross-check with our list of extras present on both sets."

"Shall I tell you what I've discovered so far about the three video films from the crime scenes?"

"Save it for the report. And have that on my desk by tomorrow." He slid off her desk and ambled over to Whitley, who was still on the phone. Slade reached across and cut the connection. "They can ring back. I need your ears right now."

"Guv!" Whitley sighed in exasperation and flung his pen down petulantly. "They were giving me the rundown on the prints!"

"And let me guess? They got sweet Fanny-fuckin'-Addams. Tell me something new. Like, has anyone been through the security tapes from the *Doctor Who* studio?"

Whitley sighed again. "D.C. Stammers went through the lot. Checked the visitors in the footage against names signed in. They all match."

"Then our killer's one of them."

"Not necessarily. There are other entrances to the building. Back studio lot doors, side gates. Which should be on the C.C.T.V. vids, but not all of them are working out back."

"Brilliant. Well, check out everyone in the logbook anyway. Just in case. I want to know where they get their hair cut, never mind what they were doing at the T.V. studio. Everything about them. Favorite jokes and sexual hang-ups, breast size, and criminal records. And I want a list of everyone who had a pass key, and everyone who didn't. I want a potted history of every twat who either works in that place or was there to deliver the tea bags. Got it?"

"Got it, boss."

"And then we're gonna visit a friend of ours..."

He strode to the front of the incident room, staring at the faces projected on the whiteboard. He sucked in his lips and frowned at one of them, nodding slowly.

CHAPTER TEN

Tommy took the call at 10:13. He was still in bed, half asleep and thinking about Jasmine.

He snatched his cell phone up after the third ring and croaked "Hello" into the mouthpiece, barely registering the fact it was his casting agency.

"Tommy?" It was Rhiannon, the main booking agent. Blonde and curvaceous, she was the secret fantasy of all the male supporting artists on the books. And while Tommy quite liked being naked in bed, listening to her husky voice tinged with just the slightest lick of Welsh, the fantasy had been pretty much usurped by Jasmine, whose image refused to fade easily now as he tried to shake his thoughts clear.

"Got a few days for you if you're interested."

"Uh, yeah. As long as nobody gets skewered or drilled this time..."

"Bad taste, Tommy. Karen wanted me to keep you off jobs for a while—especially after the police paid us a visit requesting to go through our books—but I didn't think that was fair. Innocent 'til proved guilty and everything." There was a bland sing-song lilt to her voice, as if she were discussing the weather. Karen was the owner of the South West theatrical agency and pretty hard-nosed.

"I *am* innocent! Jesus, Rhi, I've been through this with you! But I'm grateful to you anyway. I really need the work right now to take my mind off it all." And he *had* been through it all. The agency had called him in after the *Arthur* incident and grilled him again comprehensively after the *Doctor Who* murder. But they soon realized he had nothing to tell them he hadn't already imparted to the police. But he could understand Karen considering him to be some kind of Jonah.

"That's okay, lovely. Three days. Wiltshire. It's a World War One drama to commemorate the centennial this year. Sound good?"

"Sounds great. Do I get to be a Tommy?"

"Don't think so." She didn't get the joke, or she was ignoring it. "Set in a field hospital in France. You'll be a uniformed orderly."

"Wiltshire's standing in for France?"

"Yep. Got a lot more to call, Tommy. You in?"

"I'm in. And thanks."

He lay back in bed, wide awake now. Well, that was a turn up. Three days work might just cover the Gas and Electricity bill hanging over him. And now, without Trish to help, finding the money was suddenly a major consideration.

He considered phoning Jasmine, and his thumb even hovered over her contact icon, then he sighed and dropped the cell beside the bed and rolled out from under the duvet. The relationship dogma of the twenty-first century rang in his ears: don't want to be seen as too keen. He was heading for the shower when the doorbell rang.

He considered ignoring it, but the ring came again, insistent. Could be important. Could even be Jasmine. He shrugged into his purple dressing gown, a little (a lot!) turned on by the thought of answering the door to her in just a flimsy gown. The delicious fantasy lasted as long as it took him to open the front door and find the stern faces of Slade and Whitley on the front step.

"Morning, sexy," Slade quipped, striding in without being invited. His more taciturn companion followed.

"What now?" He resisted the urge to swear. "I was just about to have a shower!"

Slade consulted his watch. "Lazy fucker, aren't you? The rest of the world's been up and at it for hours."

The two coppers were already scouting out the premises, Tommy noticed with a flare of panic. *Don't Go in the Woods... Alone*—had Wayne forgotten to take it? What about *Driller Killer?* He was definitely up shit's creek if Wayne had left either of those behind when he collected the stash from the cemetery behind the house and brought it back here to check. Slade wandered into the living room, peering around at the framed pictures. A poster from *The Great Rock n' Roll Swindle* seemed to meet with his approval judging from the nod; an original oil from his favorite artist, Rick Melton, of a naked girl in a cemetery, on the other hand, did not. He cursed himself for not taking it down. Slade settled himself on the sofa, again without being invited, and motioned for his lapdog to do the same.

"Coffee," the detective said. It wasn't a question.

"There's nothing m—"

"—more you can tell me. Yeah, I know. If I had a hot whore for every time that's been said to me, I'd be a very happy man, eh, Trev?"

The DS smiled discreetly.

"Two sugars, dash of the white stuff. One lump for D.S. Whitley."

Tommy sighed and walked out into the hall, heading for the kitchen. While he made the coffee, he performed a mental inventory of the house. Had he left anything around that could possibly be construed as incriminating to suspicious police eyes? Any dodgy horror novels, a violent thriller? Everyone had one or two of those lying around, surely? All his video nasties were gone, he was pretty sure of that. He had some horror DVDs, along with a lot of Sci-Fi and comedies, but they were pretty innocuous. He hoped so anyway.

He carried the two mugs back into the living room. Slade took his with a wry smile. Tommy sat down in the armchair.

"Those were the days," he said, staring at the *Great Rock n' Roll Swindle* poster. It depicted the Pistols in broad cartoon caricature on their infamous boat trip down the Thames to mark the Silver Jubilee. Steve Jones was vomiting into the river.

"You were too young, though. Bet you don't remember nine-nine-nine either?"

The question threw Tommy for a moment. He thought of the barely played CD in the rack. *"Concrete?"* he said after a pause, wondering where this was going.

Slade sat back expansively, giving Whitley a smug grin. "I'm beginning to like this bastard, after all. A little bit, anyway. Where's the wife today, Tommy? At work?"

Tommy tried not to reveal the stab of bleakness that suddenly ran through him. He looked at his hands. "She's uh..."

"She's what, son...?"

He looked up. "She's left me." He met Slade's eyes for a second, then looked away, out of the window at the suburban street beyond. Another gray one. Bin men collecting the rubbish. A small child on a scooter fleeing its anguished mother.

"That so? Any particular reason?"

"No. I mean, not really. We grew apart, that's all."

"Grew apart... So where's she living now?"

"Does this matter?" he snapped. He controlled himself quickly. "She's staying with a friend. Laura Charles. She lives just around the corner."

Slade wrote the address down. "Just in case. You never know where our inquiries may take us." He grinned cheesily. Then the grin left his eyes and he leaned forward again. "Have you heard of a student called Harry Cribb? Media student at U.W.E.?"

The sudden change of tack confounded Tommy. "Uh. No. Should I?"

"He would be the first victim in this case you *didn't* know." The eyes, hard and blue, didn't budge from Tommy.

"Another one?" He paled. And yet he felt a sudden vindication, too. After all, if there had been another murder and Tommy wasn't involved in any way, then surely that could only help his case?

"You sure you don't know him?" Slade produced a photograph depicting a long-haired, bearded man in his mid-twenties. He was giving a doofus smile for the camera and looked happy and relaxed, sitting on a park bench in the sun.

Tommy shook his head.

Slade got up off the sofa, crossed to the bookshelf against one wall. While the top row was dedicated to novels and various bios, the rest of the shelves were taken up with DVDs. Not a VHS in sight, he thought with relief. Slade was scanning the titles. A few Hammer films, a couple of Westerns, the *Spiderman* trilogy, even a few Pixar animations. Nothing extreme. Slade looked disappointed.

"You got any more films?"

"No. That's all." And it was. Now that Wayne had cleared him out, bless his northern sockies.

Slade picked out one of the Hammer films. *Frankenstein and the Monster from Hell.* "Looks gruesome..."

Tommy shifted uncomfortably on his armchair. "Not really."

Slade replaced the DVD and clicked his finger at Whitley. "You mind if my D.S. here has a little look about upstairs?"

Tommy frowned. They needed a warrant for that. He'd watched enough films to be quite certain of his rights. But making things difficult for the cops would only prolong their harassment. And besides, he was pretty sure he had nothing left to hide. He shrugged. "Sure. Why not?"

Whitley got up and left the room. Slade sipped his coffee thoughtfully. There was silence between them for a moment or two. Then Slade said, "Got any more work lined up?"

Tommy felt a tightening across his chest. He knew what Slade was insinuating, and the thought had, of course, crossed his mind already, as it obviously had Karen's and Rhiannon's: would the murders continue? The idea of going to work again tomorrow filled him with a kind of dread. He'd considered stopping altogether but desperately needed the money. Besides, he'd always loved it before—before the deaths. He nodded weakly and told Slade about the WWI show.

"Nice," Slade said. "About time the Great War got a bit of attention. Let's just hope it doesn't get the *wrong* attention, eh?"

Tommy didn't answer. Slade pushed on. "But you don't need to worry. I shall be keeping a *very* close eye on you, sonny."

"You think..." He found he couldn't say it.

"Who knows?" Slade finished his coffee and stood up just as Whitley returned. The DS shook his head at Slade. "Who knows? But we're ready for the sick fuck this time. And while the odds seem to be leaning toward the killer targeting productions you and your bessie mate, Mark Hamm, are involved in, you can relax in the knowledge that there'll be a police presence on all productions in the area from now on. Will that make you sleep better at night?" He put out a hand to touch the naked painted breasts of the cemetery girl, stroked them thoughtfully with his forefinger. "Incidentally, will Mister Hamm be joining you tomorrow?"

Tommy said, "I'm sure you know already, don't you?"

Slade smiled thinly. "Ah, your agency been talking, have they?"

"The answer is, I don't know. They never tell me who else is booked for jobs. But I'm sure they'll tell you."

"Yes. I'm sure they will." He turned to DS Whitley. "I think we're done here. Anything else you wanna ask our friend, Trev?"

Before the DS could answer, they heard a rattle of keys in the lock and the front door open. Slade gave Tommy an enquiring look. Tommy was too busy wondering how this new situation might complicate things.

Trish entered the living room. She glared at Slade and Whitley without speaking.

"Missus Wallace?" Slade stepped toward her. The last two times they had called, Trish had been out, although the neighbors made sure they told her about the visits even if Tommy had been reticent about them himself. "D.I. Slade, D.S. Whitley."

"What do you want to know this time? Hasn't he told you everything?" She stared at them warily.

"Don't worry, Missus Wallace. We won't keep you very long. Just here making a few more routine inquiries. I'm sure he's told you all about the case."

She glared at Tommy. "Not really. We don't speak much about anything anymore."

"Indeed. That's unfortunate. But you are aware of what happened?"

"Of course. I read the newspapers. I watch the T.V. They're calling the case the Video Nasty Killings, I believe."

Slade winced. "Yes, well. *Some* papers are calling it that. But while you're here, Missus Wallace, maybe you could give us your impression of the whole situation?"

"I don't follow. I just came here to collect a few things. I'm not stopping." She looked at Tommy demonstratively. She brushed a long swathe of brown hair from her eyes. She looked defensive and tired.

"Only take a moment, Missus Wallace. Save us chasing you up at your friend's house."

She sat down on the sofa vacated by the two policemen. "What do you want to know?"

"Well, for a start, is there anyone you know of who might hold a grudge against your husband?"

Tommy started. "Then you *do* believe I had nothing to do with it?"

Slade stuck his hands in his pockets in a nonchalant manner. "We're chasing every possibility, Thomas. Missus Wallace?"

She glanced over at Tommy again. "Oh, there are maybe one or two extras he moans about. But nobody he's described to me dislikes him enough to want to hurt him. Is that what this is all about? You think the killer's really after Tommy?"

"I don't think anything of the sort, Missus Wallace. Just answer the question, please."

Tommy's hands were beginning to tremble. He had considered the possibility, of course, but more from the angle of someone wanting to frame him. But to hear it voiced aloud like this... Was *he* the actual target, then? Had the other two deaths been mistakes or warnings of some kind? Was he being toyed with? The idea shook him. Then maybe it *was* time to get out of the TV business. But then, might not this hypothetical enemy track him down whatever line of work he took? If they could kill someone in a secure TV studio with scores of people around...

"No," she said finally. "Nobody springs to mind. I thought you might be here because of the coincidence of Tommy having..." To Tommy's horror, he realized she was glancing over at the DVDs on the bookshelf as if searching for the missing video nasties. His heart stammered.

He got up quickly.

"Of course, it's a coincidence," he said abruptly. "And that's all it is. Me being on set at the time of two different murders, I mean."

"What else would you mean?" Slade cocked an eyebrow at Trish. "Missus Wallace? You mentioned your husband 'having' something. What would that be?"

Was she going out of her way to make him look guilty? She shrugged. "Nothing. I meant...what Tommy said. Of course, it doesn't look good, what with him being at the scene of the crime both times." She sighed. "But I'm pretty sure he's legit. I've been married to him for six years. I think I'd know if he was a murderous psychopath by now." She glanced at him briefly, and there was almost a soft look in her eyes. Tommy gave her a little smile back, and suddenly felt a gush of affection for her, as well as regret.

Trish frowned, checked her watch. "I promised to meet Laura for a drink in five minutes..."

"You sure?" Slade took another step closer to her, taking his hands out of his pockets to be ready for action.

She got up. "I'm sure. He's a good man. Just not the right man." That was for Tommy's benefit. He thanked her with another little smile. "Now, if you don't mind, I just need to get a few things from upstairs." She paused and looked at Tommy. "There is another reason I came 'round." She looked uncomfortable. "Are you all right?" She was trying to look contained and cool, but her lower lip trembled.

Tommy nearly reached out a hand to her. Nearly, but no cigar. He looked away from her, then at Slade. "I'm fine. Really." The moment was gone. Another five minutes, and so was she. Slade and Whitley took a little longer taking off, but eventually Tommy was alone again.

He suddenly felt like crying. He pulled his cell out and rested his thumb on Jasmine's contact icon. Again, he resisted calling her. He thought of Trish's mask of indifference momentarily dropping, and sadness held him close. He switched on the *Jeremy Kyle Show* and waited for the emptiness to leave him.

CHAPTER ELEVEN

The first person Tommy saw on set the next day was Rona. Although he didn't realize it at the time, she was the star of the whole show. He'd seen her in other stuff, a few TV series, even a Bond film, looking glamorous and sexy with her long dark hair and make-up accentuating her large brown eyes. But today, he didn't recognize the rather plain-looking young woman strolling head down toward him as he sat outside the cosmetics trailer sipping at his first cup of tea.

She had no make-up, was dressed in a scruffy sweater, her hair was tied back peremptorily, and she was stuffing a piece of toast in her mouth. She smiled thinly, awkwardly, at Tommy, and some of her toast broke off to fall down her jumper.

"You've dropped a bit," Tommy said stupidly. It was one of those irritating comments that men sometimes make to women to show they are in control, to belittle them. This really wasn't how Tommy meant it, but he realized as soon as the words were out how they sounded.

Rona reddened, then walked past and up the steps into the make-up truck. She would emerge half an hour later looking like a voluptuous vision in a WWI nurse's uniform, but by then, Tommy had other matters to occupy his attention.

Like Jasmine, for instance. He had suspected Mark would turn up, and—subconsciously—he hoped Jasmine might, too. But lately the same faces had continually been showing up on different productions as the casting agency worked their most reliable and effecttive extras as much as they could, so he had believed, as a newbie in this line of work, she might not get picked. He was delighted to be proved wrong.

He had already spotted Mark. The smug bastard saluted him as he walked past, resplendent in his officer's uniform. Of course, Mark would get the best costume—Tommy had already seen his own rather tatty orderly uniform, a couple of sizes too small and with holes in the cap and sleeves that looked like they'd been gnawed by a rat. Seeing Jasmine, however, improved his state of mind a *whole* lot, even if it was only 7:00 a.m.

She wasn't in costume yet and looked gorgeous in tight jeans and an Arran sweater. Her tawny blonde hair was wild and spilling around her cute, cheeky face. Her lips parted in a libido-boosting smile when she saw him, and she hurried over to join him. He got up from his plastic chair to embrace her, spilling a few drops of tea on the ground as he did.

The sun was just rising over the trees that bordered the production unit base, and her hair came alive under the rays. Her freckles glowed, too, and her eyes twinkled.

"Why didn't you tell me you were on this?" she scolded him, finally releasing him from the hug.

"I almost rang you last night. But then I thought if you weren't on it, you'd only feel left out." That hadn't been the only reason; he'd been feeling depressed after the cops left, thinking of Trish, and really didn't have the heart to talk to Jasmine. He realized now what a mistake that had been; she had transformed his mood with one smile.

"Silly," she trilled, stroking his cheek. Desire flared up under her touch. He wanted to snog her face off right there and then. Only the sight of Slade and his stooge Whitley restrained him. There they were, like cartoon cops, eyeing everyone with measured disdain. He'd clocked the uniformed constables on the gate when he'd arrived and had supposed it was only a matter of time before he bumped into his best mate, Slade. The DI spotted him, and Tommy saw him nudge Whitley and point over. Oh, fuck. Not now, just when he was starting to enjoy himself.

"P.C. Plod and Big Ears, twelve o'clock," he quipped to Jasmine. She giggled, smiling sweetly at the detectives as they crossed the grass that would soon turn to mud under the first of the early summer rains.

"Mister Wallace, how lovely to see you again," Slade said drily, giving Jasmine the once-over.

"You knew I was coming."

"Yes, I did. But I wasn't expecting you to be accompanied by such a charming companion." He gave Jasmine a lewd wink. She smiled back expansively, either immune to his creepiness or completely unaware of it.

"And you are?" he asked her, his eyes tracing the slight curves of her breasts under the sweater.

"Jasmine Paal. I'm playing a nurse."

"Are you? Well, you can take my temperature anytime, love." He winked again. Then, as if realizing how cheesy that was—even for him—he turned abruptly back to Tommy. "So, can I expect any dead bodies today, Wallace?"

Tommy sighed and saw Whitley shaking his head in disbelief behind his superior officer.

"Rather tactless, Detective Inspector."

"They do seem to follow you around, son. Regular flypaper for corpses, you are. But *I'm* here today, and my peepers are wide open." To demonstrate this, he bugged them at Jasmine. She giggled unsurely, glancing at Tommy for guidance.

Slade was about to continue on this theme when somebody else snatched his attention away—Rona descending the steps from the make-up truck, her nurse outfit half unbuttoned, the lace-up bodice underneath showing a tantalizing glimpse of seriously impressive breasts. Slade's eyes finally made it up to her face. She glared back at him for a moment, clearly a little taken aback by his unabashed lechery. Then she gave him a brilliant smile. If the sun hadn't already found its way out, it might just as well have stayed in bed and let Rona's dazzling smile do the job of brightening up the day instead. Even Jasmine's grin tarnished under the shine of those perfect teeth.

Tommy was staring, too, unaware that Jasmine's smile had faded, that the twinkle had darkened somewhat in her eyes, brown and cute, too, but rendered almost plain compared to those of the lead actress. Rona's eyes were huge and sensitively protuberant; they sucked you in and held you, oh lucky male, as she favored you with her attention. *What a transformation from the scruffy, clumsy girl who had spilled toast all down herself,* Tommy thought.

Tommy realized he was gaping, too, like the detective next to him, and only gradually became aware of Jasmine's displeasure. He chucked the finished tea cup in the bin next to him and clutched her hand in his. She continued to watch Rona impassively.

"Miss Capley..." Slade strode forward to intercept the actress as she descended the steps. She continued to dazzle him with her smile, her eyes inquisitive.

He shook her hand, holding it a little too long, obviously reluctant to release it. "Detective Inspector Slade, and this is..." He realized Whitley hadn't followed him over and suddenly seemed a little lost for words, like a schoolboy with a crush.

Rona came to his assistance. "Very reassuring to have you here, Detective Inspector." The smile was relentless. She thrust out her half-glimpsed breasts as she adjusted her belt.

"Especially in light of these awful...crimes recently. But I do hope you don't think we could possibly be in danger?"

"Not at all, Miss Capley. Purely a precautionary measure. We have a police presence on all productions in the area as a result of recent events. But you're entirely safe with us around, so don't you fret." He was clearly back on familiar ground now, and he even managed to drag his eyes away from her formidable chest for a second.

"I'm *sooo* glad to hear it. I feel much safer already, with a big, strong policeman like you around."

Was she taking the piss? It was difficult to tell. Tommy thought it was probably just the way she was—or, as he was soon to learn, the way she was with men. Females didn't receive half as much attention. He should have realized that immediately from the way she virtually ignored Jasmine. Those big, brown eyes that had flirted with James Bond himself left the detective for a moment and rested on Tommy. He quailed inwardly, fearing she would lambast him for his clumsy words earlier. But her smile eclipsed any such fears.

"As you can see, I've wiped myself down now. Not a crumb in sight." She brushed demonstratively at her chest, and Tommy felt Jasmine's grip on his hand tighten.

"Er, so I see," he said pathetically, his cheeks burning.

"Enough of that, Wallace. Put your damn eyes away!" Slade stepped between them and took Rona by the arm, escorting her away from the make-up truck. "Is there anywhere more private we can go, Miss Capley? I need to fill you in on a few details and precautionary procedures."

Hypocritical fucker, thought Tommy, but couldn't help grinning. He became aware that Jasmine had released his hand. She was watching him with obvious disappointment in her eyes.

"Jazz... He's talking shit. I wasn't..."

Any more proclamations of innocence were thwarted by the arrival of Jen, the runner. He'd had the pleasure (and it *was* a pleasure) of working with her on numerous productions. She was a comical northern girl, cuddly and dry-humored. She took one look at them and shook her head. "Tommy Wallace, you just can't leave the girls alone, can you?"

"Not helping, Jen."

"Time for that later. I need you both in costume. Then hair." She eyed Tommy's quiff. "That'll probably have to go for a start."

As it turned out, the quiff stayed, although they göt2b glue'd it to his forehead, as well as giving him a sharp back and sides. "Count yourself lucky," the hair stylist told him as she finished plastering his hair down with the strong gel, "I could have given you a middle parting. Very popular in World War One." She pointed at a series of sepia photos of real contemporary Tommies tacked to the wall in front of them.

"Yeah, thanks for that," Tommy said with heartfelt gratitude.

He emerged from the trailer to find Jen waiting for him. "What are you waiting for, Wallace? Go and eat your bloody breakfast!"

He gave her the thumbs up and headed toward the catering wagon. He ordered the full Monty: two sausages, fried egg, mushrooms, black pudding, toast (buttered), beans, and hash browns, and as he carried the heaped plate up the two steps onto the supporting artist dining bus, he reflected how several days of this would play havoc with his waist size.

He groaned as he saw Mark Hamm sitting at one of the few free tables left. He glanced around, hoping to see Jasmine, but no such luck. Mark looked up and gave an expansive smile.

Tommy approached him, ready to pass by and squeeze onto someone else's table, but Mark pulled a look of mock hurt.

"Nice uniform. Shame about it being too small." He gestured at the empty seat opposite. "Don't you want to sit with an old pal?"

Tommy paused in front of him. "Not really."

"Don't tell me you're still sulking about that audition business. I told you, you just weren't right for the part."

"I don't give a fuck about the part.."

"Then what's your beef, fella? Not blaming me for that unfortunate *Doctor Who* business, surely? I've had enough suspicion from that paragon of police procedure, D.I. Slade, thank you very much." A look of enlightenment dawned on his permanently spray-tanned face. "Ah, the lady. Always the lady with you, isn't it, Tommy? Do you think we didn't know about your dirty, little secret? Always chatting up the girlies on your porn sites..."

To shut him up—and he was speaking very loudly—Tommy sat down opposite him. "They weren't porn sites, you asshole."

"Dating sites, whatever. It's all porn in the end, isn't it? You're only looking to get off, after all." He stuffed a whole black pudding in his mouth and talked while he chewed. "But I told you not to worry about Vicky. I'm sure if you tracked her down on Facebook or somewhere, you'd find she was perfectly all right." He leaned forward conspiratorially, poking his fork at Tommy. "But then I'd say you're not too bothered anymore, right? You got another lady in your sights now..."

Tommy did his best to ignore him and took a bite of sausage.

"Very attractive she is, too, young Jasmine. Doing very well in our little film."

Tommy finished the sausage slowly, refusing the bait.

"Don't you want to hear how it's going? Or has Jasmine been satisfying your...curiosity?"

Tommy forked some bacon into his mouth, glanced out the window at the collection of trailers and trucks that constituted the production unit base. He spotted Slade emerging from a trailer and Rona standing in the open doorway. She gave him a wave and disappeared back inside. Crew members were smoking in the morning sunlight, preparing themselves for the long day to come. Tommy recognized several of them from other productions, other SAs, too, with whom he'd worked on many occasions—it really was like an extended family. He tried to shut out Hamm's drone, but it kept coming.

"Well, she's hardly been used yet, so she won't be able to pass on much detail. But I can tell you this..." He leaned forward over the table again, fork extended, a baked bean impaled on one prong. "...the director's a genius. Hitchcock, DeMille, Truffaut, Tarantino—dwarfs, man. Dwarfs, compared to this dude." His face was flushed with admiration and excitement. "And I've never even seen his face. He wears a latex mask every time I work with him. The mask of an average, conservative, middle-class *Daily Telegraph* reader. Some kind of statement, I guess. Like I said, he's a genius. There's real *power* in the movie. It's a highly stylized faux Snuff film—at least, that's one dimension to it. A disturbing epic with simulated snuff scenes to provide frisson. You probably guessed that from the fake Vicky audition footage anyway, but yes, that's the theme, the *motif* the director is going for. It's going to be intense, my friend. The most threatening movie ever to be made. Forget *A Serbian Film;* it pisses all over *Snuff.* Think *Cannibal Holocaust* for the twenty-first century. But even that doesn't come close. This is going to smash it out of the park, Thomas, old bean. This ain't gonna wow the critics so much as whack them over the head with a shovel while raping their intellect and senses, too. This is a real thinking and feeling man's film. The audience will be so engaged, they will never, *ever* be able to forget it!"

Tommy gazed at him. Mark was so absorbed in his speech that all efforts to antagonize Tommy had been dropped. Spittle flecked his lips, his face flushed with the emotion he so obviously and genuinely felt for the project, his eyes bugged. Tommy had never seen him so emotive about anything before and almost admired his passion. But as he listened to Mark's words, a dreadful fear began to collect in his gut. He dropped his knife and fork and stared unblinking at Mark as he spoke.

"My God... It's you..."

Mark stopped talking and sat back, bewilderment furrowing his brow. "Huh?"

"It's you and that bloody film—or at least the director. I should have known it when I saw Vicky's audition footage."

"What are you blabbering about now?"

"The deaths, you bastard! The copycat video nasty murders. You just gave the game away: *Snuff, Cannibal Holocaust...* What, are the killings just some kind of fucked-up publicity drive for your sick movie?"

Mark actually chuckled. He, too, put his utensils down and grinned at Tommy.

"Yeah! You're right. Why didn't I think of it? Brilliant publicity!" His grin dropped, and he leaned forward again, his face serious, eyes hard. "You seriously think I would be involved in something like that? Now I really *am* fucking hurt. You're right; someone is playing snuff, or something very like it, but it's nobody involved with my film. This is just a horrendous coincidence."

"And you actually believe that? Or are you just—against all previous evidence—a good actor after all?" Tommy stood up, shoving his plate of half-eaten breakfast against Mark's with a definitive clink.

"Fuck this. I've been blind. And I don't believe in coincidences. I'm gonna have a little word with Detective Inspector Slade...see if he doesn't believe in them either."

"You'll be wasting your time, Tommy. But go right ahead. Hell, if Slade does launch an investigation into the film, it'll drum up even more publicity, so thank you very muchly." He winked, and the grin was back.

Tommy emerged from the dining bus and stood for a moment on the bottom step, breathing in the fresh morning air. He was giddy with conflicting thoughts. But there was one way to solve this without involving Slade. Mark had been right: all he had to do was check that Vicky was still around to disprove his theory. If that audition stunt had been just that—a stunt—then maybe he was being paranoid about Hamm and his "epic" faux-snuff opus. He reached for his cell and switched it on. Jen came up behind him, stroking the back of his neck affectionately. "Line up, Tommy."

"Hmm?" He was concentrating on trying to get a signal on his phone.

Jen laughed ironically. "You've got two chances of getting a signal out here, sunshine—fat and none."

Tommy sighed and dropped the cell in one of his wide WWI jacket pockets. This would have to wait. Hamm was probably right, though: what sane filmmaker would publicize their film with real-life atrocities? It was paranoid nonsense. Hamm had just freaked him for a moment when he mentioned notorious video nasties in relation to his precious film project. But then he could always rely on Hamm to display his customary lack of sensitivity, even when people they had known were actually being killed around them. He pulled the moth-eaten cap down further over his brow and followed Jen round the back of the dining bus to where a line of supporting artists was already patiently awaiting inspection. Tommy stood next to a blousy middle-aged lady with graying hair dressed as a nurse. She eyed him saucily and elbowed him gently in the ribs.

"Tommy Wallace, if I'm not mistaken?"

She leaned into him, prodding him with her not-inconsiderable breasts. She air-kissed him demonstratively while he wondered who the hell she was.

"Lovely to meet you at last, cock," she said, her voice carrying the slight lilt of a Scottish accent. And the penny dropped.

"Lana..." He groped for the right surname. "Lana Fordham,

right?" Her lack of make-up had thrown him, as it had previously with Rona. But while the star was allowed to don some slap for her role, supporting artists were actively discouraged, aiming for World War I verisimilitude. Lana was attractive in a slightly ravaged way, and it was easy to see why he had initially failed to recognize her. Lana's Facebook profile was far more glamorous, albeit far more airbrushed.

"Nice to see you in the flesh, as it were," she cooed, pushing her breasts at him again. He backed up a step, her overt femininity slightly overwhelming, a second-rate Rona without the charm.

"It's not just our agency Facebook page I've seen you on, though, is it?" She tipped him a sly wink.

Tommy's mind was still curdled by all the unpleasant associations Hamm had stirred up, and he was slow to grasp her meaning. "Huh?"

"Morefishinthesea.com. Ring any bells?"

"Oh fuck. You're not on there, are you?"

She giggled, and her breasts bobbed against his uniform. "Voluptuousnymph67. Her interests are horse riding, walking on the beach, and acting. Sound familiar? I've seen you on there a few times and was tempted to pop a little something in your inbox. Maybe you'd like that?"

"Er, yeah... Maybe." He looked around, hoping Jen would signal for them to leave for the set. But the make-up and wardrobe bods were taking their time moving down the line, checking everyone thoroughly. Jasmine arrived at the end of the line and grinned gorgeously at him. She looked so cute and desirable in her figure-hugging period nurse outfit that he forgot all his dark thoughts and beamed stupidly back.

Lana followed his gaze and audibly *humphed*. "Have you had any luck on there yet?" she asked, willfully detaining him with her words.

"Sorry?" Did she mean on *Jasmine*?

"Morefishinthesea.com. You spend enough time on it. I'm guessing you're checking out all the possibilities."

Tommy smiled at her apologetically. "Excuse me for a moment, Lana..." He rather hoped it would be for the whole of the day. He trotted over to stand next to Jasmine, who stroked his arm coquettishly.

"You look great," he told her. The sun was already climbing well above the fringe of trees that bordered the base now. It was going to be a beautiful day. Even the sight of Mark Hamm appearing around the corner of the dining bus and taking his place in the queue with a supercilious air couldn't tarnish it.

A minibus took the twenty or so supporting artists to the filming location in two trips. Tommy and Jasmine were in the second load. It only took three or four minutes to reach the site. The minibus followed the curve of a mud track around the belt of trees, and suddenly, the full extent of the set was spectacularly revealed. There were several gasps and *oohs* from the SAs as they admired the collection of freshly constructed wooden wards, huts, offices, and cabins that were spread around the site. Canvas tents were erected, too, and wooden walkways spanned the grass between wards and cabins. In the distance they could see a perimeter wire fence and, at the end of a straight track, a mock-up of a sentry gate, complete with barrier and guard hut. Most impressive of all to Tommy were the vintage Ford Model Ts parked at the head of the basic drive.

The minibus unloaded them next to a large tent. Jen was waiting for them. "Come on, lovelies," she chirped. "This is your Green Room for the next four months."

She led them inside. It was gloomy and smelled of canvas and hemp. A rough circle of plastic folding chairs had been placed centrally. Most of these had been bagged already. Lana waved at him and patted the one spare seat next to her, but Tommy shrugged non-committally, with an apologetic smile. He turned to Jasmine.

"Nicer outside, I think." She nodded happily. He grabbed a free chair positioned against the wall of the tent and carried it out for her.

"What about you?" she asked sweetly.

"I'm happy standing," he replied, peering at the set. It really was large and impressive and exact in every period detail. Opposite the Green Room tent, the main unit camera was set up on the grass, preparing to film a scene outside one of the wards. The principal actors were gathered on the walkway next to a huddle of make-up and wardrobe assistants. He recognized a couple of the principles but couldn't remember their names, though he was sure one of them, a tall brunette with a sharp face, had been on *Coronation Street*. He searched for Rona, but the voluptuous star was nowhere to be seen.

He turned back to Jasmine. "Quite happy to spend the next four months on this. Especially if you're going to be here, too."

She smiled up at him. He meant it. This whole setup was looking great. Four months of regular work with the hottest girl he'd ever pulled. Bliss. And yes, he wasn't going to waste any more thoughts on dark and depressing things. Why should he? He reached for Jasmine's hand and squeezed it.

"Excuse me a sec, Jazz. I really need a pee," he said and glanced around for Jen. She was emerging from the tent, listening to instructions in her earpiece. Tommy waited for her to acknowledge them before speaking.

"Where's the honey wagon, Jen?"

Still listening to the First AD on the wire, she gestured toward the perimeter fence. He could see a couple of uniformed police officers patrolling the fence, and beyond it, a white trailer. He jerked his thumb up at her and headed across the grass toward the perimeter.

As he threaded his way around guy ropes and past wooden cabins, he heard the First AD's voice echo across the location, amplified by a megaphone. "Quiet, please. Turning..."

He slowed his pace a little, although it would have been impossible to hear him from this distance, and waited for the inevitable follow-up. It came soon enough: "And... Action!"

He smiled to himself. He loved his job.

It was only now, as he neared the perimeter fence, that he could truly appreciate the scale of the location. It easily covered three square miles or more and was situated on private parkland. He could see an impressive old mansion nestled three hundred yards or so beyond the fence amongst well-maintained grounds. Beyond the mansion and its protective border of woodland, he could just make out the picturesque Wiltshire town of Malmesbury. He marched on slowly through the tall grass, heading for a gap in the fence at one corner. A WPC was guarding the gap, talking to what looked like another detective (a plainclothes black woman), and beyond her, a truck containing security belonging to the production was parked. The WPC and the plainclothes DC watched him approach indifferently.

He nodded to them politely, and while the WPC didn't react, the black detective smiled back. A very attractive smile. He saluted theatrically and passed them on his way to the honey wagon.

He could hear someone rummaging about behind the door marked Female, and was about to climb the two steps up to the male compartment next to it, when the person who had been rummaging emerged, adjusting her petty coat under the nurse uniform as she did so. She saw him looking and smiled widely. He froze on the step, unsure what to say and awkwardly aware that her bodice was even more undone than before.

"Hello," she said openly and with such warmth and charm that Tommy's mouth opened to reply but couldn't quite form the words.

"Nice uniform," she cooed, adjusting her skirts a little more.

"It is," he stammered, meaning hers.

"Mine's a real fucking pain in the ass," she retorted, and a little belch followed the words, tainting the glamor somewhat.

"Yeah?" He attempted a smile but was sure it was goofy, so he dropped it almost immediately.

"Gonna be fun this, isn't it?" she persisted, tugging at the dress so her breasts lunged out from between the lace of the bodice even more.

"Absolutely!" He struggled to keep his eyes level with hers.

"That is, if we don't get horribly butchered, eh?" She tipped him a wink.

"Er, yeah. Let's hope not..."

She cackled lewdly. "Yeah, let's fucking hope not, eh, lovely?" She gazed around at the collection of huts and tents spread around the wide expanse of parkland. "Be a shame, wouldn't it? After they've gone to all this trouble. The set is fucking amazing, don't you think?"

I saw you naked in Game of Thrones, *that's what I think,* he felt like saying. *I saw your splendid ass and boobs. I saw you kissing James Bond, too.*

"I shouldn't worry about anything. There is a strong police presence to protect you—*us.*"

She faced him again, a voluptuous smile swallowing him whole. "Oh, I'm not worried, sweetie. But if you're referring to the Dicktective who spoke to me earlier, I feel a *whole* lot fucking safer already." She chuckled sarcastically. "That copper couldn't find a hard-on in a whore house. But if the killer has big boobs, we'll be fine, cos he did spend rather a long time staring at my tits."

Tommy found himself laughing along with her. She was so engaging and infectiously down to earth. "I can't imagine why," he quipped, shocking himself with his own temerity.

She laughed raucously. "I like you!" She finished hitching her dress around. "Right, I'd better hustle over to the set. Mustn't keep the darlings waiting. Laters, lovely." He heard her rip out another belch as she strode away across the grass. Tommy was still chuckling to himself five minutes later as he returned to the Green Room tent. Star struck? Hmm. Just a tad, maybe. He thought about mentioning his conversation with Rona to Jasmine, but then, reflecting that most of it centered around the largeness of her breasts, he thought it better not to.

The Dicktective of whose skills Rona had been so wonderfully scornful was, at that moment, sitting back in a swivel chair, which, like the trailer in which it was located, had been "borrowed" from the production for the foreseeable future. The Second Assistant Director, a rather attractive, slender blonde called Helen, had been politely but firmly asked to vacate her own office by the forceful DI, although he had asked if he could buy her drinks that evening as compensation. She had just as politely and equally as firmly declined his kind offer and re-housed herself temporarily in Wardrobe's spare trailer, where she continued to monitor the production as skillfully as ever, albeit with a host of uniforms smelling of hemp for company.

"Okay, Trev. This is how we're gonna play it." He tapped a pen against his chin and stared at his DS across the small metal desk. "I want a list of every T.V. show and movie currently in production in the region cross-referenced with every video nasty on the nineteen-eighty-three D.P.P. banned list. Anything that looks like a match in terms of location, setting, period, theme, et cetera, et-fucking-cetera, I wanna hear about it. Who's best for the job?"

Whitley sniffed, staring out of the window behind his boss. "Jason Stead. Pete Brack. One of those two could chase it up."

"No, fuck them. They're plodders. No imagination." He threw the pen on the desk. "Nandu Get D.C. Nandu to do the work. She's the one who knows most about all that 'nasty' shit. In fact, she's come up with some corking ideas already. Just shows what the fuck I know, eh?'

Whitley cocked a brow. Slade actually asking a female to participate? Unheard of. "There's a problem with that, sir. You've already allocated her to watch over the uniform boys on perimeter patrol."

"Fuck, yeah. Bollocks. Can't ask her to do everything, I suppose. Did she get back to you with that report on any suspicious film school dropouts?"

Whitley nodded. "Nothing that screams psycho in there. She's been doing her homework on the nasties all right, coming at it from an M.O. point of view based on the previous killings, but she hasn't been asked to cross-check the vids with current productions."

"Like I said, can't expect the lass to do it all. Us boys have to get a lick in as well sometimes. Tell you what, *you* fucking do it. Pull off that list from Helen Hotcheeks's laptop and get cracking. I want to know, first of all, if any of the nasties could possibly be relevant to a World War One setting. Any films on that D.P.P. list where a sick nut-job goes to town with a fucking bayonet or wears khaki while he's sawin' some tart's head off, or—I don't fuckin' know, use your imagination. You *do* have some, don't you, Trev? Crack on." He got up and turned his back, gazing out across the unit base toward the belt of trees masking the location site. He could see Helen chatting to a sound man, and his gaze took in the long legs sheathed in a particularly tight-fitting pair of jeans. "That is some ass."

"Guv?"

Slade continued to stare out of the window. "I'm beginning to wonder if I got into the wrong business, Trev. T.V. sets are swarming with tits and ass. Fucking criminal, it is." He sighed, then added, "Now get the fuck on with your job. Crime won't fucking crack itself." He lit a JPS and concentrated on the slender vision in blue jeans just beyond the window.

Wrap was at 8:00 p.m., and by then, Tommy and Jasmine were pretty exhausted, as were all the SAs and crew. He'd spent several hours crossing back and forth outside the main hospital ward, carrying bowls of pretend poo, pails of water, or sometimes struggling along with another male orderly under the weight of a long and cumbersome ladder. It was repetitive, unexciting work. Wipes, as they called it in the business. But Tommy was genuinely happy for the first time in months. Every time he passed Jasmine, whose job it was to walk in and out of the ward in her starched-but-fetching WWI nurse uniform, he would flash her a cheeky grin. He always got one back. The sun was warm on his face. The birds had become accustomed to the First AD's persistent megaphone barks of "Action" and had settled in the trees beyond the set, warbling happily.

Occasionally, Rona had been placed in the shot, delivering dialogue to a swarthy-faced, unpleasant-looking actor who was wearing a period eye patch. In between takes, she would give Tommy a ravishing smile that he hoped was not spotted by Jasmine. He soon came to realize, however, that he was not the only male on set to benefit from her fulsome charms; she smiled at every man in uniform. He quickly came to sense the unspoken hostility toward her emanating from the females on set. It was quite natural, he supposed, for the girls to feel a little jealous—hell, even his own delightful Jasmine; Rona was gorgeous and positively oozed sex and charisma.

But despite his overall enjoyment of the day, Tommy was nevertheless grateful when Jen announced wrap and they piled wearily into the minibus to be whisked back to base.

As he changed out of his uniform in the wardrobe trailer, Tommy reflected on what a pleasant contrast today had been to his previous two assignments. No death, no terror. Perhaps Slade wasn't as useless as he had suspected and might actually know what he was doing. The police presence at the set certainly lifted morale. Yet despite the fact most people had avoided mentioning what might well be on their minds following all the recent press speculation regarding the Video Nasty Murders, as they had become known, Tommy was sure the fear was still there.

He waited for Jasmine outside the ladies' trailer, and she finally emerged, even more glamorous in her tight jeans and pretty sweater. He walked her to her Fiesta, and after declaring how much he looked forward to seeing her again at work the next day—which was actually going to be a night shoot—he kissed her goodbye and walked over to his Polo.

Entering his empty house reminded him of Trish. He thought about giving her a ring just to talk things through, but the goodbye kiss from Jasmine stalled him. He sat in front of his PC, powered it up, and almost instinctively found himself immersed in Morefish-inthesea.com. He had no real idea why he was doing this. Wasn't the enticing thought of Jasmine enough to keep him occupied? Deciding it was more habit than inclination, he scrolled through the online faces, pausing with his mouse over the radiant face of Blonde-Venus. He hovered over the Send Message bar and then moved the mouse on. Jasmine was the real deal. He didn't need some haughty bint who never responded to his messages. He moved to his Inbox instead, having noticed the single glowing green digit indicating he actually had mail.

His excitement was dampened upon opening the message to find it came from VoluptuousNymph67. Or, as she was known to her mother, plain old Lana. Not that she looked particularly plain in her profile pic. She was airbrushed to the gills. He sipped at the decaf coffee he'd made for himself and read the message.

Hi Sexy

You looked FAB in your costume today. But then I'm a sucker for a man in uniform.

Just been reading through my messages. You wouldn't believe the illiterate perverts that seem attracted to me. If one more idiot refers to me as M8 or "hun" or writes "Your looking gr8" I will be forced to remove myself from this site. Text speak is the choice of children and morons. I'm getting bored of replying to them all with the reminder that "your" is a signifier of possession, not a contraction of my state of being. I'm sure it completely baffles them, darling. I shall be forced to block the whole lot. But anyway, what a wonderful day today was! Look forward to seeing you tomorrow, lovely.

That made him smile, and he decided he would be kinder toward her the next day while also making it clear how he was interested in Jasmine alone. Okay, he might allow room for a brief flirt with Rona, too, if he got the chance, but then hell, he was only male, after all!

He typed out a brief response.

Hi Lana. Er, I mean, VoluptuousNymp. Gr8 to C U too, hun

He closed the computer and went downstairs to watch the tail end of the 10 O'clock News. What a change a day had made to his state of mind. Even the crisis in the Ukraine couldn't distract him from happy thoughts. Of Jasmine predominantly, of course. But

Rona took her place in there, too. The throb of his cell phone in his pocket—it was still set to silent, one of the main on-set rules—pulled him from his pleasant reveries. He was so dog-tired he thought of ignoring it, but the chance that it might be Jasmine made him change his mind. A buzz of excitement rewarded him when he saw the caller's name.

"Feeling a bit lonely..." Her voice was a purr.

He perked up immediately. "Can't have that..."

"So what do you propose to do about it?"

Approximately forty-five minutes later, he was pulling up outside her flat in Redland. His mind felt tired—hell, if he was honest, so did his body—but the thought of visiting her flat was just too good to pass up.

He buzzed flat No. 5 on the second floor and waited for Jasmine to let him in. It was a standard residential semi split into apartments. Three-story, gray stone. Nondescript. A cat watched him from beside the bin.

The intercom crackled and the door lock popped open. He let himself in to the plain hall and took the red-carpeted steps two at a time. She was waiting for him in her doorway wearing a gold negligee and a wicked smile. Her small breasts peeked out at him through thin lace. Tommy's fatigue evaporated.

She kissed him briefly before pulling him in and closing the door behind them.

He had time to look around her living room only briefly—small, pink settee with pink cushions, a teddy bear lolling against one of these; a small plasma TV, bookcase, coffee table—before she was pulling him toward the bedroom.

"Not even going to offer me a coffee?"

"Fuck coffee," she said, posing coquettishly in the middle of the small bedroom. A soft lamp glowed over the pink duvet and pillows. A chest of drawers with one drawer open, stuffed with lingerie, and a rather shabby wardrobe were the only other items in the room.

She pulled him against her, and they were kissing again. First, softly, teasingly, molding against each other's lips, finding their way, then picking up passion, tongues tender but insistent. She stepped away from him long enough to pull the gold negligee up and over her head and toss it aside. His eyes devoured her. Her flat stomach bore a silver jeweled stud, the small breasts were tinged with a faint flush. Nipples as pink as the material of the bed summoned his lips.

He knelt before her and let them go to work.

Afterward, they lay in bed, drained from the day and the ecstasy of their lovemaking. Tommy's tongue ached from questing into every orifice. Intoxicatingly, he could taste her on his lips, and if he hadn't been so exhausted, that would have aroused him all over again.

Yet he couldn't sleep. Not now. She breathed softly beside him, her eyes watching him drowsily. In a playful mood brought on by the afterglow of sex, he reached out to pull at a pair of knickers, a small fold of which was lolling out of the half-open drawer next to the bed. "Does everything have to be pink?" he asked.

"What are you doing? Don't touch those!" Her voice was uncharacteristically sharp, sharp enough to make him withdraw his hand and turn toward her.

"Dirty are they?" He smiled at her suggestively. Her face relaxed again, and the tired anger was gone. "What have you been up to behind my back? Sleeping with your special director? Does his latex mask turn you on?"

Her smile became lascivious. She pulled the duvet down so that her pert nipples were revealed. "*You* turn me on. Now get to work! I'm hungry again..."

He got to work. Tommy had always done as he was told in the bedroom.

An hour later, when her soft breathing had settled into rhythmic sleep, he let himself out and climbed into his car, bone-tired and cock-happy.

Back home, he sat in front of the TV, reluctant to end this perfect day. Eventually, he fell asleep during the repeat of a Lee Mack sitcom and finally dragged himself up to bed at 3:00, for the first time in years looking forward to what the next day might bring.

On the night before her world turned red, DC Nancy Nandu was dreaming of video nasties.

She'd been watching a download of *Nightmares in a Damaged Brain*. Not a good one to fall asleep in front of. The dreams were vivid and full of action, color, and torment. They morphed from the psychotic breaks of the film in question into a horror-run down night-mare alley, taking in all the DPP 39 tourist sights along the way.

The Technicolor fun—yes, this dream was *definitely* not mono-chrome—began in a seedy bedroom. The child protagonist of *Nightmares in a Damaged Brain* was entering the room, wearing a face mask and carrying a fuck-off axe. There was a woman's decapitated head sitting in a spreading tide of gore at the foot of the bed and a corpse sprawled on the floor below, more blood pulsing from the neck stump. But as Nancy lay rigid in fright under the blankets, she realized her immobility was not simply due to fear as she drifted into the next detour in this dreamscape to discover straps were holding her down in a different bedroom, in a different bed. From the medical restraints that bound her, she knew which film she'd blundered into this time. The door was being forced open, and she knew a bearded giant would soon be through, a mathematical compass protruding from his left eyeball.

Here he was now, her friendly bedside visitor. He didn't seem bothered by the restraints (or at least the dream didn't) because she was now being born aloft and carried down a hall that went on forever. And she could hear the soundtrack music now. An electronic symphony of damaged synapses that grew louder, louder—surely her neighbors would hear it next door and wake her!

The bearded killer took her into the kitchen, and that was where she knew she really *had* to stop this dream. Right now, please. *Right* now! Because this was *the* scene. The Worst Scene Ever. The Big Bad of video nasty clips.

Someone up there was obviously listening, however, as just before the monster from *Absurd* could reach the oven, she was snatched away, into another scene, another film. The soundtrack to her terror became more elegiac, more composed, just as disturbing. She was running through the *House by the Cemetery*; she was backing away from the Freudstein Zombie rising from the tomb in the hall-way (didn't every house have one?), poker at the ready in one decomposing fist. His head resembled a block of lamb in a Greek Take-Away, and when he opened his kebab mouth, there were maggots, and they tumbled from his lips in a white wriggling waterfall. She could hear them pattering on the carpet. *Her* carpet.

She jerked awake. She'd knocked over the glass of wine that had been standing on the little glass table next to the armchair in her convulsions. The red drops continued to patter onto the carpet.

The TV was still playing. Another suppurating wound of a film—*Beast in Heat*—but enough was enough! She reached for the remote, still shaking from the dream, and killed the TV. Then she leaned back against the armchair cushion and listened to the thunder of her heart.

Part Two
And... *Action!*

CHAPTER TWELVE

Slade and Whitley arrived at the production base by four the next afternoon, ready for the night shoot. The Bentley roared up the bumpy access track and lurched to a halt on the grass car park in front of the unit trailers. Slade switched off the engine, killing the loud music (*Whips and Furs,* the Vibrators), much to Whitley's relief. And DC Nandu's, too, who also occupied the car.

Slade scowled at them. "Whassup? We can sit right here and listen to a few more tracks if you like?"

Whitley and Nandu proved how much they liked that idea by the speed with which they jumped out of the Bentley.

Slade followed them, trudging toward the production office trailer. Helen greeted them politely.

"I've got constables patrolling the perimeter fences and more guarding the entrance, just like yesterday," he told her redundantly. She already had her production security personnel on the job liaising with the police force. She nodded. As he continued, he couldn't help noticing the top buttons on her blouse were undone and part of her cleavage was showing. "As this trailer has the only outside line on the site, I'll need to stay on the spot, but D.C. Nandu will be glad to give you any advice or help you or your T.V. bods might need out on location." Nandu smiled sympathetically at the Second AD.

"I'm sorry about the lack of a signal, Detective Inspector Slade," Helen replied smoothly, ignoring the crawl of his eyes. "It doesn't make any of our jobs easier. Though we do have H.T., which serves most of our needs. But I'm sure you must have your own," she added pointedly.

"Of course. But I need to be contactable from outside at all times." He smiled broadly at her. "Ooh, and while you're here..." he added, settling himself in Helen's swivel chair. "Any chance of a coffee? White, one sugar?" She stared at him for several seconds without answering. Whitley rolled his eyes at Nandu.

Whitley sat at a smaller porta-desk against one wall of the trailer, poring over Helen's laptop. The Handheld Transceiver next to his coffee cup burbled and crackled every now and then. Slade spent most of the next hour on the landline, checking on other productions in the area. There were a few: a supermarket sitcom in Bristol; a crime serial set in Clevedon; a children's Sci-Fi in Bridgend, South Wales, out of Slade's area, strictly speaking, but as he'd told DI Hughes, he was now in charge of the whole case wherever it took him; a period drama in Wells dealing with witch burnings; a sword-and-sandals prime-time show for Saturday nights; and the continued antics of *Casualty* in Cardiff (*Doctor Who* was still on hold). Slade was particularly interested in the Wells drama (burnings) and was in half a mind to visit, but the combined presence of Hamm and Wallace on this particular set compelled him to stay for the time being. He would make regular telephone checks on his officers looking after the period drama, though. Finger on the pulse, or fucking what!

If Slade had had his way, every production in the South West and Wales region would be on hold. He had assumed his Super would share his opinion, but what Slade obviously failed to perceive (as his Super pointed out to him condescendingly) was that there was more at stake here than simply solving a crime. Politics was rearing its big ugly head, too, and the British TV and Film Industry still had a lot of clout, especially when it came to MPs. So there it was: productions so far unaffected by recent occurrences would continue to film despite the murders, and Slade would just have to spread his force thinly to cover them all. So Slade continued his calls, concentrating first on those productions that Whitley had highlighted might lure the killer, swiveling in his chair to watch evening fall outside the trailer window as he did so.

He returned his attention to the Wells period piece, which might link to three films on the infamous list: *Blood Rites, The Burning,* and *Don't Go in the House.* He cross-checked the latter two first because of the fire motif. Whitley had scribbled in biro next to these titles: "The first has a nutter with a face like a Southern Fried Chicken chopping peeps with a HUGE pair of shears, and DGITH has a sick fuck torturing babes with a blowjob." Slade was pretty sure his DS was confusing his terms here but really didn't want to guess what had prompted the lexical mash-up. *Blood Rites* was a period slasher ("supposed to be a bit shit," was Whitley's considered lit crit). Slade sighed and moved on to the Clevedon crime drama purely because of its theme of murder (Whitley's comment: "Might tie in with *Terror Eyes* because of bumbling cops and decapitated heads in fish tanks"), although there was nothing overtly violent about this rather cozy sleuther by the look of it. He would need to check with the production to see if they had any fish tanks in the script, or, indeed, decapitated heads. Next up was *Casualty,* which linked with two films: *Dead and Buried* ("Nurse whacks needle in eye of patient") and *Visiting Hours* ("Looney on loose in emergency ward—this one's got Captain Kirk in it."). Slade was of the opinion that they could probably discount the A&E soap, though. His hunch told him the killer wouldn't strike at the same studio twice.

But sitting in a warm office drinking coffee could get dull, even for a man with Slade's leisurely proclivities, so when the call came through from his department, he was, on the whole, quite glad of the distraction. He'd been on the point of delegating the production checks to Whitley, who had just finished working through the list of extras present at the previous crime scenes that were also booked for future TV jobs. Again, Hamm and Wallace were the only common factors, the DS reported. This confirmed Slade's opinion that he'd parked his ass on the right production. Standing up to stretch and pondering whether he should go and check on Rona Capley, the telephone pulled him out of his pleasant reverie. He snatched up the receiver on its second ring.

He listened as DC Pete Brack relayed what had just come through to the station, and his lazy mood abruptly vanished. "Fuck's sake!" He slammed the phone down, looking distracted.

"What's up, guv?"

"Get your fat ass off that chair, Whitley. We're out of here." He grabbed the HT off the desk and contacted DC Nandu.

"There's been another one. Myself and D.S Whitley are going straight to the S.O.C. just outside Bristol. You're in charge here. Position a uniform in this office to man the landline. Anything fucking unusual happens, I want to hear about it straight away. But I want you out on location where all the action is. We'll be back as soon as we can." The walkie-talkie crackled, and Nandu's voice was serious and to the point: "Copy that, guv."

Within seconds of speaking to Nandu, he was down the steps of the trailer and hurrying toward the Bentley, with Whitley trying to keep up.

"We got the wrong production?" Whitley asked as they climbed in.

Slade started the engine. He killed the music as it blared out in response. He wasn't in the mood for punk. "No. This is another old one. Just been found. An anonymous caller tipped off the local Bristol bobbies. They contacted the department. Fuck it all: I was looking forward to a quiet night."

"Could be worse, guv. Could have happened here."

Slade swung the Bentley in a bumpy curve and headed down the track to the B road, nodding at the two constables at the entrance. He wound down the window. "Keep an eye out, boys. D.C. Nandu's holding the fort for the next hour or two. Spot anything odd, get on to her." They stood back, and the Bentley bounced off the track onto the road to Malmesbury.

The room stank of human rot.

"Another old one" couldn't possibly have prepared Whitley for the scene that awaited them. Even Slade, who had taken the info firsthand, lost his jaded composure.

The two detectives stood in the bedroom with its peeling paint and cobwebs and looked at the girl on the bed.

She had been in her early twenties. They even had a name. Jim Tavell provided that as soon as they arrived. "Vicky Hebworth. Model. Does occasional extra work on films and T.V. Reported missing six weeks ago by her boyfriend and parents."

Slade nodded grimly. "Check the boyfriend out," he said to Whitley, who was scribbling in his notebook. He sucked in some air, then immediately regretted it.

She had been pretty, maybe beautiful, once upon a time. Slade ignored the wound in the forehead and what was embedded in it for the moment, taken in by the cobalt blue eyes, now glazed by a film of death, the taut cheekbones marbled by putrescence. Rigor mortis had propped open her once sexy mouth. Maggots had fed on her bottom lip and played on the tongue, which was now greener than pink. She was naked. Her nipples were beginning to sink in, the aureoles dark. There was a sheen of rot replacing the tan that once bronzed her sleek legs.

"Take the bra off, Vicky."

She looked off camera, toward the man who had spoken. He nodded once.

She did as she was told. The pink, shiny bra dropped to the bed.

"Now stand up and drop the knickers, too."

She hesitated a bit longer this time but eventually pulled them down her thighs. They pooled around her ankles. She stepped out of them and stood shyly, sexily, nervous, yet proud. She had a great body.

"Hammer blow to the left clavicle," Jim Tavell said. He held up the evidence bag with the tool inside. "Claw hammer. Only one blow from this, by the looks of it. Certainly not the cause of death."

"No, that would be the fucking great nail sticking in her brain," Slade snapped. Tavell glanced at him.

"Sorry, Jim." Slade rubbed his forehead. "Just tired, that's all."

"Tired of this sick bastard, like all of us," Tavell answered.

Slade nodded slowly. He felt a deep, uncontrollable fury rising. He took in the other wounds peppering the naked body. More nails. Jim Tavell's pretty female assistant was holding a bag containing the nail gun that had fired them.

"Kind of the fucker to leave us with the murder weapon." His fists were clenched. Always worse when the victims were female. Always.

The light went out. Vicky hadn't been expecting that. The bedroom was so quiet she could hear her own breathing (faster now) and a rustle as the camera moved. Were they filming in infra-red? She heard a clink of metal. Boot steps across the bare floorboards. Then dreadful, sickening pain as something hard and metal smashed into her shoulder blade, just above her naked left breast.

Vicky screamed.

"Any videos this time?"

Tavell nodded. He gestured at one of the other SOCOs, who brought forward two separately bagged items.

"*Two?* He's fucking loving this." Slade scrutinized the boxes through the plastic of the bags. "Couple more for your list, Trev. Or maybe this means two you can cross off." He read out the titles. Whitley scribbled them down. *Toolbox Murders, Snuff.* There were no comical annotations this time.

She fell back on the bed, sobbing, screaming. But nobody would come, would they? She knew that. The house was empty. It stood on its own, miles from anywhere. She had walked right into this, like a sheep into the slaughterhouse. Baa-ing all the way. Her vanity had led her down this path. But what was wrong with that? What was so wrong with being beautiful and wanting to make a living off her beauty? She cried without sound as she thought of her mother, waiting for her at home, and Dan, her new boyfriend whose texts would never be answered. She rolled off the bed. "Don't, please! What are you doing?"

She heard a clink-kerchunk of some metallic item being loaded. Then a hollow percussion sound. She felt the agony seconds later.

"Present occupier?" Slade turned to a uniform who was standing respectfully back, trying not to gape at the beautiful corpse. The hideously beautiful corpse.

"Uh, yes, sir. Jezac Pincker. Romanian national. Emigrated here six months ago. Construction worker. Been renting this cottage for five months. Present whereabouts unknown, sir."

"A construction worker who can afford a place in the country like this. Something doesn't add up, does it, son?"

The constable nodded, then shook his head. "Er, no, sir."

"The tip off..." Slade continued. "Details?"

"Anonymous caller, sir. No details. But er..."

"Yes?" Slade's voice was steely.

"Male with Eastern European accent, sir."

Slade dismissed him with a curt nod. He turned to Whitley. "I want to know everything about this Pincker bastard. Every building site he's worked on both here and in Romania. Get onto Interpol. I want his background. I want to know who he interacted with here and over there. I want to know what his parents do, whether he's been married, whether he's gay. I want to know who delivered the fucking milk here. I want to hear from the postie. I want..." He paused, gathering his breath. "I don't just want this fucker's history, Trev; I want to know what hair gel he uses, what kind of burgers he likes, how big his fucking cock is!"

He turned away. He needed air again. But he knew stepping outside this quiet, lonely house of death secreted in the woods five miles from Bristol would not take away the sight of those staring bluebell eyes, the once pink gloss of the lipstick, now moist with decay. He doubted he would ever be able to look at a pair of naked breasts again without seeing the dreadful subsidence of those aureoles—as if some sadistic child had pressed in the plastic tits on a doll—and the nipples themselves with their new shade of putrescent blue.

Through the pain, a memory. Of happier times. Cold, so cold, but what excitement! A movie set—her first! Goodwood Racetrack. The glam costumes, the vintage cars, the good-looking extras, the men, always the men...mum... Mum!
Cold... So...cold...

"Let's go, Whitley," said Slade, turning his back on the room, on the dead girl staring after him with those blue, blue eyes.

CHAPTER THIRTEEN

Tommy could have had no idea that within just a few short hours of arriving at the WWI set for the night shoot that he would be fighting for his very life.

He was busy carrying bowls of fake shit in Ward 2 when the attack came.

The First AD was struggling to restrain his temper, although to be fair to him, it was a complicated shoot, and a couple of the supporting artists were not helping matters. Lickie, for one: a great bumbling oaf of forty-five who was continually moaning about his back when called upon to carry one end of a stretcher containing a wounded soldier. The SA on the other end kept quiet, even when Lickie decided he knew better than the AD about how far across the room they should carry their charge. His ad-libs were kind of anachronistic as well. But when Tommy added one of his own—the director had called for improvised vocalization—it was Tommy who received a dragon glare from Hetty, the frosty bitch who had a co-starring role along with Rona, albeit in the less-glamorous role of Matron. She put her finger to her lips pointedly as she glared. Tommy carried his shit and shut up. Hetty was defiantly Old School: extras should know their place and speak when spoken to. A real contrast to Rona's natural warmth.

The First AD finally twigged that the scene would be a whole lot easier if he got rid of the useless fuck who was doing all the moaning, despite the fact Lickie had signed a medical fitness form like everyone else before joining the production.

Lickie stood down, still muttering. Tommy barged past Hetty a little too forcefully (nearly knocking one of the period oil lamps over as he did so and earning another icy glare) and took his mark for the next shot, not realizing that, at that very moment, the two constables guarding the main entrance were having their very own little bit of drama, of a decidedly more violent kind.

They had seen the headlights approaching up the country lane and paid the vehicle no inordinate amount of interest. Even when it pulled in through the open gate, the glare of the lights obscuring the occupants behind the windshield, they simply sauntered over to check, not expecting the back door to burst open and a veritable giant to leap out and come running at them.

He topped seven feet and was dressed in a dirty, stained, and curiously seventies-style suit with big lapels and flares. But it was the face that brought the two constables to a halt, momentarily freezing all rational thought, all professional decision.

The face was peeling and horrifically pockmarked, flaps of skin hanging loose to reveal weeping wounds beneath. Bloody eyes glared wildly, promising nothing but violent death. The teeth were bared like a rabid dog's.

If all that wasn't bad enough, the huge right hand clutched an axe. The axe swung out at the nearest constable—his name was Steven Keill, and he had a sweet wife and two-month-old baby waiting for him at his little semi in Gloucester—and took him under the chin, lifting him off the ground. The giant held him up in the air for a moment, inspecting the wriggling copper like he was a pike swinging on a fishing hook, then shook him free and lunged at the second officer, who was scrabbling belatedly for his walkie-talkie.

The giant's left arm swiped the officer's helmet from his head contemptuously while his right followed through with the axe, smashing the blade deep into the exposed head. The skull parted around the weapon, and the brittle crunch was loud in the clear spring evening. The cameraman behind the giant caught all the action, his features disguised under the latex mask of a bland, middle-aged man, which only made it all the more surreal and disturbing. Two more grotesque figures lumbered forward from the back of the Transit.

The giant stooped to retrieve the axe, placing one size fifteen boot on the dead officer's chest. This copper's name was Jeff Barnes, a lonely bachelor with children from a previous marriage who wouldn't be missed as much as Steven, although his mother would certainly grieve for him. The killer had no time for such considerations, however, as he tugged the blade from its socket. The axe pulled free with a soggy belch of blood and brain that pitter-pattered on the giant's work boot.

The four intruders proceeded through the open gateway toward the production base two hundred yards beyond.

DC Nandu first became aware that all was not right in this peaceful country park in Wiltshire when she approached the Subaru containing the production security guard. The man inside appeared asleep, his head slumped forward. She noticed the bloody gash of his throat a second before huge hands clamped over her face from behind.

She was lifted into the air as easily as if she were six years old again, being bounced in her father's loving grip as he pretended to toss her. This grip was not so loving, and the toss was not pretend. She flew into the night sky, the country mansion half a mile away upending as she came down again, smashing into the chicken wire perimeter fence. She rolled on the grass, stunned, and the creature that had thrown her was shambling slowly (no hurry, it seemed) toward her.

She groped for her walkie-talkie, but the giant took it calmly off her, like her father used to take away her favorite doll when it was time to carry her up to bed. She stared up at the awful face and recognized him. She had done enough research, after all. This was a proper bogeyman, all right. The real deal, thank you very much. His face adorned the scariest cover on the whole DPP 39 list—and there certainly was a generous damn choice of scary covers to pick from for Nancy Nandu, Detective Constable, one month into the job and already showing definite signs of promise.

She reached out ineffectually to ward off those huge hands, but they batted aside her attempts while the giant emitted a guttural growl that was as Video Nasty as his face.

She saw the cameraman with the hideous Mr. Bland mask holding out his Red One camera at her, and for a moment she clung to the fragile belief that this might just be a publicity hoax, a stunt, just some student filmmakers screwing around—and oh, that would be fine with her. Oh God, yes. *Oh God!*

She saw the other two figures lumber out of the shadows, big, yes, but not quite in the same league as the Anthropophagous—because that's what he was, the bastard. He was the Beast from the second title on the official nasties list (alphabetically speaking), and her research had really paid off, hadn't it? All that downloading was coming up with pay dirt. She could die with the knowledge that she knew the identity of her killer. But that was absurd, wasn't it? *No, no!* Absurd *was the title of the first nasty on the Banned List.* She managed to stop the insane giggle before it escaped. The Anthropophagous Beast was played by a seven-foot-two Italian actor whose name DC Nandu couldn't remember right now, and frankly, it didn't really make a whole lot of difference, did it? She was going to die; that was the real deal. Like the security man in the Subaru. Like the student axed in the bathtub, the prop wrangler drilled in the TV studio, the Geordie speared wearing a bear trap as a headgear fashion accessory.

So what is my *video nasty death going to be?*

DC Nandu had never been a screamer. In school, when the racists in her class called her a black bitch, trapping her in the toilet stall and telling her they would paint her white, she had not screamed. When they scratched her face and ripped her hair, she had not screamed.

She would not scream now.

Her mind frantically replayed everything she knew about *Anthropophagous the Beast*, not for research purposes this time, but to calculate exactly how her death might come to her. Calculate. She would stay cold, speculative; she would prepare for her death, and when it came, she would not scream.

The Anthropophagous Bastard held both her wrists up above her head in one hand, began ripping her jacket open with the other, a huge knee holding her legs down all the while. Buttons flew from her expensive leather jacket (*hand-crafted in Covent Garden*). Her mind, so agile, continued to race even while her body was immobilized. The brutal hand ripped at her blouse next. Another crazy thought. *He'll be disappointed by my breasts. They're small. He won't rape me. He won't kill me.*

Axe. There had been an axe killing at the start of the movie. Or was it a machete? She couldn't remember. She recalled a man on a beach and a weapon splitting his head. But she wasn't on a beach! There was no beach for miles. So this wasn't consistent with the MO! Other deaths, Nancy: think! If you're prepared, you can defend; isn't that what her training officer had told her in rookie class?

But all she could think of was a greatest hits package of kills, a frenzied montage of throat-tearing, axing, and gouting blood. And the fetus-eating scene, of course. How could she forget that? Anthro had ripped open a pregnant woman's belly—or actually just reached under her sweater by the looks of the parsimonious effects sequence— and pulled out an unborn baby, commencing to scarf it down with vile relish. Her research had uncovered the startling fact this scene had even had a few seconds of footage broadcast on the nine o'clock news back in the early '90s amidst a second wave of "nasty" hysteria. The anchorman had referred to it as belonging to a snuff film. She reflected ironically, and with mounting hysteria, that their research just wasn't on the same fucking par as hers. But at least she would be spared that horrific fate. She certainly was not pregnant.

Her blouse was ripped down to her navel now. The Anthropophagous dribbled and growled. Those filthy red eyes roved over the little black bra cupping her little black breasts, and if he was disappointed, he didn't show it. The eyes rose to hers. She wanted to shout at that made-up face, that understudy of an actor, *"You're not real. You're just some sick fuck playing a part. A copycat psycho. Take off the make-up, fucker!"*

The Anthropophagous Beast ripped away her bra, and the growls became lower, more guttural still, blood-chilling. She looked up at the three figures behind him, all staring down at her patiently. There was the burned one, with the face like a torqued walnut. She'd seen his film, too, but the title skipped her mind just now. He held the biggest pair of gardening shears she'd ever seen in his melted hands. Next to him, his companion from hell was an atavistic throwback, naked but for rags around his groin like the most hideous Tarzan she had ever seen. Shaggy fur appeared to grow from his back and arms—it looked cheap, like wardrobe could only afford to sling an animal rug over his shoulders, but she knew no wardrobe girl had dressed this monster. His face was Morlock-wild, eyes maddened, sharing the same appetite for destruction as his buddy, the Anthropophagous. Plastic-faced Mr. Bland with the camera stood proud in his smart suit, sharing the terror. And with the exception of Cameraman and his terrifyingly normal mask, she suddenly knew none of them were faking it. This was no make-up masterwork showcase. This was...oh yes, this was *alllll* real, baby. She remembered how her Daddy would stroke her hair when it was plastered against her forehead with nightmare dew. *Don't worry, honey*, he had crooned at her. *It's not real, baby.* Nancy, of course, knew differently. She knew *them*. She could name them.

She opened her mouth to do just that.

But screams were all that emerged.

The scene in Ward 2 was in the can. The gate was good, and now they were resetting outside for an exterior shot. Rona was smoking a ciggie and chatting to Hetty. Rona had asked Tommy for a light, and he'd proudly used the authentic WWI replica lighter the props guy had entrusted him with for an earlier smoking scene. Hetty was responding to her with disapproving nods and grimaces. Tommy looked away before he got too irritated, and Lana flounced up, all bosom and winks. He groaned inwardly, wishing Jasmine had been in this scene to keep him company instead of cooped up in the Green Room tent waiting to be called for the next one. His tongue still felt stiff from licking Jasmine's body in every inventive way he could think of, and his lips tingled at the memory of her taste. That brought out a smile, which Lana took as meant for her.

"I saw you staring at Rona again," she mocked. "They'll be bringing out a restraining order against you if you don't watch your cute little ass."

Tommy opened his mouth to reply—and everything changed forever.

Four figures were stalking toward the film unit. Spotlights raised on cranes picked them out, glinted from the axe in the giant's hand, the shears of the Burned Man, the hand-held Red carried by Mr.

Bland. They were walking slowly, stepping over guy ropes and tent pegs, no hurry. And Tommy knew them, of course. Anthropophagous the Beast, the ugliest of the nasties; Cropsy, the summer camp caretaker in *The Burning*, horribly disfigured in a prank gone wrong; the homicidal Bigfoot from *Night of the Demon*, the most violent entry in that maligned subgenre. And...

Tommy squinted to take in the details of the latex mask worn by the cameraman—and Mark's words came back to him: *conservative, middle-class Daily Telegraph Reader*—but distance obscured it. "We need to get out of here..." he half croaked, half whispered to Lana, who was just starting to notice the figures.

The Irish director was swearing at the First AD as delays continued to plague the camera set up, far too involved to take notice of four clowns in elaborate costumes narrowing the gap between them. Jen did, though, and Tommy saw her step away from the huddle around the monitor to intercept them.

"Jen, no!" Tommy croaked again. Then louder: "Jen, WAIT!" He was running now, not sure what he was doing, but aware that he was the only one here—apart from Mark, thanks to his involvement in his latest project—who could recognize the implications of the bizarre costumes and make-up worn by the four intruders.

Fast as he was, his reactions were way too slow to save Jen.

Cropsy took her out.

The shears extended, opened to embrace the cheerful runner's neck, closed again. Cropsy stepped over the body, red shears opening for more deadheading.

Some of the make-up and wardrobe girls started to scream. The director looked up at last. He hadn't seen Jen die and was annoyed at this potential further delay to his schedule. "Who the fuck are you? What are you doing on this site?"

The video nasty killers ignored him. They kept coming. The First AD stepped forward to intercept them, likewise unaware of Jen's fate. He was a big chap with a shaven head, slightly camp. Anthro lunged at him, pounding him to the grass, sawing at his neck with the axe, growling, slobbering.

That was it. The tide broke. Make-up and wardrobe girls were scattering into the night, sturdy prop guys joining them. The Irish director ran toward Tommy, smashed him aside, and disappeared into the night. Tommy nearly fell, but Lana held him up. Her face was ghost white but set, calculating. "Into the Ward!" she yelled at everyone. "Quick! We can lock them out..." Tommy wasn't sure what good that would do them but guessed it might be worth a try.

The sound guy had jumped up from his control seat next to the director's monitor, moving faster than Tommy had ever seen him. He heard Lana's suggestion and clearly decided it was a good one because he was the first to launch himself inside the wooden cabin. He would have shut the door there and then, too, if Tommy hadn't been close behind him, forcing it back. The night was alive with screams. Where the fuck were the police? He'd seen them all evening, prowling the perimeters, but now, when they were *sorely* needed—not a blue uniform or plain clothes in sight.

There was Hetty, stumbling grimly toward the ward, hitching up her matron's dress as she ran. Behind her, Rona, beautiful eyes wide and scared, her mouth open, coming up on Hetty fast.

Tommy stood back against the open door, scanning the knot of screaming crew members, actors, and extras as they streamed lemming-like toward the ward, now that someone had imposed a course of action on their brains. He was searching for Jasmine and praying that she had heard the commotion from her tent and somehow got away.

There had been about fifteen people involved in the night shoot. Jasmine and two others had been sent to the Green Tent. Six or seven were already in the ward, the rest either running toward the door or scattered into the night. There were a dozen places to hide, Tommy conceded, and probably a lot of them better than concentrating themselves into this one location. Sitting ducks, anyone?

Almost everyone who was coming was in the ward now. Mark slowed as he trotted forward, his eyes wild, confused. As if all this might be a dream—certainly not part of his smug schedule. He entered the ward without looking at Tommy. Rona was last. She glanced at Tommy as she squeezed past, but his eyes were fixed on the Anthropophagous Man who had peeled off toward a huddle of huts and tents at the west side of the set—toward the Green Room tent. *Toward Jasmine.*

Somebody was yelling at him to close the door, and he snapped out of his inertia, starting to do just that. But somehow, over the hubbub of screams, sobs, shouts, scraping of period bedsteads and chairs inside the ward, Tommy heard a more distant scream, and this one was definitely female. Jasmine? He couldn't tell. He froze in the doorway, his self-survival instincts urging him to stay, his passion spurring him to run after Jasmine. It might not be her. Knowing he was selfish and not caring right then: *Please, God, let it be someone else!*

"Shut the fucking door!" The sound engineer's white beard flecked with spittle as he shouted.

Bigfoot was mutilating the First AD's body, worrying it like a dog. A wet squelch and the creature tugged something free. The AD's head bounded off the wooden wall of Ward 2, just above Tommy, leaving a red smear. Bigfoot lumbered forward, face feral, hands open wide.

Tommy closed the door then.

They couldn't lock it, as there was no key. This was a period set; it didn't need that much verisimilitude. The designer hadn't anticipated the ward might need to withstand a siege.

Lana snapped into action. "We need to barricade the door! Use beds, chairs, anything!" That galvanized the stunned group of TV folk somewhat. While the make-up and wardrobe girls huddled in the middle of the room with Hetty, looking absolutely traumatized (and Tommy certainly couldn't blame them for that), Tim, the Third AD, and a stocky grip whose name Tommy didn't know seized a bed and brought it over to the doorway. Tommy helped them angle it across the door—which luckily opened inwards.

"What the fuck is going on?" The sound engineer again, his eyes bugging with terror as he turned from one frightened face to another. Tommy stepped back, not confident at all that the barrier would hold. He performed a rapid check of the room. "More beds!" He and Tim proceeded to position another bed on top of the first. Lana helped stack chairs and a period bedside table behind them. It was flimsy, but it would have to do. His breathing coming in heavy gasps from the effort and adrenaline, Tommy glanced around at his fellow siege victims. Besides himself, there was Rona, Lana, Tim, Mark, Hetty, Juliette the make-up girl, Sally from Wardrobe, the sound engineer, and the grip. The rest had fled or died. Tommy watched Juliette helplessly thumbing her cell.

They could hear a snarling from outside.

"Who *are* they...?" Rona was looking for answers as well. Nobody had any. "What the fuck do they want?"

Tommy crossed to the window.

Anthropophagous was back, and he had a companion.

Jasmine was tucked under one arm, screaming and wriggling, looking like a petulant five-year-old in its monstrous Daddy's grip.

CHAPTER FOURTEEN

Slade was driving like a maniac cop.

"Set up," was all he would tell Whitley as they hammered down the M4 toward the Malmesbury turn-off. As soon as he'd tried to ring the production base on leaving the SOC and got a dead tone, he'd known the score. When none of his officers, including DC Nandu, responded to their walkie-talkie sets, he was convinced of the worst.

"Fucking diversion, Trev," he elaborated as the miles toward their destination continued to diminish—but still too slowly for Slade. Whitley had listened to him barking orders into the car radio. The nearest substantial force to Malmesbury was Swindon, and a squad was now mobilized. They would probably beat Slade to the film set, but not by much, judging from the speed the Bentley was doing.

Slade was going all out: "Scramble a copter," he had barked at the Avon and Somerset Transport Department over the two-way radio.

The walkie-talkie squawked back at him. Some junior officer not knowing whose ass to stick his thumb up. "What d'you fucking mean it's already mobilized? I don't care how many chav joy riders are out enjoying themselves on the roads, get a fucking chopper over Malmesbury. *Now!*" He cut the connection, continued to glare straight ahead at the M4 vanishing point.

"Fucking bastard tipped us off to clear the way, Trev. We fucked up."

"We've got several officers there already, guv. They can handle themselves."

"They're not expecting anything. They'll have changed down a gear after we left. You know it, I know it." He was doing 100 mph, and it still wasn't fast enough.

Jasmine was screaming. And Tommy was watching her through the window. She was out there with four killer freaks, and he was watching the view.

Anthro dropped her casually on the grass. She struggled to get to her feet, and Anthro helped her, scooping her upright with one hand on her throat. He held her there half gasping, half screaming.

Then the lock broke on his courage, and he made for the door.

"What the hell do you think you're doing?" Lana barred his way.

"She needs me! I can't just watch them kill her!" He made to push her out of his way, but she stood firm. Tim the Third came up behind him, grabbed his shoulders. "She's right, mate. You can't go out there. They'll kill you as well."

"*Let me through!*" He shrugged Tim off and pushed Lana roughly aside. He began tugging at the beds, trying to make a gap to slip through and open the door. Then a voice stopped him.

"It's me who should go."

It was Mark, and when Tommy swiveled to face him, his rival's face had lost both its tan and its smugness. He approached Tommy slowly, and that confusion Tommy had noticed earlier was still there, along with the fear. "I know them."

"What the fuck d'you mean?" This was from the sound engineer. Tommy didn't have time for this. Jasmine was still screaming outside.

"You *know* those freaks?" Rona's face was like that of a shocked child. Terror had made her a ten-year-old again.

"It's him, isn't it?" Tommy said, staring out the window again. Anthro was still holding Jasmine upright, and she was still struggling. Next to him, Mr. Bland with the camera—and he was still too far away for Tommy to be able to distinguish what caricature that mask was supposed to represent—was filming the cabin patiently. "The director..."

"He promised me all the snuff footage would be faked. I never believed... I never believed he'd do *this*..." He followed Tommy's gaze out of the window. "It was such a controversial idea, a faux snuff film with no credits, filmed in such a masterful way that everyone would believe it was real. A diatribe against our brutal, meaningless lives, he said. A horrific allegory for horrific times. Shock through Art." Mark's voice was wavering, his eyes lost in trauma. "He said he'd be the new Hitchcock, the new Kubrick. Beyond all those. He said—"

"It doesn't matter what the fuck he said!" the sound engineer cut in. "If you know him, go out there and talk to him. Tell them to stop!"

Mark bent to continue tugging the beds free from the door. Tommy hesitated. "Did you know they killed Andy? And Graham, the wrangler?" Before Mark could answer, Jasmine screamed again. There wasn't time for this bullshit.

Mark pulled the beds free at last. He straightened, gasping, his face earnest with terror. "No! Of course not! The director said it was all an unfortunate coincidence, but it would make great publicity for us... Silver lining, he said." His voice trailed away shamefully.

Tommy grabbed him by the scruff of his uniform and thrust his face into Mark's. "Coincidence, my ass!! You must have guessed! With all your talk of nasties earlier on the dining bus... You *must* have suspected something!" Another memory clicked into place: "And then there's your ringtone... Teddy Bear's fucking Picnic. I remember hearing it on *Arthur* and wondering where I'd heard it before. Now it's just come back to me... Funny it's the theme tune to the film that inspired Andy's death... Don't you think?"

"No, I—" Mark looked down, faltering. "I couldn't... I wouldn't!" His face was ghost-white. "He said it was going to be used on the movie soundtrack. He wanted me to install it on my cell for..." His voice became a whisper. "...advertising purposes." He looked up again, like a schoolboy pleading his innocence. "I didn't know... I...don't know much about video nasties. I didn't connect the dots..."

"Chuck the fucker out with his mates!" Sound Engineer again, and Tommy was getting sick of his voice.

Rona was weeping now, and surprisingly, it was frosty, old Hetty who took it upon herself to look after her, stroking her hair, hugging her soothingly.

Mark looked up again at Tommy. His chin became firm, his eyes resolute. "I'm sorry. I know we've never got along, but please believe me now. You can see why it's me who has to go out there and put this right." Tommy said nothing for a second, then gave a quick nod.

Mark slipped through the gap they had made and yanked the door open. They all watched him step outside. Tommy made to follow him, but Tim and Lana restrained him.

They watched through the window as Mark approached the four grim figures. Jasmine quietened her screams a little as she saw him come.

Had Mark's fear all been a ruse? It could well be that he knew a lot more about nasties and death than he had let on. Was he, in actual fact, going out to join his accomplices?

Mark held up his hand as if welcoming his pals. Tommy couldn't see his face as his back was turned, but he seemed to be addressing the cameraman with the bland latex mask. The Director.

The cameraman was filming Mark, just as he had done in their "epic" snuff movie to end all snuff movies.

They all heard Mark's voice clearly through the half-open doorway, carried on the spring night air. "What are you *doing*? This isn't what you promised! You told me it was all going to be simulated. Have you lost your fucking mind?" *More games?* Tommy clenched with indecision. Should he rush out now, before anything happened to Jasmine?

The cameraman/director didn't bother answering. He gestured to Bigfoot, and the brute with the cheap "fur" gave a gibbering roar and lumbered forward. It was a sound that embodied all video nasties. The growl was amped and muffled at the same time, like a deep electronic vibrato. One filthy hand seized Mark by the crotch, jagged nails tearing material and flesh. And squeezed. And ripped. Blood began to hose the grass before him. Mark was screeching and begging, but he'd overstepped the mark, his role was played out. With a final wrench, Bigfoot swung his hand up in the air, clutching its raw trophy, and Mark let out the most god-awful scream Tommy had ever heard. He spun, pissing blood from the root of his amputated cock, lurched away from the four killers. They let him go. They were done with him. Mark was clutching his groin, the front of his officer trousers wet and dark with blood. He made it two yards, then went down on his knees, and then his face.

Jasmine screamed. Oh boy, did she scream.

Behind Tommy, most of his companions joined in.

Ten miles to go 'til they reached the turn-off to Malmesbury.

Whitley tried DC Nandu's frequency again on the walkie-talkie. Nothing. Same with the other officers. Swindon came on: they were in Malmesbury now, five miles from the TV location. Another car was on the way from Gloucester.

"We'll get the fucker this time, Trev." Slade's face was set, his eyes concentrating on the road. They flew past a service station. Six miles.

The rookie from Air Support came over the radio. "A broken fuel pipe? I don't fucking care! Fix it! I want it covering the unit base in ten minutes!" Slade slammed the steering wheel in rage. "Fucking amateurs." He glared at Whitley in disbelief. "One chopper's got a busted fuel line, and the other's deployed out past Gloucester. They seriously think I'm stretching my neck out over nothing here!"

Whitley continued to ineffectually press the button on the two-way radio. Nothing but dead air answered him.

It happened very quickly then.

At a gesture from Mr. Bland, Anthro released Jasmine. She took a hesitant step forward, looked back once, then toward the cabin. Took another step.

Come on, Jasmine! Tommy struggled against Tim and Lana, but the latter was stronger than she looked. He watched Jasmine take another step, unable to stop himself from recalling a similar scene in *The Wild Bunch*, where General Mapache releases the militant bandit, Angel, and he takes a step toward freedom, two steps, not believing he is actually going to make it—and then the blade in Mapache's hand flashes and Angel's throat opens. Red. All red.

Please don't let this be an Angel moment. "Let me *go!*" He managed to pull free and made it to the door. Anthro's hand swatted Jasmine's head, almost gently, almost lovingly, and she went down. Tommy yelled inarticulately.

And the four killers began to move forward.

Anthro stepped over Jasmine's slumped form as they came, Mr. Bland filming all the way.

Tim had him in a firmer grip this time, helped by the prop guy, and together they dragged him back around the beds, then let him go to concentrate on slamming the door shut and barricading it again.

"They're coming!" This from Sally, the wardrobe girl. Her voice quavered on the brink of madness.

"We need weapons." Lana was once again taking charge. She scanned the wooden cabin for anything they might be able to use to defend themselves with. A portable gas fire in one corner, period bed pans, blankets, chairs. Nothing particularly useful.

Rona, still reverted to childhood, was peeping out from Hetty's starched bosom, her eyes impossibly wide. Hetty continued to stroke her hair. "It's all right, dear," she crooned repetitively. Tommy felt like screaming, *It's not all right, it's not fucking all right!*—but he knew that wouldn't help anyone. He took a peek through the window. The killers had closed the gap now. Ten yards from the door. Eight, seven— Tommy saw the latex mask on Mr. Bland clearly now.

He staggered back from the window.

Like Rona, he had reverted to childhood. He was being driven to school by his truculent father. It was a memory as clear and pristine as if it were a scene restored for a Blu-ray remastering. His father turned to him and said, "Behave at school. I can't afford for you to let me down. My reputation depends upon it." The twelve-year-old Tommy was staring at his father's profile in the car, and the thirty-seven-year-old Tommy was staring at his father's features molded into a latex head mask and worn by a psychopathic killer.

The world had tipped. Helter-skelter madness. This was the moment when Tommy felt sure it could be just one big, bad trip after all.

Until Bigfoot crashed through the door, all video nasty growls, red eyes, and brute Neanderthal rage.

He shoved the beds aside like they were made of balsa wood, seized the sound engineer, held him by the throat with his furry left hand while opening up his belly with his right. The claw punched through the leather jacket, plaid shirt, and flesh and came out clutching loops of filthy intestine. The sound engineer shut up for the first time since the siege began.

Bigfoot dropped the guy and stooped to unravel those gray, slimy guts, like a deranged kid playing with a string of grubby sausages. He slung them around the room in a welter of blood while good people screamed and screamed again. Tommy saw Rona's face red with blood splash-back; Hetty had let her go, was backed into a corner. Cropsy followed his murderous mate inside the ward, molten face a burn scar from Hell. Lana swung a chair at him. Cropsy parried it with his shears, then closed the blades and lunged them through Lana's throat. Blood frothed and bubbled around the steel. Lana's eyes locked on those of her killer, sadness mixed with agony.

Anthropophagous was in now. He'd found his prize: Rona. He snatched her with lecherous glee, peeling down the nurse uniform with one huge hand. Hetty ran forward to protect her friend. Cropsy, his toasted-marshmallow face grimacing horrifically, snipped at her out-flung right hand, clipping her fingers neatly, leaving just a thumb and four pulsing stumps. Hetty dropped in a faint. Cropsy gouged her chest with the shears, stabbing manically.

Bigfoot had Tim up against the wooden wall, was sliding him toward the window. The pane shattered beneath the force, and the killer pushed the AD's head through the broken gap, rubbing his neck against a particularly jagged piece of glass that jutted downward. Flesh parted. Blood came.

Cropsy snipped here, deadheaded there, like a maniac gardener. Sally was down, Juliette, too, missing limbs, gouting from various wounds.

Bigfoot scooped up the grip by his neck. Swung him toward the gas fire that his greedy little eyes had spotted in the corner. He pressed the side of the grip's face against the super-hot surface of the cylindrical heater. The well-built young man struggled gamely, but no cigar. Bigfoot was so much more macho. The grip's face turned orange under the heat, sizzling, searing, flesh patching, popping.

Anthro had exposed Rona's considerable breasts. He held her up with one hand, admired her nakedness for a second while she sobbed and dribbled and beat at him ineffectually. His other hand, huge and dirty, began to desecrate her. First stroking her right breast, then pawing at it, animal-like, then ripping, *wrenching*.

The ward was red.

And Tommy?

Tommy saw it all happen, but Tommy was in a bad dream. His father had come into the cabin, only his father's face was false somehow, and he looked thirty years younger. But, of course, it wasn't his Dad...

That would be impossible.

As impossible as three monsters from video nasty land taking on life and breathing, killing form?

His Dad was filming the carnage. The Red One swung smoothly in his hands, and Tommy could see the eyeholes in the latex mask, and behind those, real eyes, blue eyes. But that was wrong, wasn't it? Because his father's eyes had been brown.

That was when reality kicked in, and Tommy's mind cleared. He was the last one standing. He saw what Anthro had done; he saw what Bigfoot had done. He saw Cropsy with his shears, and suddenly Tommy knew what *he* had to do.

His hand delved into his jacket pocket, came out clutching the little gold WWI lighter. He flicked the wheel, and the flame came. He spun, tore one of the old white sheets from an overturned bed, thrust the flame against its starchy material.

Cropsy watched him, shears open wide but making no threatening move toward him. Flames erupted from the sheet in Tommy's hand, spreading quickly. He tossed it over Cropsy's head. The killer spun aside, but the sheet settled on his right arm, and flame rolled up it in a blazing stream.

Cropsy thrashed wildly, and the flames engulfed him in fast-forward time.

He made no sound as he burned.

Tommy's father (no, not his father, it was *not* his father) filmed that, too, then signaled to the others. They were leaving.

Tommy let them go, pressed back against one wall, breath pumping in and out, watching Cropsy burn.

The flames popped out one by one, and a charred corpse lay on the ground. The face was undeniably burned, but the exaggeratedly melted features had disappeared. The face of a normal man was revealed, blackened, blistered, dark hair half-seared away. But *normal.* Tommy knew the mask hadn't dissolved under the heat; it had simply *gone.*

Tommy swiveled his head to the left so he could see out of the broken window. The three killers were striding across the grass. Anthro stooped, pulled the slumped form of Jasmine up on his way. Tommy stumbled toward the door. This time he *would* save her. The doorway telescoped away from him. Blackness wanted him.

He reached the outside step and then dropped like a sack of bolts.

CHAPTER FIFTEEN

The patrol car took the winding country lanes at a steady fifty. There were three officers on board, two male coppers in their forties and a WPC[11]. Sergeant Bailey was not impressed with the call out, particularly as it was from a different department, *especially* because it was from Slade, for fuck's sake.

They all knew Slade, all knew his reputation. He was a '70s throwback, a renegade, a retard, as far as they were concerned. Yes, they would answer the urgent call, but only because he outranked them, even if he was a Bristol boy. Fucking City Coppers. It was all choppers and riot squads with them. They needed to take it easy. Swindon was a quiet beat. Joyriders, burglars, and the odd perv flashing his dick. And here was Slade with his latest bugbear. Four murders on this case already, and still, Sweeney Slade hadn't pulled a perp. About time he put his own squad in order before he called hardworking coppers out in the middle of the night to chase fucking wild geese.

They took the last bend before the Malmesbury Estate, and Constable Probert changed up to fourth as the squad car eased into the final stretch. Headlights were turning out of the entrance ahead, and they were on full, blinding the PC. Probert flashed his in warning, but the lights came on, still full beam.

"That bastard's going fast," Bailey said.

---

[11] Woman police constable

WPC Greene stiffened in the back. "They're coming right at us, Sarge!"

She was right, Bailey realized. He could see the Transit now as their own beams picked out the dirty white of its bodywork, the filth obscuring the windscreen.

"Turn the fucking wheel, you prick!" he roared at Probert. The PC locked the wheel to the left. Tires screamed. It looked like they might just make it. But the Transit put on its own little burst of speed and hogged the center of the road, coming on like a steel bull.

The front grill powered into the driver's side, slamming the car across the road and tipping it up and over into the ditch.

Bailey's world revolved. His neck lurched against the safety belt, the side of his head smacked against the glass of the passenger door. The car was on its side, its engine screaming like a heavy metal guitar solo. Probert hung above Bailey, suspended in his belt, blood dribbling from his open mouth. WPC Greene was moaning in the back.

Bailey took control. He reached forward, twisted the ignition key to off, then unbuttoned his belt. Next, he used his riot stick to smash out the windscreen. He certainly wasn't getting through his door: that side of the car was wedged deep in the ditch. He forced his way out through the shattered glass, sliding down the upended hood into the mud of the ditch. He put out his hand to help Greene follow him, then scrambled around the car to try to get at Probert. No good: the driver's side was up in the air. He would have to scramble across the hood again and pull him out through the windscreen.

"Get an ambulance!" he yelled at Greene, "And backup!"

A huge figure appeared at the side of the road. Bailey looked up. The figure owned a face right out of horror hell. There were two others behind him. The Transit was parked behind them, its grill buckled. The engine idled.

The chopper was overhead now. Slade could hear it as the Bentley flew along the twisting lanes. Swindon had gone dead on the walkie-talkie. This was a proper blackout. This was crazy. But he had communication with the copter, and they were telling him the worst: Swindon patrol car upended in a ditch. Bodies lying in and beside the road. Three: all uniformed.

Slade hammered the Bentley around the last bend. "And the T.V. guys?"

The pilot responded dolefully. More bodies. No sign of life anywhere.

The chopper was over the grounds now. Slade could see the strobing search beams lighting up the night. He saw the crashed patrol car up ahead and slammed the brakes.

He and Whitley got out and ran over to the first of the bodies. A woman. Pretty once. Now her eyes, her breasts, were gone. Slade straightened, didn't need to look over at the other two corpses to appreciate how badly mutilated they were.

Whitley was crouching over the corpse of the sergeant. Slade had never liked him; Bailey was a bully and a minor racist. But he was a police officer, and he certainly didn't fucking deserve this. His intestines were looped in the dust of the road.

"The fucker's been *eating* him," Whitley said, shocked despite his experience of many depravities during twenty years on the force. "Bite marks on his fucking intestines, guv. The mad bastard was scarfing down Bailey's *guts*!"

Slade stood in the country road at two o'clock in the morning and had nothing to say to his DS. He stared at the bodies scattered like disfigured toys, and his mind reeled.

The chopper droned overhead. The two-way radio in Slade's Bentley crackled, just audible over the sound of the rotor blades. He could hear the pilot's voice clearly. "Repeat: no sign of life. I'm going to take her down beyond the perimeter fence. *No wait!* Three people running toward me. Waving. Survivors, DI Slade: we have survivors."

Slade came out of his daze, strode to the car.

"Copy that. On my way in."

He climbed back in the squad car and headed for the entrance. They passed the other police vehicle parked just inside the open gate. PCs Keill and Clarke were positioned in their seats, almost reverentially. Slade took one look at the blood, the gaping wounds, and drove on up the track.

The chopper was coming down beyond the trees, its blades whipping the branches, the searchlights flicking among the cabins and tents beyond. As Slade bumped the Bentley over the track past the unit base, he saw more bodies, some lying in the grass, one—Helen, the Second AD with the cute ass—sprawling halfway down the steps from the production office trailer Slade had requisitioned from her. Blood was drying on her ruptured chest. Her upside-down eyes were leveled on Slade's as he passed.

CHAPTER SIXTEEN

Tommy came out of his coma several times during the next day, and each time Slade was there, right by his side, and each time he looked more impatient than ever. *My new best friend*, Tommy thought dreamily. *But did he bring me flowers or grapes?* Then he'd be off again, drifting, falling. Once, he woke momentarily to find Slade had metamorphosed into Trish, with tears and a concerned face to boot, but the next time he surfaced, it was Slade again, and there certainly weren't any tears.

The final time he came around, Slade was still there, sitting at his hospital bedside. A nurse was bringing him a cup of coffee and Tommy thought how normal everything seemed, and how much he wanted a coffee, too. Then the memories crashed in, slamming any vestigial feelings of comfort or contentment right out of the park.

He opened his mouth to speak. One word: *Jasmine.* It came out clogged and indecipherable, but the nurse had seen he was awake and was darting forward to check all his vitals. Slade put his cup down and stood, too.

"How is he, nurse?"

The nurse checked Tommy's temperature. Then spoke to the patient, ignoring Slade. "It's okay. You're all right. You're quite safe now."

Tommy tried again, this time with partial success, "Jasmine..."

He looked up at Slade.

"You need to give him some space, Detective Inspector," the nurse said. "He might be awake, but he's been through a terrible ordeal. I've already told you all this. He's certainly not ready for your questions yet."

But Tommy was struggling to sit up. "Jasmine!" he said again, louder and stronger. "Slade, I need to know... Has she been found?"

Slade put a hand up to the nurse. "I'll be gentle, don't worry." He stepped closer to the bed. "You mean Jasmine Paal?" He was scrutinizing Tommy with his steely blues. "She's the only person unaccounted for, I'm afraid. And I can't say whether that's good or bad news. She a special friend of yours, son?"

The nurse handed Tommy a cup of water, and he sipped at it slowly at first, then downed the lot. He said, "What do you mean, 'unaccounted for'?"

"Just what I said. She's not among the dead, and she's not among the survivors. She either ran and is hiding somewhere in shock, or they took her."

Tommy was trying to get out of bed now, but the nurse definitely had other ideas about that. She forced him back under the covers.

"Oh, no, you don't. You need rest. Your body is recovering from shock. You're not leaving here until tomorrow morning at the earliest."

Tommy fell back against the pillows. He *was* exhausted, that was true enough, more drained than he'd ever felt, but he couldn't just lie here while...

"Are you sure she's not...among the dead?" he managed to ask Slade at last.

Slade nodded. "Look, son, I know this might be hard to believe, but I'm not actually here to give you a kiss and a get-well card." The nurse shot him a filthy look, which he ignored. "If you want your friend found alive and well, we need to get on this as soon as possible. Which means we need to find out as much as we can about the attackers, and from where we're standing, you're the best witness we've got."

"You said there were survivors?"

"Three. A prop guy, head of wardrobe, and a cameraman. They were lucky. They didn't listen to whoever thought it was a bright idea to hole up in a flimsy cabin."

Tommy thought of Lana, how brave she'd been, and what Cropsy had done to her.

"I got one of them," he croaked. "I burned the bastard..."

Slade looked impressed. "Was that you? Good work. You're not as useless as I thought—er, sorry, nurse." He waved a placatory hand at the nurse as she checked Tommy's monitor one last time and then withdrew from the small, private ward. "Yeah, we've got him in the morgue, but there's not much to go on. The other survivors said there were four of them, all dressed in masks and costumes."

Tommy thought about that, thought about the way Cropsy's mask hadn't so much melted as vanished completely, leaving a normal, albeit burned man behind.

"I don't think they were costumes."

"What's that?" Slade frowned. His cell was ringing, but he ignored it.

"I said, they weren't costumes. They were real." He knew it was insane, and voicing it aloud only made it sound even more so.

"I don't get you."

"They were characters from video nasties—no, that's not right either..." He struggled to express what was half-buried in the tired fog of his brain. "They were *real*. Like they'd just stepped out of the films, or been summoned from them. I know that sounds crazy, but if you'd seen them, if you'd seen the way Cropsy..." He paused, struggling for breath and conviction. "...*changed* back into just a normal bloke after—after I burned him..."

"Cropsy?" Slade looked interested and skeptical all at once.

Tommy rested his head back on the pillow. But only for a second, one precious second of rest, before he was lifting it again to ask the question he couldn't let go. "That doesn't matter now. I'm guessing you found more video nasties at the murder site. But you need to be out there searching for Jasmine. *That's* what matters."

"And where do we look?" Slade frowned at Tommy. "You think my boys are sitting around playing with their dicks? Why the fuck d'you think I've been wasting my fucking day nurse-maiding your ass when I should be helping the squad lead the search? Because I think you're cute? Fuck's sake, wind your neck in and start giving me something to work on. Like, for a start, everything you've got on these jokers, cos you obviously know a hell of a lot more than you've been telling us so far."

Tommy sighed, and his head fell back again. Of course, Slade was right. He *did* know more, and now seemed the right opportunity to spill. He thought of the director with the Mr. Bland face. He thought of Anthropophagous the Beast, Bigfoot, and Cropsy. "Get me a tea, and I'll tell you what I know."

And he did. Or at least most of it. He told Slade about the audition at the Factory for the low-budget film; he told him all about Mark, how he'd begun to think he was involved, the way he'd enthused about the Snuff Film to end all Snuff Films—including Hamm's insistence it was all *faux.* He told him about the ringtone that tied him in with Andy Hill's murder, about the fact he was always there when someone got killed (at this point, Slade had interrupted with, "A bit like you, eh?"). He told Slade how Mark had showed bravery in the end and gone out to try to stop the killers, how they'd... He swallowed the rest of his tea almost in one gulp before he could continue about what Bigfoot had done to Mark. He told Slade all about the killers and the individual video nasties from which they came, how they had been more than copycat killers, more like the real deal. Here, Slade had put on his skeptical face again, but that was fine; he could wear that face as much as he liked, just as long as he found Jasmine.

He was about to tell Slade about Mr. Bland, too, about the face mask he was wearing, but something made him hold back on that info. Some misguided sense of loyalty, maybe (loyalty to whom—a father he'd never liked?). Or maybe it was trust issues: Slade was not the most sympathetic of audiences. Were those the motives that kept his mouth shut? No, not those, or not exclusively those—more the feeling he just might need to keep some cards close to his chest...

Slade took it all in. He got on his cell and gave orders to Whitley to check out the factory and the film's website for any clues. Then he popped his phone back in his jacket and sat down again, his eyes never leaving Tommy.

"Why you?" he said.

"Why me what?" But Tommy averted his eyes, pretending there was still tea left in the bottom of his cup.

"Why were you the only one left alive in that ward? Any ideas? Because I'm a good fucking listener."

Tommy sighed. He didn't know what to say. He didn't understand it all himself. Not by a long way. He knew there was a personal aspect to all this; that had been made obvious to him last night. The face mask was just the culmination of a long list of clues. But he wasn't ready to talk about his family life to Slade just yet.

"Maybe because I killed one of them? I don't know. Maybe because they didn't expect us to fight back..." That was flimsy, and he knew it, and Slade knew it, too. The detective said nothing for a moment.

Tommy thought of a way to change the course of the conversation. "The body of the killer... *Cropsy*. Have you identified him?"

"Hey, who the fuck's asking the questions here? The bozo in bed or the one with the badge?"

"The bozo with the badge," Tommy said quickly.

"I'll let that fucking go." Slade almost smirked. "Yeah, Romanian national. Jezak Pincker. Mean anything to you?" Tommy shook his head slowly, wincing when it made his skull ache worse. "He was renting a house where we found another murder victim. A Vicky Hebworth..." He stopped talking when he saw Tommy's reaction. "I take it you know her?"

Tommy felt sick. He reached for the polystyrene cup of water, realized it was empty. Slade didn't offer to refill it for him. "Go on," he said.

"She was the girl in the audition video. The one Mark said was fake. And now I'm beginning to think he really believed that, too. I met her on another film set. She went missing—"

"Six weeks ago. Yes, we know all that. Why didn't you come to us with all this before?"

"Like I said, I thought it was fake. Bad fucking taste, but fake. That's why I walked out of the audition."

"And why do you think you were invited there in the first place?" His eyes were like a terrier's who has just spotted a squirrel nibbling a nut slap dab out in the open.

This time Tommy stared him right back in the eye. "Maybe so they could do the same to me as they did to Vicky." Then, emphasizing each word: "I don't. Fucking. Know."

Tommy thought of something. "How did they manage to get away? Surely three sick fucks who looked like freaks and who were probably splashed with blood would stand out a bit in Wiltshire at silly o'clock in the morning?"

Slade looked a little uncomfortable. He stood up from his chair, walked to the window, gazed out at the Bristol traffic. "They must have taken the opposite direction to us down the lanes and gone to ground. They could've just parked up in a sleepy town—Malmesbury, for instance, only a few miles away—and we wouldn't have known. We had no visual on any vehicle—although we're assuming they had one judging from the damage done to the Swindon squad car." He coughed. Tommy imagined he'd practiced this speech a few times before standing in front of his Super. "The chopper was too late getting to the S.O.C. I set up an A.P.B. as soon as we got there, but it was—"

"Too late?"

Slade turned slowly back to face him. His eyes were more dangerous than any criminal's right then. "You think I'm not taking this seriously?" His voice quavered slightly as a sudden spurt of rage threatened to engulf him. "They took one of my best officers, and they *crucified* her upside down on a fence, for fuck's sake!" He put his hands on his hips and breathed in sharply. Then, "I'm going to *nail* these fuckers! I'm promising you that."

Tommy could almost believe him. Then he thought of Anthropophagous peeling off Rona's right breast like he was tearing off a particularly juicy hunk of raw steak, and his bowels contracted. Wherever Jasmine was right now—if she was even alive—she was going to need a lot more help than this anachronism of a detective could ever provide.

CHAPTER SEVENTEEN

While he was dressing the next morning, impatient to get the hell out of this room that stunk of Slade and his own sweat, Trish came in to see him.

The tears were gone—had he dreamed them?—and her face was guarded again, although she smiled warmly at him and gave him a hug. She looked tired, and despite the careful air of concern, he got the impression she would rather be elsewhere. He couldn't blame her for that. Her tears had been for what they had lost, not because she wanted him back. He looked at her and, returning her smile, wished she was someone else.

"How are you feeling now?" She hadn't brought him anything, and he was kind of glad about that. The last thing he needed now was pretense.

He tied the laces on his boots and checked the room for any belongings before remembering he didn't have any; they'd brought him straight here from the set, and he hadn't left any there either.

She tried again, "You must still be in shock. The nurse told me you have to take it easy for the next few days."

He nodded, wondering if she was going to move back in, if only just to nursemaid him. He hoped she wouldn't suggest it, or that they start again. It was too late for that. And was *he* too late? To save Jazz?

He followed Trish to the elevator, still unable to say anything to her.

"It's all over the papers," she said as they waited for the elevator. "All over the T.V. as well. Our house has been swarming with reporters." *Our* house? "It must have been awful. I can't even begin to think what it must have been like for you."

"Don't try," he said, and it sounded harsher than he'd meant it to.

The doors opened, and they entered the compartment. Trish pushed the button for the ground floor, and for a moment, there was silence between them.

"I came to visit, you know. Yesterday."

"I know. I remember...vaguely."

Neither of them could think of anything else to say.

They were waiting for him in the lobby. Hospital staff and police officers were doing their best to keep them back. Tommy waded through the reporters like they were a tide of filth, ignoring the barrage of questions. Outside, strong sunlight blinded him momentarily, and the paps seized on his hesitation to surround him.

Trish held his hand, and he let her, suddenly glad she was there for the first time. "Leave him alone!" she shouted. But then a familiar face was pushing through the throng and ushering them toward the Bentley parked outside the hospital.

"Get in, quick," Slade barked at Tommy, opening the back door. He glanced at Trish, hesitated, then said, "You can come, Missus Wallace, but I'll be taking Tommy on a little journey and then over to the station. You would be better off at home."

Tommy looked up at her as she waited on the curb, indecision all over her face.

"It's all right, Trish. I'll be fine."

She nodded briefly, and was that relief on her face? He was no longer her problem. If he had known he would never see her again, he might have jumped back out and hugged her so tight, so very tight, and apologized for all the shit he'd put her through, all the minor infidelities, the flirting, the websites, the texts. Everything. He would have kissed her and begged if they could start again—*Let's make it work this time*—and all those other things he could have, *should* have said and didn't.

Trish watched the Bentley pull away and wondered what the future held for her now.

She knew the marriage was dead; she hadn't loved Tommy for years. She was just as sure he felt the same. She was certain he had cheated on her, too. God knows he spent enough time on his PC up in the bedroom. She couldn't blame him if he had. She thought of her own infidelity, but there was no room for guilt, only sadness. The sadness of something ending, something that had been good to start with but wasn't any longer.

Yes, sadness was the legacy of her failed marriage with Tommy. Maybe there *should* have been guilt, but she hadn't quite worked out how she felt about Mark's death yet. Shock, of course. But she knew she had never meant anything to him, or he to her. It had purely been about sex, and she was sure he had been using her in his constant battle of one-upmanship with Tommy. But that was fine; she had been using him, too. She wondered if Tommy had ever suspected her little affair with his detested rival. She thought not. It would have destroyed him.

The Bentley turned a corner, and Trish hesitated a moment, then walked slowly to the nearest bus stop and waited for her new life to begin. It would start on the Number 55 to South Bristol, she was completely convinced of that. She boarded the bus when it arrived but couldn't stop the sadness that climbed on with her.

"Where are you taking me?" Tommy asked as he sat back against the smooth leather and the Bentley screeched away from the curb, reporters diving hurriedly out of the way. Slade didn't seem to give a fuck who got under his wheel today.

"A little trip, son." He sounded grave. Whitley sat next to him, quiet and pensive as ever. The Bentley bullied its way through the morning city traffic, eventually escaping onto the M32, then stretched its muscles and flew.

Slade said very little during the journey, and Tommy was glad of that. He seemed to be bristling with some secret knowledge but was not ready to impart it quite yet. Tommy let him keep it. As long as it wasn't about Jasmine, he didn't care. Slade had answered his initial questions in that respect, and there was nothing more to be said. Jasmine was still missing. Of course, she was. He hadn't expected a bumbler like Slade to find her. So they drove in silence. Slade played no music, and neither did he speak to Whitley.

They changed onto the M4, heading west for a few miles before switching to the M5.

When they turned off at the junction for Dursley and the Slimbridge Wildfowl Trust, Tommy began to feel uneasy. He sat still, watching the familiar landmarks slip by: Tortworth Court, Cromhall Quarry, Renishaws factory.

Finally, when he saw the cluster of trees on top of the hill that overlooked the small Cotswold town, he could keep silent no longer.

"Why are you bringing me home?"

"Not home, son." That was all he got. The Bentley prowled through the narrow streets of the old market town, eventually slowing outside the lychgate to St Mary's. Two police officers stood at the entrance, holding back a few provincial paparazzi. Slade nodded at the officers as they entered the churchyard. The sleek car nosed its way up the drive between the sleeping stones and parked in front of the church. Tommy knew now what to expect. He caught a glimpse of a large, yellow forensic tent half-obscured by the church, and then Slade was telling him to get out.

Slade and Whitley marched him around the back of the church, where more graves and tombs drowsed in the sun. The tent was about ten feet high and twice as wide. SOCOs were milling outside it like bees around a hive.

Slade pulled Tommy up just before they got to the entrance flap. "You know what's in here, don't you?" he asked, his face expressionless.

Tommy nodded. "What have they done to him?" he asked quietly.

"Brace yourself, son," was the Detective Inspector's only answer.

Then he lifted the flap and gestured for Tommy to precede him.

The first things he saw were the videos. A circle of them around the grave, like a ring of fairy mushrooms. Big, plastic, ugly. He glanced at the titles, at the lurid artwork—anywhere but at the grave itself.

Slade stood behind him. A gray-haired SOCO Tommy recognized

from both the *Arthur* and *Doctor Who* crime scenes was talking to a female associate. They stopped and turned to look at Tommy.

He took his time. He'd taken in all the video nasties propped around the mound of disturbed soil. He had nowhere else to look now. Slowly, he raised his head.

His first impression was that his father was sitting up in bed. He was perched on top of the soil, leaning back against his own headstone, and he was clutching a video nasty between his withered hands. The bones were peeking through the flesh like he was wearing fingerless tramp mittens. He was holding out the VHS box for them to see, and Tommy didn't need to read the title. The close-up of a rotting hand breaking through earth on the cover was familiar enough to him.

He raised his head some more.

His Dad would have been staring right back at him, if he'd had eyes. But, of course, after five years in a grave, there was no question of that. His hair was gone, apart from a thin clump of grass-like strands sprouting from the greasy skull. The flesh that remained on cheekbones and forehead was mottled purple and yellow. The teeth jutted from naked jawbones that had lost their gums and lips. It looked like Tommy's old Dad was snarling at him. Even in death, he disapproved.

"Take your time," he heard Slade say in a low voice behind him. Take his time for what? To pass on his best? Wish you were still here, and all that bullshit? Well, he didn't. His Dad was dead, and that was that. Had been dead for five years. Just because some sick fuck had dug him up and planted video nasties around his grave didn't make him any more amenable to conversation with his son.

There was a worm tucked in the breast pocket of his filthy burial suit. It waved cheekily at Tommy, then fell out and plopped into the soil below. Tommy had seen enough. He turned to face Slade, his expression set, giving nothing away. And to be honest, there wasn't anything *to* give away. He felt emptier than ever.

Slade was gauging his reaction, and if it threw him a little, he barely showed it. They would both have been great at poker. "*Zombie Flesh Eaters*," the Detective Inspector said after a moment, reading out the title of the VHS Tommy's Dad was holding. "Does this one in particular mean anything to you?"

Tommy shook his head. "It means they've got a sense of humor, however sick it is."

Slade nodded slowly, thinking. Then, "You don't look surprised by all this."

Tommy said nothing. He inclined his head toward the still-open tent flap. His meaning was clear. Slade stepped aside to let him out, then followed.

They stood in the sunshine, Tommy deep in thought, Slade watching his every expression.

Finally, Tommy said, "No, I wasn't expecting this. But I should have seen it coming. Or something like it."

"So, are you going to fill me in?" Slade had pulled a pack of cigarettes out of his jacket pocket. He offered one to Tommy—a token kindness, which Tommy refused.

"He was my Dad. He used to be an M.P. But you know all that already."

"There's more to it, isn't there?"

Tommy nodded again. He looked older, so much older than when Slade had first met him—what, three weeks ago? But then, that was hardly surprising.

"Shall we go?" Tommy said, gesturing at the Bentley. "This place brings back unpleasant memories." He wasn't sure if he meant the churchyard or the town itself, but at the end of the day, the two were now inseparable in his mind anyway.

The drive back to Bristol was another quiet one. Tommy knew they were holding back on the interrogation until they got there, so he put his head down and got some sleep.

Too soon they were pulling up outside a block of gray offices in a suburban district of Bristol, and Whitley was opening the door for him.

They took him down several corridors and into an interview room.

"Do I need a lawyer?" Tommy quipped mirthlessly.

Slade ignored him. A uniformed officer brought a tray of coffees, and Tommy sat back and waited for Slade to begin. But Slade seemed to be taking his time, too, as if he wanted Tommy to speak of his own accord. Finally, he lost his patience and tossed a handful of photocopied sheets over the desk to Tommy.

Tommy barely looked at them; he'd seen the headlines before. He put his hands up and told them what they wanted to know. And as he spoke, it felt like he was shedding years. Who knew a visit to Slade's office could be so therapeutic?

"He was my Dad. Not a particularly good one, but he was all I had. You've read all about it here..." He tapped the photocopies. "...so you've already joined the dots. Between me and the killings, I mean. But it doesn't explain the motive, does it? Is that what you're hoping I can help you with? Well, I can't." He leaned back and took a gulp of coffee. It was strong and harsh, just what he needed.

Slade picked up one of the photocopies and began to read aloud. "'Rape of our children's minds.'" Strong stuff, eh? Wait for this bit; you'll love it. 'So how many more women will be savaged and defiled by youths weaned on a diet of rape videos?" He glanced at Whitley sitting beside him, then across at Tommy. "Shall I go on? Here we go, then. 'It's time to turn back this tide of degenerate filth.' Or how about this one. 'An electric drill slowly grinding away a man's brain.' Sound familiar? 'Nazi Death Camp Sadism, complete with the screams of the Jewish girl victims, played for kicks. And rape, rape, rape... Britain fought the last World War against Hitler to defeat a creed so perverted that it spawned such horrors in awful truth. Are we insane? Are we bent on rotting our own society from within? Are we determined to spur to a gallop the forces of decadence that threaten to drag us down? Years ago, children went off with their Saturday sixpence to see Roy Rogers and Trigger. Now, for fifty pence, they gather in sniggering groups to watch *SS Experiment Camp.*"

Tommy began to clap his hands together slowly, ironically. "You could have written those words yourself, Detective Inspector. Very good. So very you."

Slade lowered the sheet. "You think this is funny? I thought you were worried about your girlfriend, but all you can do is sit and sneer."

Tommy put his cup down. "You're wasting my time. I could be out looking for her myself. Instead, you're reading me tabloid propaganda from the nineteen-eighties. Do you really think this is helping?"

"If it gets you to tell me everything, then yes, I would fucking say it is. For one thing, all this was just the start, wasn't it? The scene was set for the big hero to arrive. Let me remind you." He read from the photocopy again, "'No one has the right to be upset at a brutal sex crime or a sadistic attack on a child or mindless thuggery on a pensioner if he is not prepared to drive sadistic videos out of our high streets.' That was another M.P., not your old man. But it paved the way nicely for Mister Tim Wallace, Conservative representative for Gloucester South, to step boldly in and save the nation. Don't you think so? Far from being ashamed of your old man, I'd say you should be fucking proud of him."

"Yeah?" Tommy feigned indifference. "Of course, you would say that. You're a copper. You've got a *Daily Mail* mentality—no offense meant."

"None taken. Or maybe a little. So what exactly was so wrong—in your eyes—with facilitating a Bill of Parliament that swept all this shit out of our video shops, off our streets, out of our fucking homes?"

"It's easier than chasing actual criminals and solving real crimes, I suppose," Tommy said bitterly. "Just chuck a video shop owner in the nick for six months for having a banned film on his shelves and the nation's moral security is restored. Listen, the introduction of that Bill was just the start. It brought about one of the most draconian censorship measures in the world. Great Britain—the nanny state. What price democracy when all the evils of our society can be symbolized in video tape? Burn a few nasties and the coppers, the M.P.s, the muck-raking tabloids—they can all pat themselves on the back and say a job well done. Except it wasn't, was it? Since the introduction of the Video Recordings Act in nineteen-eighty-three— the Act my own father was instrumental in getting passed—crime is now officially higher for all offenses except murder than it is in the United States. And that gap's narrowing, too. You must know all this. You're an intelligent man." Tommy sat back again, his eyes challenging Slade.

Slade smiled coldly. "You've done your homework then. But you're wrong. If all this is to do with society's efforts to defeat the spread of video nasties, then we obviously didn't go fucking far enough. These copycat murders prove that. We've got softer, more lenient—look at the wild shit that's allowed in the shops today, on the internet, on our fucking T.V.s! Possessing a copy of *The Evil Dead* used to be a prosecutable offense; now my own kids—if I fucking had any—can watch it on the box right after fucking *Coronation Street*. No... If you ask me, your Dad was a fucking hero, but he didn't finish the job. Now it's my turn!"

Tommy shook his head in despair. "Films don't kill people. People kill people. I'm not arguing about this again. And my Dad was certainly no hero; he did it purely to further his own parliamentary career, not through any altruistic notions of saving society. He was an M.P., remember? I've spent my whole life trying to escape my father's lunatic legacy, and now some sick fucker is holding me directly responsible for it. I can't—"

But Slade stopped him there. "So you agree that's what this is about? That what your pop set in motion has come back to bite you in the ass? You're a scapegoat for some maniac who holds you to blame for your Dad's actions? But that's ridiculous, isn't it?" Slade obviously thought so, but it was still the only motive he could grope for in this whole mess. "It doesn't hold up, does it? I mean, like I said, you can watch far more disturbing shit on the T.V. these days than was in most of those videos. If anything, your Dad's efforts were futile. So why target you?"

Tommy stared at him thoughtfully. "I'm all out of ideas. You're the Detective, you find out. I take it you checked the Factory?"

"Deserted." Slade chucked the photocopied sheet of paper on the desk. The air con picked it up, tipped it onto the floor. Tommy watched it drift.

"So you're no nearer to catching these bastards?"

Slade sniffed defensively. "We didn't have a lot to fucking go on, did we?"

"No," Tommy answered sarcastically. "Only about twenty corpses and several video tapes left at the crime scenes. What more do you need, a signpost and a signature?"

Slade leaned over the desk and pushed his face in Tommy's. "Then maybe you'd better give me yours because you're the most fucking likely suspect from where I'm standing!" He kept the position, face enflamed with anger, until Tommy turned away. "You're the only bastard to survive that ward massacre. You've been at the scene of the crime every fucking time, and you've even got a motive for the murders. You're rebelling against your old man. Classic case of chip-on-the-shoulder syndrome."

Tommy laughed. "You're right. You've got it all sewn up. Thank fuck you're on the case."

Slade sat back, controlling his anger. He let a smile play on his lips. "Except I'm not as stupid as you think. I know you didn't do it—"

"Hallelujah. Give the man a banana."

"—but I might just chuck the book at you anyway. Just cos I fucking can."

"A real badass." Tommy rubbed his eyes. "But I'm tired of this bollocks. Are you gonna find Jasmine and bust these fuckers, or are you just gonna concentrate all your resources on giving me a bad day?"

"I was hoping you'd be able to provide some vital clue. But it does seem I've been wasting my time."

Tommy looked up, measuring the man's integrity. Despite all his headstrong, anachronistic bullshit, there was a man in there, admittedly pretty well hidden, that *maybe* you could rely on. Tommy decided to give him a break. "I don't think there's anything more I can add to what you already know and what I've already told you. Mark didn't tell me much about the film he was making, or the director, for that matter. Jasmine didn't give me much either—I already told you in the hospital that she was involved in the film, too. I'm beginning to think she was the lure all along."

Slade looked interested. "Lure?"

"If they really did want to get at me, they knew the best way of doing it."

"Because you've got a weakness for a pretty face?"

"Because I liked her," Tommy said, refusing to rise to the bait any longer. "They used her to get to me."

Slade considered that. "So they might use her again."

"Meaning?"

"I don't know..." He shifted tack smoothly: "So now we know you're more informed about video nasties than you were letting on before, can you provide us with any clues as to what they might be planning next, or even where they might be hiding out?"

"Shit, do you seriously not think I would have told you that already if I did know? I've as much idea as you. And yes, I *do* know about the nasties. I collected several of them just to piss my Dad off..." His voice tailed away. "But that doesn't matter now. If I had *any* clue as to where they were holing up, I'd tell you. You can rely on that." He thought for a minute. There was something playing at the back of his memory, skipping just out of reach... He shrugged. "I guess you've checked out all productions currently filming..."

"All productions in the South West and South Wales have been put on hold indefinitely," Slade answered firmly. "It wasn't a popular decision, believe me, but the Chief Super could no longer argue in the face of all the media scrutiny and public outrage. Rona Capley was a very popular actress..." He looked rueful for a moment. Tommy said nothing, trying to blot out the memory of what the Anthropo-phagous Beast had done to that very popular actress.

"We're checking out every low-budget film company known to exist, and searching for those that aren't," the Detective Inspector said at last. "No fucking camera is going to be left unturned. We're checking eBay and Amazon for video nasty purchasers; we've got officers looking into every fucking car boot sale in the South West. We're looking. And we will find them."

Tommy nodded, though he was far from convinced. He was think-ing of the way Cropsy had transformed from a hideously disfigured monster into a regular Eastern European guy when he died, but he thought Slade's overworked brain really couldn't cope with bringing up that anomaly again right now.

"There's just one thing bugging me," Slade added, finishing his now-cold coffee. "Why the change in M.O.? I mean, beforehand, the killers were content to murder one at a time and leave single videos behind that fit the crime or the location. Why suddenly go berserk and slaughter a whole load of folk and leave a glut of videos behind."

"It depends which videos they left behind," Tommy responded. "You never told me that bit."

"A whole helter-skelter of video nasties..."

He glanced across at Whitley, who had kept quiet throughout the entire interview. The DS reached inside his jacket and withdrew a notebook. He flipped some pages (*Just like a* real *cop,* Tommy thought) and read out a few titles. "*Anthropophagous the Beast, The Burning, Night of the Demon, The Living Dead at the Manchester Morgue, SS Experiment Camp...*" Slade shut him up with a gesture.

"Any of those ring any meaningful bells with you? I can recognize the connections to the M.O.—we've checked the contents of the films and can see the bastards took inspiration from the Nazi film to crucify D.C. Nandu, and the deaths of the officers on guard and the Swindon force were right out of the Lake District Zombie film. Then there's the gardening shears from *The Burning* and the various killings from the Bigfoot flick... I guess I don't need to go into the details as you've lived through them. But is there anything else you can add?"

Tommy could but didn't see how telling Slade the killers from those particular films were actually the perps the Detective should be looking for would actually help either of them right now. He'd seen the way Slade reacted to these notions in the hospital. He suspected

Slade considered his theory that the killers weren't simply wearing disguises but had somehow actually *become* the monsters was a crock of shit, a paranoid delusion brought on by trauma. So he kept quiet. But he did say, "You've certainly done your homework, Detective Inspector," in a tone he hoped was not dismissive. He was tired of being antagonistic. He was tired of thinking about murder and carnage. He was tired.

Soon after, they let him go home.

The house was empty when he entered it, the police car having dropped him off. No sign of Trish. And apart from one or two paps looking bored across the street who raised their cameras in a decidedly desultory fashion when they saw him, there was no sign of the throng of reporters she'd said had been picketing the place since he'd been in hospital either. They'd obviously gotten bored.

There was, however, a small parcel addressed to him on the doormat. He was about to pick it up and open it when his cell rang.

It was Wayne, and suddenly Tommy remembered what had been eluding him for the last hour or so. Wayne was at a horror film festival. He'd told him in the Crown the other week that there would be stalls selling video nasties on the premises. What he hadn't told Tommy (because he hadn't known) was that the Festival was premiering a new film—albeit an unfinished work print—by an unknown but burgeoning new talent. Wayne was ringing to ask how the hell Tommy was coping after his terrifying ordeal, of course. But he was also ringing to tell him the film was starring the late Mark Hamm, and that it was just about to begin...

Tommy screamed down the phone. He told Wayne to get the hell out of there. He didn't wait to see how Wayne responded to that. He was too busy ringing the number on the card Slade had given him.

He forgot all about the video-shaped package still lying on the doormat.

CHAPTER EIGHTEEN

Slade was in the incident room when the call came through. He was standing by the whiteboard. Sitting would have implied inertia, and he wanted to be seen *doing* something, even though there was very little he could do at the moment. He deliberately avoided looking at DC Nandu's empty desk. That would have distracted him with rage, and he needed to think very clearly right now.

He was staring at Whitley as the DS pored over his video nasty research, checking synopses of all the films on the DPP 39 list in some vain hope that a clue might be there, some hint as to where the murdering bastards had holed up.

Whitley continued to scribble notes next to each title.

"I want details of every location used in these films, Trev. Whether it's a wood cabin, park, tenement block, or public fucking toilet, I wanna know about it. No matter how irrelevant or insignificant you might think it is, note it down. The fuckers seem to be treating these films as their manual. We can do the same."

Whitley carried on annotating as he spoke. "There's quite a few concentration camps on the list, guv. I'm guessing they're not hiding low in Auschwitz or Buchenwald."

"And cut out the fucking sarcasm. This is deadly serious. A girl's life is at stake, and probably many more if these lunatics aren't brought in soon. Not to mention my career..." He paused, then poked a finger at Whitley. "And yours, Trev, old son. So crack the fuck on and get me something I can stick my teeth into. Or we'll both be back in uniform... Only the hats we'll be wearing will have big yellow Ms stitched on the front, and we ain't never gonna get rid of the smell of burgers."

With that dire warning ringing in his ears, Whitley dutifully cracked the fuck on.

Some locations were improbable, if not impossible. He crossed out all the Nazi films (three); ones set in far-flung locations (*Mardi Gras Massacre*); the cannibal capers set in exotic jungles (two); goat-shagging films set in Greece (one); extraordinary adventures in the Himalayas involving Yetis and Werewolves (one!); and zombie extravaganzas set on Caribbean islands (one). Whitley had seen the last one himself when he was a teenager. He remembered the stupefying scrap between shark and zombie but didn't think the film could add anything to the case beyond being an ironic prop held by Wallace's unearthed old man.

He cross-checked the films against locations most likely to be available in the UK, particularly the South West, and compiled a generic list—deserted schools, slaughterhouses, laboratories, abandoned houses of all description—and popped them all into a search engine. Slade seemed satisfied for the moment and left him to it.

That was when Tommy's call sent the shit all over the place.

"Slow down!" Slade barked into his cell. "I can't understand what you're saying. What the fuck do you mean a horror festival? How did you manage to not mention this to me before? What part of 'tell me everything you know' did you not understand? You *forgot?* Well, that's okay then. Let's hope the killers *forget* to make your girlfriend the newest star of their video nasty re-enactments or whatever the fuck they're doing. Just...stop freaking out. Ring your friend back and tell him to get out of there, taking as many people as he can *without* causing a mass panic. I'll get the local boys round there pronto." He clicked his fingers over at Whitley, who rose from his desk. "And don't you get any fucking ideas about going up there yourself. We'll take it from here." He cut the connection and rounded on the DS.

"Trev. Get the fuck up to Burnley. That wanker Wallace forgot to inform us about a horror film festival taking place there right now. And guess what? It's only showcasing a certain low-budget film starring the late Mark Hamm. Now Mister Wallace is of the opinion that this might be a significant cause for concern, as it seems to be the premiere of this sick piece of shit. I happen to agree with him. I don't know what to expect. But I can always count on one thing, and that's finding an overflowing septic tank at the end of every rainbow. Bound to be trouble of some kind if this sick film's involved. So take some D.C.s with you. I'll get the local force over there right away." He noticed a look of confusion on Whitley's normally stoic face. "Yes? What's wrong?"

"Burnley, guv?"

"Yes, Burnley. I don't fucking know where it is either. Lancashire somewhere. Coal pits, flat caps, and whippets. Look it up on a fucking map on your way. Or better still, join the fucking twenty-first century and use your sat nav. Just get the fuck up there."

Whitley glanced at the clock on the office wall. Slade caught that, too. "Yeah, five o'clock, Trev. Which means you won't get up there 'til at least eight. So you're gonna miss *Eastenders*, I'm afraid. Get going!"

"You not coming, guv?"

Slade had already discounted that idea. "This could be another diversion, like the one that took our eyes off the ball at Malmesbury. Not gonna let that happen again. I'm staying down here right next to our friend Wallace. Because I have a strong hunch he's gonna be at the center of any action." He reached for his office phone, intending to alert the Burnley police force, Manchester, too. He looked up to see Whitley carefully tucking his Parker pen inside his jacket pocket. "You still here, Trev? You and me are gonna have a serious falling out if you take any longer getting your fat ass out of this office."

He snatched up the phone and began hitting buttons as Whitley strode out of the office with as much dignity as he could muster.

Tommy spent a minute seriously toying with the idea of ignoring Slade altogether, getting in his car, and driving up to Burnley right there and then. He had visions of the director and his monstrous video nasty henchmen introducing the premiere of his film on stage before sending his bully boys out to rough up the audience. Jasmine might even be there, to be offered up as a sacrifice or whatever sick act the man might have in mind for her. But two things stopped him. The first was that he knew if anything was going to happen, it would be all over anyway by the time he got up North to Burnley. The other reason: he had a sneaky (not to mention disturbing) conviction that the killers had something else in store for Tommy, and that he wouldn't need to travel 300-odd miles to find it. However, he did remember Slade's instructions regarding Wayne and promptly thumbed the recall button. He got a dial tone, then two, three rings. Surely, the silly fuck hadn't ignored him and switched off his phone to settle down and enjoy the movie.

The fourth ring did the business.

"All right?" The northerner sounded confused but very much alive.

"Did you do what I told you to and get the fuck out?"

"Well, no. Of course not." Wayne sounded indignant. "Just because you've been at the center of all the action doesn't mean you have to start getting paranoid. I paid fifty quid for this festival. Just calm down and have a cup of tea. You've been through a lot. There's nothing to fret about. It's just a film."

Tommy squeezed the cell 'til the plastic creaked. "Wayne, listen to me *very* carefully. You need to get up out of your seat right now and tell the festival organizer or the projectionist, or whoever the fuck will listen to you, to switch the film off. Then you need to get everyone to leave the cinema. You need to do this *right* now, Wayne. These are direct instructions from Slade. Trust me; he is not taking this lightly either."

There was a lengthy pause on the other end. Tommy could hear someone shushing Wayne. He could also hear the soundtrack of the film: footsteps, some ragged breathing—and while he couldn't tell whether the frantic breathing was from a male or female, it undeniably encapsulated the sound of fear—the odd crash and thud, but no music. A workprint, of course. Unfinished, Wayne had said. Then his friend came back on, his voice lowered into a whisper, "You're getting me in trouble here, Tommy. I'm actually getting shushed! First time ever..." He giggled a trifle nervously.

"Are you seriously not fucking listening to me!" Tommy closed his eyes and pressed his head against the cool wall of his living room. Then he spoke more calmly, his words measured, clear. "Wayne, how long have you known me?" He didn't wait for an answer. "Ten years? Eleven? In that time, have I ever bullshitted you? Have I ever fucked you around?"

"Once or twice, yeah!" came the emphatic reply. "What about

that time I was tripping out of my head on ecstasy at your place and you still made me drive all the fucking way back to Burnley!" His voice was angrier and louder now. "Just because you were worried Trish would find out what we'd been up to. Some friend you were. I could have been killed."

"Exactly. You could have been killed. But you weren't. Not that time, Wayne. Now I'm making amends for that day. I'm making it up to you, if you'll just let me. If you ever want to see Burnley Town play again, you had better just fucking listen..." His voice was going weird because the tears were coming. He had to remain in control. But Wayne wasn't listening.

"You're making me miss the film, you know. I think you're just jealous because you're not the center of attention right now. I know you've been through a terrible time, mate, but this ain't all about you. Now shut the fuck up and let me watch it..." There was a pause. Then, "It's not very good. I know it's advertised as an unfinished film 'by a maverick new wunderkind of underground cinema'..." His voice took on a sarcastic tone. "...but this is a bit rough. Oh, there's your mate, Hamm. And fuck it, he's certainly living up to his name. Hang on... Ouch. That was actually pretty nasty. I can see what the director's aiming for, but it's quite primitive. Bit of a Snuff copycat, if you ask me, although it does have a certain...atmosphere. You still there?"

"Wayne, I don't want your commentary. I want you to do as I say and get out. Please. If you're my friend, you'll do it. You're right; this isn't about me (*oh, but it so was*); it's about you saving your own silly, Northern neck. I don't want you to die. I really fucking don't." He'd quashed the incipient tears but not the awful premonition of catastrophe he felt (*knew*) was imminent.

Wayne still wasn't listening. He seemed to be getting a thrill out of letting Tommy know what he was missing. It was as if his friend felt left out by Tommy making all the papers and now wanted to relish his very own role, however small, in the unfolding drama. "Like I said, you're worrying about nothing. There's no director or evil maniacs present, just the film. And the more I watch it..." His whisper trailed off.

"Wayne! *Wayne!* Are you still there?"

Distantly, as if his friend were slowly nodding off to sleep, or was in a daydream. "Yeah... Still here... Chill out, Tommy boy... I'm really starting to..."

"What? Starting to what? Wayne, get off the phone and tell everyone to get out. Please. While you still have the chance!"

"I feel a bit...weird." Wayne was sounding even more distant now. His whisper became practically inaudible, then suddenly was back in range for his next words: "This film is seriously fucked up... I've never seen anything...like it...fuck. Fuck. It's almost as if..."

Tommy felt the frustration exploding inside him. The one thing keeping him from slamming his cell against the wall was the fact Slade would almost certainly have contacted the local constabulary by now and they would be on their way. Wayne would be okay. Tommy could trust Slade. Couldn't he?

"As if there's something nasty in the..." Wayne's whisper was coming and going now. Like he was tripping. "...in the celluloid itself. That's seriously fucked, man. This film has power. There's evil embedded in the print. I can feel it. I can *see* it... Do you get what I'm..." Drifting again. *Losing him,* thought Tommy. Something was happening up there. The audience was being subjected to some kind of suggestive influence, and there was nothing he could do to stop—

"Seriously evil," said Wayne, in a tone of almost grudging respect. "Can't talk now, Tommy. I'm watching..."

"*Noo! Don't watch!* Jump out of your seat, Wayne, my old friend, and get out of there. If you ever thought anything of me, do this now. For me. For your old buddy. *Please.*"

"Someone's entered the cinema late," Wayne was saying in that same tripped-out tone. "That's weird... That's very fucking weird."

"What's happening? *Wayne!*" When the fuck would the local coppers arrive? Surely, they must be nearly there by now. A horrible thought: *if* Slade had contacted them, that was. Or would he be a complete dick and try to do the job all by himself? But it would take him hours to drive to Burnley...

"Some fucker's just come into the screening room..." Wayne giggled again—just like the time they were tripping on magic mushrooms, Tommy thought. "He's dressed in a black boiler suit and a ski mask. Reminds me of something. Oh, and he's got a wheelbarrow with him. He's pushing it...up the central aisle...toward the stage. Big bastard. And the barrow...it's full of..." Here, his voice dropped out again. Tommy pressed his ear against the sweaty plastic in a frantic effort to hear.

"*Full of what, Wayne? Full of WHAT?*"

"Tools. The barrow's full of work tools..."

CHAPTER NINETEEN

Tommy couldn't have hung up on Wayne now, even if he wanted to. He had to hear this through to the end. That it would be a bitter and very bloody end, he had no doubt whatsoever. That Wayne no longer possessed the ability to think for himself and respond to Tommy's pleas, he was equally as sure of. But that wasn't going to stop him trying.

"Wayne. Something very bad is going to happen. I can't tell you how important it is that you *get the fuck out of that cinema!*"

No response. The frantic breathing on the cinema soundtrack suddenly erupted into screams. Ragged, agonized. Female. A vile thought that made Tommy almost drop the cell—*Jasmine's?*

"Wayne! What's happening? Is that Jasmine?"

Wayne was back. Drugged sounding, but quietly coherent. "Did you fuck her?"

"What! What are you talking about? Has anything happened?"

"You did, didn't you?" Tommy could just about hear him over the screams—and they *were* Jasmine's; he was sure of that. "Was she good? I bet she was a screamer." He was chuckling now, a low, nasty guffaw that didn't sound like Tommy's good-natured friend at all. "Nice little tits as well. You didn't tell me she was shaved down there, you naughty boy..." Again, the spiteful, cruel chuckle. "Good actress as well as a good body. She looks great up on the big screen— especially with no clothes on. A good screamer, all right. If I didn't know any better, I'd say she wasn't acting. Maybe that fucker with the flamethrower is really going to burn her. He's dressed in an asbestos suit, just like the maniac in *Don't Go in the House*. You remember that one, Tommy? We watched it together at your place. Yeah, they've copied the scene from that film. Your tart's hung up naked from the ceiling, and the Incinerator Man's gonna cook her up." A titter, edged with madness that caused a cold, cold hand to slide down Tommy's back. "Maybe this *is* a real Snuff film." A pause, then: "I'd fuck her, too, before I burned her. Did you come in her mouth, Tommy, you cunt? Did you fuck her *mouth?*" Wayne's voice rose in sudden sadistic fury. This time, nobody shushed him. Tommy could hear general sounds of restlessness among the crowd, as well as several low shouts. No panic yet. The screams from the sound-track stopped.

Tommy had never felt so helpless in his life. Had they killed her, too, filmed her death, and then inserted it into this atrocity of a film? He had to know.

"Is she all right—on screen, I mean—is she still alive? I think it's all real, too, Wayne. I think you're right. You're actually watching real Snuff clips, and I need to know...*please* tell me, Wayne... Is she all right...?" He could feel his own sanity crumbling, and Wayne certainly wasn't helping assuage his fears. He seemed more interested in what was happening around him now than the action on screen.

"The fucker in the boiler suit's handing out tools from his barrow. And it's just clicked who he reminds me of. He's dressed like Cameron Mitchell in *The Toolbox Murders*. Go on, give 'em out, Cam. Ha, there's kind, eh? What a helpful fellow. And he knows just what they're gonna use 'em for, doesn't he, the sly fucker? Drill with power pack, check; nail gun, check. Claw hammer, pickaxe, scythe, shears, rake, shovel, check. I could bore you with what films inspired those items, Tommy, but you already know." Again, that nasty grit of sadism in his voice. "He's got it all, this bastard. A regular Handy fuckin' Andy. The D.I.Y. Guy of Death. Toolbox Murders? Fuck that. The Wheelbarrow Butcher, more like." He was laughing again, delirium lacing the manic chuckles. "Yeah, he knows what he's up to. Wonder what I'll get? Nah, he'll probably run out before he reaches me. Just my luck, eh? Story of my sodding life. Someone else always gets there first, whether it's with the girls, the jobs, or the fucking toolbox weapons. Life, eh? It's a fucking blast." His manic ranting stopped suddenly. Tommy could hear other screams now, and they weren't coming from the screen.

"Ooh, that's good," Wayne suddenly hissed, loud in Tommy's ear—*where the fuck were the police?* "Oh, fuck, *yeah*! That was brutal, man! Got to fill you in, good buddy, can't have you missing out on the action. Some fat fuck just ran up the aisle with a pickaxe. Buried it in another guy's face. Took his fucking eye out! Literally. He's fucking levering it out as I speak! Ha ha. They're all at it now. Some bald cunt's getting his head battered in with the claw hammer. Gotta love a man's dedication to his workmanship. Another blow should do it. Fuck—did you *hear* that? Skull's cracked. Yep, I can see a sludge of brain peeping out through a mess of bone. This is *sooo* much better than sex, man. Are you getting all this? You should be here. You really should. All those years of watching crappy video nasties, and now I'm living through the real thing." He was cheering raucously now, like a fan at a Millwall Vs West Ham match. The Wayne Tommy used to know had gone. The audience's screams were strident, deafening, drowning out the film, drowning out everything but Wayne's vile commentary.

He almost disconnected then, but something stopped him. He knew he was probably going to hear his friend's death very soon, and this was the last time he would speak to him. He desperately wanted to hear something that would signal the arrival of the police, but still nothing but screams and the dull, sickening sounds of violence. He should call Slade, tell him his worst fears were realized. His thumb hovered over the red disconnect button on his cell. But there was something else he needed to know first.

"Is the director there?" *That was important, right? If the main man was there, then the police would catch him.* "Is anyone filming it all…?"

Wayne's blood lust had abated slightly. When he spoke again, he sounded distant and disconnected again. "No. No cameras. Toolbox Man's just enjoying the show. He's on his own, far as I can see. He's finished handing out his death tools, and he's just standing on the stage in front of the screen like the master of all he fucking surveys." Then his tone sharpened again. "Gotta love that dude. Cool as death."

You're going to die, Wayne, and there's nothing I can do about it.

More screams, louder now, as the tide of murder and mutilation swept closer to where Wayne was still sitting like a Roman at an amphitheater, watching the deaths of others all around him while waiting patiently for his own.

Then Wayne said, "There's a lot of blood. I don't like this anymore. I'm..." Silence for a beat. "...scared. I'm scared, Tommy." And then, heartbreakingly, Wayne began to cry. Tears were already rolling down Tommy's own cheeks. *Why didn't you leave when I asked you to? Why?* He knew the answer to that, though, didn't he? Wayne had said the film had power. The film hadn't *let* him leave.

Wayne sobbed for a few more minutes, and then he stopped.

Tommy disconnected the phone.

CHAPTER TWENTY

Of course, by the time Whitley arrived, it was all over.

But then he already knew that, and so did Slade. The DI had filled him in on the slaughter over the car radio as Whitley was still plowing up the M5. Thirty dead, fifteen mortally wounded. The local boys were all over it, as were the press. Slade was not happy, yet Whitley sensed he was relieved it hadn't happened on his patch for once. Slade told him Tommy Wallace had heard the massacre during a cell phone conversation with his friend who was attending the festival. When Whitley heard how the festival crowd had turned homicidal, he nearly ran off the motorway.

"What the fuck's going on, guv? This is all so—"

"Fucked up? Tell me about it. This is way off the scale. According to the Manchester boys, the mad bastards were tearing into each other with any weapon they could get hold of. It's like that Jonestown incident where the crazy pricks offed themselves cos of some guru. We need to find this fucking guru, Trev. Do your best."

"Do you want me to turn round, guv?"

"Why the fuck would I want you to do that? Muscle in on the local boys and get every scrap you can. It's still our case, remember?"

Then why aren't you up here leading it, you lazy fuck? "Gotcha, guv. Halfway there now."

"Put your fucking foot through the floor. I want something we can use before the Burnley and Manchester Plod step all over it with their clumsy size tens. I would ask you to seize the film print, but the projectionist burned it before setting fire to himself in his booth." His sigh crackled with radio static. "Grill the survivors. Liaise with S.O.C.O. You know the score. You don't need my fucking hand to hold all the time, Trev. And find out all you can about some bastard in a ski mask."

"Guv?"

"One of the director's hired killers, by the sound of it. Wallace said he pushed a wheelbarrow full of work tools into the cinema and handed 'em out like some hellish usherette doling out lethal fucking ice creams. I've spoken to the flat cap in charge in Manchester, and the daft cunt didn't have any answers. Make sure *you* do by the time you're through. Back me up properly for once. Understand?"

"Yes, guv." *Fuck you, guv.*

But by the time Whitley got there, of course, the Burnley and Manchester forces were all over it with their size tens, and not only did they actually have some answers, but they really didn't look overly impressed by the arrival of a DS from Bristol.

The Greater Manchester DI was a thickset, no-nonsense bruiser called Maclean. He had a haircut and eyes that said, "Don't cross me, you soft, Southern wanker," and he had a habit of picking at his teeth with his tongue. But he had something very interesting to tell Whitley when he met him in the foyer of the old Cinema where the festival had been held.

"Never seen anything like it," he muttered. "What would make them fucking flip out like that?" It was a rhetorical question. The DI was still obviously shaken by such a big multi-homicide on his patch, and Whitley could tell he wasn't particularly interested in any contribution from a lowly DS. Whitley peered past him into the auditorium. Stretchers were still being brought out, though most of the bodies had already been taken to the morgue. There was a smell of blood and popcorn. Not a good mix at all. "We didn't make it in time, even though we followed up on your tip-off as soon as possible."

I'll bet, thought Whitley. *You didn't get off your fat ass in time because you thought we were making a fuss over nothing, didn't you? You thought—and I can read it in your bulldog face and squinty little peepers—you thought,* Bollocks to those Southern cunts, what the fuck do they know? *So you finished your tea, popped another éclair in your fat gob, let a fart rip, and eventually strolled down here with a couple of sleepy P.C.s. That's how it went down, isn't it, Detective Inspector Maclean?*

"It was all over surprisingly fast. Done and dusted before we got here. Just bodies, and people screaming in agony and terror. But at least the killing had stopped. Fucked up doesn't cover it. Nothing we could do." Maclean looked away, surveying the blur of activity that was the SOCO team. "And before you ask, your D.I. has already spoken to me about the film that was shown. It's just ashes, along with the projectionist. Lucky the whole building didn't go up when he poured whiskey over himself and lit the old Zippo. *Whoosh.* Crazy bastard. But as for how the film got here—I've been through it all with the festival organizer. All communication between him and the production company—Sinema Extreme or some shit—which provided the print was done by email. It arrived by courier yesterday. Sender's address is a smoke screen, like the website and email address. Nothing to go on there."

"You spoken to the survivors yet, sir?"

Maclean swung his tiny eyes back onto the DS. "What, you think we're all grooming our whippets up here and cooking black pudding?" The Northerner's shock and confusion were transforming into anger now (something he was more comfortable with), and who better to vent it on than some lowly DS from Laaandon Taahn or wherever the fuck this asshole pounded the beat? "Course we fucking have! And I'm surprised your D.I. hasn't come up here himself instead of sending his sergeant."

Whitley smiled mirthlessly. "We're spread thinly, sir. In case you've forgotten, we've just had a major incident down our way, too."

"You being cocky, Detective Sergeant? Because if you are, you can fuck off back down to London and sip your pina fuckin' coladas and pay five fuckin' quid for your poncy lattes, ya Southern muppet. We've got this covered. You're just in my way, right now. Are we clear?"

"Bristol, sir." He could imagine how Slade would have handled this no-necked bastard. They would have been brawling on the floor by now.

"What?"

"I'm from Avon and Somerset, based in Bristol, not London. Doesn't matter. Sir, I know this is inconvenient for you, but my D.I.— who's heading up this case as you know—has given me clear instructions that I need to talk to all the survivors. I really hope you're not going to make that difficult for me."

"Difficult for you, you uptight little carrot-cruncher? Fuck, no. Why should I bother? I've got enough on my plate without flushing your pointy head down the toilet." He swung his back on Whitley, then changed his mind and came back for more. "I'm sure your D.I. will be interested to hear one thing we found out, though. And I'm sure you'll hear exactly the same thing when you interview the survivors."

"What's that, sir?"

"Apparently, there was some bastard dressed in a boiler suit who started the whole massacre off. One of your copycat killers, I'm guessing?"

"Sounds like it, sir. Did he get away?"

Maclean smirked and stopped worrying his teeth with his tongue for a moment. "No, he didn't fucking get away, sergeant. This isn't fucking *Bristol*."

Whitley brightened. Maybe they could finally get somewhere if they had a live suspect. "So where is he now, sir? In custody?"

Maclean tilted his stubby head toward the auditorium. "He's in there. But you won't get much out of him."

"Why's that, sir?"

Maclean smirked again. "The bastard's plan worked *too* well. Not only did the audience kill each other, they took out the bastard in the ski mask, too. Ironic that, don't you think?"

Whitley nodded slowly. He really wasn't going to find out much up here after all. "Sir, you mentioned a plan. 'The bastard's plan.' Is that based on any evidence?"

Maclean worried his teeth again for a few seconds before replying. "You'd better go and speak to the survivors, sergeant. You need to get up to speed a bit. 'Speed' being a word you might need to look up in a dictionary, seeing as your boys probably all drive tractors on their beat down there in Wurzel Country."

He turned and followed a SOCO back inside the auditorium. Whitley hesitated a moment and then went after him.

Just around the same time Tommy was about to get up from his armchair and find the parcel on his doormat, Slade was hearing a pretty unsatisfactory report over the phone from Whitley in Burnley.

Slade listened carefully as Whitley backed up Wallace's statement that the festival crowd had actually turned on each other due to some unknown influence affecting their minds. Slade was more inclined to believe the vending machine must have been spiked with a nasty strain of LSD mixed with MDMA[12]—either that or mass hypnosis—rather than the wild theories put forward by Wallace about the film itself being to blame. Slade was also very interested in details of the masked man in the boiler suit, whose identity had as yet to be discovered. Slade would have put money on him being another Eastern European, though. He was almost as impressed with the irony surrounding the suspect's death as his opposite number up north. But it left him no further forward in the case, and time was running out. The media were reaching a frenzied point. The Super had given him 24 hours to get a solid lead in this case or he would be replaced. Slade finished speaking to his sergeant and paced the incident room, glaring at the DCs hunched over their desks. They were all working around the clock, and as yet, not one of them had dared complain.

When the call came from Jim Tavell, Slade was ready to hear something solid. He listened carefully to what the SOCO had to say, his face giving nothing away to the detectives who glanced up at him. He said, "You sure? Okay. That's put the shit among the daisies. You find out anything more, let me know," and hung up. He rang Wallace and got his voicemail. He tried again with the same result. He swore, rammed the cell into his jacket pocket, and left the incident room.

He was driving toward Wallace's house with not enough sleep and a foul taste in his mouth. It was 8:30 in the evening. At home, Tommy was almost finished unwrapping his parcel.

He'd been so distraught about what was happening with Wayne at the festival that he'd forgotten all about the item on the doormat.

It was only after he'd tried ringing his friend repeatedly and each time succeeded only in reaching his voicemail, that he'd given up and dialed Slade's number. If he'd suspected the Detective Inspector would have trouble believing his story, he was proved firmly in the

---

[12] Ecstasy

wrong. Tommy's naked anguish had been responsible for that. He was a supporting artist, for God's sake, not a proper actor—Slade knew he wasn't exaggerating. The DI had moved into action straight away, and after telling Tommy to stay put and keep him informed of any more developments, he hung up and got on with sorting out the mess that was the Burnley FearFest.

Tommy sat where he was for nearly an hour, dazed, empty, drained. Finally, he roused himself, determined to fight off the despair. He needed to be alert; he needed to be ready. For what, he couldn't have said, although he could have put a fair bet on at Lovetogamble.com that it was not going to be pleasant.

It was dark outside the window. He didn't bother closing the curtains. Leaving the lounge to grab a coffee, he noticed the package on the doormat.

It was rectangular—VHS shaped—and that sent a dart of fear into his heart. He hadn't ordered anything, certainly not a tape. He knew who had sent it before his shaking hands finished tearing off the plain brown wrapping. There was no sender address, no note inside, just a plain VHS Maxell tape with one word scribbled on the plain white label: JASMINE. On the carpet near his armchair where it had fallen, his phone went unheeded as Slade called for the second time.

He carried the tape to the DVD/VHS player tucked under the TV and inserted it without further delay.

It wasn't very long. It didn't need to be. It looked like the same scene Wayne had described at the festival: a man dressed in inflammable gear with a propane tank slung over one shoulder and sporting a menacing fireproof visor of the type used for furnace and incineration work. Or used by sick maniacs in video nasties for torching women in their underground metal dungeons.

He had known it would be horrible, but the reality was so much worse. He resisted the urge to switch it off because he had to know. He had to know what Wayne had failed to tell him—did the maniac in the asbestos suit really burn Jasmine, or was it just a movie scare? He stayed with it, all five minutes of it. He watched her squirming and wriggling, dangling naked by her wrists from shackles fastened to a hook in the low ceiling. Unlike its pristine metal counterpart in *Don't Go in the House*, this room was hewn from rough stone, dark and dingy. Jasmine was pleading with the maniac, begging him to let her free as a crease in the tape scrolled down Tommy's TV screen.

Tears streaked her cheekbones with mascara; her eyes were wide and terrified, her body slick with sweat. Tommy cried, too. He clawed at his face, raked his fingers through his hair like a mad person. He waited for the ordeal to end, for the killer to move forward with the wicked-looking flamethrower he carried in his huge, gray fire gloves.

The killer turned toward the camera—toward Tommy!—and held up the flamethrower, then casually ignited it. A tongue of flame licked out, steadied into a bright orange gout as the bulky figure turned clumsily around to face the girl suspended before him.

Holding the flamethrower in his right hand, the killer extended his left glove, stroking Jasmine's smooth thighs. The hand moved higher, teasing the viewer (this little clip had an intended audience of one), fabric fingers investigating her private parts, tousling the short strip of pubic hair, caressing the lips below. Jasmine tried to twist away, but the hand gripped her hard between her legs, the big thumb holding her steady while the fingers explored brutally. Jasmine screamed in pain, in outrage. Tommy was panting now, the sobs breaking out of him. He stood up, fists clenched, wanting to, *needing* to turn away, but unable to do so. He *had* to watch this, his very own private video nasty.

The hand holding the flamethrower moved closer to her sleek, naked body. Jasmine's eyes were fixed on it and the little tease of flame that puffed out from the nozzle. She screamed one last time, her vocal chords tearing. Then the screen went blank.

The tape was still running. Tommy saw another tear run down the screen. Video snow-blossomed, then cleared. A message popped into focus, huge, blood-red capitals:

JASMINE IS ENJOYING HER ACTING DEBUT. SHE WILL ENJOY IT FAR MORE IF YOU COME AND SHARE IT WITH HER. BUT SHE WON'T ENJOY IT AT ALL IF YOU INFORM THE POLICE WHERE YOU ARE GOING. SHE WON'T ENJOY ONE RED HOT, BURNING MOMENT OF IT. DO YOU WANT TO SEE HER ALIVE AGAIN? OR DO YOU WANT TO SEE A CRISPED, OVERDONE ROAST HANGING FROM THIS HOOK WHEN YOU ARRIVE? YOUR CHOICE... MAKE THE RIGHT ONE. SHE'S WAITING. JOIN US. JOIN US AT THE VILLAGE WHERE NOBODY LIVES. YOU REMEMBER IT FROM YOUR CHILDHOOD, I'M SURE. NOW IT'S THE HOME OF THE NASTY. COME ALONE OR JASMINE BURNS.

Tommy replayed the message once more. Hope mixed with utter dread. Was she still alive then, or was this just one more twist of the knife? *Make the right choice*, the message had read. But there was no choice at all, was there? He had to go, and he had to go alone. He switched off the TV and made for the front door, grabbing his phone from the floor and car keys from the hook in the hallway as he went. He saw the missed messages from Slade and dismissed them. He switched his phone to silent and left the house.

Outside, it was very dark now. The dashboard clock read 9:01 when he fired up the ignition on the Polo. His headlights picked out the empty residential street. He didn't need to consult a map or plug in a satnav. He knew exactly where he was going.

DC Pete Brack was dozing at the wheel. That was all right, though, because it wasn't moving. The engine wasn't even switched on. There wouldn't have been much point, as he was on surveillance duty. He was supposed to be awake, alert, Slade's eager watchdog. But five hours of sitting in this suburban street had taken its toll. Tommy Wallace was in his house and he wasn't going anywhere, and Brack just couldn't keep his eyes open any longer.

It wasn't until Slade's strident voice came over the car radio that he remembered sleeping on the job wasn't what he was paid for. He jerked wide awake, cursed his boss, and reached forward to pick up the transmitter.

"You awake, Brack?"

"Course I am, sir."

"Anything from Wallace's house?"

"Nothing, sir."

"I'm on my way over right now. If he goes anywhere, don't stop him. Just make sure you follow him and report to me immediately."

"Yes, sir."

"And Brack..."

"Sir?"

"If you fall asleep again, I'll have you policing my toilet with a brush every morning after I've had a heavy fry up. Are we clear on that?"

Brack swore again but made sure the connection was cut before he did so. Across the street, Tommy was letting himself out of the front door. Brack nearly missed him. It was only when the Polo coughed into life that he looked around.

Fuck! Close one...

He waited until the Polo had reached the end of the street before firing up his own Peugeot and following at a discreet distance.

Tommy had no idea he was being tailed. He was concentrating on keeping to the inner-city speed limits while terror built in him relentlessly. The last thing he wanted was to be pulled over now. But soon he was escaping the city up the dark stretch of the M32, the night pricked with a scattering of stars. The rind of the half-moon lent a curdled light to the fields streaming past him on both sides. The needle hovered around seventy-five. Another ten minutes and he was veering off the junction that opened onto the M4.

More fields, more stars. The lights of Bristol were behind him now. The M4 gave way to the M5.

Fear was his only companion on that journey. He knew he was probably driving to his death (and which video nasty-inspired fate would be his?), but this was a course with no sane choices. He knew now that he loved Jasmine. *You don't really know her,* a small voice in his head retaliated, but he ignored it. Refusing to answer this challenge was not an option. Fear pushed his foot down on the pedal, and fear yanked at his mind and heart.

Join us at the village where nobody lives. You remember it from your childhood, I'm sure...

Join us...

Tommy knew that particular entreaty was chosen specifically to resonate (*Evil Dead,* anyone?) Whoever created the message—and Tommy had a pretty damn good idea it was the bloodthirsty maniac known only as the Director—was clearly enjoying the game.

But who was he? And why had he gone to so much gruesome effort to target Tommy in particular? His overworked mind ran through the possibilities again and again, but none of them added up, or they seemed ridiculously mundane in light of the atrocities committed.

A video shop owner who received a sentence for selling videos banned as a direct result of his father's intervention in Parliament? That was beyond absurd. Somebody wanting revenge for some past deed of Tommy's? But he had no enemies—apart from Mark Hamm, currently residing in the Bristol City Morgue. The leader of a cult of video nasty devotees who blamed him for the "sins" of his father? That might account for the obsessive attention to detail, but again, what, exactly, was to be achieved by all this horror? It was madness. And sometimes that was the only answer. Why search for logic in the insane? Or rationality in evil?

He dismissed his frantic reveries. He would know soon enough. When he reached *the village where nobody lives.*

And, of course, he remembered that. His friend had once delighted in telling him how he'd burned down one of the empty houses. A teenage prank that had cost him six months in a youth detention center.

He barely slowed to take the exit ramp onto the same B road Slade had driven him along earlier that day. But the destination was slightly different this time. He thought of his father sitting up in his ruptured grave with his hands outstretched like a Big Issue seller begging for small change. He thought of Jasmine's naked body twirling from the hook. The gloved hand exploring her, the excited tongue of fire from the flamethrower. The needle crept up to sixty-five as he hurtled around bends and twists in the country road. He bypassed his hometown, heading east. Seven miles. He'd cycled there as a boy. It wouldn't take him long now. The needle crept higher. He didn't care who tried to stop him now he was near his goal.

Only one thought was riding him.

Jasmine. And the flame.

Brack knew he hadn't been seen by the object of his stealthy pursuit. He kept far enough back on the motorway to avoid suspicion and kept Slade in the loop. Slade's Bentley, in turn, was maybe ten miles behind Brack, and catching up fast.

"He's probably heading back home again. Keep me notified."

"Sir." Brack cut the connection before Slade's evident irritation built up again.

The Polo was taking the Dursley exit, as Slade had guessed it would.

Brack followed.

Tommy guided the Polo through the narrow lanes, forced to drop his speed as he prowled through quaint Cotswold villages. Wortley fell behind, two houses and a post box. Then Hillsley, with its pub frequented by old country hunters 'n' shooters. He remembered the Inn from his teenage years. He used to sit in there with his fellow rebels, tipping out handfuls of change (just enough to buy one pint) and goading the landlord with their unruly presence without quite tipping him over the edge to the point where he barred them.

Up the hill toward Hawkesbury Upton and its more violence-prone pubs. This was farm laborer land, and the inhabitants of the ugly village were not renowned for their liberal philosophies. He hung a right at the duck pond, the moon floating in its dark water, and was soon descending a narrow lane overhung with trees. The moon was shut out immediately, and darkness pressed in.

Tommy hadn't been down here since he was a teenager. He hadn't been present the night his crazy friend burned one of the empty houses down, but they all used to come here fairly often, riding down from Hawkesbury Upton on their 100-cc motorbikes, glugging cheap cider from plastic jugs and flaunting the laws without even thinking about it, in a way only the young can.

Halfway down the steep lane, Tommy steered the Polo into an open gateway and parked on the rough track. He killed the engine and listened to the silence. An owl announced its presence, the distant cries of sheep, nothing more. He sat behind the wheel for a moment, not moving. He could just stay here. He could stay here and live a little longer. Or...

He got out of the car and opened the boot. He pulled out the car jack, then closed the boot as silently as he could. He waited, listening, before walking to the road and descending the hill, his breath fast, his pulse thumping.

The cell in his pocket throbbed. He didn't even check it, so he missed his last chance to talk to his wife. He had turned his back on her a long time ago; one more missed call wouldn't make any difference now.

He kept to the side of the road, hidden under the shadow of the trees. If his tormentor had expected him to just drive in like a lamb to the slaughter... Tommy reached the bottom of the hill and peered around the last of the thinning trees.

The hamlet of Hawkesbury lay nestled in a dell surrounded by steep hills and woods. It consisted of four cottages and a manor house. Twenty years ago, there had been five cottages until some idiot thought it would be funny to put a match to one of them. With the sole exception of the manor house, the buildings had been abandoned twenty-five years before when a severe case of sinkhole subsidence took out one of the cottages and nearly killed its occupants. The surveyors discovered an ancient cave system under the village that was threatening to swallow the whole hamlet, stone, chimney, and gable, at any moment. That "any moment" had stretched out to twenty-five years without any of the houses disappearing into the abyss beneath, but the signs of instability were evident. And even in the dim light of the half moon and a hand-throw of stars, Tommy could see the cracks in the cottage walls had become significantly wider in the years since his last visit.

Wire fencing and warning signs corralled the cottages, but this attempt at protection was showing signs of age, too; the metal signs with their bright red lettering had slipped and rusted; the fencing peeling back or trampled to the ground by wind, weathering, and uninvited visitors.

Yet despite its neighbors consisting of a decayed and crumbling set, the manor house had continued to be tenanted. The last occupant—and for all Tommy knew, the present occupier, too—had been a prog rock musician, big in the '70s, not so big in the decades that followed, but obviously retaining enough dosh to purchase the imposing building that dominated the hamlet.

Tommy scanned the cottages huddled behind their tatty wire defenses, searching for any sign of movement. Nothing. The tall façade of the manor house was dark. He thought he heard a car engine from further up the road he had just come down, and he pulled back under the trees to wait, but after a few moments of silence, he turned to survey the hamlet again.

Where are you, you bastard?

Hefting the metal car jack, he stepped cautiously out from the tree cover and crossed a swathe of overgrown grass to the first cottage, praying the moonlight hadn't picked him out to any malicious observer. The fencing had buckled here, and Tommy stepped easily over the portion that lay on the ground. He huddled behind the crumbling stone wall, his breathing the loudest thing for miles.

But if he stayed in hiding too long, might not the killer assume Tommy had rejected his challenge? What would happen to Jasmine then? He remembered the message on the videotape. *A crisp, overdone roast...*

He inched around the wall, peering into the broken windows of the cottage. Too dark to make out much detail, although he could have sworn there was a figure in one room, sitting in a chair in deep shadow. He froze, straining his eyes, but the figure didn't move. It could have been anything: a coat slumped over the chair, a mass of cobwebs? He moved around the corner of the house. The distance to the next cottage was fifty yards of pitted, moonlit road. A large portion of the fence on this building had fallen away, too. Tommy dawdled for five seconds, heart as tight in his throat as the crowbar was in his fist. Then he picked his way back through the gap in the fence and ran toward the next house.

He scrambled through the hole in the wire and thudded against the wall of the cottage; a large piece of cladding slid free, shattered on the stone flagstones beneath. He closed his eyes as terror engulfed him, his breathing out of control, and waited... Waited. The silence continued. He opened his eyes, edged toward the corner of the cottage, passing another shattered window that revealed nothing but rot and shadow within, and peeked around. The last two cottages were on the far side of the dell, but they looked just as dark and dilapidated.

He looked toward the manor house. The front door was open.

He was sure it had been closed before. Had he been seen? Was this his invite? So what did he do now? Continue to scrabble around the hamlet in the dark, or face his fear head on? *But to go through that open door was certain suicide...*

He thought of Jasmine, twisting and turning slowly, suspended from a hook in the dark. He thought of the man in the fire visor, itching to turn his flame on her.

Tommy sucked in a deep breath that reeked of mold and nettles and stepped back through the hole in the fence. Then he proceeded slowly, like a dead man walking, toward the manor house.

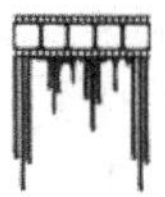

Brack had been following Tommy discreetly—a little *too* discreetly, he thought for one panicky moment when he nearly lost him at the Hawkesbury Upton duck pond. Which way had the bastard gone? He killed his engine and listened. There, to his right, down the road that led to Lower Hawkesbury, he heard the grumble of an engine. Then it was gone. He switched on again, picked up the dashboard radio transmitter, and contacted Slade.

"Where the fuck are you now?" the gruff voice crackled at him.

"Still on his tail, guv. Going down toward Lower Hawkesbury."

"Could have sworn he'd return to his hometown. Never the fuck mind. I'll reset my satnav. Not too far behind you. And Brack...?"

"Sir?"

"If you lose him..."

Brack switched off the transmitter and followed the signs, his car soon slipping into the thickest shadow he had ever known (he was a city boy; the country made him irrationally nervous).

He almost drove past the Polo, hidden, as it was, in the entrance to a farm track. He reversed and pulled in behind it, switched off the engine, then climbed out. Whatever fucking wild goose chase Slade had sent him on had better be worth keeping him away from The Star and Dove. Tonight was the Star's Pub Quiz. Brack's team always— nearly always—won, and he'd have been sipping free pints acquired from the losers right now. Maybe chatting up the tasty young (too young) barmaid, whatever the hell her name was... Instead of all that glamor and excitement, he was strolling down through a country lane in the dark, trying to keep his best Peter Bowers out of the fre- quent dollops of horse shit that littered the road.

What the fuck was Wallace doing snooping around in the back ass of beyond in the middle of the night anyway? Another thought, which was a little more disturbing than the idea of losing a night at the Star and Dove: what if Wallace had been involved with the mur- ders all along, and Brack was now walking into a trap? Had Wallace realized he was being tailed and led him down here into the dark on purpose? Maybe his homicidal accomplices—the freaks the survivors of the Malmesbury Massacre had spoken of—would be waiting for him, too...

Why the fuck hadn't Slade provided him with backup before sending him off here on his own? He hesitated, straining his ears for any sound, his eyes struggling to make out the shadowy road ahead. He switched his mobile to silent and continued slowly down the hill.

The manor house was erected on a slight rise, which made it seem even more imposing. Although it was only a much smaller replica of some of the country piles Tommy had seen around the Cotswolds, it was still impressive enough, in a pocket-sized nobility kind of way. The compact façade was gray and embraced by ivy. Three stories of blank windows, a pillared portico, and faux battlements spiking the night sky: the entire building reeked of contained decadence, *nouveau riche* aspirations, and aristocratic pretensions on a reduced scale. Was this an example of irony on the part of his nemesis? To locate his squalid Video Nasty Empire in the very heart of picturesque, conservative England? Tommy suspected that was *exactly* the intention.

He stepped onto the pebbled driveway leading up to the house, and the open doorway was a dark tunnel ahead of him. It wasn't until he was within ten yards of the entrance that he noticed there was light of a kind; a candle flickered deep within a large hall. At least, he guessed it was large as the flame only illuminated the table it stood upon and a few yards of marble flooring around it. Enough to guide him forward and give an impression of space, but not to show him who was waiting in the thick darkness inside.

He climbed the three wide stone steps to the portico. The silence was heavy on his ears. He couldn't even hear the sheep now.

He took a last look behind him, then breathed deeply and faced the door again. It was time. He remembered Gary Gilmore's last words as he walked toward the firing squad. *More than appropriate*, he thought, as he moved slowly forward.

Let's do it...

Part Three
Cut!

CHAPTER TWENTY-ONE

Clutching the car jack tightly in his sweaty fist, Tommy entered the house.

He moved as lightly as he could, not wishing to alert anyone to his presence, yet each step on the marble flooring of the spacious hall seemed amplified in the silence. He tried to breathe through his nose only—and was his heart audible, too, in the echoing gloom? He reached the table with the candle and hesitated. Oak paneling was just visible on the walls around him as his eyes adjusted. There was the occasional shadow of furniture, the cold pool of a mirror on one wall, oil paintings hanging just out of reach of the fluttering candle flame. The hall seemed empty. A corridor led off to the left. He hesitated. And heard the scream.

It was coming from down the dark corridor, and so distant that his first thought was that it might be a night bird or a fox. He strained his ears, and there it was again: undeniably female. He knew he was supposed to follow the sound right into the jaws of whatever trap awaited him, but he had not come this far to turn his back on Jasmine now. That it was her faint screams he was hearing, he had little doubt. She was alive…and that was enough to compel him to move. He crept ahead into the darkness, which became thicker as he progressed.

Yet after a few more steps, he became aware of a glimmer. The flash of a blade? No, another mirror, reflecting a flicker of light from around a corner where the corridor veered to the right. Tommy inched forward, then peered around the bend. The corridor ahead stretched into dimness, yet there was a slight illumination, an unstable glimmer, beckoning him on. The screams sounded louder now, edged with nerve-slashing pain and terror. His heart clenched at each one, his fist tight around the car jack—which now felt ridiculously inadequate. Who knew what monsters from the Vid had been summoned to guard her? And how crazy to even believe that was possible! But he'd seen the proof already, hadn't he? Anthropophagous and Friends.

He forced his breathing into a regular rhythm and continued on. The intermittent screams and sobs drowned out the sound of his shoes on the marble flooring, and Tommy felt he could increase his pace a little. He passed occasional antique chairs and sideboards, one of which he nearly stumbled into. But the flicker was becoming more prominent, and he could finally recognize its source. He advanced ever so slowly to the entrance of a room on the left, from which a wash of harsh light emerged. The sobs came from inside.

He paused next to the open doorway, fist squeezing the bar even more tightly, though the metal was slippery with sweat. He pressed his head against the wall next to the door jamb and slowly, so slowly, leaned forward to peer into the room.

The room was almost as large as the central hall. The far wall and those to either side had been fitted with banks of video screens. All showed the same image: Jasmine in the torture dungeon. She was still twisting on the hook, her eyes closed, moaning brokenly. Just in front of the doorway, a leather sofa sprawled decadently, facing the monitors. A figure was slumped against the cushions, the head fallen to one side. The face had acquired a dirty blue-bottle sheen, moist with decomposition, but Tommy still recognized him. The musician had obviously been dead a good few months. Ever since the new resident paid him a visit, deciding this really was the perfect lair. His hair, once long and blond, was now gray and clipped short around a balding pate, where maggots had taken the place of follicles, rupturing the scalp. The eye on the side of the face visible to Tommy had begun to sink inwards like a cheap prop.

Strangely enough—and boy, Tommy could appreciate the biting irony—the '70s legend had once provided the music to one of the larger-budgeted nasties, and Tommy had the soundtrack at home on vinyl. The keyboard wizard was doubtless playing his last Moog solo in Prog Rock Hell... Tommy stared at the dead man on the sofa while screams broke from the speakers in the walls and felt again the resonance of so many echoes from his past returning to taunt him.

Tommy completed his tense scan of the room. He spotted another door, this one closed, on the opposite wall below the largest screen. Apart from the corpse, the room appeared empty. When the voice boomed suddenly from the speakers, Tommy felt his heart gripped just that little bit harder.

"Welcome to Hell."

Tommy stiffened against the door jamb. Had he been seen? Or was this a trick to summon him from hiding? His eyes flicked around the room again, but it remained resolutely empty. He became aware that the image on the multiple screens had changed. They no longer showed Jasmine. Instead, his father's face watched him from every angle of the room. Young again, as he had been at the time of the Video Recordings Act, which he had so primly facilitated. And hadn't Tommy resented him for that? And how he wished he could return to those simpler times, when the only horror in his life was safely contained in eight inches of plastic and a reel of magnetic tape...

Staring at the multiple images of his father, he could no longer feel the old resentment and shame. He remembered how he had been pilloried at school when his father first began his campaign. And then a year later, in the pub, when the reality of the Act had become clearer and real people were losing their stock, their livelihoods, their right to *choose* because of something his father had precipitated. He remembered the son of the local video shop owner pinning him against a wall in the Falcon Inn, his mates urging him on, his podgy face florid with indignant fury. Uncomfortable memories that flashed back in an instant, relived now as he stared at his father's face on countless screens. But he knew his father wasn't to blame anymore. How could he have envisaged his self-serving actions would result in this? A Video Nasty helter-skelter, Slade had called it. And if Slade had been wrong about many things, that wasn't one of them. No, Tommy's father was not the monster here. He was just a weak man, with one eye on his career and the other on the prize money: respect, approbation... *Acceptance.* Well done, Mister Wallace, you did a fine job there. Join our club and have a cigar. You're one of us now.

His father spoke again, and even though Tommy knew the words coming from the lips were not his (how could they be?), the voice most definitely was.

"If you're looking for your slut, she's down below. She's dying to meet you again." The mouth moved in different time to the words, badly synched. *Just like most of the nasties*, Tommy thought wildly.

"If you hurry, you might find her in time. She's looking particularly hot at the moment, I must say. So tempting. Such pretty flesh."

The mocking voice drew Tommy into the room. He irrationally considered smashing the screens, but what good could that possibly do him or Jasmine? He twisted his head from right to left, from one screen to the next, but the face duplicated fifteen or so times had paused. Video flack skidded across the monitors. Then the image unfroze, and Tommy's Dad was replaced by Jasmine. The burning man was fondling her again. Her sobs picked up from where they left off.

"*Where is she?*" The cry burst from him before he could stop himself. He spun on impulse and ran from the room, heading down the corridor deeper into the house, the shadows closing over him again, the sound of her sobs dwindling.

Detective Constable Peter Brack was whispering into his cell phone as he paused at the bottom of the hill to survey the empty cottages. He'd discarded the walkie-talkie for obvious reasons. Too damn loud. Slade sounded tired, and that made him frostier than ever.

"Have you lost him?"

"No, sir. I mean...he must have gone into one of the houses."

"For fuck's sake. Ask you to do one simple thing. Any sign of trouble?"

"No, sir. Quiet as a graveyard. But maybe we should call for backup, sir."

"And why the fuck would we do that? If I fuck up one more time, it's all over. Case pulled. You know that. Scotland Yard or some other bunch of wankers will come marching in. You'll be pensioned off for a start, Brack, you useless bastard."

No, I rather think it'll be YOU who gets shunted off to Bournemouth, Sladey, spending the rest of your days shuffling around tea shops and wearing slippers while you watch Lucifer *on T.V., ruefully chewing on tea cakes and regrets.* Brack bit his lip and said nothing. He was scared. He needed the company of another officer, even if it was Slade.

"Where are you now, guv?"

"Some shit-arsed, retard village called Hillesley. Only two or three miles, Brack. Try not to soil your pants, I'll be there before you fucking know it. And make sure you've located Wallace before I arrive."

The cell went dead. *Bastard.* Brack pocketed it and stealthily followed the road as it wound between the derelict cottages.

He was passing the first building when the guard dog emerged from the shadows inside. This particular guard dog was seven feet tall, bearded, and clad in what looked like a hospital johnny soiled with dried blood. Tommy would have immediately recognized him as the psychotic killer with the out-of-control tissue-regeneration from the sequel to *Anthropophagous.* Twice as violent as his first incarnation, this homicidal giant was far from *Absurd.* Tommy had always believed the French title to be far more apposite: *Horrible.* Of course, Brack was aware of none of this background detail.

Absurd didn't bother hiding his presence anymore. The fencing clattered as he pulled it further apart as he came for the policeman. Unlike his Anthro forebear, this big bastard remained silent, apart from ragged breathing and the stomp of his huge boots as he lumbered after his prey.

DC Brack whirled. He saw the abomination heading his way, massive hands spread for mayhem, and promptly did what his guv had told him not to, and soiled his boxers. Even though he was a trained officer with three years of service, he knew he had no chance against this brute. He knew he was going to die.

He thought of turning to run but also knew he'd never make it. So he held his ground, ready to get the first punch in. Absurd slowed long enough to swat the detective's head with his huge right hand, and the copper went down. The giant scooped him up effortlessly under one arm and carried him back to the cottage he'd emerged from.

Now and again he would find a fire burning in a grate inside a room off the passageway, or a candle strategically placed on an occasional table to abate the darkness. Mood lighting, just for Tommy... He soon found himself at the heart of the house where a large stairwell wound impressively upward into more gloom. But it was the open door to one side, revealing a far smaller set of steps leading downward, that interested him.

The steps were hewn from stone and crawled with more flickering light, this time coming from below.

His shoes kicked up echoes from the first two steps, forcing him to increase his stealth. He didn't have far to go; the short flight brought him down to another door, this one half shut, just allowing him a glimpse into the stone dungeon beyond. And it was certainly more of a dungeon than a cellar—at least it was now. The hook was probably a new acquisition (unless the '70s muso had been prone to dangling naked ladies from the ceiling between doodling on his Hammond), and the shackles gleamed with sweat and dried blood.

The first thing he realized was that the hook, and the shackles suspended from it, were empty.

Jasmine was still in the room, however, and she was very much alive. Tommy's jubilation was short-lived; her torturer in the bulky asbestos suit was still there, too, fuel tank slung over one shoulder, flamethrower cradled in his arms.

Jazz was sitting in a corner, still naked but no longer crying. She was staring at the floor, as if dulled by terror, lost in a trance. Her persecutor stood in the center of the room, motionless, his back to the door. Waiting? For Tommy...

This was it, then. Tommy had never been a man of action. He'd avoided fights at school, been drawn reluctantly into them at college. He didn't know how to swing a punch to make it count. And now it really was going to count. But he had his car jack, and even though he quailed inside at what he was about to do, the sight of Jasmine, huddled and grimy with sweat and tears, spurred him on.

He pushed the door open wider and slipped through.

Jasmine slowly raised her head. Her eyes opened wide. Wider. Tommy put one finger to his lips and hefted the car jack.

And Jasmine smiled.

CHAPTER TWENTY-TWO

But the smile was wrong. It was wrong in a way that tipped Tommy's heart upside down. It was a smile that shat on everything he'd grown up to believe was good. That smile said, *yeah, your whole life: what a joke.* He'd never believed in God, but he'd been brought up to have a general sense of what was right. And this...?

This was not right.

Not by a long way.

She was smiling a cruel, cat-got-the-bird smile. Her eyes were coldly triumphant.

"He's right behind you," she said. The Incinerator Man began to turn, flamethrower leveled like a bulky rifle. "Good boy."

The dark visor nodded at Tommy, who stood rooted with utter despair and shock. But then, instead of turning the weapon on Tommy, the man in the bulky fire suit swung back to face Jasmine. He ignited the spark plug, squeezed the trigger, and the nozzle puffed out a tongue of flame.

Jasmine's expression changed from one of gloating, to first bewilderment, then horrified understanding. The Incinerator Man lumbered toward her.

"Wha-what?" she stammered, leaping to her feet. "What are you—?" Her terror was as naked as her body as the truth hit home and stayed there. "You *promised me!*" She put out her small, delicate hands—the ones that had touched Tommy in intimate places with their glossy pink nails. The killer from *Don't Go in the House* increased pressure on the trigger and hosed her down with flame.

The stream of fire stretched out like a livid rope, groped her delicate, sweet flesh, and lashed it with ignited propane. The fire stream caressed her breasts, melting them into bubbling black craters. Jasmine fell back against the stone wall, her body a thrashing candle flame, shrieks from hell ripping from her lips. The flamethrower barrel moved upward, saturating her face with its blazing torrent. Tommy saw the soft brown eyes he'd stared into while making love to her transform into smoking blisters, the nose flake away like a charred piece of barbecue. The face blackened with the intense heat. The screams stopped. The lungs were melted crisp bags, the lips a fall of ash. The body slid down the wall, leaving a dark stain. Smoke filled the room, along with the stench of cooked female flesh.

Tommy, mind reeling, body numb, watched the whole horror show. It was only as Jasmine's executioner began to turn to face him again that he moved.

Slade didn't bother with stealth. He saw the two parked cars and ignored them, driving the Bentley right down into the heart of Lower Hawkesbury, parking up next to the first cottage.

Brack had stopped answering his phone. That might mean he was very close to Tommy and couldn't speak, or it might mean he was in trouble. The latter seemed unlikely. The place looked innocuous enough. Although what the fuck had inspired Wallace to come here at this time of night was beyond him. But Slade couldn't afford any more mistakes; he had to grasp any lead that came his way. Tommy's nocturnal adventure was one such. He tried Wallace's phone again. Straight to voicemail. Slade hesitated. He still didn't know exactly how far Tommy was implicated in all this, although he definitely believed the extra was just a victim. But Slade didn't want to announce his presence yet, just in case Wallace led him to whoever *was* responsible. However, if Wallace wouldn't answer his phone, Slade would just have to leave a message. Maybe passing on the evidence Jim Tavell had recovered from Jasmine Paal's flat would flush Wallace out and push things to a head—or warn him if he was walking into a trap. He'd tried to inform him earlier, but the bastard—like that other bastard, Brack—wasn't picking up. He waited for the beep, then spoke quietly and seriously into his phone. "We searched your girlfriend's flat, Tommy. Looking for any clue as to the identity or whereabouts of the director she worked with. We found something else. Vicky Hebworth's bloodstained knickers in a drawer. We believe she's involved, Tommy. It's imperative you inform us if you hear anything from her."

As he climbed out of the car and approached the ruined cottage, he considered again whether to call for backup. No, he would trust his instincts as a copper for thirty years and play this by ear. He glanced up at the manor house, the dominant building in the hamlet. It was as dark as the cottages. Where the fuck was Brack?

He scanned the cottage in front of him, stepped gingerly over the flattened section of fencing. He tried Brack's mobile again as he stepped up to the wall and peered through the shattered window. He could see nothing but vague shadows—maybe a chair?—and swathes of damp cobwebs hanging from the walls and ceiling. The phone continued to ring. A sound answered it from inside the gloom of the cottage. A low vibration, only audible because the night was so quiet, and whatever was vibrating was throbbing against something. Brack's phone. He strained his eyes to make out the details inside.

And the cottage lit up like a scene from hell.

Brack was sitting in a chair facing the window. He was strapped into a bespoke electric chair, which was rigged up to a generator and a control panel, now visible as the amps started to build up. Brack's mouth was gaffa-taped, his eyes bugging wide. They locked on Slade just as the giant who had switched on the apparatus threw the lever connected to it and pummelled Brack's body with three thousand volts. As his body arced, a camera fixed in the wall captured every frame. White foam began to dribble from Brack's mouth, flecked with traces of blood like swirls of raspberry syrup in semolina. More blood trickled from beneath the metal cap crowning his head, and a gout blew from his nose. His executioner leered at Slade and increased the voltage.

Slade snapped into action. He scrambled around the side of the cottage until he found the half-open door, then threw his weight against it. It grated open reluctantly, but he was in, the living room beyond the decomposing hall still lit by the eerie glow from the chair. Sparks fireworked. Brack's final moan was just audible above the thrum of lethal electricity, and then he slumped forward against the straps.

Slade didn't even think. With no time to even call for backup (and how he regretted his earlier hesitation now!), he hurled himself at the giant.

Absurd roared and let go of the lever. He spread his hands as if for a catch and lunged forward to meet Slade. The DI tripped over a piece of broken furniture on the floor, and it was this that saved him. The giant's bear hug closed above his head as the policeman went down.

Slade rolled onto his back, thrusting himself quickly to his feet again.

No weapon. No fucking weapon! This wasn't the US-of fucking-A! And if he survived this, he was going to put his strongest request yet to the Home Secretary, demanding that all senior ranking officers should be equipped with handguns. But right now, he had more pressing concerns.

The giant swung to face him, eyes ferocious and promising nothing less than total dismemberment if he got his hands on Slade.

Slade glanced around the room, looking for any item he could use to defend himself.

A rusting saucepan; the broken back of a chair—the same item he'd tripped on; a plastic washbowl filled with rank water on the floor nearby. Not an impressive arsenal by any means. He feinted to the left, then dove toward the bowl. The giant hesitated, thrown by the duck, then came at him like a locomotive. Slade scooped up the bowl, whirled, and dashed the contents into the bearded face, then threw the bowl as well for good measure. Pathetic. The bowl bounced from his head harmlessly, yet the giant paused regardless, wiping at his eyes and growling in frustration. Which gave Slade just enough time to seize the chair-back and smash it across the monster's skull. Absurd swatted the broken furniture aside, and Slade backed up against the far wall. *Nowhere to go, good buddy.* The saucepan lay at his feet. It wasn't even worth picking up. So he didn't. The giant was giving him a snarl-smile. *You are so fucking dead,* that grimace said. Slade knew it. No more jollies to Prague, no more tits. He thought of Judita and their seedy transaction and swore if he got through this, he would fly straight over to the Czech Republic and beg her to marry him.

He swung a punch at the bastard, but it didn't even connect.

The giant closed his hand over Slade's fist and crushed it like it was an egg. He clamped his other hand around Slade's head and did the same to that.

Absurd moved slowly out of the cottage and headed for the manor house. His hands were smeared with blood. Some of Slade's brains had dribbled onto his fingers, too. The giant didn't even notice.

The car jack slammed into the killer's bulky fire visor with enough force to send him to his knees. The visor tipped forward off the man's head, revealing the face beneath. A loser's face. A sleaze-bag with "victim" written all over his features, and Tommy remembered the lank hair and dumb-fuck attempt at looking crazy from the video nasty that had inspired the Incinerator Man's MO. Tommy no longer cared how the man could be here, in this dungeon, with a face identical to the actor as he had appeared thirty years ago. He didn't fucking care.

Tommy's second blow landed on the man's right arm, and the flamethrower dropped. The propane tank slipped off his shoulder, clanked on the stone floor. The third blow rolled Incinerator Man on his back. He was starting to rear up again like an upside-down bug attempting to right itself when Tommy dropped the jack and picked up the flamethrower instead.

He didn't waste time going for the asbestos-protected body, but aimed for the self-pitying face and squeezed the trigger all the way.

The killer's head blazed like a Roman candle. Tommy paused long enough to sling the propane tank over one shoulder, then turned his back on the pitiful squeals and the smell of burning flesh that filled the room, and made his way back up the steps.

He prowled the dark corridors, face grim, eyes a little mad. He was heading back for the room with the screens, guided by the instinctive knowledge that his tormentor would be waiting for him. His mind was red. Red as the flames that had consumed Jasmine. Red.

CHAPTER TWENTY-THREE

He could hear the tag lines from the end of the corridor.

The flamethrower was still ignited, and his eyes were crimson with reflected flame.

"Everyone has nightmares about the ugliest way to die..." The melodramatic voice-over beckoned him on, closely followed by another choice snippet: *"Prepare yourself for the ultimate experience; this video cassette will change your attitude to life..."*

He reached the room in time to hear the most famous one: *"To avoid fainting, keep repeating it's only a movie, only a movie, only a movie..."* The words dwindled into silence as he stepped up behind the leather sofa, staring at the screens.

There they were: the DPP 39, each video nasty taking its individual turn to show off on the screens, one offensive clip after another, the fifteen monitors showing different films at the same time. He saw throats ripped out alongside dismemberment, rape, eye-gouging, scalp-ripping, chopping, burning... Endlessly looped. A treat for the senses, a riot of the cheapest gore and terror. Horror stripped down to its primal bone in grainy VHS.

And in amongst the narrated tag lines, Tommy caught snatches of dialogue—quotes from Nasty Hell: *"They'll eat your eyes first, then your nose and lips while you're still alive, then your brain, and then you'll die..."*

He stalled before the phantasmagoria of vileness. He could see it now for what it was—had he really fought with his Dad to defend this shit? The words attacked him from all three sides of the room.

"I was sure the best way for the filthy lesbian to die was for her to burn..."

"Too real to be simulated, too shocking to be ignored..."

"Brother eats brother, mothers devour their offspring in a chain of foul slaughter until nothing will remain but the bare earth, soaked in putrefying flesh..."

The volume crept up. The soundtracks battered inside his head, repeating, overlapping, destroying his mind.

"Rape her... rape her!"

"We've really put ourselves in the shit this time, staying to film the last bit."

"The more you rape their senses, the more they seem to like it."

"A vile film for vicious sex criminals..."

"Violence beyond reason, victims beyond help..."

And one more insistent than all the others, burrowing like a hate worm into his soul: *"The actors and actresses who dedicated their lives to making this film were never seen or heard from again..."*

He raised the flamethrower. His finger was on the trigger when the screens blanked out. Then flickered back into life, depicting his father's face again. He seemed to be delivering a lecture from fifteen screens, although he only had an audience of one.

"In nineteen-eighty-three, The *Daily Mail* and other tabloids whipped up a moral fury that instigated the rise of the nasty for their own selfish reasons—to sell papers..." His father frowned in digitally manipulated disapproval. "But the papers did too good a job of demonizing it—of making it a definable essence. They made the monster potentially tangible in every household that possessed a V.H.S. player. An as-yet formless creature with the sole aim of creating and perpetuating evil. It stretched out tendrils and began to exert a subtle grip on weakened minds in living rooms across Great Britain. Our insulated isle reveled in the intolerance, hatred, and seething violence it encouraged."

Tommy's fingers twitched. He ached to burn those screens, that pompous face that was his own kin. The talking head continued its monologue: "But then the right-wing politicians saw their opportunity and conservative oppression crushed the burgeoning force of evil by driving it underground—entirely unwittingly, of course—and again not through altruistic motivations, but to further their own careers."

The images changed again, and now a man occupied all of them, a man unfamiliar to Tommy. Pasty-faced, scarred by acne, his hair lank and damp and falling over his thin face. This face shunned the sun as much as society had almost certainly shunned the person it belonged to. The narrator elucidated all in Mr. Wallace Senior's educated tones: "Here was a man unloved by the beautiful, who grew to cherish the stark ugliness rooted in us all. A failure of a man, a student of cinema who had no discernible talent. A man of mean tastes and squalid desires. A perfect vessel for the Nasty to further its cause. For along with the laxer moral focus the twenty-first century brought, a more liberal attitude toward censorship arrived, too, and the Nasty made a resurgence."

Tommy listened, despite his hatred and his anguish—which was becoming a dead thing numbed by the horrors. He watched the face on the monitors, and the voice lulled him, as it had when he was a child with the occasional bedtime story. His grip on the trigger loosened.

"Obsessed with video nasties, this failure, this Abject Man, had channeled all his non-existent talents into making cheap underground horror films on D.I.Y. D.V.D., which stimulated nobody. But inspiration was at hand. When this Shunned Man undertook a lonely video nasty marathon in his flat one long weekend, he was taking the Devil by the horns and singing along to all His best tunes. The essence of the Nasty, which had been fortifying its existence in the ether, fastened on his sleaze- and horror-channeled mind. It battened on him like a vampire bat gorging on sadism, joining with him, transforming him..." Tommy's father, the venerable former MP for Gloucester South, bowed his head in mock respect. "His delusions of grandeur were inflamed. While he still retained a shred of humanity, he believed his new 'enlightenment' would enable him to influence minds in a way never believed possible before, through the medium of film. He believed he would go down in history. Hitchcock, De Mille, Peckinpah...Tarantino! These would be talentless infants in comparison. When he commenced his new film, inspired by the force now roosting within him, he believed he was creating his life work. His Masterpiece. True Art. But these were the trappings of the ego of a disillusioned young man. His legacy would be far greater than personal glory... In time, the Director became something else. The Visionary of the Vile, or Mister Nasty... Call him what you will; he is humanity's nemesis."

And now the screens switched again. Tommy's father was gone, replaced by a montage of real death, real horror, all too familiar to Tommy. He saw Andy Hill, impaled on a tree. There was Graham, the wrangler, his forehead leaking brains around the thrusting drill bit. There Rona, her breast ravished brutally; Lana, Mark, everyone from the Malmesbury Massacre. He saw Vicky in her Snuff bedroom... Finally, he saw a young man he didn't recognize at all, dying in a blood-filled bathtub—and even though he didn't know him, he knew what he *was*. A virgin, a prototype killing. An experiment to kick the whole foul process into play.

Tommy could read much in those flickering images of butchery. He could see into the mind of the monstrous genius the loser had become. He saw how the first killings had been clumsily performed, probably by the Romanian criminals—and one had almost certainly been an extra on *Doctor Who* the Director had recruited with promises of financial gain. *And it wasn't until Malmesbury that you perfected your Art, was it, and the physical spirit of the Nasty was invoked? When the killers became something more than a gang of immoral henchmen and transformed into monsters that had stepped right out of the videos themselves...real artists at work!*

As the last of the real death scenes froze on a close-up of Vicky's scared cobalt eyes, Tommy perceived the extent of the web he had been ensnared in. The Director had been systematically remounting the most horrifying scenes from the list of banned films, and, in so doing, had fed the vileness hidden inside himself and instigated— "The end of civilization..." The Honorable Mr. Wallace was back. "The end of rationality. Rome, Greece, Mesopotamia...all fell through their own decadence. And the greatest civilization of all time will go the same way, destroyed by the basest, innate desires that lurk in the human soul, baying for horror, for horror and for blood." A pause. Silence filled the room, apart from the soft burn of the small flame drooling from the nozzle. "That is his gift to humanity: to let everything slide into the chaos of depravity and total violence. Not so much a director then, but a conductor leading the Orchestra of Horror that will play out over mankind's final credits. Believe me: this *is* the End."

Another change. This time the screens all showed the same image of a young man and woman who were vaguely familiar to Tommy. They were bound to wooden chairs in what looked like different ruined cottages—maybe the two Tommy hadn't checked out when he crept through the hamlet earlier. It was only when the giant from *Absurd* untied the young girl, snapping her bonds easily, that Tommy recognized her. He'd last seen her in the Factory audition waiting room. The monster carried her to an oven and opened the door. The oven was already lit. Tommy could almost feel the heat escaping in waves. He didn't want to observe the giant force her head inside, didn't want to see her face begin to pop and blister, her dark hair to sear and fall, but something made him keep watching. On another screen in a different cottage, her audition companion was waiting his turn. Fat bulged over the rope fastening him to the chair. His head drooped. When Absurd had finished baking his friend's face away, the giant would come for him, too. Tommy could see what awaited him: a circular saw at a cutting table. It wouldn't be long before that blade was set in motion.

When it was all over (and Tommy had to see it all), Jasmine returned to life on the screens.

Naked, writhing, on the hook. Then, an edit cut and a close-up of her face slackening in horror as she realized the extent of her betrayal. Tommy would have appreciated the irony, but his mind was too full of Red. He watched her burn for the second time that day, her death amplified, multiplied, a world of flame and terror that filled his eyes, his head.

Jasmine... Media Whore extraordinaire. Fuck anyone, anything, for a role. The morality of an S.S. Doctor locked in the body of a hooker. A dangerous combination. She fucked you for a role, after all. Fucked you over as well. A strutting player led by ego, nothing more.

He saw it all now, so clearly...and the Red bloomed.

He swung the flamethrower toward the screens. He would burn them all. And if this nightmare film was here, he would find the master print and burn that, too. Burn everything. *Burrrrn.*

His finger caressed the trigger as, for the last time, his father's face replaced Tommy's lover all around the room.

"That's a wrap," the former MP said simply, and the door in the far wall opened.

CHAPTER TWENTY-FOUR

The Honorable MP for Gloucester South was still talking from the screens, although the figure with his face that emerged beneath them was silent.

The latex mask was terrifying in its impassiveness, the suit conservative and gray. The man's hands lifted as if orchestrating the pompous words from the speakers.

"In nineteen-eighty-three, the English middle class was appalled by the thought of incendiary material being viewed by the great unwashed—the working class; centuries previously, the gentry were similarly threatened by the invention of the printing press making penny dreadfuls available to the barely literate masses. This film is *my* printing press. And I am going to make you a part of it in a very special way."

The man approached Tommy slowly until he was barely five feet away. Tommy focused all his hatred and revulsion and the burning need for revenge on that one insignificant figure, and the urge to squeeze the flamethrower trigger was almost uncontrollable. Yet the man seemed unafraid, and the words that detailed Tommy's destiny continued to spill from the screens all around him. His finger tensed but did not squeeze.

"Clips of death and depravity from all the choicest of the nasties have already been inserted into my film to compliment the real deaths your friends so kindly provided for me. The brutal Mother of all Nasties is almost complete. Just one more act of processing before the DVD is mastered and released into stores. And yes, the orders have already been placed. Advertising hype and false credentials have prompted contracts with major distributors. Nobody will know it's the same film that caused the deaths of fifteen people up north in its festival test run. This is the next big thing, Thomas Wallace. All the terror, all the hideous violence that attended the work print premiere—amplified a thousand-fold by the unexpurgated D.V.D., complete and primed with its final encoding. Can you guess what that encoding is, Thomas?"

Tommy didn't want to guess. He wanted to burn. He would start with that mask. The symbol of repression throughout his life. He'd burn that mask right off. But yet again he stayed his hand as the words from the speakers continued to burrow into his brain.

"Human encoding is the answer... Your personal fear programmed into the master tape—the son of the Repressor, the stultifying moral crusader of the '80s—what symbolic irony... Not only will you endure unbearable agony and terror in your starring role as the victim in an endless Video Nasty Greatest Hits—you will physically experience every drilling, stabbing, burning, and eye-gouging on repeat mode—but your horror encoded into the film will stimulate the essence of evil dormant in each frame. When the D.V.D. is viewed, its malevolent influence will be amplified because of your contribution, and it will reach out to the minds of all those who watch it. Like you, they will be mentally conditioned to believe they are actually experiencing the scenes in the film, and the resultant madness will induce homicidal urges on an unparalleled scale."

The voice stopped.

The nozzle of the flamethrower lifted. Tommy grimaced. It was not a smile. The flame dribbled from the barrel. His finger tensed, ready to propel ignited propane at the instigator of all his woes.

And a huge hand closed on his arm from behind, forcing the barrel down.

Another hand clamped around his face.

The giant began to lift him off his feet. Tommy could smell the sweat and blood on the killer as he struggled in his massive arms. His finger closed on the flamethrower trigger, and a gout of fire streamed out, engulfing Absurd's right leg.

The giant released him with a roar of pain and fury. Tommy hit the floor and rolled, the fuel pack falling off his shoulder as he did so. He depressed the trigger again and held it there, giving Absurd another pulse of flame that took him in his bearded face. A rhino screech, and the monster flailed, beating at the flames. Tommy regained his feet, swinging the barrel to face the Director, the attached fuel pack clanging along the floor as he turned.

He pressed the trigger. A hollow click. The dribble of flame dwindled and died. Tommy dropped the flamethrower, quickly scooped up the tank, and swung it by the attached hose. It smashed heavily into the Director's mask.

A rent appeared in the latex. The Director reeled back. He reached up, clasped the mask by the fake haircut, and tugged. The face Tommy had seen on the screens earlier was revealed. The pasty face was even pastier now, liquefying with rot. The pockmarks were filled with mold. As Tommy watched, one of the eyes slopped out of its socket and rolled down the cheek, dislodged by the blow. The Director idly plucked the other free, too, and dropped it to the floor along with the mask. A video spool was exposed where each eye had been, protected by grimy transparent screens. Tommy could even see the fingerprints smeared on the plastic—*just to add to the horrible verisimilitude.* Mister Nasty was a VHS man through and through. Tommy didn't scream or laugh, although he felt tipped toward both reactions. The Director's mouth opened and a loop of videotape drooled out. Tommy flinched back. The conservative shirt beneath the suit was bursting open now as the Director's belly ruptured, and a seething coil of magnetic tape tumbled over his belt, questing, snaking, imbued with slithery life.

Life really does imitate film, Tommy thought as the loops reached for him.

Absurd came up behind him, his burned face smoldering, breathing like his lungs were on fire, too. His massive hands pushed Tommy toward the jungle of tape, and the tape embraced him in its coils.

He was dragged toward the editing suite beyond the inner door, and his thoughts were no longer fuelled by rage. His anger was done. There was no more. His heart was the color of sadness. He saw Trish: it was their first date all over again. Summer evening in the beer garden of a country pub. He remembered the ale he had drunk (she had gone for a glass of red). She had laughed when he called his bag of crisps moon flakes, and his pot of cockles Sea Beasts. Her hair so dark, her face sensual, eyes kind. Her features fading now.

I'm sorry.

He saw his father's face (but never his mother's, dead when he was six). They were sharing a glum supper. His father buried in the newspaper. He remembered staring at the conservative side-parting of his hair, flecked with gray. He remembered wanting his attention, and always failing to get it. But now his father was looking up at him, and he was smiling. Tommy saw the smile crumble to soil, and a tear down his cheek became a worm dribbling from the socket. Tommy's Dad was sitting up in his grave to beg for forgiveness. They had failed each other for the last time.

I'm sorry, too, Dad.

He saw Jasmine, and the night of passion in her flat. He looked into those mild brown eyes as he thrust, as he thrust into the dark, and her face blew away in a shower of ash.

Tommy's cell phone clattered to the floor as he was dragged, unresisting now, through the door. The fall activated the screen and revealed a text had just been received. Tommy could see the sender's name at the top of the screen. BlondeVenus. Tommy started to laugh. Slowly and quietly.

The Director and the giant placed Tommy in a chair in the editing suite and fixed a metal helmet over his head. The reels of tape dangled from the Director's torn belly and twitched from his mouth.

This is MY film, Tommy thought, and the world turned red.

ABOUT THE AUTHOR

After some very dark wilderness years indeed, staying with treehouse-dwelling unrepentant cannibals in New Guinea and seeing things that really shouldn't be seen in Java, Leo Darke has survived the real horrors to create fictional ones instead, though some actual experiences will inevitably creep into the pages of his books... As well as writing, Leo spends his time working as a supporting actor and creature performer in TV and Films, whether as a tortured sinner in Da Vinci's *Demons*, sword-fighting on *Atlantis* and *King Arthur*, being a zombie in *Generation Z* or as one of *Doctor Who*'s regular Daleks and Cybermen. He has written four titles for Grinning Skull Press: Lucifer Sam, Pandemonium, Sawney Bone, and Mr. Nasty.

Book Two in the *101 Ways to Hell Series*

SAWNEY BONE

LEO DARKE

Author of *LUCIFER SAM* and *PANDEMONIUM*

PART ONE: HOLE

Father's shout.

Eat the world—and the cave stinks of horror.

I sees the sun spurt blood over the deathless sea. I squints at the rocks with their *hoods o' weed skulking on that goriest o' shores. I sees the world in my head, and I'll eat it all.*

The grisly man crouches at the mouth of the cave and scratches irritably at his rank beard. *Eat. I'll eat 'em all.*

Across the sea, the mound of Ailsa Craig drips with blood from the wounded sun. The grisly man gazes at the blood, can taste it on his lips, feel it ooze down his jaws. He stretches gnarled hands toward the sun, thirsting for redness.

Behind him, from the depths of the cave, comes the pig-stuck roaring of his spawn. He snarls back into the darkness. If any are unwise to venture near him now, he'll scoop them up by their chicken-bone ankles and slap their brains out against the roof of the cave. He hears his hag of a woman spit and curse and the sound of stone on flesh. It excites him; he wants part of the violence. He is about to scamper into the throat of the cave when a sound reaches his sensitive ears.

His grotesque head tilts upward, nostrils working eagerly. His body, clad in a filthy jerkin and a loincloth of rotting seaweed, stiffens; a man of rock with death screaming in his mind. He listens, breath stilled. The echo of hooves can just be detected from far above.

He moves.

Like a human crab with scabbed flesh and slimy hair, he sidles over the rocks beyond his cave, swarms over piles of sick, pale weeds, and sprays through the first tongues of the advancing tide. He needs be hasty.

The carriage road winds toward the edge of the world.

The cliff tops hang above a gulf of twilight. The horizon is a band of blood, splitting the dark of the sea from the dark of the sky. Blood. The old woman at the Inn talked of blood and other horrors. Her ghoulish babbling gains more credence as the evening sucks light from the heavens.

Beware the cliffs of Bennane.

The knotted crone burbled gleefully upon the subject, and the words have taken root in his head, will not be tugged free. Now they grow with his fear, take on awful shape.

Folk disappear, lad.

A shriek swoops at him from over the lip of the crags. His heart stammers. A seabird, wailing horribly as it circles its cliff-top nest. The traveler urges his horse onward, the steady tattoo of hooves on the rough road mingling with the agitated screams of the gull. Far below, the sea pushes hungrily against the rocks.

He must reach Stranraer before dawn, and this guilty road is his only route. Why should he fear?

The gull ceases its mournful cries. The hollow trembling of the sea below... Night seizes him.

Father's shout.
Mother's scream.
"Derek, mind the road, for God's sake."
Gulls.

HOLIDAY

1972

Father's shout.

One large hand left the steering wheel, formed into a fist, swung around into the back seat, pounding the boy's right arm like a fleshy demolition ball. The Avenger veered dangerously across the coastal road.

Mother's scream.

Father twisted round again to confront a big, blue vista of sea filling the windscreen. He bore down hard right on the steering wheel. Tires screamed in agony. The car bucked madly, barely managed to cling to the narrow road, and pulled away from the cliff edge.

The boy rocked against his brother, who elbowed him viciously back onto his own side of the seat. As the car steadied itself again, the boy nursed his arm, fury building, out of control like his Dad's driving. "Bastard. *Bastard.*" He shrieked the colorful word—it sounded so good, so *right*—at the back of his father's bullish neck. Father's oversized head (Freak. *FREAK!*) began to swing toward him again.

"Derek, mind the road, for God's sake," Mother whinnied. The boy watched his father's profile as it swiveled to confront him, his bulbous left eye bloodshot with rage. The boy leaned forward and stabbed the index finger of his right hand into that mad bull's eye. Then he was scrabbling at the back door of the Avenger, ignoring the bellow of pain from his father, the frenzied octaves of his mother. The door swung open, the gray surface of the road ground past. The horizon of sea and sky beckoned him on. He took one quick look back, saw the gloating expression on his brother's young face. *Go on,* his expression read. *Do it. We all hate you. Jump.*

The boy jumped.

He hit the grassy verge at the side of the road, and the breath left him with a punch more brutal than those even his father regularly dealt him. His body rolled on, tossed by momentum, plunged through the rusty web of an old wire fence and down, down. Sea, sky, and bracken, merging crazily. Down. A rock thumped his left kidney, bounced him into the air, winded. He landed in thick ferns, his frame suddenly numb. The sea rolled closer.

Something was leaning over him, preventing him from falling farther: a tall, white object that reared incongruously up from the bracken. It rocked when he collided with it, but it did not fall. The boy wondered dimly through his pain why a refrigerator should be stuck out here on this wild slope. Perhaps the seagulls kept their fish fingers in it. Not funny. Too much *hurt.*

Unconsciousness beckoned, but he wasn't going to let it take him away. The hurt kept him alert. Far, far away it seemed, he heard his father's bellows as he searched for his son.

The boy's agony urged him to be sensible and wait here until his father found him, but his hate forbade it. Instead, he forced himself to his knees and crawled away from the rusting fridge, away from the sounds of searching.

A glimmer of sand: a beach lurked beneath the tumbling hillside. He could hide there. The bastard with the swinging, balled fists wouldn't find him there. Ever. And then they would all be sorry, he promised himself as he half-crawled, half-rolled down through the ferns onto the dirty, white beach. He thought of his mother's careworn efforts to stop the violence; the jagged bursts of fury into which his father would ignite, chasing him round the kitchen table, chasing him up the stairs, always chasing him.

And when he caught him...

Waves rolled in. Spears of sunlight glanced off rocks that rose from the beach like petrified monsters. Seaweed was strewn thickly over the sand, off-white innards bloated by the surf. Gulls mourned.

The child heard more cries from above: his father's angry voice fading, to be replaced by his mother's pleas. Was he supposed to believe she really cared? The boy wasn't going to fall for that one. He knew what would happen if he let himself be found. The rage of his father unleashed, an unstoppable thing. He considered crawling onward into the wall of waves ahead, allowing himself to float off into the glorious burst of the setting sun exploding across the sea. He inched forward, sobs chugging up from his chest.

When the surf licked at his hands and his knees, bare below his shorts, he knew he couldn't go on. The cold pulled him back from the brink. He stood shakily. The bastard mustn't find him; he must keep that thought uppermost at all times. His legs wobbled as they carried him along the shore, but the pain was not so fierce now, although his left kidney felt as if it had been flattened. But he would not cry anymore. That was all over.

As he limped on, the heather-covered slopes surrendered to sheer cliffs. Gulls rose and fell around the tops of the crags, white and gray confetti scattered by the wind. Their sad cries mingled with those of his mother, the pounding surf a steady backbeat.

The beach ended where an arm of rock pushed out into the frothing sea. Automatically, as if he must keep as much distance between himself and his parents—his *family*—as possible, he began climbing around the outcrop, and the cave was suddenly there.

He forgot to breathe. A hole like a screaming mouth gaped from between shoulders of rock in a dry, narrow inlet. Above, the cliff face bulged out into a stern forehead, sweeping up, up, so the boy had to crane his neck to follow it. His gaze leaped back to the mouth of the cave, from which a spew of boulders dribbled down a slight incline of shingle and weeds toward him. The weeds were thicker here, piled like ripped white bellies on the rocks, and the violent stink of it prised his nostrils wide. But his eyes were wider. The boulders formed an ogre's staircase leading up to adventure.

The hole pulled him. There was no choice, really; even if he had wanted to turn away, he couldn't. Not now. There was something here for him; he knew that somehow. Something special. He clambered up the boulders toward the screaming mouth, sliding and slipping over the weeds clinging like wet hair to the rocks. The crack widened to greet him as he neared it, then closed abruptly over him. The sobbing of the sea faded.

The cave was dark, and it was full of horror.

The ten-year-old could smell it. He could taste it. But he could see nothing beyond the first few yards visible in the faint light from outside. The cave opened into a fairly large chamber after the constricted opening. Then, as he groped his way onward, hands out-stretched, nothing but blackness. He felt the damp roof lower over his head and the rough walls squeeze him in as the opening chamber gave way to a narrow tunnel. Now and then, his hands would sink in-to cold emptiness as they traveled along the walls, side passages lead-ing into deeper mystery. Terror squeezed him like the walls as he ventured farther in, and he wondered why he should savor it so. He sucked it inside his lungs, breathing it deep.

And it was the best thing he had ever experienced in his life.

With the pulse of the sea distant now, he eventually reached the end of the cave. Here, he felt the tunnel open up into another cham-ber, smaller than the first, where a wall of rock prevented further progress. On an impulse, the boy squatted on the cold ground, small, alone, drinking in the delicious wine of this new fear he had dis-covered.

Bone.

He had been sitting for several minutes, his hands distractedly exploring the floor of the cave around him when his fingers slipped across the smooth, brittle object. His heart inflated with a burst of horror. His subconscious mind identified it before his rational one would dare. He tried to focus his eyes on the find, but the dark would not let him, as if the object should remain unseen, hidden.

Bone.

Yes, a bone, a special kind of bone. And it refused to pull free from the crack of rock in which it was embedded, so he applied both hands, laughing wildly.

The double row of jagged teeth rasped against his palms as he wrenched, as if nibbling his skin in welcome, or hunger. The shape of the football-sized bone seemed oddly malformed, he thought as he caressed the bulging forehead and poked his fingers into the hollow sockets, which surely were set too far apart. His special fear rode him, spurring him on, and so intent was he on his efforts that when he heard the voice, he wasn't sure at first whether it was merely the sound of his own excited breathing playing tricks on him in the cave. A drip of water from the roof, the wind beyond the cave mouth? Then it came again: his name whispered through the dampness and the dark.

He paused to listen, but only the wailing of gulls reached his ears. Had his father followed him down onto the beach, was he calling him still? But it hadn't sounded like someone calling, more like someone sighing. He returned his attention to his find and, with a final exertion, managed to pull the skull from the crevice.

He cradled it eagerly, his heart stamping so loud that it could have been the heartbeat of the cave itself. And over the beat, the whisper came once more...

A whisper coaxing him with secret words. He bent his head to the filthy jaws and listened to what they had to tell him.

Beyond the mouth of the cave, the gulls mourned ceaselessly.

The family holiday was over.

"Father..." the child breathed, sitting in the dark.

PART II: THE SLAUGHTER
1993

CHAPTER ONE

"I want the sickest film you've got," the man said.

Jack had watched him enter the video library. He was the first customer of the day (always the worst?), and Jack had never seen him before. He was quite sure of that. He wouldn't have forgotten a face like this one in a hurry. A sly face, long, and somehow uncomfortably handsome in a bitter kind of way, as if the features were only reluctantly good-looking and tried to twist themselves slightly out of true to spite the man to which they belonged. There was a flick-knife viciousness in the eyes, which were so dark as to be almost black. The cut of his thin lips was dangerous. The man's eyes slid over the tightly packed video shelves lining the narrow passage leading to the counter.

Jack took in the long, dark overcoat, the square-toed biker boots emerging from the turn-ups of his black jeans. He looked as if he'd edged violently into his thirties and was lean and sharp as a pirate's cutlass.

I don't like you, Jack thought as the stranger approached the counter. *Nope. Not at all.* He felt himself worm under the nasty chisels the man used for eyes.

The stranger slicked a blade of jet-black hair away from his eyes. There wasn't a trace of color anywhere on his body; from his frost-white face to the heels of his dark boots, he was every inch Veidt's Cesare, nightmare-walking into Jack's life. His lips tilted into a serial-killer sneer.

I REALLY *don't like you.* Jack's guts tensed, and his teeth clenched the way they always did when he found himself in circumstances he wasn't happy with.

"I don't mean just sick," the man continued in a voice laden with grave dirt. "I mean *vile.* Mind-bendingly repulsive." He spread his hands on the counter and cocked his head forward. Jack noticed how long and thin his fingers were, all rough and grimy like raw, stringy carrots, the sort of vegetable fingers you'd stuff in the sleeves of a scarecrow.

Jack summoned a cheery grin that read: *Love to help, mate, even if you are the most unappealing creep I've ever been forced to serve,* and said, "I'm afraid we don't stock mind-bendingly repulsive films, chief. Not even merely vile ones. Sorry." He *was* actually, or rather, always had been up to this point. He loved horror films. But right now he was suddenly quite happy with the situation. "This is a clean shop. No under-the-shelf nasties here." He marveled at his own smugness.

The man wiped one hand idly along the countertop, his eyes never leaving Jack's. The sneer remained. *He's going to flip into violent mode any minute.* Jack performed a rapid mental check of the video library for possible weapons with which to defend himself. Unless he was prepared to fight off the sick bastard with a copy of *BEE Movie* that leaned patiently against the computer waiting to be put to bed, there really weren't many options.

The stranger turned around to survey the shelves of the small video vault that, with its low roof, narrow passage, and subdued lighting, resembled a fox's bolthole. *I'm trapped in here,* thought Jack. *Shut in with Mister Mind-Bendingly Repulsive. How was that for typical Tuesday afternoon entertainment?*

The dark man pulled a video box down from a shelf. The naked light bulb shimmered on the plastic cover. Jack read the title and wiped his mouth nervously. *The Boogeyman.* Mister Vile weighed the box in one hand as if deliberating whether or not to rent it. Jack could feel a ring of sweat under his collar. *This is stupid. So he's unpleasant and creepy, but that doesn't necessarily make him dangerous.*

"Evisceration," the man breathed. "Decapitation. Dismemberment..." He drew out the last word lovingly as he faced Jack again, and his snarl was pure Jack-O'lantern.

Jack knew he was as pale as the stranger now. He groped for

reassuring reasons for the man's behavior... A joke? Some ridiculous gag dreamed up by his mates to freak him out? He dismissed the idea. His friends didn't have the imagination to come up with something like this.

So why was this happening to *him*? He'd never done anything to deserve this persecution. The only comforting thing he could think of was that if the man wanted to see a film, he was going to have to become a member, and to do that, he would have to do normal, mundane stuff like producing a driver's license and bank statement. Safe sort of things. Of course, he could already have joined when Jack wasn't working, but even then, he'd have to show his card, and Jack could fix something on him, like an address that would make the man just a customer and not a homicidal maniac.

"Do you think this might give me what I want?" the man waved *The Boogeyman* at Jack.

Jack steadied himself. *Get a grip, you prick.* "Depends what you're looking for, I suppose."

"I just told you what I'm looking for. Grotesque mutilation is all that will satisfy me. I'm looking for blood; I'm searching for guts."

Blood. His slug-black pupils were swollen like they were gorged with the stuff. *You're freaking yourself, Jack.*

His voice came out through a dry crack. "Well, you won't find much in that film." He was determined to keep some kind of customer-friendly slant to the conversation, to pretend he wasn't disturbed at all by the man's behavior. No way, no how. If he showed fear... The Video Shack had never seemed more like a fox hole than right now. He forced the bravado. "It's been cut, mate." *Wrong choice of words.*

"Cut?" The man might as well have slavered like a hound, he was that delighted as he closed on his prey. "Like a throat? Like an eyeball peeling before a razor?" A grim smile. "No, you mean censored, don't you? Our sanity and senses protected by moral guardians. The butchery butchered. And that's a sad irony because I'm in the mood for a little dismemberment right now. I need inspiration."

Jack looked away quickly. The man's eyes were so dark as to be impenetrable. If the man was playing, there was absolutely no way of telling. "Never mind," the stranger continued, "How's about..." He trawled along the horror section near the till and came up with a find. "This one?" He held it up for Jack. *The Mutilator.* The cover showed some backwoods retard wielding a bloody big axe.

"Nice title, don't you think? Just rolls off the tongue."

"This is a wind-up, isn't it? Either that, or you've got a serious problem." *So much for the pretense of normal customer service.* The words were meant to be bold, but Jack's voice carried an embarrassing wavering note that spoiled the illusion.

The pumpkin grin vanished. The long face tautened like a whip before the crack. Silence for a fistful of sweaty seconds while Jack swallowed dryly.

"Does it look like I've got a problem? Don't I look perfectly in control to you?" He pushed *The Mutilator* across the counter toward Jack. *By pick, by axe, by chainsaw ... Bye, bye*, the cover blared luridly at him. Jack glanced at the misanthropic hillbilly straddling the tagline and went right off the film. He'd watched it twice himself and thoroughly enjoyed it—horror films were the reason he'd chosen to work here, after all. He got to see all the latest releases free-of-charge. But he'd suddenly lost his taste for this one.

He turned his attention toward the computer sitting on the counter before him and nudged the pad on the keyboard in an attempt to defuse the situation. The customer index file flickered up on the screen. "Are you a member?" he asked with reasonable calmness. "If you want a video—mind-bendingly repulsive or otherwise—you need to be a member."

The stranger didn't answer. Jack looked up, and the man nodded once, slowly. Progress of a sort? "So, what's your name?"

Nothing. Jack drummed his fingers nervously on the keyboard, but he wasn't going to look up again. He could wait here all day, if it came to it. He was being paid to sit here.

"Bane," the dark man said finally, and his smile would have given a crocodile bad dreams. Jack looked up. He could see his own pale, lugubrious face echoed in the stranger's bulging pupils. He snatched himself back from the brink and punched the name into the computer. A response leaped up instantly: MISTER BANE, THE SLAUGHTER INN, BUCKINGHAM ROAD, BRISTOL.

Jack blinked stupidly at the entry. Maybe it *was* all a gag, after all. But if it wasn't his mates pulling this stunt, then what about Mary? Mary being the blonde Video Vault worker *Jack* had been trying to pull for the last year. The Slaughter Inn, for Christ's sake. *Mister* Bane, the man with no Christian name. Everyone had to give their Christian name. It was library policy. No exceptions. So, this *was* just a prank, after all. Of course, it was. Hilarious. He should have been annoyed, but the relief felt too good. Mary, bless her. He smiled at the dark man with confidence for the first time. Where did she find *this* geezer? He had to admit he'd fallen for it brilliantly, what with the horror-video angle and the sicko in search of a macabre fix and everything. If Mary hadn't made the joke too obvious with the Slaughter Inn gag, he'd never have cottoned on.

Except as he beamed foolishly at the dark man, he suddenly knew it *wasn't* a joke. No way, no how. Which just made the whole thing grotesque. Ghoulish.

As if reading his thoughts, the stranger pulled a pack of Death cigarettes from his coat pocket and lit one.

"I live just down the road from you. Isn't that nice and cozy?"

For a moment of pure panic, Jack was sure the man knew where he lived. Then he realized the stranger must be talking about the video shop. Buckingham Road was indeed just down the road from here. But as Jack lived roughly opposite the shop, it didn't make a whole load of difference.

"I...never heard of it," he stammered. The *Slaughter* Inn. *Jesus.* He pulled himself together and rummaged through the A–Z drawer of tapes behind the counter, found what he was looking for, and stuffed *The Mutilator* cassette into the plain plastic customer box with *Video Vault* emblazoned on it, and then pushed this across the counter to the man. The sooner he got what he wanted, the sooner he would go. Hopefully.

The man sucked hard on his Death cigarette, which was as black as his hair, and tossed three pound coins down beside the film. He scooped up the box and turned to leave. *He's going*, thought Jack, feeling like he was ten years old again and morning was coming after a long, scary night. But the stranger *wasn't* going. Not yet, anyway. He stopped halfway down the aisle and turned his unnaturally dark eyes on Jack once more.

"Tonight's Opening Night," he said, flashing Jack a farewell rictus grin. He bent his head slightly as he strode toward the door, and his boots clicked hollowly on the wooden floor.

CHAPTER TWO

Neighbours was just finishing when Dennis announced his return to the flat with the usual demonstrative slam of the door. Jack twitched awake in his black plastic armchair, the one he'd rolled a mile from where he'd found it sitting in the rain outside a house on Ravenscourt Road. Why? Because he'd fallen in love with it on sight. And he was way too tight to buy a new one. He yawned with a mixture of relief and irritation. Irritation because he'd fallen asleep in front of *Neighbours* again, and relief that Dennis was home so he could discuss the day's bizarre events with him.

"I keep telling you... This shit cheeses your brain," Dennis grunted, flopping onto the threadbare sofa and looking more than a little aggrieved that he'd missed it himself.

"I like to keep tabs on reality," Jack told him.

Dennis began to roll a cigarette, bored with the conversation already. He was a funny-looking bastard, and Jack never tired of telling him so. Although the electrician was only twenty-nine, he already had the face of a world-bitten East End villain from the 50s. His small eyes glinted only occasionally now with a fading memory of their former juvenile mischief. More often these days, they were cloaked with cynical bitterness. Back in his adolescent days, when he had something to prove, mainly that he wasn't a prick despite his name, he changed his hair color from week to week, and often he would have to bend low to get his comical spiky coiffure through doorways. That was the Dennis Jack always looked for and very rarely found of late: the manic, dare-all, bumbling rebel without a clue who was always there for his mates and always got them in trouble. In the last decade, he'd wised up, cropped his hair, and lost the joke. Now he looked like his Dad, Dennis Senior, who was also an electrician and who also resembled one of the Krays' bodyguards, but without the bitterness. Dennis's old man was a jolly, innocent soul; Dennis was dangerous.

Jack watched the Six O'Clock News for a while. Dennis said nothing. Jack guessed his old friend was already plotting some new adventure that would take him off and out of himself to some distant haven for a short period and then return him here again, more cynical and disappointed with life than ever. Four years ago, Dennis had done what Laurel and Hardy had done to more amusing effect before him and ran off to join the Foreign Legion. Ran, as in chased. The police wanted to chat with him about certain things. Petty things, on the whole. Nicked car stereos, the odd bit of B & E. Oh, and, of course, his girl had left him. The clichés made the man, but Jack wondered if he might not have done the same himself if a girl like Sam had dropped *him*.

Dennis had left his family, his friends, and his drugs far behind to find himself caught up in a nightmare of his own making. Wild adolescence had received a good kicking, and a bitter man had emerged on the other side. During the first week in the Legion, he spent every night tied up in a closet with a pair of soiled Y-Fronts for a gag as part of some disgusting initiation ceremony. Seven nights breathing in someone else's shit. *What was that like, Dennis?* Jack had often wondered. Unsurprisingly, it wasn't Dennis's favorite topic of conversation. No wonder he was a different person from the naïve, boisterous clown he used to be back in the good old carefree days. "I'll tell you one thing the Legion did for me," he once said in a matter-of-fact tone: "I'll never be scared of anything again." Jack rather envied him that quality, if nothing else.

After a year or so, Dennis found himself promoted and in charge of a tank unit ordering the shelling that obliterated a nest of Iraqi snipers in the Mother of all Wars, and he became the recipient of a Legion d'Honneur as a result. He'd come back on leave a hero. Jack always thought that was quite strange, really, when he remembered the drunken wreck Sam had turned him into by giving him the elbow a few weeks before he took off for Tangiers. They used to use him as a doorstop down at the Crown. You'd always find him lying on the floor at the end of the night (and often at the beginning) with a bottle of Famous Grouse clasped in his paw. So he came back a hero, and suddenly the sun shone where he shat. He didn't like to talk about his heroics, and Jack respected him for that. It's funny what they gave you medals for, and Dennis obviously thought so, too; he deserted while on a tour of Canada a few months later.

"Fancy going out tonight?" Jack asked his flatmate. A strange excitement had seized him ever since the dark man left the video library. His uneasiness only intensified it.

"*Coronation Street*'s on," Dennis answered without apparent irony.

"There's a new pub opening tonight in Buckingham Road. Sounds interesting." Jack stared at the *Clockwork Orange* poster on the wall above the TV, and the anticipation was thick in his belly like hot soup.

Dennis nodded wisely and puffed on his rolly[13]. Anna Ford told them about rape in Paisley and tins of dog food laced with arsenic placed in many chains of a well-known supermarket.

Jack flicked the channels with the remote control—*Batman, The Addams Family, Home and Away*—then flicked back to Anna. Baroness Thatcher was shaking hands with Jimmy Saville. "Something pretty scary happened today..." Jack trailed off. It wasn't that interesting to anyone but himself, really, as evidenced by Dennis's total lack of response. Saville's face filled the TV screen. "Twisted bastard tried to put the frighteners on me," he continued regardless. "And then invited me to his pub's opening night." He mimicked Saville's creepy voice. "'Ow's about that, then? And wait 'til you hear the name of the place..." Dennis gave all the signs of being able to wait a very long time, so Jack put him out of his misery: "The Slaughter Inn. Crazy, eh?"

Dennis turned his head slowly to look at him, then turned back to the television. Jack's pulse was quickening just from saying it aloud. Alex the Droog met his gaze from the poster on the wall. One eye winked at him, laden with false eyelashes.

"Just as long as it's dangerous," Dennis mumbled around his roll-up. "I need some danger tonight. I need reminding I'm still alive, now and again." Which sounded pretty funny when he'd just been looking forward to *Coronation Street*. He exhaled smoke at the TV screen, obscuring a particularly hideous political correspondent. "And as long as there's women. I don't care what sort, just as long

---

[13] Hand-rolled cigarette

as there's some sort."

"You never know your luck, Dennis; Sam might even turn up."

Dennis yawned to show his huge indifference to the subject of his ex. "Better make sure I get into a beery mess, then; I wouldn't want her to think I'm getting all civilized these days."

While Dennis lumbered about in the bath, Jack made a couple of phone calls. The night was definitely beginning to sound promising; Joe was free from delivering pizzas that evening and would see them there, so Jack wouldn't have to cope with Dennis alone. He thought of ringing Nigel but decided he wanted to enjoy himself for once. So he phoned Sam instead, after first making sure Dennis couldn't hear a thing; the ex-Legionnaire didn't take much provoking these days.

Sam was doe-eyed, svelte, possessed the most luscious mouth in the known universe, as well as mahogany curls that ivied down around her small, perfectly shaped face. Along with Mary from the Video Vault, she was the most eminently desirable female Jack had never gone out with. He'd kissed Sam once at a Christmas party when Dennis was unconscious in the toilet, and he'd remembered the taste of her ever since. She'd made it quite plain the next day that it was a drunken kiss only and gave him the "just a friend" speech. But he'd never given up hoping. She'd dumped Dennis when she realized he was an electrician with an attitude and was never going to change, and there was no reason why a video clerk should have any better luck. But he would never give up, even if Dennis had wisely seemed to do just that long ago. She was dating a property developer these days. Jack hoped she wouldn't bring him along tonight.

"Oh, it's you, Jack," her voice purred along the line.

Don't sound so thrilled, he thought, but batted on regardless. Yes, she agreed finally, she would come: The Slaughter Inn sounded pretty off the wall. She asked Jack if he minded her bringing Thomas ("My name's Thomas, *not* Tom") along, too. "Of course not," Jack answered in a strangled voice. The telephone went dead to her husky Honor Blackman farewell.

He took his place in the bathroom. Dennis had left him a gift. No, he'd been more than generous and left him two: one unflushed in the toilet bowl that greeted Jack as he lifted the lid to take a leak, and another made of pubic hairs forming a nest in the bath as he stepped in to take a shower. He whizzed the wiry hairs along the bottom of the bath and down the drain with the shower head, then turned the lukewarm jet on himself, the water becoming rapidly colder with each second, just so he wouldn't forget Dennis's third gift.

He wiped the steam from the mirror and examined himself as he toweled his body. *Hey, good lookin'.* Well, almost, if you were *especially* forgiving, as his mother used to say in her tired way. It was the closest she'd ever come to joking with him, and with the memory came a sense of wry pain. But she was right; his face was a little too long and his nose a little too large for him to win many beauty contests, but hell, it showed character, didn't it? Maybe a dash of gaunt attractiveness if he held his head at a certain angle. His brown eyes held a slightly lost look. "Is that acid casualty with the bewildered hair a friend of yours?" a female wit once asked Dennis in a pub. His flatmate had taken particular delight in repeating *that* one to anyone who would listen for the next six months.

Jack entered his bedroom and began drying his hair. Whenever he tried to impose a style onto it, he failed miserably. Its natural state was a brambly anarchy, and short of cropping it completely, there was no way of getting around that fact. He reached into the wardrobe and chose his favorite shirt—a black, silky number fraying slightly at the cuffs and collars from overuse—and pulled on a clean pair of crisp black jeans. He made an abortive effort to brush some order into his hair and gave up when it looked worse than before he'd started.

"Hurry up, ladyboy," Dennis hollered from the hallway, already opening the door to the flat.

Jack shouldered his way into his leather jacket, hunching it around until it felt good. He patted the twenty quid note stuffed in his back pocket and joined his friend at the door. Dennis looked him over with undisguised amusement, a roll-up jammed between his lips. He was dressed in his usual casual get-up of brown suede jacket and faded blue jeans. "Where d'you think *you're* going? The High School Prom?"

"If I am, I don't think much of my date." He was ready.

For the Slaughter.

The phrase repeated itself inside his head as he strode down Southley Road and turned onto Buckingham, while Dennis stomped moodily along at his side.

CHAPTER THREE

Thomas arrived early. It was an annoying habit of his. No, strike that; it was one of many annoying habits. Sam hadn't finished applying her make-up, and she did not want to have to do it while he prowled around her small flat, distracting her with inane comments like: "Still slapping the cement on, Samantha?" She *hated* being called Samantha. He only called her that when he was in an irritable mood. Well, that made two of them now.

"Why don't you make yourself a coffee and watch telly for a bit." She knew that would get him; he hated waiting.

His expression clearly showed what he thought of that idea. "You said you'd be ready by eight," he said reproachfully.

"It's only ten to. Sit in the lounge and stop panting down my neck." She watched his reflection in the dressing table mirror. He was rooted behind her now, staring at her back, and it didn't look like he was going to shift. "Please?" He wavered, hands in the trouser pockets of his Armani suit. It *had* to be Armani. Thomas never liked to disappoint in the unoriginality stakes. He was almost at the door when he turned back.

"Are you sure you want to go to this pub?" he said, leaning against the bedroom door jamb.

Sam sighed and put her eye pencil down. He wasn't going to give her any peace. "Of course. It sounds a laugh."

"It sounds like torment. It'll be full of ugly people with bare armpits and music to make your head bleed."

She regretted asking him along now, but who the hell else could she have turned to? Her best friend Sue was out with her boyfriend (as usual), and she couldn't go on her own. No, she had to drag Thomas with her, if only to spite Dennis and show Jack she always had *someone* on her arm. But that suit...

"Couldn't you have come more casually dressed? How many times have I told you to loosen up? There'll be nobody there *you'll* want to impress."

"I *am* loosened up. And I don't need to impress anybody. I just like to look good. What's wrong with that?"

"You'll look stupid." She picked up her lipstick and tried to dismiss her irritation. It was a hard job. She could see it staring back at her in the mirror. There must have been a time when he didn't annoy her, but she'd be damned if she could remember when that was. But she only had herself to blame. What did it say about her that she needed to go out with people like Thomas? Self-centered high achievers who liked control. Did it make her feel in control, too, to run with the ruthless executive set, when all she would ever be to them was just another asset? Is that what she really wanted?

He was fidgeting with the door handle now, pushing it down and allowing it to spring back up again noisily with the impatience of all greedy people. He obviously had something on his mind. She could wait.

"When are you going to grow out of them, Samantha?" he said after a pause.

She put down her lipstick. There it was. It had been a long time coming, but it was something between them they both knew was there, although neither had openly acknowledged the fact before. It had been gnawing away at him ever since he met her. Now, at last, he was letting it out. She turned around, and he was pouting sulkily the way he always did when he didn't get what he wanted. His sweptback, pure Gecko hairstyle had a little too much Brylcreem, his eyes were a little *too* sweet, his chin a little too infirm, she thought, and wondered why it had taken her so long to see it, or so long to admit it. Tonight, she could see him naked and it wasn't as appealing as it used to be. He was a selfish little boy, and she was growing tired of little boys.

He waited for her to respond. When she didn't, he pushed on regardless: "I mean, they're not exactly your type, are they? They've got no style. No class."

She considered stopping him right there but decided to let him run on, have his little say. Then she could have hers.

"I mean, what *are* they exactly? An electrician with a criminal record, a rental clerk who gets off on video nasties...and a pizza delivery man, for Christ's sake! Worse, a pizza delivery man who thinks he's Brian fucking Jones. It's as if they're all competing to see who has the worst job. You should have moved on, Sam. You really should. A long time ago. You're just clinging to them from some deluded sense of—I really don't know what—surely not loyalty? It's embarrassing. They probably despise you anyway for trying to improve yourself. They're really not your problem anymore. You've got new friends, a different set. Let them go."

She crossed her arms, her face expressionless. "All done?"

He shrugged, but she noticed he couldn't look her in the eye. He had been compelled to say it, she could see that, and now that he *had* said it, she could suddenly see just how big the block really was he carried on his shoulder.

"They threaten you, don't they?"

He met her eyes; they were small, bewildered, and, yes, a little afraid. He put on a complacent grin. "Yeah, hell, I just can't compete..."

"That's just it; they worry you because *they* don't *have* to compete. They don't think a fat salary and a fast car are that big a deal, and that really *bothers* you, doesn't it? That sort of undermines everything you believe in." She got up, and she was feeling good for the first time in... Yes, she was feeling—what? Clean. She eased into her black suede jacket. "And you're wrong. They might be beer-guzzling slobs, they might never be achievers, and they might not speak with the right accents, but they'll *always* have class. It's something you wouldn't understand. Now, take me to the ball; we're late."

She swept past him down the short hallway to the door of her flat. He stayed where he was for a minute, digesting everything she'd said. She looked at him quizzically and realized she didn't have to worry about rushing back before midnight; the pumpkin had already appeared, and she was taking him with her.

"History and present day collide, and in the pandemonium that follows, Darke has crafted a quality narrative that is both comedic and dripping with tension. An entertaining folk horror tale a thousand years in the making."
— Dave Jeffery, author of *Tooth & Claw* and *A Quiet Apocalypse*

LEO DARKE

PANDEMONIUM

Book One in the *101 Ways to Hell Series*

Part One
The Guide Book

Chapter One
I Hate Pink Floyd t-Shirt

Billy was listening to an album of Pink Floyd cover tracks when the aggressive thumping at the door roused him from his chair.

He'd nicked the CD off the cover of the latest edition of *Mojo;* or rather, it had eased itself away from its meager gum fastenings and into his hand. Practically fell off. Listening to it now, to the various bands' interpretations of "Wish you Were Here" on this Tuesday in mid-April, he was reminded of two things: how much he loved the original tracks, and a t-shirt once worn by Johnny Rotten. He forgot all about these conflicting lines of thought when the ferocious banging on the door made him move to the laced net curtain to peep out. Another random thought occurred to him as he did so, about being caught "peeping," this one courtesy of material from Mickey Flanagan, the cockney stand-up comedian—because the lace didn't completely cover the left-hand corner of the lounge window and the "peepee" could see Billy peeping from his position outside the front door.

The sense of calm created by the music, vanished. He knew this visit must have something to do with Aura before he even reached the window and saw the thug standing there.

The man was in his early forties, stocky, wearing a scruffy, brown hoody and dirty jeans. His face was brutal and slightly deformed in a way that was difficult to pinpoint; there was something about the cast of the features that didn't sit quite right. And as he glared at Billy through the pane of glass, his expression certainly didn't hint that he was calling around to check the meter. The man jerked his head toward the door. *Open it, you fucker.*

If the man had something to tell him about Aura, then Billy wanted to hear it, despite his feeling that the man wasn't bearing good news. As he stepped into the short hall to open the door, he wondered if he'd pushed it just a little too far with her. As soon as he opened the door, he knew he had.

The man's dark hair was tousled and messy. It looked like he had a blotch of moss growing on one cheek, but it was probably paint, as he looked like a painter and decorator, albeit one potentially born in Innsmouth… His slightly askew eyes were menacing and dark.

"You Billy?" The voice was guttural, and a thick country accent dragged at the words.

Billy nodded, a clench of unease right in the middle of his gut. The Pink Floyd tribute album was still playing (a band he'd never heard of called Beak had reached "Welcome to the Machine").

The thug cleared his throat. "I'll tell ya this once. Don't try to contact Aura no more. No calls, no messages, nothin'." He ticked off the instructions on his fingers as he spoke.

Billy stood there in his socks and an insubstantial Judas Sinned t-shirt and bristled. "I just want to know she's all right," he protested. He sounded like a stalker, even to himself now, though he knew it wasn't like that.

The thug took a step closer. "I'll say it again: you keep away. You don't try to find her, you don't try to contact her."

He wasn't going to get any info out of this oaf. Billy's anger overcame his desperation to know more. "Who the fuck are you coming to my house and threatening me?"

The thug moved with terrific speed. He actually growled in fury as he lunged at Billy with demented eyes. The shock of the charge took

Billy completely by surprise. He was bowled over and landed on his back in his own hallway while the thug slammed a big army boot down on his chest, effectively pinning him there. The man had wigged out big time. He tried to rain punches down on Billy's face and would have caused some real damage were it not for the narrowness of the hall impeding his blows. Unfortunately, the close walls prevented Billy from rolling away to either side, too, trapping him on his back beneath the boot that was now grinding viciously into his chest. He managed to deflect the majority of punches with his own hands, which just infuriated the thug even more.

The man was grunting and cursing as he gave in to his inexplicable hatred. "You cunt, you *cunt!*" he spat repeatedly as he stomped and punched. Billy strove unsuccessfully to push upward against the weight, "Shine on You Crazy Diamond" playing now through the open door to the lounge. Maybe the thug, like Rotten before him, hated Pink Floyd, too. Maybe Billy should have been playing the Cockney Rejects instead. At least he would have been in the mood for a scrap. As it was, he was only conscious of three things now: what in the name of hell the neighbors would be making of all this and what state his designer t-shirt would be in after the unprecedented wear and tear. The third consideration bothered him the most however: for Aura to send this animal around to warn him off (and there didn't seem to be any other explanation than that she'd sent him), he must have seriously pissed her off. There could be no going back after this. And that hurt more than anything this psychotic ape could do to him, and it also drained any desire to fight back. His anger and inability to accept the abruptness of her distancing herself from him had resulted in this. The flurry of unanswered calls he'd made to her mobile number certainly could be construed as unreasonable—and desperate. Nobody liked desperate. Billy had never before done desperate. This is what it tasted like. This was the fruit it bore. Billy was ashamed: this was conclusive proof that he'd blown it for good. She obviously never wanted to see him again.

"Get the fuck off me!" Billy managed to gasp as the boot continued to bear down on him, cutting off his breath. Then, a little more lamely: "The neighbors will have called the cops by now!"

The thug didn't respond to either utterance. His fists continued to try to mar Billy's unremarkable good looks, but the close walls continued to hamper him from getting a proper swing. Billy grasped the man's boot and tried to twist it off his chest, but his position gave him no leverage. "You *fucking* cunt!" the thug elaborated on his previous litany, and then suddenly lifted his boot and turned to go.

Billy pushed himself up on one elbow, stunned by the whole unpleasant, albeit surreal, experience. The man was about to step out of the house, his back to Billy. Billy jumped to his feet, adrenaline coursing through him, and shoved the man from behind, propelling him through the doorway. "Get the fuck out of my house!" he yelled this time. It was the thug's turn to be caught by surprise, and he stumbled over the doormat, allowing Billy to slam the door after him.

He stood there panting for a minute, trying to understand everything that had just happened. He jumped as a terrific crash jarred the wooden door in its jamb. That heavy boot had been put to good purpose again. Billy tensed, waiting to see if his assailant would repeat the kick, but there was silence from outside.

His thoughts were manic quicksilver crazy. He had not been prepared for a fight. He was in his socks, for God's sake! And Pink Floyd was not the most aggressive of soundtracks. He certainly didn't feel inspired to chase out after the man. But he knew he had to.

He darted toward the closet, searching for his All Saints mock army boots. He shouldered his way into a leather jacket for added measure, finished doing up the laces, and made for the door again, collecting a poker from the fireplace as he went. Surely the bastard would have disappeared by now, he hoped (and was that why he had taken so long to do up his boot laces? Was he actually just a coward who didn't deserve Aura in the first place?) and yet simultaneously didn't hope. With the thug gone, his last connection with Aura would be gone, too.

When he opened the door, there was no sign of the malevolent visitor outside on the street. But Billy could see his next-door neighbors approaching along the pavement. So they had missed the entire show then. That was something, he supposed. He really didn't want to have to explain why he was brawling with a stranger in his own doorway. The neighbors on the other side of Billy's terraced house were always out during the day, so that didn't matter.

He crossed the street to avoid the approaching neighbors, conscious of the poker clutched in his fist. He marched quickly to the side street on the right, wondering if the thug had nipped down there, but apart from the back of an old pick-up truck disappearing around the corner at the end, there was no sign of anybody.

He hesitated, realized his breath was pent up after the fury of the attack, and released it. He honestly felt more disappointed than relieved. Aura was gone. He'd lost her forever. All the phone calls to her voice mail over the last two weeks, the messages he'd left—his concern and agitation increasing with each one, until the dreaded "desperate" kicked in when she hadn't replied to any of them—had left him here, on this street corner with no answers, an aching chest where a size ten boot had ground, a bruise on his chin from the constant flailing fists, and a poker in his hand. What a hero.

He turned and made his way back to his house. The tumult of emotions the violent visitor had unleashed was beginning to ebb. The shock fading, replaced by despair. That was it then. Should he hate her for sending this (speed-fueled?) slightly deformed crazy to his house? Could he hate her? *Did he even know her?* The answer to that had to be no. He had no idea where she lived or any detail about her past whatsoever. The last time he'd seen her, two weeks ago in the elegant grounds of Tortworth Court, she had run away inexplicably. But if this attack proved one thing, it was that she had appalling taste in acquaintances. He remembered that afternoon, dusk creeping over the mansion house and the ornate gardens…and recalled what else he'd seen there among the gathering shadows of the trees. He remembered his unease, too. *No, it had been real FEAR, not unease; don't hide from the truth, sunshine.* He had been distinctly scared. And now this: violence and strangeness seemed to follow Aura around. Perhaps he was better off rid of her after all.

If only it was that easy, he told himself as he withdrew the keys to his house. If forgetting could only be that easy... His neighbors were letting themselves in next door. He nodded politely, his attention distracted by the dirty boot print on the white door. Was that to be Aura's legacy? Was that all he had to remind him of her charms? That, and the whistle of course... He could hear it now, as he closed the door behind him, and his overworked heart kicked into overdrive for the second time that day. The CD had run its course, and the house was otherwise silent, apart from the tuneless warbling. It was faint today. Sometimes it seemed to be coming from right behind him, loud and sharp, and, of course, there was never anybody there when he turned around. He froze in the hallway, the same hallway where ten minutes earlier he'd been sprawled on his back defending himself from a manic assailant, and listened to the indistinct whistle. It was always the same three notes, protracted, eerie, relentless. Right now it was trembling on the edge of inaudibility, wistful as a half-remembered dream, fading, fading... gone. He breathed again, the tension that seized him each time he heard the whistle easing away. There had been far worse times. He could handle it in the daytime. It was a very different matter when he heard it alone at night...

This was Aura's other legacy, of course. The one that had followed him since he had first met her, and which was beginning to drive him mad. The jury was still out whether the whistle was all in his head, just like the budding relationship with Aura seemed to have been.

He sat in his armchair and wondered where it had all gone wrong.

Chapter Two
Not the AA Guide Book to
101 Best British Walks

She was standing in the travel section, looking at a guide book to British Walks.

Billy had never seen her or the book before, and his attention was aroused immediately. Not by the book—he worked in a bookshop all day every day for God's sake and was surrounded by the buggers—but by the beautiful creature holding it.

She was slender as a water nymph, tall, maybe five-eight. Long, sleek legs in tight blue jeans and knee-length fawn boots. Her poncho was fawn, too, swaddled around her slight figure as if she was really feeling the late March chill. Her long, blonde hair fell in waves around her elfin face. She felt his gaze on her even from ten meters away and looked up.

Billy felt a shock vibration jolt him, as if he'd just stumbled into a live cattle wire. Her eyes held his for a moment, kaleidoscope-blue flecked with a mosaic of gray. The gaze was lost and wild, and even in that first moment of meeting, he saw the conflict there, an excitement mixed with sadness. She smiled shyly at him, dropped her gaze back to the book. Billy was already moving, stepping briskly toward her, no idea what he was going to say, just more convinced than he'd ever been about anything in his life before that he had to go and say *something*.

He paused at a loaded trolley that was next to her, waiting for the travel bookseller to shelve its contents. She looked up again and flashed that winsome smile, and Billy could see that her teeth were white and slightly sharp, although the side molars were slightly (ever so *slightly*) uneven. Now that he was close to her, he could see that her nose was a trifle prominent, too, though not unattractively so. It was shaped in a seductive curve rather than being oversized. And anyway, what was it they said about imperfection? It accentuated the beauty of everything else or some such bollocks. But it did in her case. It really did. And she was, startlingly, self-consciously beautiful.

Billy rested both hands on the edge of the trolley, trying to affect a nonchalant air. Now that he was here, he was a fish gulping on a beach. Stranded by foolishness, totally out of his comfort zone. Her electric eyes didn't waver, scrutinizing him…measuring him. But for what? But it was more than that, too. There was a quality to those eyes that stirred more than obvious attraction in him, teasing away at something beneath the surface of his memory that had been long buried. He could see the same suggestion of recognition in her gaze, too. But that was ridiculous. He'd never seen her before in his life.

"Hello," he said after the silence began to become unnatural, even if, for some reason, not awkward.

She smiled again in answer, her cheeks showing the slightest hint of a blush.

He wrenched his gaze away from hers and looked down at the hardback book in her hands instead. It looked old and battered, and he guessed it must have been in the shop a long time to be in such a well-used state. Her right hand obscured part of the title, but he could make out most of it: *The Olde British Guide to 101 Walkes through…* The rest was hidden. Were the extra E's a sign of when it had been written or just a postmodern affectation, he wondered. The book was fat, the dust jacket tattered, and she was holding it open at Walk No. 21, he noticed.

"Walk 21… Where does that take you?" he asked, and immediately felt foolish. It was his turn to blush.

Again the long, measuring gaze before she answered. And when she did, her voice was quiet and soft, with the slightest tremor of a West Country burr. "I expect it will take you exactly where you need it to."

He laughed. What kind of answer was that? Was she a little touched? Instead of deterring him, however, this hint of eccentricity only intrigued him more.

"And what does that mean?"

"It means whatever you want it to."

Ooookayyyy. He grunted in amusement. "Enigmatic, eh?"

She tilted her head coquettishly. "Me, or the book?"

Where the hell did he go from here? Everything she said seemed to pull the rug from under his feet. He realized a female member of the staff was watching them chat from the till by the door, but he refused to acknowledge her. *Julie, damn her.* Always watching him, flirting blatantly and sometimes inappropriately, and while normally he received her attentions gracefully but with no real interest, right now he really didn't want her interfering. In an effort to make it look as though he was helping a customer and not trying it on with an attractive female, he reached for the book as if to offer the blonde girl some advice.

"May I?" he said.

She handed it over readily enough without a word, and he glanced at the page she'd been studying.

WALK NO. 21. DEEPEST, DARKEST SOMERSET

Beneath the title there was a paragraph of text written in old-fashioned English, followed by a sketchy map of a circular walk, and beneath that, a step-by-step guide on how to follow the route.

"Interesting, isn't it?"

He looked up. She stepped around the trolley to peer over his shoulder at the book, and he breathed in her scent. A faint aroma of blossom clung to her. It stirred his senses, quickened his pulse, and again, there was a vague memory associated with it that was just out of reach.

She took the book from him, closed it, and looked up earnestly. "It's very old. How wonderful to find such a book in a shiny, new shop like this."

He was still trying to catch a glimpse of the rest of the title, but again, those beautiful, slender fingers were obscuring it.

For lack of anything better to say he mumbled, "It *is* very old. Obviously been thumbed through a lot. Looks more like an old library book than something we would stock. I shall have to order in some newer copies." As conversational gambits went, this one was pretty dull, so he pushed on with: "Do you walk in Somerset a lot then?" It was better than "Do you come here often?" but only marginally.

"Oh, yes. I spend all my time in deepest Somerset."

He felt another thrill at the delightful accent that furred her words. He suddenly longed to hold her, to breath that May blossom aroma in deep, and nuzzle the long, pale neck. She was so close he could snatch her in his arms right now and not care about what anyone thought. Not even Julie, who, he noticed, was still watching them, a look of intense irritation on her face.

"Maybe I'll take a walk there myself," he said.

Her smile dropped, and she stared at him earnestly. There was confusion in her eyes now. She pursed her lips. "Yes," she said hesitantly. Her gaze fell for a second. "Maybe you should."

"Maybe even Walk number 21," he added.

Her eyes locked on his again. There was no trace of playfulness now. She looked deadly serious. She said nothing but held his gaze until he looked away, puzzled by her intensity. Over the blonde's shoulder, he could see Julie moving around from behind the till, her attention still fixed on him and the girl, her expression dark. Over in the Sports section, Jerry was watching them, too, a cynical sneer on his face as he paused in his shelving task. The blonde was oblivious to the reaction she was causing amongst Billy's colleagues, however. She stepped away from Billy and over to the tall stack of Travel books. She popped the book into a vacant slot in the British Isles section (next to an *AA Guide to Country Walks*, he noticed) and turned to face Billy again. The smile was back, shy, tentative.

Julie Everly was watching Billy alright. Oh yes. The *fucker!*

Didn't take much to distract him, did it? Blonde hair, good legs, and blue eyes. In fact, everything Julie *herself* had. What was so special about this tart, she wondered as she moved out from behind the till, ignoring the old lady who was approaching with a book to purchase. She stepped closer to find out exactly how much flirting was going on. The bastard usually saved it for Julie, even if (being *brutally* honest with herself) she knew deep down he wasn't that interested. Didn't stop him from responding to her insinuations and obvious desire for him, though, did it? He'd given her enough signals that one day he might give in and take her out. Julie had persuaded herself that the only reason he'd deferred 'til now was because she had a boyfriend. But hadn't she made it clear what a waste of time and space this particular boyfriend was? She'd certainly told Billy enough times, for God's sake. How he never paid her attention, never took her anywhere, never treated her. Just came home from work and watched sports on the TV. What kind of relationship was that? Julie wanted more. She sensed that in Billy there was real potential boyfriend material. Billy wouldn't settle for watching the soaps and maybe once in a blue moon (or even once a fortnight, if she was lucky) slipping her a quick one before falling asleep, as if the act had bored him into unconsciousness.

She saw him break off his flirting with the "special" customer as he became aware Julie was watching him, and she marched quickly over to where Jerry, the tall, skinny Scouse was making a poor imitation of a bookseller shelving stock.

"Look at him," she hissed. "Bastard hasn't done any work since she walked in."

Jerry smirked. "Don't blame him. She's a belter."

Julie glared at him. "What's so special about her?!"

"Let me see..." Jerry paused dramatically. "Sophisticated, slim, great legs, long, blonde hair—"

"*I've* got long, blonde hair!"

"—pretty."

Julie gaped at him. That hurt. "You wanker!"

"That I am," Jerry agreed cheerfully, a wicked grin on his face. "And proud of it. But to be honest..." he trailed off as he studied Billy from across the shop. "I don't know why you're so into him. He's not exactly Josh Hartnett." Indeed, he wasn't. Billy was in his late thirties, tall enough, slim enough without being skinny (unlike himself, Jerry thought ruefully), and his face was pleasant and reasonably good looking, and yes, he still had his hair (unlike himself, Jerry thought even more ruefully.) But really, he wasn't all *that*. "Face it Julie," the Scouse continued cruelly, "he ain't interested."

"Fuck *you!*"

"No, thanks. We already did that, remember?"

"You really are a twat, aren't you?"

He smiled smugly at her. "I think you've got a customer."

She turned to see the old lady waiting patiently at the till. She sighed and stormed over to serve her.

Billy stared at the mysterious blonde. He didn't know what else to do or say. He couldn't move, couldn't think of anything beyond this beautiful girl who seemed to trigger so many impulses inside him, some of them completely inexplicable.

"What's your name?" he said simply. His attempts at flirtation were gone. He was serious now, as serious as she had been a moment ago when he mentioned the Walk. He *needed* to know.

"Aura," she said, and then she was gone.

It wouldn't be the first time she would walk out on him, and he would soon become familiar with her disappearances. That is, until the final, most devastating one of all. But right now, it felt like the sun had died in his world. He watched her leave the shop, walking past Julie without looking back, and everything in this corporate bookstore suddenly seemed meaningless and mundane.

She was gone, and Julie was heading for him instead. What kind of poor substitute was that? Then, ashamed of his lack of charity, he summoned a smile for his colleague. To his surprise, she turned her head away, blanking him, and strode purposefully away across the shop. Going to report him to the manager for flirting with pretty customers maybe? *Jealous mare.*

Billy sighed, and then he remembered the book. He crossed over to the shelf where Aura (and wasn't that a great name?) had replaced it. For a moment, he couldn't find it. There was the *AA Guide to Country Walks*, but next to it was a book on farming. Maybe he hadn't watched carefully enough when she put it back. He stepped back and scanned the rows of books. All sorts of walking guides—circular paths around Bath, around Bristol, even around Portishead, but none dedicated to Somerset. And they were all paperbacks, too. Not a hardback in sight.

He scratched his head. Weird.

Slightly confused, he turned away from the Travel section, ready for his lunch break.

It was as he was crossing the shop that he heard the whistle for the first time. It was faint, almost submerged under the classical music playing over the shop's speaker system, and he didn't think too much about it. It was probably some old fool whistling out in the central hub of the Galleries, the shopping mall complex the bookshop belonged to. So he promptly forgot all about it and hurried over to the staff room door before any customers could stop him with a request.

An hour later, as he let himself back out onto the shop floor, his stomach full of tomato soup and cheese sandwiches, he heard it again. A little louder this time.

He searched around for whoever could be producing it. The shop floor was fairly busy with Friday afternoon shoppers, but he couldn't see anyone whistling.

The flat, tuneless warble seemed to be coming from over by the Erotica alcove, where the dirty old men hid to read the pornographic photography books (Frank, the portly security guard attached to the shop had caught a middle-aged man actually pleasuring himself there once; it was no wonder the female staff were calling for the section to be moved to a more conspicuous location), but when Billy leaned over the balcony on the raised section overlooking the alcove, there was nobody there.

A little disconcerted, Billy put it to the back of his mind and headed for the Travel section again, thoughts of Aura more appealing than those of a bodiless whistle. He was determined to find the book now that lunch was out of the way, and this time, it didn't take him very long to track it down.

The classical music pumping around the shop came to a stop as the CD was changed, and in the sudden silence, the whistle was clearer, louder. It seemed to be coming from all around him, the three protracted notes changing interminably. Probably an electrical fault with the speakers, he decided and focused his attention on the book, the spine of which he could now see clearly—right next to the *AA Guide to Country Walks*, where it should be. He pulled it out carefully and glanced at the cover. It bore the illustration of a path meandering through typical English countryside, the meadows and hills simply sketched. But it was the title that riveted him. The piping whistle swelled in his ears as he read it:

THE OLDE BRITISHE GUIDE TO 101 WALKES
THROUGH…

And if he'd expected the location to be Somerset, he was in for a surprise. For some reason (maybe it was the creepy whistling), the word that was no longer concealed by Aura's slender fingers chilled him right down to the marrow. It was probably a publisher's whacky attempt at humor, maybe referring to the difficulties experienced by ramblers finding the right paths through overgrown terrains. Probably. Maybe. But (and he couldn't, for the life of him, explain why) he didn't think so.

The word Aura had hidden was HELL.

INTERLUDE ONE
ROMAN BRITON, 364 AD

"Enough of your complaints! We have a job to do, so let's do it before this squad is whittled away even more by Celtic demons."

The squad of battered and filthy legionaries regarded their centurion with distaste that bordered on rebellion. If it hadn't been for the fact they were stuck in this heathen island of dark forests filled with creeping, savage Britons and no way of returning to their homeland, they would have long ago gutted their leader with his own *gladius*.

The squad originally consisted of ten legionaries. The troop's original leader, the *Decanus* with whom they had exercised and drilled, not to mention shared every night in their squad tent for the last eighteen months, had been replaced for this mission by a more experienced centurion, and they were missing their erstwhile commander with each hour they had to spend in this new bastard's company. He wasn't a bad man, and that was his problem; he was far *too* dedicated. He obviously believed in this crazy suicide mission, probably because he had one eye on promotion. They'd already lost three men in sneak attacks, and while that wasn't the centurion's fault, it was clear to everyone but him that this mission was doomed to failure.

They glared up at him now as they sat on the damp grass and rocks of the small clearing, shivering from the cold and the gloom and the incipient threats of attack from the depths of the forest.

Laccus Sciro, a stocky, swarthy legionary with a foul temper and a cruel sense of humor, regarded the tall centurion with barely guarded contempt. Of course, this quill pusher of a centurion hadn't allowed them to light a fire. Their old *Decanus* would have. He would have brought an amphora of good Roman wine along for the trip, too. Which was probably why the poor bastard had been replaced with this Ceasar's arse-licking fucker instead.

Sciro turned to the soldier beside him, ignoring the centurion. "A real fucking mess," he muttered darkly, not quite loudly enough for the officer to hear. "This bastard's leading us to certain death. We just going to take it?"

His friend, Antoni Martus, shrugged, glancing at their leader hostilely. He was lithe, with sneaky features and a prominent nose. He spat in the grass without answering.

"What was that, Sciro?"

The centurion stepped toward the bulky legionary, one hand on the hilt of his sword. His face was set and hard. He would not take *any* more bullshit from this pack of lazy scum.

Sciro glowered up at his leader. "Nothin'."

The centurion stiffened. This was just another example of their disrespectful attitude toward authority. If they were back in camp and a common infantryman had addressed his officer in such a manner, he would have been cleaning the barracks for three months. Why the hell had they given him this bunch of insolent, not to mention indolent, gamblers and whoremongers to do such an important job? It was almost as if the *Pilus Prior* who had delegated them for this mission had known it was doomed to failure and didn't want to waste his best men. But what did that say about the centurion? He believed in this job even if nobody else did, and he was going to do his damnedest to prove the *Pilus* wrong and complete the mission as planned.

He kept his hand meaningfully on the sword hilt. There was a long silence while the two Romans glared at each other.

Eventually, Sciro lowered his eyes. "Nothing… *sir.*"

"Then get on your feet. Now!"

The seven legionaries climbed up slowly and reluctantly, their bodies tired and aching from the long march through this hellish forest and the incessant cold and rain.

Sciro was last up. He withdrew his sword from its scabbard as if to check it was clean and dry. His eyes met the centurion's as he did so, and they locked gazes for another handful of seconds. The officer's hand was still on the hilt of his own weapon. The other soldiers fell silent, watching the conflict of wills eagerly, wondering who would make the first move.

Sciro grinned wolfishly and then slowly, so slowly, sheathed his sword in its scabbard. He scratched at the two days' worth of stubble on his jowls and watched as the officer nodded abruptly, then turned away to continue the march.

He led them on through the dripping trees. Mostly oak and ash, thick boughs and trunks making the darkness of night that much darker, more threatening. Painted Celts could be lurking behind every bole, waiting to skewer them with their primitive javelins and swords.

Sciro, last in line, was no longer grinning as he glanced furtively around him at the impenetrable gloom. He hated Briton. Hated it with a passion. No wonder the indigenous people were so wild and barbaric, so utterly savage. They lived out their brutal existence squatting in mud huts and praying to dark Gods while Sciro's countrymen back home erected magnificent palaces, temples, and cities that were glorious testimonies to their advanced civilization. What did these pigs have that could rival those achievements? He gritted his teeth. Megalithic monuments and arcane stone circles. It was pathetic, and it stirred a deep hatred in his soul. If it hadn't been for the stubborn refusal to accept Roman civilization into their lives—to accept *sophistication*, for fuck's sake—he could have been deployed back to Rome years ago. Back to the warmth, the wine, the food, the women of Rome.

He thought of the women here. Mud streaked, clad in filthy, stinking furs, their hair crawling with lice, their teeth snaggled (if they had any), their bodies gristly and sharp-boned. It was no wonder some of the legionaries turned to each other for sexual comforts. Not that Sciro would ever stoop to *that*, of course. He would wait until he got back to Rome, and then he would spend all his *sestertii* on the elegant ladies of the most beautiful city in the world.

But right now he was squelching through mud, with a biting wind penetrating his tunic, his head aching from lack of sleep, his balls itching from wet leggings, and wishing the centurion would trip in the dark and fall down one of the various clefts and gullies that riddled this endless forest. Now *that* was an idea…

Ahead of him, the puny form of Aurelius Piccano halted momentarily to adjust his sandals, causing Sciro to walk into him. *Clumsy fuck!*

Sciro was tempted to push him over in the mud as the smaller soldier knelt to refasten his buckles, but he resisted the urge. He shouldn't waste his aggression on his friends… He patted the legionary on his head as he passed him. "You can pull rear duties now, Piccano, you useless prick," he said in what, for him, was an amiable tone.

Piccano straightened swiftly, blanching at the idea. "The centurion picked you, Sciro," he argued petulantly, his small, round face puckered up with anxiety.

"Fuck you, and fuck *him*," Sciro replied, walking on and leaving the smaller man to look nervously around and (especially) behind him.

At the front of the troop, the officer had heard the mutter of voices and glanced back to see what was causing the commotion. Hadn't he told them enough times to keep silent while they were on the march? Their enemies were all around them. These really were the most clueless cowherds he'd ever seen. He certainly wouldn't dream of calling them soldiers. He halted the file of legionaries momentarily with a raised hand, making sure the disturbance at the back was finished before beckoning them forward once more. Sciro, of course. Always Sciro. The way he'd played with his sword, openly mocking his officer—openly threatening him. The centurion half expected to wake from one of their infrequent rest breaks to find the evil bastard squatting over him with that sword blade resting against his neck.

As far as missions were concerned, this one really *was* going all the way…

…to Hell.

Chapter Three
Closing Time

It was closing time, and Billy was glad of that. The last customer was ushered out by the portly Frank, and as usual, the "loss prevention officer" (hey, Frank, fancy title for a security guard) nipped off sharpish, leaving three members of staff to close everything down.

Those three members consisted of Billy, a stout, former football hooligan turned philosophical bookseller named James, and the truculent Julie.

Billy wished he could have locked up on his own. At this time of the evening, he just wanted to get the hell out, not have to put up with Julie's weirdness or James's constant chatter. But tonight there was another reason he wanted a bit of privacy. He'd been thinking all day about the book Aura had been reading. He'd been too busy serving a flurry of Friday afternoon customers all eager to snag a good book for the weekend to get around to checking it out properly until now. He could see James up on the raised area where all the Mind, Body, and Spirit bullshit was, tidying up the mayhem customers had left it in. He couldn't spot Julie anywhere, thankfully.

He crossed to the Travel section, half expecting not to be able to find it again like earlier, or heaven forbid, discovering it had actually been sold. But no, there it was, in plain sight, wedged next to the AA guide book. He was pulling it from the shelf when Julie appeared from the customer orders office and, spotting Billy, immediately made a bee-line in his direction.

Billy groaned to himself but looked up with a forced smile.

It wasn't that he disliked her. How could he dislike someone who so obviously thought he was wonderful, even if he couldn't, for the life of him, work out why she felt that way. She was only 25 after all, and Billy was 38. There was a world of difference between them in terms of tastes, interests, and general character that could not be put down solely to the age gap. Her constant attentions toward him were kind of flattering, but they were, at times, a bit cloying, too. And she was very persistent. Like right now.

She glanced at the book in his hand, and irritation creased her freckled brow. She obviously remembered who had been looking at it earlier. Julie was pretty enough, Billy couldn't deny, in an anodyne, underfed, prickly kind of way. Her blonde hair was thin and a little lank despite the curler she obviously used to energize it. Her eyes were faded blue, sharp as a seagull's, as was her pointed nose. He wasn't really attracted to her—or maybe only slightly (he'd once almost kissed her at a colleague's leaving do, but that was after a fair few pints). If he might have relented before, however, the arrival of the ethereally beautiful Aura into his life had really put paid to any chances of anything happening between Julie and Billy now. She looked like a faded black-and-white photograph next to Aura's Technicolor glory.

"What's so interesting about that bloody book?" she asked him, unable to disguise the note of petulance in her voice.

He shrugged, feeling caught out and a little cornered. He wished she would leave him alone. He felt a needling compulsion to investigate the book and whatever secrets it might hold.

She scanned the title and laughed mirthlessly. "Walks through Hell, huh? Sounds like a pleasant way to spend a Sunday afternoon. You planning to take your new friend for a stroll?"

He ignored the sarcasm, then indulged in some of his own before he could stop himself. "It's six-thirty, Julie. Your boyfriend will be expecting you."

Annoyance flared up in her pixie face. The end of her pointed nose crinkled. "You trying to get rid of me?" Then she added her own spin to his words, a spin that appealed to her, however far-fetched it might be. Her expression brightened. "You're jealous, aren't you?" She reached out a bony hand and touched his bare arm (he was wearing a standard branded corporate t-shirt emblazoned with the name of the bookshop franchise). When he didn't flinch, she took that as encouragement and stroked his skin in what she guessed was an erotic fashion.

"There's no need to be, you know," she said, lowering her voice huskily.

Billy detected the note of passion in it, and despite himself, he felt a little aroused. God, he was a man after all! Yet he gently pulled away and glanced at his watch demonstratively. His urge to check the book out properly was stronger than any lust Julie might stir in him, especially now that Aura had arrived on the scene.

"Time to close this baby up," he said jovially. He could hear James thumping down the stairs from the raised area. Julie heard him, too, and that spurred her on.

"You know there's someone in this shop I really like, don't you?"

Billy felt trapped. "Julie," he began, but she put her hand on his chest to stop him.

"Listen to me. There's someone who makes me feel more alive than I've ever felt before. Every time I hear him speak, I want to kiss him. When he's serving on the till and calls for the next customer, he always shouts out the same thing and…"

He almost laughed. "What thing?"

She smiled, and her hand moved down his chest a little, a subtle caress. "He calls out, 'Yes, please,' and…" She chuckled and flushed. Her cheeks looked like freckled bacon for a second. "And I go all weak at the knees…"

"Weak at the knees, eh?" James popped his head around the tall shelves of the Travel section and smiled broadly, his round, frameless spectacles reflecting the fluorescents above. "Who's causing that? Not Billy the Kid again, is it? When are you gonna make an honest woman of her, Bill?"

"For fuck's sake, James! Haven't you got a home to go to?"

"Too right. As soon as you two love birds have finished flirting, of course. Don't let me stop you though."

"Nothing for you to peep at here," Billy told him.

"James, you're a prick," Julie snapped angrily.

James beamed. "Is that any way to refer to your Assistant Manager?"

Julie shook her head in irritation and walked off toward the staff room.

Billy cleared his throat. "You might as well clear off, too, James. I just wanted to sort one more thing out and I'll follow on."

James glanced at him curiously. "What you up to? Not like you to linger after time."

Billy averted his gaze. "Just something I forgot to do earlier. You don't want to miss the start of the England game do you? Just leave me the keys. Won't be long." Billy knew exactly what buttons to push to decide it for James. He handed the shop keys over and turned to leave. "Cash drawers are all in the safe. And don't forget to check Goods In, for fuck's sake. You know what happened last week." Last week involved a rather daring but ridiculous plan by a rival bookshop owner (although, in this case, it was a stall on St. Nick's Market) who decided it would be a brilliant idea to hide in the parcel unpacking room until after the shop had been shut and then help himself to a sack load of free books. It wasn't so much that he forgot about the alarm as he was convinced he could get away quickly enough with his booty before anyone responded to it. If it had been left up to Frank, the shop's corpulent security guard, then he would have been right. However, he forgot one essential thing—the shop was part of the Galleries Mall shopping center. Every alarm alerted the 24-hour security staff for the whole complex, and they hadn't eaten as many pies as Frank over the years.

"I'm heading there now," Billy told James, and he walked across the shop, still clutching the guide book. He was aware of a curious niggling in his mind, almost like an urge for a fix, like a junkie wanting to be alone so he could find a vein. A silly analogy, he told himself, but the sense of compulsion stayed with him as he hurried to Goods In. He was just pushing through the double doors into the unpacking room when he caught sight of Julie out of the corner of his eye. She had her coat on and a grim expression and was heading for the main doors. He breathed out, and then the doors swung closed behind him and he was alone in the shop.

James had already killed the canned music, so the shop was eerily silent. Billy crossed to one of the PCs on the long desk and placed the book next to it, intending to check out the ISBN and gain a little more information about the Guide. He nudged the "stock analysis" key on the board and turned to pick up the book again. He frowned, scanning the back, then flipped open the inside cover. He flicked through to the publication info page, his frown deepening.

No ISBN. That was unusual. But not unprecedented. No barcode either. Just how bloody old was this book? It looked like one of the old books he used to take out from his local library back in the early eighties. He remembered a copy of the *Everyman Frankenstein* that had looked every bit as battered as this.

Even the pages were yellowed, for God's sake. But then maybe that was the intention, the faux antique-look marketing to match the kitsch title, which he could only assume was a postmodern attempt at humor.

Except this book looked anything but postmodern. And absolutely nothing about it hinted at any intentions toward humor on the part of whoever had compiled it. He examined the publication page more carefully. Published by Hobbemarke House, Somerset. The publication history was a real eye-opener: *first edition published 1610, derived from older texts.*

For the second time since he had found the book, a coldness spread inside him. He actually looked over his shoulder, something he hadn't done in many years. The Goods In room suddenly seemed larger than normal, with too many corners not illuminated by the one small fluorescent. Stacks of empty cardboard boxes and metal racks of books were obscured by gloom at the furthest end near the fire door.

He turned back to the PC and pulled up the book search page. He keyed in the title of the book and waited while the slow machine worked its wonders. Or didn't, in this case. There was no mention of *The Olde Britishe Guide to 101 Walkes through Hell* …

He refused to be beaten. He *needed* to know about this book for some reason. He checked the cover for the editor. Of course, there wasn't one listed, not on the flyleaf or title page either. He keyed in Hobbemarke House and came up with a similar blank.

He returned his attention to the book, and flipping through it again, a brief preface caught his eye:

> *The Wayes marked in this Booke Are not for*
> *All, though all those who touch it must follow them.*
> *Those who tread them would do well to tread them wisely.*
> *Trust unto the markers, though they may alter…*
> *For the Pathes may change for those who walke them.*
> *Lest ye not enter a wilderness of the mind, tread softly, tread with care.*
> *Man is lost… May you each find your Waye.*

The light flickered and then went out.

He was plunged into complete blackness. And silence. Even the hum of the computer had been cut off. He could hear his own breathing, though, and it sounded way too loud.

"Fuck," he said to break the quiet and bolster his nerves. Then something else disturbed the silence. Faint at first, then growing in volume, as if whoever was whistling was approaching the Goods In room from across the darkened shop.

Three notes in a descending key, long and trembling, pausing as the whistler took in a breath, then resuming, becoming clearer. Billy could hear the tuneless drone right outside the doors now. He stepped away from the desk, groping toward the wall beside the doors, intending to find the switches that operated the shop's lighting system, realizing as he did so that even if he managed to find them in the dark, they would not respond. He stumbled over a box of half-unpacked books left in the center of the floor and fell to one knee. His gasp of breath was loud in the sudden silence. The whistling had stopped. He strained his ears, remaining in a kneeling position, but all he could hear was the tinnitus in his left ear and the thumping of his heart.

Then the whistle started up again from just behind his right ear, as if whoever was responsible was leaning over him in the dark. Billy cried out and lurched to his feet, heading for where he hoped the double doors were located. The whistle followed him, *reached for him….* Billy's shoes clattered over the concrete Goods In flooring, but he heard no other footfalls pursuing.

He burst through the doors, and the haunting whistle was with him, just over his shoulder. It stayed with him as he scampered through the pitch dark of the shop, colliding with tables, spilling the immaculately piled books onto the carpet. It stayed with him as he blundered into the Erotica alcove, completely clueless as to where he was going. He felt the tight cul-de-sac of books pressing around him, the whistle trapping him from behind. The three notes grew more urgent, more violent in tone.

Then they stopped. And Billy's tinnitus was again the loudest sound in the shop.

And the lights flicked on.

And everything was normal again.

Everything was *normal* again.

The Day the Music Died

When a private jet carrying internationally acclaimed rock band Cat O' Nine Tails vanishes over the Indian Ocean, the shockwaves were felt around the world. There was no wreckage, no bodies, no black box recordings to provide clues as to what happened to the musicians. They were simply gone.

Rock 'n' Roll Will Never Die

Just as the world is recovering from the loss of Cat O' Nine Tails comes news that the jet carrying the band has mysteriously re-appeared in the same air space from which it had vanished six months ago. Was it a publicity stunt? The band is unable—or unwilling—to answer that question. They were "lost. But now we're back..." with the promise of a new album with a killer new sound coming soon.

There's something definitely not right with the band, but the nation is too firmly in the grip of Cat O' Nine Fever to notice. And as the formerly affable, much-loved Cat O' Nine Tails gears up for a new stadium show, it falls to Cat's original front man, sacked years before, and the members of a virtually unknown punk band, Lucifer Sam, to uncover the real threat behind the massive publicity drive.

And, from Midnight Machinations, don't miss…

LIGHTS!

A killer is targeting TV and Film extras on various productions throughout the South West of England. The murderer leaves a macabre marker at each crime scene—a VHS video nasty, while the murders themselves mimic the killings depicted in the tapes.

CAMERA!

While the police are drawn into both the seedy world of nasties and the hierarchical system that thrives in the film industry, the killer remains one step ahead.

CUT!

It's an A–Z kill list, and the cops are in a race to stop the slayings before the murderer can chop their way through the 39 titles on the list of banned films, from *Absurd* to *Zombie Flesh Eaters*…

WALKING SHADOW
A Stone/Darke Mystery

www.ingramcontent.com/pod-product-compliance
Lightning Source LLC
Chambersburg PA
CBHW072028220726
48293CB00016B/529